A Circle of Earth

Patricia Weil

outskirtspress

DENVER, COLORADO

This book is lovingly dedicated to my husband Ray and my mother, Betty Grey, both of whom will understand why.

I would also like to acknowledge the late Laura Hruska, for her very generous work on this manuscript.

Chapter 1

They were always there with him, waking or sleeping. The ghosts that peopled his dreams.

Night rain lashed against the sides of the building, and the storm wind was fierce. But where would they have been, there together? In one of the old riverfront buildings, Henry later decided. They were high up, the five of them, on what seemed to be a third story. Floors and walls moved apart and tilted, then moved together again. Henry knew that he had to get all of them out, quickly—quickly as possible. He was afraid that the old building would collapse, with the water and wind. But the stairs to the lower floors were blocked in some way—or missing.

And cold. It was cold. A hurting cold that slid cruelly next to the skin and settled there. The room was cluttered with furniture and old packing crates, but nothing to keep them from the cold. Lillian had the children around her, all of them holding onto each other. She watched Henry. He remembered her eyes. He'd thought he'd be able to get them out by the outside fire escape, but there was a connection, there, too, that was missing. The steps were old and rusted. A shutter from the window below stood out, then banged against the building. The river was leaving its banks. Dark sheets of water, cold, cold, flew against Henry. He'd have to use the shutter to step out on—he didn't know if it would hold. He thought he could step down on it, then swing over to the escape steps. He'd have to move each of them, one at a time. He was half crazy with fear. He knew the flying shutter was rotted and flimsy. Possibly he could let them down to a lower part of the roof. But there the water and cold would beat over them. There were his children. There was Lillian. The building was swinging apart. Sheets of water cut through it. It was dark. He was losing them.

The dream ended.

And recalling it, on a bright and safe June afternoon years past that place in time, Henry was shaken—though the nightmare had left him altogether while he was with the boy. He'd had none of that odd, faraway feeling that trailed around after a dream like that one. They had been crawdadding at the trestle pond on Highway 80. That afternoon Henry had done no more than watch Rallie safely inside his daughter's house after their expedition. Betty Kate and Frank had the old Skinner house, just blocks down from Henry's own room on Alabama Avenue. On Saturday mornings Henry walked up Alabama Avenue to Betty Kate's, the same way he had once walked to the house on Water Avenue, to and from town.

The afternoon was coming to a close—people were just beginning to return home from work. Henry didn't acknowledge the fact that his comings and goings to his daughter's house were sometimes contrived to avoid meeting Frank "Buddy" Griffen. The more important thing that afternoon was that he needed some time. The matter of the dream required a good thinking about. Henry parked at the back of the Burroughs' residence, a preposterous piece of architecture called a wedding cake house, with its festoons of gingerbread trim. Here he rented a single room. The hangover from the dream returned as soon as he pulled onto the property, got out, and chained Wolf. He met no one else in the hallway, which he considered fortunate. His plan was to duck into his room at the front, then get to the upstairs shower as quickly as possible.

And Henry was, in fact, able to make himself presentable, without encountering another roomer. After hanging his muddy clothes, he released Wolf, who came around to the front, where Henry took his place on a porch rocker, drawing a Camel from his pocket, testing it between his lips, spitting a grain or two of stray tobacco before lighting it. This would be the kind of thinking that required a smoke, from start to finish.

He smoked. He thought of David Levy and felt a little better. Henry never had understood Levy's reactions to his dreams—he had few enough of them, as it was. For some reason or another, Levy always seemed disappointed in Henry's dreams. He'd ask him questions that didn't seem, to Henry, to apply. But now Henry smiled, thinking back on it. He could see the young doctor lifting his head in a quick nod, maybe lifting a finger. It was Henry's signal to go on talking. He was instructed at times to go on talking, no matter what came out, no matter how crazy or off the subject it sounded. Just keep talking—Levy stressed how important that was. Images of Levy had a way of comforting Henry. As always, Henry intended to write to him, just a line or two. In another part of his mind, he knew that he never would write; but the idea of it kept alive some feeling of connection that he wanted. Needed. He didn't know another person like David Levy; he never had.

And Levy was right. Dreams had a way of telling the truth. He had, after all, lost her; he had lost all of them, except Betty Kate. It was decades back that he lost her—he couldn't have said, even now, exactly when it had been that he knew it was so. Long before that gray morning in '32 when he'd walked over from Strayer's, out of the heart of town and into East Clanton. This after having made himself as presentable as possible, coming on weeks or more of riding the rails; his mouth tasting salty from brushing his teeth too hard. He had crossed the railroad yard, the fan of spreading tracks, and entered the back yard of the shotgun house: knowing before his foot even hit the back stoop. Knowing that she had left not just the house but had left him, Henry.

His eyes were immediately drawn to the cardboard box placed so intentionally in the doorway, between the two rooms. Mute. Confirming everything.

It could have been any number of small occasions that had been their last one, without either of them realizing it. The last time of their being together, as they had been for—it seemed to Henry—a lifetime. He recalled a certain morning at the faded little house. The girls must have already left for school. And he had reached for Lillian, there, inside the kitchen, when she was standing with her back to him. Touched her and felt the tightening travel all over her body. Her recoil. He had sat, instead, and tried to make some sort of ordinary conversation—he couldn't have said what it had been about, now. And had felt something close to panic when he realized she was leaving the room. An odd thing, that had been—that feeling, when she would be stepping no more than a few feet away. He'd been unable to move—somehow he felt that his moving would have made her go farther and faster. Made her leave him outright. It didn't make sense. His knees, arms braced against them—his whole body—locked into place at that moment. Because of how much he wanted to go after her. To shout at her. Bully her, even. All of these, things that he'd never have done, even known how to do. Words once had made a difference. But they wouldn't come then. They just wouldn't come.

Not even the morning he found the house empty. It had taken him hours, only, to locate her. She had opened the door, not thinking, absentmindedly not looking through the door pane.

So that when she opened the door, Henry stood just inside the threshold, his body blocking the door.

"You will *not* come into this house!" She fairly spat the words at him, Lillian did.

But of course he would go no further. It was the habit of his lifetime to obey this diminutive person. Her voice by itself would have stopped him. Not like Lillian—not Lillian's voice. But ragged, almost gravelly. That quickly she had worked herself into a fury, her chest moving as though she'd been running. She was fierce—he would have never thought her capable of it. She, who had always been helpless in that way of females of a particular kind. Just below his awareness, the helplessness had always gratified Henry. Because it directly informed him of what to do. He was on sure and familiar ground, then.

Now, no words would have made any difference. He would have needed as many words, Henry thought, as there had been days and minutes and hours. On reflex, he stepped back from the door, and Lillian closed it. She was no longer his wife.

As Henry smoked, recollecting, he dropped a hand from the arm of his chair, which fell on the head of Wolf; and Henry stroked the head again and again. Until his fingers stopped momentarily, remembering something. The scars. The little cluster of white scars. Long time, now. Henry would have given Wolf to the boy, his grandson; but the dog would have none of it. Now Henry stood up from his porch rocker. It was a little early, but he thought he'd walk on over for his meal, then back to the club room. It was the pattern of his evenings. As he stood, Wolf stood up with him, and they crossed Alabama Avenue there, in front of the house. He didn't want to meet anyone from the club room just yet. He had more thinking—Henry always had thinking. He walked in the way of someone absorbed, a man looking for something. For the years. Whole sections of years, years as seamless and unused as time stored in the mind of a child. They were blank years, the many of them. And because the years were gone, Henry looked, instead, for some kind of understanding. He had a lot of work to do.

He walked toward the old Bluebird Cafe, which had changed hands and been redecorated during the forties. Now there were booths with Formica tops and benches covered with red, padded plastic, which was split in various places and repaired with aluminum-colored tape. Here, Henry ate three meals a day, each day, the breakfast special #2 and the lunch and dinner specials. And here, Henry had a friend, Louise, one of the waitresses. Louise would have been, Henry guessed, about the age of his daughter Elizabeth. And under other circumstances, she might have been an attractive woman. Her hair was dyed a brittle red and had to be pulled back and pinned under a net. Health regulations. She wore a bright, slightly violet-colored lipstick, in an attempt to give her look a little flair. The friendship, now a warm one, had grown slowly. Henry liked Louise because she was cheerful—he suspected that her life had not been especially easy. And Louise liked Mr. Gray because he was quiet and courteous. Both were heavy smokers. They smoked and talked together in the comfortable way of two people in a situation that posed no threat to privacy. Nothing personal, at first. Gradually, Louise had started to talk. She had a brother that she was worried about. She knew that Henry belonged to AA, and she had questions. Many of them—which Henry was ready to answer at length. Henry would have talked at whatever length Louise needed. If she had asked him, he would have without hesitation confirmed that he had spent several years in Bryce mental hospital. But she never asked about that.

"How's John Earl?"

"Oh, I think he's doing a little better." The answer never

varied. They spoke of her four-year-old, who was, as Louise put it, going through a delicate stage. She brought the boy in with her from time to time to the Bluebird. And Henry supplied him with oddities from his catches: a stink jim, an eel, grinnell, gar, all of which he routinely saved, if he knew John Earl to be with his mother at the cafe—the Bluebird was only a couple of blocks from the river. Afterwards, he threw the fish out over the water.

The cafe was filling with noise and customers. Henry left the counter, where he had been smoking with Louise, and took his place at a booth. As he ate, he thought of his afternoon with the boy—which had been nothing out of the ordinary, but nonetheless deeply gratifying to Henry. It had been Rallie who insisted on the trestle pond. The pool, a greenish-black in color, was said to have no bottom—that sort of thing appealed to the six-year-old. They kept to the bank, along the shallow stretches of water. Henry had to keep a close eye on the boy, himself weighted down with paraphernalia. Rubber boots that came up to his knees; his vision part blocked by his hat—at one time a formal business hat, now badly stained, the brim nicked and misshapen. And the trawler was heavy. He'd built the trawl box himself, using window screening, the whole thing attached to a pole. He pitched, dragged, and emptied the contraption— which on another afternoon would have brought the boy run- ning, to lean over the thick ooze of black mud and leaves. A black ooze that at once began to twitch with the movement of trapped things. But the boy was absorbed further up on the bank. So Henry peered into the mass, picking out the crawfish and tossing them into a washtub. They'd left the truck parked high up, close to the highway. A '48 Chevy, the blue of it pow- dery and rust-marked. Wolf lay at a distance below it, in a shad- owy recess. Watching the truck. Watching the man and the boy. Ahead of Henry, the boy stood in water which was, for him, nearly knee deep. Henry suspected that he'd set up a crawdad fight. They'd been there at the pool for a matter of hours. The boy had spent most of the time in the water, taking breaks to pick dewberries. It was past time for the berries; most of them were now dry on the bush. The small hands moved from stagnant water to berries to mouth. Betty Kate would have had a fit. And the boy's t-shirt was off—Henry wondered if they'd find it. The boy was burning, Henry realized—he'd forgotten the bottle of Coppertone, one of a running supply that Betty Kate placed in the truck. The bottles managed to disappear, one way or another, or show up in odd places. Rallie's shoulders were violently red. But he had in common with Henry the fact that both could burn to a redness painful to look at, then wake up a calm and comfortable brown on the following morning. Henry made a mental note, just the same. He needed to do things right with the boy. When he left Clanton, the boy was little more than a large toddler, although he'd already begun his excursions with Henry. During his absence, Henry had tormented himself that when he returned, the boy might somehow not be there. But he was there.

The hard June day had softened when Henry finished at the Bluebird. Cicadas rattled, a sound too accustomed at this time of year for notice, the sound of the South in summer. Henry walked around to the back of the building, where Wolf lay against the warm brick, four legs stretched full, half sleeping, attentive enough to raise his head to growl at anyone who came to or went from the kitchen. This was excepting Louise, who regularly fed him a choice collection of table scraps, as did the landlady Mrs. Burroughs, as well as did Betty Kate. The dog was wiry by inheritance but extremely well-fed. He kept up with Henry as far as the courthouse, where the A.A. club room was located in the basement. Henry chuckled to himself as he walked, thinking back to the boy and his crawdad fight. Henry had never, until now, had a boy, only daughters. Rallie: Betty Kate's boy. Henry had been surprised that she agreed to name him Ralston, after the old man. He was a mean one, all right, the old fellow. But Henry thought fondly of the farm woman Emma who was his wife.

Chapter 2

Emma wasn't given to nightmares—or so she thought. And possibly it was so. If she had a dream that troubled her, she would have directly snipped it from her memory, like a child cutting out paper dolls. Emma's bad dreams had all happened to her when she was awake. And she didn't dwell much on those. Ned would always be with her, in a way that had moved beyond remembering or forgetting. Life was a fairly settled thing for her now. There was no cause to dwell back on the bad times. The twenties. The Depression—she had long since put that behind her. But there were moments when Emma's mind did turn back. An unexpected reminder, here or there. Like the letter which had arrived from her sister Mamie that morning. Even now Emma thought of Mamie as young—which for a fact she no longer was. The handwriting was young, the single page written out in the same, schoolroom script in which all of them had been schooled. And all in the same, country schoolhouse. Mamie still used a pencil, as Ralston's brother Charles had done in The Letter—that was how Emma thought of still, these many years later. That letter. A punctuation mark to everything that made up her world. That letter which arrived on an April day so many years ago. She'd waited for Charles' reply, then, nigh on a week. Yet had made herself walk as far back inside as the doorway, before tearing at the envelope. Commanded her mind not to move—stopped everything until she could get that envelope torn—and find out. Then had read its contents through only once, crumpling and jamming the paper deep into her apron pocket. There was nothing, then, but to leave the house.

There was always work to do then, it seemed. But on that day, there was little to be done to the stretches of crops. At first spring, the cornfields were no more than rows of bleached stubble that caught the sun at odd spots. There'd been nothing to look over in the orchard, which lay to the other side of the house, with the wood lot growing behind it. From the front of the house, Emma would not have been seen. The house itself sat back from the road. One of those rounded clay roads that dipped and dribbled through fields, to any outsider leading nowhere, but for Emma many years home. She had chosen her kitchen garden—there was always something that needed her attention, there.

Emma moved slowly that afternoon—which wasn't her way. It was her habit to be in motion, and she moved with the directness of a schoolgirl, a little heavy on her feet; hurrying. On the day of The Letter, Emma had to make herself move against her will. She would have liked to sit inside her kitchen, just sit, pull her arms in around her and think. The windows of the kitchen stood open. From the front, she could hear the sounds of her five children, noisy play sounds that ordinarily soothed and pleased her. But there was nothing of pleasure in Emma's face then. It had the faded look of the contrasting prints of her dress and apron.

No detail of Emma's appearance was contrived to draw attention to herself. She plaited her hair without thinking about it and twisted it into a bun at her neck. She was twenty-nine that year—and long, to her mind, a mother. Though her face was not yet lined—hadn't changed much at all, really, from the face she had as a girl. She no longer had that blank, expectant look of a girl. But it was the likable face of an honest nature. Straight featured, the shape of her upper lip pointed instead of curved. Emma was easily interested in conversation, and her eyes, blue-green in color, became still and intent when her interest was caught. Her freckles had never left her. Emma's life as a mother was not all that different, in fact, from what it had always been, except that the places had all changed around. Time was when the world seemed to move past, outside Emma, like a thing she could reach out and touch. Now, the world moved from the inside, out. She was the mother. She was the source. The world depended on Emma.

The worktable where Emma sat was crowded with cooking things. Now she lay the letter down among them, the pencil marks already rubbed down to something like faded ink. For a second time, her attention was caught by the voices of her children. She felt wealthy in her children—she hadn't lost a child then, as some women had. Nettie was her oldest. And Emma gave no thought—never had—as to whether her daughter were plain or pretty. It seemed somehow that Nettie had always been with her. There was Ralph, the one with the dark coloring, the one who favored Ralston. There was Ned, the one Emma's eyes loved to look at. Billy, the youngest—Emma had to laugh at Billy. His five years of life were a serious business to him. But Buddy—there was her oldest son, Buddy. When Emma thought of him, a smile started behind her eyes that didn't quite make it to her face. Then she heard him, whistling around the corner of the porch; Emma smiled outright at the whistling. Buddy had worked it into a fine skill, a strong, fluting whistle that moved easily from key to key. He was a handsome boy—everybody bragged about Buddy. He would be the first of the five of them to come in making inquiries about the supper. Emma's children usually started around mid-afternoon.

Satisfied at the sight of the cobbler Emma was making, Buddy left again, leaving an unusual quiet in the kitchen. Rays of afternoon sun fell into the room. She should move, Emma told herself; but she didn't. Snatches of scripture ran through her mind. Scripture: Ralston paid no attention to that sort of thing. Although his family and hers had always belonged to the Baptist church that sat at the crossroads of Dothan Highway and County Road 3. Emma remembered. Odd, that she should think, now, not of the bad times, but that her mind traveled all the way back. She thought she could still get it, the odor of sun-soaked shiplap peculiar to that building. And she could see the congregation. The Griffen family. When seated, fifteen of them in all, an entire church pew, a solemn, throat-clearing group. Emma's father spoke approvingly of Charles Griffen's family, as Charles Griffen no doubt spoke of the Swanns. Emma couldn't remember a time when she hadn't known Ralston Griffen by name. She could picture Ralston, she thought, as he had been then, in the way she would have thought of someone still there, in that place. Emma had taken just lately to stopping in front of the formal wedding portrait of herself and Ralston, a large photograph, framed and hung over the mantel. The faces in that portrait were people she couldn't make real. Herself she hardly recognized, her hair was done up, so. Emma thought of a hawk when she looked at Ralston, with his face part way in profile—he, too, a stranger. The focus wasn't as clear as it could have been. It never belonged to two people, really.

She would will herself now to stop looking at it.

"Emma."

The face. The voice.

She didn't know when he had stepped up beside her. Heat rushed into Emma's face. She took in the looks of the people immediately around her, stood for some moments, plucking her collar.

It was the voice from the photo that spoke. From that hot night a decade and more ago, now. Ralston was twenty-two when his formal wedding photograph was taken. At that age a handsome man in an unlikely sort of way. Dark, thin-lipped, with a sharp, slightly hooked nose. Most people could see that in Ralston Griffen there was something that was not altogether friendly. But he was courteous—it didn't draw comment. Ralston joked easily enough, amused himself among his cronies; with his buddies there was a certain cockiness about him. That summer of 1914, when he first became interested in Emma Swann, he'd been more than usually satisfied with himself. He'd done some traveling around the state and had bought a farm in central Alabama, for, as he bragged, little more than back taxes. He had found the farm; now he needed a wife to go with it. And in this regard the Swann sisters had been the first to come to mind. Ollie, the oldest, tiny and round, with soft blue eyes that sloped down at the outside corners. Mamie the youngest, tall and skinny, covered with overdark freckles. He would have Emma, the middle sister. Emma was pleasing enough to look at. And the girls had been made to feel pleased with themselves. Their father, Edwin, lavished attention on his daughters. It was his pride to have taught each one of them the mechanics of handling a plow. He had patiently taught each daughter to shoot. On their land the Swanns had achieved a dependable self-sufficiency, as well as a certain prosperity. Emma was the sort of young woman that Ralston wanted. The other young women he knew—there were a number—were of another sort.

"Emma." Again, the voice at her side. It was now, he decided, to make the move of asking to drive her home. Now that the dancers had broken up, the music ended. People had started to move.

Emma had never paid any special attention to Ralston

Griffen—one of the young bloods, as her father called them—until all at once he started to watch her. The Griffen family had a fine old home place for their thirteen children—that was something worthy of mention, in itself. And she had noticed for the first time that for a fact he was handsome—she had heard that remarked. The Swann sisters catalogued any and all such remarks of that nature. Among the three, a great—the great—favorite topic was that of their future marriages, any real or imagined intentions, anyone else's marriage; the marriage state in general, this achievement that they'd been led to plan for, wait for, and wish for almost all of their lives. Emma was seventeen that summer, an entirely marriageable age.

Emma had known that on the evening of that particular dance, something was bound to happen with the Griffen fellow, what with the way he had taken to staring at her. And she looked forward to basking in the little sun of a woman being openly courted. But Ralston had worked it out differently.

Emma would have never suspected the lengths of Ralston's canniness—she wouldn't have known what to do about it, if she had. In Ralston's estimation, this courtship could have been long and taxing. The Swann sisters had any number of callers. Emma could have taken it into her head to trifle with him in any way that amused her. So on that hot night, Ralston dallied. For the longest time, he refrained from dancing, leaning against a wall of the barn, in a spot where the sun faintly hit, one foot propped back behind him. As he laughed with his buddies, his eyes traveled over the details of the people who were standing in the yard. He even studied the different teams standing hitched to their wagons. He paid no attention at all to Emma. For the first hour or so of the evening, Ralston never looked Emma's way—not so much as to acknowledge her, for the sake of general politeness. But all of this was intentional. Ralston singled out a certain Jane

McGowan, a pretty girl in an anemic sort of way, and danced exclusively with her. Everybody knew that a McGowan girl couldn't be taken seriously, this family being the butt of conversational jokes—a careless, superficial sort of cruelty. At their low yields, the late plantings, the weedy stands of crops. But Jane McGowan suited Ralston's purposes for the evening exactly.

Ralston wore his best clothes for the dance—but the jacket and tie were soon discarded. The brightness of his best shirt set off his dark coloring in a way that he knew to be to his advantage. The pace of the music increased. The players whipped into a polka, a fast one. And here Ralston knew just how to overdo it. He led Jane McGowan into a whirl of a polka so fast that within the first rounds the other dancers stepped back. His knee cut into the starched crease of his trousers, as he dipped, lead, charged, with the outstretched hand that held onto hers. At his pace, there could have been an embarrassing collision; but Ralston expected no mishap. The whole gathering laughed when he swept his unsuspecting partner out of the cleared area and around one of the wagons. It was an act of splendid showmanship. Emma and her sisters tried to look anywhere but in the direction that everyone else was looking. Emma was properly mortified.

But then there had been a change, when the main fiddler began a slow, whining waltz. Ralston walked up to her.

"Emma." He held out his hand—it would have been proper to call her Miss Emma. Certain onlookers were suddenly curious.

The showmanship had served its purpose; now Ralston put it aside. He and Emma swayed together very correctly. Emma didn't look up—it was her due, now, at least, to be courted. Ralston's eyes were fixed on her face in a way that made her uncomfortable. Almost it seemed that he smirked.

"You know how to dance, don't you, Emma?" She made a depreciatory noise and looked past his shoulder. Emma did know how to dance—the Swann sisters practiced.

The evening was a jumble, from that point—Emma was not her right self. She was over self-conscious, flighty. She made conversation that was silly. Through every minute of that evening, with or without him as partner, Emma was aware of exactly where Ralston was. And uneasily. He had a kind of look about him. The eyes jeered, or they dared her—something, she didn't know how to say. She wouldn't meet them directly. Her own every move was being observed, Emma knew—no unusual thing in itself. But Ralston Griffen was different. His attention exhausted her. She felt a strain.

It was late when the dancing came to an end, but the night air was still thick and hot. Ralston's voice was a little startling in the sudden quiet that followed the music. "Emma, you go ask your folks if I can drive you home."

Ralston never properly proposed to Emma. Possibly it was an oversight. He took his success much for granted. And as it was, his behavior on that evening had resulted in the very effect he had counted on. Emma had been made unsure of herself. She had assumed his admiration to be only hers; and now the value of it, which might have otherwise been questioned, had risen inalterably in her estimation.

It was a poor conversation they shared on that slow wagon. And Emma Swann couldn't know that this paucity would be a fact of her life with the man who was sitting beside her. As she saw it, there must have been something she wasn't doing right. She raised her hands, let them fall back into her lap, conversationally—or so she imagined. "I like to wore myself out, dancing." Emma expected only to have to say a word or two, to open the conversation. He would take it from there.

Ralston glanced at her.

"Ollie, Mamie and me. We do all our own sewing." She was

hoping for a compliment on her newly made blouse. Or on her freshly washed wavy hair, not drawn back so severely in its usual bun.

"Ain't it a hot night?" The situation was suddenly painful. Emma didn't know what it was she should be doing, should be saying. She had never given it any special thought—things had always been easy. Now that she looked at it, Emma couldn't have said what it was, before, that she must have talked about with her callers—what anyone had *ever* talked about. There must have been the usual jokes and stories with those others, the pranks and foolishness. But it was complicated now, all of a sudden. Emma smoothed her skirt, made fanning motions with her hands. She felt her face burning.

For his own part, Ralston would have been content to drive without talking unless something in particular occurred to him. Thoughts of the farm absorbed him. He didn't stop to think that the pictures so full in his own mind were blank and silent to Emma; so that for him there was no suddenness, not even a break in thought, when he abruptly spoke out, "Got us a nice place, Emma. Think you're gonna like it."

Well, then it would be all right. Emma's shoulders dropped a little, a movement that Ralston could have observed—he looked ahead as he drove. Still, there was no talk, just the hot night and the night noises. Cricket sounds passed back and forth over the road in front of them, like a kind of breathing. Voices of the other travelers at different distances broke through the dark. Comfortable sounds, again. The wagon lurched over ruts in the road that couldn't be seen. But the flood of night noise, the lurching wagon, fell into an ordinary rhythm. The world was a place that suited Emma after all.

It would happen to her, Emma. She would be married. Emma smiled. She was going to be the first.

Chapter 3

In November of that same year, Henry Gray stepped out to the front porch in his sock feet, making an effort to be as quiet as possible getting out of the house. In one hand he held his good shoes and work boots, both dangling together by the strings. He would wear the boots until a convenient point on the road, then switch to the shoes. It was Sunday. His shirt was starched. With his Sunday suit he wore a bow tie that particularly pleased him, maroon with white polka dots. Henry was jug-eared, with an open, good-natured face, features regular enough, large and kindly. Henry's was a face that laughed. He had just finished shaving at the stand in the hallway and had nicked himself, leaving a little dark line to one side of his mouth.

His mother would be getting up at any time now, to start on the breakfast. But for the moment the sleeping house was quiet, like a house that had been left empty. As far as Henry could tell, there was nothing yet at that hour that moved. Then the sounds would break out all at once, his brothers and sisters, the quick hitting of feet. His mother calling out orders—Sunday morning was a lot of fuss and bother. They had to be especially presentable at the table. And Henry thought of the breakfast—the hot ham and gravy with grits and eggs, the steaming biscuits—with regret. Tucked under his free arm was a bundle of cold ham biscuits knotted in a dishcloth. There'd be at least a small scene concerning his absence at the breakfast table—he wouldn't regret missing that.

"That boy'll be one of those folks who can't abide by people, the way he takes off by himself." From his mother. And it wasn't a new complaint. The "boy" she referred to was by now a young man of twenty-two. But no way around it—he'd be out of favor with them all, again—except for Drefus, who went contentedly along on these church Sundays, to make every occasion to enjoy the feminine company. Church attendance in itself was incidental.

Henry was headed for a tent meeting, instead. This first tent revival of the season, led by a traveling evangelist named Simms, had been set up on the far side of Orville. The Gray home was three miles from the center of town in the other direction. Henry had a good distance to walk, and he looked forward to walking. It was a pleasure to put his body into good, sustained motion. Henry did his best thinking while walking. And morning was a good time. He liked to be up at first day. Daylight was breaking as he stood leaning against the porch railing. The heavy silence was pleasurable, arresting to his senses. High up, the sky was a circle of new, clear blue, unclouded. It would be sunny today and warm.

Henry couldn't have said exactly why he was drawn by this particular revival. Likely it was the break in routine. There had already been three nights of meetings. Each day Henry saw the theme of the sermon, written on the chalkboard that hung in the general store. On Sunday the message would be "The Mark of the Beast"—he'd made special note of that one. It was the title that piqued his curiosity—he wondered what it would be about. Henry pulled on his boots and laced them, picked up his shoes and bundle, and fell right away into the long and regular strides of physical well-being. The sun was well up now, falling along the shapes of trees and outbuildings with a fine, brilliant edge. It was late November, a mild time in Alabama. The trees were mostly bare, the last flakes of color pooled at their feet. Henry's senses traveled as his feet did, his eyes tracing the patterns of things, the thin lines of leafless branches, the lay of the ground. He liked to reflect that the patterns of tree limbs, veins in a leaf, his own fore-arms, the course of rivers and streams were all the same.

"The Mark of the Beast." There'd be speculation about one with a title like that. There'd be an elderly person or two who would guess at something ridiculous, like the running of the rail-roads. No one approved of the business of Yankee investors—that topic would bring up the usual rounds of complaints. Most people would be likely to guess that the mark of the beast was the dollar. Or it would be alcohol. In 1914 Alabama was bone dry. Henry had no clear thoughts worked out on the subject—he fancied the words, the mystery of them. But a picture came to his mind, a thing that troubled him. The children who worked at the mill, that little sharp line on their foreheads. And the men and women, some of the faces stupid with malnutrition. The mill owners were greedy. The mine owners upstate were greedy. Greed. He'd decided. Greed was the mark of the beast. Henry thought of the cotton mill where his father worked as manager—it was at its worst in hot weather, which had just recently passed. He would be expected to fill his father's position, once Mr. Gray decided to give it up. As a sort of unofficial under manager, he had to meddle with everything—be alert for injuries, signs of heat exhaustion, all manner of detail. The worst of it was that among the brothers his father had singled him out for the mill. An honor. That he was the chosen one. Of his own accord, he'd have never set foot inside the place. It was the single and painful bane of his existence. His plan was to escape it at the earliest possibility. He was well aware, though, that without this position at the mill, he could not have proposed to Lillian. He couldn't have asked for her hand, while still walking behind the plow. Lillian required more than that.

Now he was walking into Orville proper, not a large

enough place to be called a real town. More like a crossroads community. A clapboard church stood at the first intersection. Lillian's church, the Presbyterians. He'd gone to a service there once with her. And had been an eager visitor at first. But as it turned out, the prayers and sermon weren't any different from the scores of others he'd heard—he had hoped for some kind of difference. The religion of Henry's upbringing was one of judgment, fire, and punishment, long lamentations on the state of sin and its consequences, a text that had come to irritate Henry. He felt pummeled under the words. He minded the shouting. These reactions made him ashamed, even uneasy. It wasn't the sort of thinking people did. Everyone else appeared perfectly satisfied.

Privately, a little secretively, he had read the Gospels once through for himself, and had been struck by the gentleness of the language. He thought of an experience he'd had when he was a boy, one that came back to him from time to time. He was in knee pants then—he didn't recall his age exactly. He'd been cane fishing with his older brother, Drefus, on Cedar Creek, the two of them sitting high on the bank under a stand of small trees, not very well protected from the sun. Drefus had ordered him to be quiet, so as not to scare the fish—cane fishing required patience. Henry's eyes drifted along the line of the creek, where, at a distance, a Negro congregation was holding a baptism. The group was too far away for Henry to overhear anything much but the shouting and laughter. He watched the preacher and the new convert, both in white robes, walk out into the moving, brown water, saw the preacher raise one hand up high, then lower the other figure backwards. Henry had been instructed that each human being had a soul. What, then, was a soul? That was when it came to him, there on the bank, his strange notion about a soul: was it, maybe, that a soul was a piece of God that each person had somewhere inside him? Was it that if you put all these souls of people together, you came up with God? An odd idea, that a soul was not a thing to either be saved or cast into eternal fire. He knew that it wasn't the sort of thought he could have spoken of to anybody.

Henry stopped now at the edge of the still empty churchyard, squatted to unwrap his bundle, and ate his breakfast quickly, considering where to leave his boots before striking out across the open fields between town and the tent. He hid the boots in a weedy spot behind the feed store and felt satisfied with his planning. He felt pleased and in possession of life, altogether. It was a good thing, being alive. When he set out again, expansiveness, a feeling of physical strength, seemed to work out from his body. He raised his head, took in long gulps of morning air, just for the pleasure of it. He thought again of Lillian. She had formally said that she'd have him—he'd known by the time he asked that she would.

The area under the tent was still dark. The meeting was just beginning. There was singing under way, opening hymns from a thin collection of voices. The early arrivers were seated in clumps on the rows of benches.

"Hey, Candy. Over here."

The greeting came from an old schoolmate of Henry's, who was seated with her mother. Henry's mother, Annie Gray, had it all wrong—her son had an easy affinity for people. Dottie's special liking for Henry, of years' standing, embarrassed neither of them. He tolerated the nickname with good humor. And it was just this that attracted people to Henry, a sort of unfailing, natural courtesy. Women were particularly comfortable in his company.

"Sit here, Candy." Dottie patted the bench next to her. Henry stood.

"Won't you sit down, son?" This came from Dottie's mother, a plump, comfortable woman. And at the second invitation, Henry sat down.

The service began with a lengthy prayer of invitation and petition for forgiveness of sins. The evangelist, a Mr. Simms, was a hefty, red-faced man. He warmed quickly to his message, alternately lowering his voice and shouting so loudly as to startle his audience. Then his voice settled into a steady, mournful cadence. He droned on with passages of scripture, working up at length to his message.

It was idleness that he had settled on. Idleness was the mark of the beast. The letdown, by now, was familiar enough. Henry sighed, without being aware of it. He glanced at the others sitting around him. The others were solemn, dutifully nodding at points to the words. It was at this time that Henry noticed the mingled sweet and salt odors drifting up from the hamper beside Mrs. Wheeler. His stomach contracted, in anticipation—he would be asked to join them. He looked over the assembly of people. At the back of the tent, some of the mill workers were standing together. When outside the mill village, the workers kept to themselves. These people carried no lunch pails or hampers, and Henry understood why. The contents of the poor meals would have been an embarrassment. Now he squinted. He had recognized a woman in the group at the back, a Mrs. Jenkins, a thin woman with sagging posture. She was wearing a flowered dress. She had come in one morning with one of her boys, to ask if Mr. Gray could take on the boy to tote water. This was a common enough request among mill parents. The boy would be put to work at the spools, like the other young ones. Henry drove away the image—no child should be put to work at the spools.

The sounds suddenly stopped. For a moment there were no voices. Then a flow of relieved conversation started all at one time. Work was over for the day. People began to move. The walk home would be a release, thus a pleasure, following the workday. Coolness seeped out of the piney woods along the path from the mill village. And already the windows of the building had darkened. A white haze of lint hung in the rooms that irritated the eyes and throat, making people frantic for the clean outside air. Henry stood at a distance from his father, who had moved around all day at a pace that suited him, noticing that a group of men had formed and were look- ing in his father's direction. At the center of the group was Jenkins, a stubby man in overalls, the overalls none too clean. He had a doughy face. And the face was angry. He was staring at Mr. Gray, telling some sort of news to the others. He jerked from them, telling his story, like somebody spoiling for a fight. Men who passed Jenkins laid a hand on his shoulder, gave him small, acknowledging pushes.

Henry walked up to his father. "What ails Jenkins?"

"Had to let him go, son."

"Let him go?" Letting a man go was as serious a thing as could happen at the mill.

"That's right. Send him home. He's no good for us here." Mr. Gray straightened his stack of papers against his desk, a desk that was built for standing.

"How come?"

Mr. Gray shot a look at his son. Joe Gray was a short man, with wiry gray hair; there was no physical resemblance between his second son and himself. Generally, he was a tolerant parent.

And he depended on Henry. But this particular son of his just didn't know when to leave a thing alone. Henry meddled in things that were routinely accepted as nobody's business.

"Man's not doing his job, Henry." Joe Gray made himself be patient.

"He looks mighty shook up."

Mr. Gray withheld the exasperation. "Well, I can't help it, son. He's got to go."

Henry stood there, obstinate, waiting for an explanation.

No explanation was given. Mr. Gray turned his back to Henry.

"Well, can't he—," Henry started in.

"No, he can't!" The answer was explosive. And Mr. Gray instantly thought better of it. But it took an effort. "Henry, the man's got a problem with liquor. And that's a danger. Now, you gonna manage a mill, you got to know when to let a man go. 'S all there is to it." He slapped the collection of papers against the desk.

By this time, the others were coaxing Jenkins out of the door. Henry gave the men time to clear the mill grounds. He was impatient, himself, ready to burst for the outside air. He had never expected to be here in the mill, but had been led to it. And had not stopped to consider what work he would have freely chosen, if a choice had been put to him. Work that would be direct— clear and direct. Working the land with his hands, his animals, his implements. But then, he had chosen an unlikely sort of wife for work of that nature. A lady, who would have expected no trace of earth on his hands. He would have to move her into Clanton.

Abruptly he decided not to walk home with his father that evening. He walked to the other end of the building and left by the back stairs instead. The mill yard, whitened by layers of lint powder, was already empty. Henry stood for a while at the edge of the woods behind the building. He studied the ground, moving one foot through the linty soil. To let a man go meant turning him out of his house. There was no other labor for hire around Orville. He stood a few moments longer, hands in his pockets, then turned in the direction of the mill village.

He had hoped to get by unseen. And by the time he walked into the clay street between the rows of houses, there was no one around, only a couple of boys sitting on some front steps. There was the cover of darkness, the windows in the little houses pale blurs of kerosene light. Here the houses were identical, shotgun houses set up high on brick legs. The evening had turned chilly. Voices, the complaining of children, were for the time being shut up indoors. There was the odor of cooking fires, the smell of the privies, the sour leak of a drainage ditch. Henry felt conspicuous, even in the dark—there was something that felt like feathers inside his stomach. He had no idea which of the houses belonged to the Jenkins—so he didn't know, then, even where he was going. There was nobody to ask. He admitted it—there wasn't a thing here he could do for that family. Any little amount Henry could have given from his own pockets wouldn't have made any real difference. The offer of it, now that he thought about it, would have been an insult. No single effort to right a wrong would amount to anything in this sad, bare place. He'd have had to upend a whole way of life, to make any difference. The worst of it, when you tried to reason out the system of mills and the villages, was that there was no one person to blame.

His father was right about things, in at least one respect. A man's personal feelings shouldn't be brought into the workplace. He'd struck off to the mill village, where he didn't belong, without having any real business being here.

And he would be late getting home.

Chapter 4

Emma's wedding took place on the first Saturday in October, a day of blinding sunshine and still lingering heat. The small church, quickly filled, smelled of well-dressed people and wilting flowers. The Griffen family entered the church single file, with a quiet decorum. There was Ralston's mother—Emma was a little afraid of the woman, who didn't, in fact, look particularly agreeable. She was thin and sharp, had once been deeply brunette, and had passed on her complexion and features to Ralston. She was dressed in a sedate dark blue and she moved with a sort of wariness. The Swanns, in contrast, had to make an effort to settle themselves. Their whispering was audible, almost boisterous. Emma's mother smiled and greeted all around. A small, cushy woman, her own dress was pale and over-trimmed. And as the ceremony began, all eyes on that family pew streamed, except those of the boys, Emma's young twin brothers. The Griffens were evidently a more self-contained lot.

Emma's heels made a loud, hollow sound, as she began down the aisle to join Ralston. The pianist handled *The Wedding March* a little clumsily. Down toward the front, to one side of the pulpit, Ralston stood, hands clasped properly in front of him, with eyes so unnaturally blank, he appeared to look through the walls of the building. His hair was still damp. He wore a new suit, very formal. The change startled Emma. And for a moment her attention came to a halt at the sight of him. She didn't know this dark, strained-looking person. And that wasn't supposed to be.

If inclination had been all that mattered, she might have turned then and walked just as easily back out of the church.

But that instant was lost in other instants. For her ceremony, Emma looked generally pleased and radiant. She had never been in the position of having so many eyes fastened upon her. This was her own very special event, she had been coached; she was instructed to be cordial. Emma blushed, flushed with pleasure. The unusual color was becoming in her face. She was an unexpectedly pretty bride, although physically not at her best. The night before, her mother and sisters had made a pile of the boys' socks, winding and tying Emma's hair up with them. Emma had slept on a head full of loose, uneven knots. Then, later in the morning, there had been the trying ordeal of three pairs of hands, her sisters' and mother's, dressing and ringleting her hair. She had chewed on her lips, to redden them, so continuously that one side of her mouth was puffy.

Now, as the wagon was being loaded in front of the Swann farmhouse, Emma's parents and sisters were subdued. They were losing her. Clanton was over one hundred miles away. But for Emma, the time for such thoughts had not arrived. The day still belonged to her—and she would prolong it, to suit her pleasure. She had never been more than fifteen miles or so from her home. They were going to Clanton—she had always heard of Clanton. They had a farm that belonged to Ralston. And Ralston was her husband—it still didn't seem quite possible that in that brief space of time he had, once and forever, become her husband. Emma's parents had been generous to a fault with their household contributions. So much so that there was no room left for the two trunks which held her special wedding items. Things that the sisters had sewed so lovingly over the summer—things that would have given Emma the most pleasure, if not the most material comfort. They would have to be shipped into Clanton by parcel post. Now the trunks stood by themselves in the yard. And this was too much for Ollie and Mamie, who had worked with such tender enthusiasm. They hung back on the porch and cried.

As the wagon began to move away from the house, Emma too cried a little, from the easy emotion characteristic of her family. "Do you think we'll ever get there?" It was a silly question, she knew, made in simple excess excitement. Emma laughed at herself, wiping her eyes.

Ralston answered with an obliging chuckle. He drove attentively, his legs propped high on the edge of the wagon.

Emma had been often enough into Malvern proper, a little crossroads town, surrounded by miles of unvarying fields, planted to corn and peanuts. The afternoon had peaked, but the sky was still hard and glaring.

"Wasn't it a pretty wedding?"

Ralston's answers were single or double syllables.

"You know, I've never been as far as Dothan."

"That so?" The truth was that Ralston wasn't listening. His thoughts were everywhere and anywhere—surely not on that seat on the wagon. For Ralston, too, the world was in motion, the present little more than a means to an end.

She felt a pressure to keep up some conversation, though Emma wasn't at her talkative best. For one thing, she was too stunned by the heat, dressed as she was without regard for the climate, in long sleeves and gloves, along with stockings and a many-flounced petticoat. Wet rings had formed under the arms of her traveling dress. For some reason Emma became conscious now of the ugliness of her sun hat, which she'd had to tie on, owning no other—her freckled skin blistered in the sun. She was suddenly conscious of all sorts of things. Those wet circles under her sleeves—it was unseemly for a woman to sweat. The sound of her own high voice, beside someone so quiet. She was by now self-conscious of just about everything about herself. She carried a small crocheted handbag—a wedding gift—and so relieved the strain somewhat by busying herself with it.

Just beyond Malvern was the Edwards' place. Emma's mother had written ahead to this Mrs. Edwards—whom nobody had met—whose family had a room to let for travelers. From one place to the next, Emma and Ralston would have to look for this sort of arrangement. There'd be no hotels before Greenville.

The room seemed too brightly lit, to Emma's eyes. Her embarrassment began right there, with the introductions. They were Ralston and Emma Griffen; and there they stood, two awkward young people newly married. They had stepped just inside the doorway to the front room, facing this woman called Mrs. Edwards. The damp places in Emma's clothing had cooled, but she felt hot prickles now under her skin, on her face and neck. Mrs. Edwards seemed a kindly enough sort of person, though Emma wished the woman would lower her voice! A tall girl in pigtails stood a few steps behind her mother, staring. From the farmhouse kitchen came the sound of laughter and masculine voices. Caught off guard, Emma stood there, in that unfamiliar parlor, wanting nothing so much—never would again—as that no one else should enter that room. These people were going to *know*. Everybody in that family was going to *know*! It had been years since Emma had first learned about what happened "down there" when a woman got married. Ollie had been the first one to find out. At first, the sisters had been incredulous. It couldn't be true. Why, their parents—. This reflection made all three of the girls lapse into a sudden, frowning silence. They considered the married women that they knew, who all acted perfectly natural, going about their business as though nothing had happened. Each girl had to carry the new information off by herself for a while. The topic of "down there," so often discussed, had not been mentioned during the months prior to Emma's wedding.

To her relief no one else came up into the room. The family and voices disappeared upstairs—it must have been, Emma thought, earlier than usual. Mrs. Edwards had left a cloth-covered supper tray in the large downstairs bedroom. Afterwards, Emma could never remember what it was they had eaten. She had gone rigid with quiet. As she ate, she listened to the sounds from upstairs, footsteps, conversation, the banging of closets and drawers. When they finished their meal, Ralston blew out the lamp, and the two of them moved around in the darkness, removing their clothes. The bedroom windows stood open, but the heat of the day was still thick in the room. Since her introduction to Mrs. Edwards, all speech had left Emma. She gave not a thought to keeping up her running, small conversation. Her mind had blanked to everything but the embarrassment. Never would she have believed that any embarrassment could be this terrible. Yet it grew worse. She felt its vibration fairly pass over her body—felt, even, a little faint, a thing she never had patience with in other women. Ralston had never touched Emma, apart from chaste— possibly obligatory—parting kisses at the parlor door.

Then an unforeseen complication appeared. Emma's corset— it had hooks as well as lacing. She stood facing away from the bed, immobilized by this predicament. Ralston could see the still, white shape of his wife, and he was familiar with the problem. He stepped up behind Emma, loosened the stiff piece, then returned to the bed. Emma drew out the business of exchanging her chemise for a nightgown as long as was possible. She was dry-mouthed. She was starkly horrified. But there was nothing for it—she moved into her side of the unfamiliar bed. The soft mattress gave way immediately, causing her to slide into Ralston. Without thinking, Emma took hold of the bed frame underneath. Then in a sitting position, braced herself against the bed board.

"Emma."

She couldn't. They needed more time. She *couldn't* be asked to!

"Emma."

His voice was a sound coming from a distance. Her consciousness had departed from everything but the embarrassment. Ralston tugged at her elbow. Again without thinking, Emma jerked at the touch.

"Emma, we got to get some rest."

But that was not what he meant. Both of them knew what he meant.

Speech would not return to Emma that evening. She remained stiffly propped against the bed board. When Ralston finally slept, she inched down into the bedding and dozed. Sometime during the night Ralston woke up, stood first, then stepped around to Emma's side of the bed. And as Emma woke, he roundly patted her stomach. It was an odd gesture, a little like affection, a little like sounding a melon. He raised Emma's gown and entered her so quickly that she had no time for much reaction. Her mother had warned her that it might hurt, reassured her that the hurt wouldn't last. And true, there was the hurting and scraping—but for not much more than a matter of moments. Then it was over. Ralston rolled back and stood up again, obviously relieved. He had acted more in the interest of resolution than from curiosity about Emma's body. He slept again immediately. But Emma lay for a long time in the dark, open-eyed with astonishment. So, this, then, was it. This was the marriage act.

On the following morning there was an awkwardness between the two of them. The Edwards were up before daybreak, like any farm family, the household moving about quietly by lamplight. Ralston and Emma made the simple changes necessary for their day. But their self-consciousness was soon overcome by something stronger. Expediency. Both felt an urgency to be on their way, to make good time. The sky was graying as Ralston hitched the mules and Emma said goodbye to Mrs. Edwards, alone with her now, one married woman to another—though of course nothing was mentioned. The night had moderated, the clean air almost cool. Beyond this farm lay new, open miles and the towns of Enterprise, Elba, Luverne. Now Emma's sense of adventure returned to her. And Ralston's good humor. He chuckled as the wagon moved off the Edwards' place and onto the road. Both felt a sense of expectation. They were going—now they were rightly on their way.

The Edwards house seemed to move little, over the course of that long morning. It sat there over the flat fields for what seemed to Emma like hours on end, its roofline bobbling like the rigging of a ship. The Wiregrass roads were deep in sand throughout the summer. The wheels of the wagon fell into the ruts beneath, making it difficult to steer out again. As the morning brightened, they entered stretches of pine woods, where the mosquitoes were vicious. Ralston swatted and slapped. Emma was unexpectedly shy about dabbing oil of citronella on his neck, his ears and forehead.

The afternoon fell into a heat-soaked lull. She couldn't have said exactly when the trouble began. Emma elbowed Ralston, hard—hard enough to cause him to look over at her with astonishment, to see her swallowing as though she were about to be sick.

"I want to go home."

"What?"

"I want to go home!" And the outburst of tears began. What had she been thinking about, Emma asked herself now, coming off like this, with a man who was little more than a stranger? This thing she had done—it had been a mistake. She hadn't thought long enough. She had moved under water. Now, she surfaced, and the reality of it washed over her. The weeping became ragged. Emma's face had broken out in fierce red blotches.

"What do you mean, you want to go home? We got a farm, now, Emma, our own place." It would have been more appropriate to point out that they were married. But the word "married" would have been too new and too foreign to Ralston's tongue. And in some way too intimate. It would have referred, unavoidably, to the events of last night.

Emma didn't actually hear him. Her speech was stupid. "But I never thought—."

"What do you mean, you never thought?"

"I just didn't, that's all."

Ralston had no answer for this. He didn't know what to do with a weeping woman—it embarrassed him. He looked at her. She didn't look back. He might have patted her a little on the shoulder—but that wouldn't have been quite the thing. Another type of woman he would have jollied. But his mind made no parallels between Emma and that kind of woman.

"You'll like it when we get there." It was a feeble response.

But Emma had quieted down. Because there was nothing else to do. And because she was quiet from simple amazement.

The dry plants were heavy and noisy, made a swishing sound rattling together, as Emma walked back out through the corn rows from relieving herself. Then the silence was sudden, like the invisible fields were at night. And like *he* was silent. He seemed to have nothing to say to her. She wept while Ralston slept. She wept messily, with the swipe of a hand, as she fetched water and moved along, bumping the bucket. She grew less talkative on the seat beside him. The long stretches of pine woods would never come to an end—she knew it. They passed an occasional, isolated farm or a junction with a store and some houses, none of it anything to look at. Enterprise, Elba, Luverne, as it turned out, hadn't been much more to look at than Malvern, just a larger collection of buildings and streets. And there was nothing of playfulness on that wedding journey of gritty and tedious days. Although there might have been—the Swanns were an affectionate family, given to teasing and practical joking. With even a hint of an invitation, Emma could have invented some fun. But did *he* know how to go about having fun? She hadn't the nerve or heart to try.

They were a solitary pair of travelers. At night Ralston un-hitched and tethered the team, and the two of them slept under the wagon on blankets, a single sheet pulled canopy-like over their heads. Emma found herself tiptoeing in the dark—the truth was that it made her uneasy. She felt exposed, even unsafe. She would have never imagined that there could be so much silence in all the world! And all that empty, listening darkness. His silence beside her—it wasn't natural. Was it something she'd done? Something about her, herself? She thought back to their courtship. His calls at the house. For sure he was the courteous sort, a little on the side of too quiet at times, but winning and conversational with her father, respectful to her mother, and with Ollie and Mamie agreeable, if not forthcoming. The two of them were rarely alone during that period. When they were, Ralston tended to hold his hat in his lap—he called dressed in a suit and tie—twirling the hat from time to time and generally staring ahead of him. So, he was shy of her, then. That was understandable. Emma eased the situation along for him with agreeable chatter—or so she thought. Ollie and Mamie were often there, sometimes the twins, frequently Mr. Swann, to whom Ralston directed most of his conversation, amiable talk of weather and farming. Emma had no standard of comparison for a serious courtship. And from Ralston there was nothing inspired, certainly none of the sort of behavior that would have left the sisters giggling behind the front door— they had listened once or twice.

Still holding his hand under her elbow, Ralston roughly escorted Emma—almost lifting her off of her feet—out the hotel door and into the street. She had no idea if they were being observed. But it was all right. Because at last he had claimed her. Acknowledged and claimed her—at least, Emma told herself that. She'd made a mistake in judgment, she knew. But she was out of her depth in Greenville—she was too young to know better. Maybe none of that mattered, after all.

Emma Swann had no conception of wealth. Comfort and modest prosperity, yes. Her own family was modestly prosperous, the Griffen family more so. But wealth—she didn't know how to imagine it. The simple accumulation of what Emma's world called valuable would never have constituted wealth. And it was precisely that which had gone into the making of Greenville, Alabama, a trading center for cotton—along with all the social distinctions and contrivances that went with it. A gravel road had been the first difference. Then, the gravel road leading into town gave way to brick pavement at the junction just past the outly-ing cemetery. There were spired stone markers and plots fenced off by grillwork, all of it draped by the overhang of live oaks. Then the houses began. Emma would have never believed such extravagance, the sheer overpowering size of them. The columned bulk of them dwarfed anyone out on the porches or lawns. It was enough to bring back her chatter, which Emma understood by now to be no more than conversation held with herself.

At the first intersection, two large and handsome churches sat facing one another from opposite sides of the street. Then the business section began, a spectacle for Emma. The stores—there were so many of them! Emma had only seen general stores. She had never seen a really smart buggy. She had also never seen large numbers of black faces at any one place. She glanced around. Nobody else seemed alarmed—Emma had been taught to be afraid of Negroes.

For Ralston, too, all of it made for entertainment—but he was proud about it, a little furtive. He only glanced at Emma as he tied the mules and she climbed down from the wagon. Emma must have assumed that Ralston was behind her as she walked through the front doors of Butler's Hotel. She wore an old calico, once an orange and gray print, now faded to near uniformity. She held the hated sun hat by the strings. But she entered the double doors of Butler's with a pleasant smile of greeting on her face. She saw that the lobby and restaurant were extravagantly lit, though the sun was still bright outside. Potted palms stood on either side of the entrance and along the hallway. The floor was made up of octagon-shaped, colored tiles. Toward the far end, the hall was wet and gleaming, where a Negro woman was passing a mop. A partition and ferns separated the entrance to the restaurant area, close to which two women sat, drinking tea. They looked at Emma, then back at each other, with only the subtlest change of expression.

A man in a formal suit with a looped mustache stood behind the reception desk. Emma was aware that the man's eyes were on her, saw him withdraw them, just an instant too late. Afterward she wondered why it was that she kept on walking. She recalled that the Negro woman had stopped her mopping and stood, hands resting across the handle—staring. Emma stepped up to the desk; the man behind it carried on his business as though no one were there. It was possible that he didn't know how to deal with the delicacy of this situation: country people wandered in, from time to time, but this young woman was by herself. Young though she was, Emma had her own female intuition. She hadn't stopped to think—why, just last night they'd slept under the wagon, fully clothed. Now hot shame crawled over her. She should give some sort of explanation, that they were on the road and such. But the man wouldn't look at her. Emma had never been outside of surroundings that were familiar, where her family was known and respected. She couldn't have said to this stranger that she was Edwin Swann's daughter. She was not—she understood that much already—in a place where that remark would make any difference. She would have backed away then, if Ralston hadn't stepped up behind her and taken her elbow. He cleared his throat, and Emma looked up. Ralston's face had gone stiff. The clerk glanced up once, then slammed the register drawer. Emma noticed that he batted his eyelids. Those few moments under Ralston's eyes now executed his punishment in full. For that stare had, in its potential for cruelty, the assurance of a perfect and delighted execution. The clerk must have wondered in those few moments if he would be bloodied, strangled, or worse.

"Let's us be on, Emma," Ralston said, in an unexpectedly

gentle voice. But he stood at the desk for a few moments longer, aware of the small but exquisite torture he was inflicting. Then he smiled very slowly. "Good day to you, sir."

Emma was led away. The touch at her elbow was not gentle. Yet it was a new feeling. He was protecting her. Claiming her. Emma said nothing. She was afraid of him, had the truth been known to both of them. Without a pause in his stride, Ralston looked down at her, directly into her eyes. It was the first time he'd ever done so. Possibly he was assessing her. Emma didn't grasp that his own vanity was outraged—for she was, after all, his.

When later they brought the wagon down a side street to a neat bungalow with a room to let, Emma listened with a little surprise to Ralston's introduction. "Pardon our appearance, ma'am. We've been traveling."

She sat drawn into herself on the seat, while the pleasantries and information were exchanged. Something in the "we" of his words struck Emma. She knew, too, that in this day's experience there was something too large for her understanding.

Chapter 5

The mill whistle sounded, a long, monotonous blast. Noontime. The noise of machinery was quickly replaced by a blur of voices and the movement of feet. Henry shuffled down the back stairs with more noise than was necessary, excessive energy, and on this particular Thursday, especially good humor. The stairs stopped at the wall where coats hung and pails were stacked. Henry passed a youngster bending over to pick up a lunch pail.

"Something in your pocket, son."

A couple of feet away a tall girl was lifting a coat off a peg. "Spider, miss!" Henry smacked the wall with his palm, then pushed something into her hand. The girl smiled. She knew the one about the spider. What Henry had given her and the boy were pieces of hard candy, cheap candies from the general store, lingering tastes of sugar and flavoring delectable to the mill children.

"Hey there, June bug!" This greeting to a little girl named Eloise, who was also taking her coat from a peg. Eloise would get the peppermint, a favored piece. The little girl's color was wrong. It disturbed Henry.

Now he ducked inside the door to his father's office, to collect his own things. "That little skinny one out there, with the pigtails," he spoke of Eloise, "she ought not to be here at all."

Mr. Gray was used to these opinions of Henry's. It had occurred to him that his boy was a dreamer. They'd never had one like that in the family—it was frankly a curiosity. But he would get over it, Mr. Gray told himself. In this same son there was something that plumbed true and right, in a way that was absent in the others. And as for Henry and his running opinions, if he'd realized Mr. Taylor was also present, he would have withheld his launching comment. The two older men had grown up together, had the habit of meeting during the day between business hours. Mr. Taylor was a drawling, self-satisfied man of some leisure. The family owned land; he ventured one business experiment after another with the capital. And Henry, who by habit observed all the rules of good manners, was embarrassed to be caught in his unguarded, at-home behavior. He snatched up his coat and cap in a rush, while the older men watched him, then looked back at each other. Mr. Taylor had a high opinion of Henry, and the behavior amused him. He often remarked to his friend Joe that Henry had, as he put it, fine prospects.

The truth was that Henry's loathing of the mill had increased to the point that he had to allow it these little exits. He hated being shut up, any place. But this place he hated just walking into—the smell of it by itself annoyed him, stinking and stale, the air itchy with lint dust. He grew irritable, a thing not in his nature. He broke out at times in a very fever of restlessness. Once, after closing time, he struck off in the direction opposite to home. And in the cover of first dark took off his shoes, tucking both under his arm like a football, and ran—he didn't stop to think why. Had run down a little dribbly sand road between cornfields, run to the point of punishing himself, run until exhaustion brought him the relief of mental and physical calm. He didn't remember what he'd told Lillian about the sand in his clothes. He and Lillian had been married since that summer, and she was several months pregnant. At times during his work day, Henry remembered these facts with a sort of wondrous surprise, like a child forgets and remembers a new possession.

Today was Thursday, the last Thursday of the month. Once a month at this time Henry drove into Clanton for a meeting with the owner of the mill. It was Henry's job on these Thursdays to collect the payroll, discuss the quality of the threads, collect samples of newly-baled cotton for his father's inspection. He was also instructed by his parents to "check on" his older brother Drefus, who rented a room in Clanton, one of three brothers, the much-loved family ne'er-do-well, about whom the parents complained, fretted, and secretly grieved. Drefus was wild. They could do nothing with Drefus. As with himself and his father, Henry and Drefus had no noticeable family resemblance. Drefus' face and features were narrow. His ears lay close to his head. But the two of them had been together all the slow, indistinct years of a boyhood. Of his brothers and sisters—there were five of them—Henry loved this one most, the brother under whose arm he'd grown up, who had taught him to fish, to hunt, and to fistfight. Before Lillian, Henry would have scarcely recognized himself, without Drefus beside him.

Now Lillian accompanied Henry on these once-a-month business excursions. There was no reason, of course, that she shouldn't have, at least as far as Henry could see. They made it into a special sort of a thing, between themselves working up an anticipation of the day, a weekday, that had all the flavor of playing hooky.

That noon it was obvious to Joe Gray that Henry was splitting to be off. "You're in an awful big hurry there, son." He was amusing himself at Henry's expense. Mr. Taylor looked on. "You're gonna have to hold up, though. Mother wants you to go by and pick up some shirts she's got ready for Drefus." The delay, any delay, was maddening, but Henry nodded, nodded again to Mr. Taylor. He was already moving.

Once outside the building, he broke into a peculiar-looking stride. Henry's legs were long, and he worked the legs at full tilt, hopping a little with each step. The family home was a good twenty-minute walk away. He'd have to make it shorter. But the effort was futile. When Henry arrived at the house, coming in through the kitchen, he saw that his mother had the shirts intended for Drefus rolled into three damp balls, ready for ironing. There was nothing to do but sit it out.

"Well, how's my boy?" Each of her sons was "my boy" whenever he happened to arrive at the house. Mrs. Gray stepped forward and spread her arms, but it was a gesture—she didn't embrace Henry. She turned up her face instead, for him to kiss. She was not an especially demonstrative mother, except with Jay. Possessive and competent, yes. Above all, she was fiercely opinionated—even if the orbit of Annie Gray's opinion was small. She favored religious topics, which to her mind consisted of right and wrongdoing. Though as a rule Annie Gray placed no particular curbs on her tongue; even she would have never openly said to Henry that he had married above himself—no more than any of the McClintons would have made the inverse statement to Lillian. For himself, Henry knew only that there was a fineness in Lillian. A sort of quality that directly satisfied some nameless thing in himself.

"Well, has she been feeding you?" Mrs. Gray made a show of looking over Henry. Her grin had just a touch of spite. "Looks like you could use a bite. Now, you'll have to wait a little, while I get these shirts ready." She brought a cake plate in from the dining room and set it in front of Henry. Only a slice or two of the cake had been eaten. His mother made a pound cake that was weighty on the fork, and Henry cut one piece, then another. It had been hours since he felt any trace of his breakfast, and his need for food imposed on him. Food. That was the only drawback to these Thursdays. Lillian's cold lunches. Henry fervently hoped that Rosa, their hired help, would have cooked a hot dinner. Otherwise, Lillian would have packed what she called a cold lunch, in a hamper. Henry's small and dainty wife, so committedly a lady, was a lamentable cook, performing the various tasks of cooking with such stoic dislike that the very ingredients of the food seemed transformed in the process. Efforts surrendered, failed altogether, beneath that dainty hand. It amused Henry to watch his wife, frowning and poking over the stove. She was near childlike in size, in her smallness intensely feminine. He looked at her mouth, the way the clean little top lip rested against the lower. In all the little details, nature had been kind to Lillian. Her hair was thick, a dark auburn. She pulled it back, twisted, and pinned it hard each morning. But by midday it would have worked loose and curled around her face, which was full, slightly square. She had very round, dark eyes. Lillian's movements, her posture, all had a kind of delicacy about them. She was anything but a practical person.

With her pregnancy, there were nights now when she didn't want to sleep. Henry, always an easy sleeper, would find himself awakened at odd hours, tickled or poked. Lillian lay in the dark, propped on an elbow. She knew that she was being silly about the baby, but she couldn't seem to help it.

"Henry, what do you think the baby will look like?" A pointless question, of course.

It would take Henry some moments to wake up. "Well, we wouldn't want him to have my ears." He folded his pillow around his head, preparing to sleep again. Lillian pulled on the pillow.

"Henry, do you want a boy or a girl?" And so it would go. He indulged her at these times. She was foolish these days with contentment.

"That gonna be enough for you?" As Annie Gray watched her son eat, Henry watched his mother lift and sling the iron, without any effort that he could perceive. She was a strong woman, as tall as her husband, not fat, but thick through the middle. As Henry ate and his mother ironed, he looked at her in a way that was new, that had come to him since he himself had been married. He wouldn't quite allow that he was looking at his mother as a woman—looking at her now as the girl who had been his father's bride. As a girl, Annie Rivers was said to have been very pretty. Henry had no way of knowing that the thick body had once been small-waisted and sweetly curved, the smile dimpled, the eyes laughing. Or that Joe Gray had been besotted by his young wife. But he noted, now, with surprise and dismay, that there was a lack of refinement about her that must not have been apparent to young Joe Gray. In spite of himself, he compared his mother to Lillian. Henry was still giving serious attention to the cake, which his mother noticed.

She inclined her head toward him. "Henry, has that girl learned to cook yet?"

This wasn't a question.

Henry replied mildly enough. "She's doing reasonably well."

"None of those girls ever expected to have to cook for themselves. When everybody knew the McClintons hadn't had a thing for so long, nobody but them remembered. 'Course, now, she's got that colored woman."

Henry had finished the cake and was restless. Now Mrs. Gray turned to face him. "She won't be off this afternoon with you to town, traipsing around in her condition?"

Henry chuckled again. "She'll be off, all right."

The answer had been a mistake. It brought Mrs. Gray's ironing to a halt. "You mean to say she'll be off to town in that wagon on these roads? What business has she got in town, anyway?"

"She wants me to take her to the library."

"The library?" Henry may as well have said a house of ill repute.

"What business does she have at the library?" This time Mrs. Gray's incredulity was genuine. "The library." Her voice dropped a few notes.

"She likes to read," he answered over his shoulder, as he walked outside to smoke. Lillian was the only person Henry knew who read for pleasure. Mrs. Gray's reading was exclusively biblical. She continued, through the door, "Myself, I don't hold with too much reading of books."

What she didn't know was that Henry's liking for reading books was even stronger than Lillian's. On their hooky Thursdays, the thing the two of them looked forward to most was their visit to the Carnegie Library, a dome-shaped building of gray stone, with a dim and silent interior, managed by a Miss Calder, a sour woman who disapproved of the public in general, with some exceptions—Lillian was an exception. The young librarian had thin fingers, with large, bony knuckles. The hands, clean to the point of looking boiled and scrubbed, annoyed Henry. He couldn't help it. He hated the hands, hands that were proprietary, hands that so stingily doled out the riches that they controlled. Henry would go directly to the reserve room, where material could not be withdrawn without Miss Calder's special permission—which from Henry she withheld. He didn't think of handing the matter over to Lillian. The reserve area smelled of aging paper and wiped down dust, but Henry had grown fond of the smell. He prowled the periodicals for facts—the *Clanton Times* had mostly editorials. But he was impatient. He wanted even more to get at the books.

For it was here, in this small room, that Henry fed his starved love for history. He seemed always just to get started—there was never enough time. Henry found that he was enthralled by the past, as though some revealing and secret thing could be found there—something that must be, had to be, if not reclaimed, at least found out. The history selection on the reserve shelves tended heavily toward Southern regional history. Now, propped up in a straight-backed chair, Henry read a volume-long account of the Battle of Clanton. He was lost in the pages. The old arsenal had been located just short town blocks from where he sat now and read. It was a firsthand account of that battle, and it affected him strangely, that the events had been so near. Almost, Henry wanted to stand up and walk out somewhere, to find out that very place, and with it, in some way, that time. He read rapidly, in great gulps, so that when Lillian came for him, he'd feel a little like he'd been waked up from a nap. He had to make a conscious effort to relocate himself.

Lillian went about her own business, leaving Henry to read. She knew that it was the reserve room material that her husband craved. She could locate certain war novels for him. She had to fall back repeatedly on westerns. She stood in front of a stall of softcover books, a serene little woman in a loose blue dress and a string of pearls. Already she had a stack of books on the floor beside her. She skimmed others or fell into reading them. Unconscious of herself, Lillian was one of those women who made a kind of picture. Eyes tended to look back at her for pleasure.

Now Henry's eyes locked onto his mother, who, placated a little, started in on the last shirt. His time urgency heaved. He didn't have to be reminded that his mother saw no value in reading. For all of his years in that house, there had only been two books besides the Bible, those Henry had hidden in the windbreak spot behind the cornfield. He had borrowed them, he told himself. Over the period of time that he secretly toted the books back and forth from the schoolhouse, he'd been edgy, almost guilty—but not quite. The hidden books were always in his mind in some way. He was possessed of a secret sphere of delight. Like any of his schoolmates, Henry hadn't been much for reading, until about his sixth year in school. It had all been a tedious business at first— school was a thing that had to be put up with. It began at the general store, Henry's sudden pleasure in the skill. He found that he could tell himself things. He didn't have to ask. He could read the information on boxes and cans. He could make out the larger print from where old Mr. Chittom sat, cross-legged, reading his newspaper—it didn't cross Henry's mind to ask to see it himself.

Nothing connected with schooling had ever been linked with pleasure. His teacher in grades five through eight, an embattled Miss Lewis, moved her students through days of unvarying routine, through drills of facts that were pointless, through endless and torturous calculations. One Blue East and One Blue West, a classroom wit had once called her. The name stuck. Her blue, bespectacled eyes looked out in opposite directions, and they were not kind. Miss Lewis was ready with the ruler or cane, although Drefus was the only one of the Gray children to actually get it. Henry wasn't the caning type. Miss Lewis knew the caning type, so that his sudden, odd behavior puzzled her. Henry took to throwing spitballs, at odd times, usually on the way out of the building for recess, so that there wasn't time for Miss Lewis to stop the class for a caning. She made him stay inside, instead, this being what he had counted on. For he had made a discovery. Miss Lewis owned books. There was a bookshelf near the platform where her desk sat, most of them books used for math, spelling, or recitations. But there were a few on the lower shelf that Miss Lewis didn't use. The one that caught Henry's attention was the *New Encyclopedia, Volume 5, L-N*. He was struck by the word: encyclopedia. Now there was no possible reason that he could think of for making a word so long. He took a quick look at the book one day after school was let out, just long enough to see that there were pictures. Then the throwing of spitballs began. He had to time it just right. If he did it too often, even on the way outside of the building, Miss Lewis would have stopped the lot of them and caned him right there. And he had to choose just the right victim. Most of Henry's schoolmates just smiled or laughed at a spitball; some of the girls interpreted the behavior as flirting. But there were certain troublemakers. Lillian McClinton was one, a small girl with fat ringlets. He regretted having to choose Lillian—years later he asked himself if he had already loved her. He could count on her to make a fuss. The spitball he launched at Lillian hit her cheek with an unintentional sting—he had flicked it hard. The little girl at first just looked at Henry. The big eyes became enormous; the lower lip bunched up. For a moment, he was outright sorry. But he was right. She had made a fuss. A big one. The McClinton children were part of that group that Miss Lewis treated differently. Henry's first awareness of social distinctions came from observing this difference.

But the recesses seemed even shorter inside the stuffy school building than in the freedom of the yard. It would take him a year, Henry thought, maybe more than a year, to read all of the heavy book—even, it seemed, to read the section on Man. The *New Encyclopedia*, which was far from new, had fallen open just at this section. Maybe at one time old Miss Lewis had used it. In the middle of that section was a double page, a chart, with pictures. And a caption. The Faces of Man. Arranged over a map of the world were artist renditions of the torsos and faces of men with strange features and clothing. Henry studied each one of the drawings, wondering if all of them really existed. Now, Indians he already knew about—more than most people, in fact. A family of Grays had gone off to Texas in a Conestoga, to settle, they had thought. But in the long run only turned around, most of them, to head back to Alabama. They had been full of stories about Indians. Negroid. This torso and face Henry studied with outright disbelief. The face was blue-black, the head slightly elongated. There was a large metal ring through the nose. Negroid. Negro. But the illustration didn't look like Jessie or Nathaniel. Someone must have made it up. Jessie and Nathaniel looked a lot like each other, with round faces and button-like noses. Their skins were the color of the polished wood trim on Henry's mother's settee. Henry hadn't thought of the boys for a year or so, but now he could see them again. He had missed them. The Hobson family had lived in a small, rickety house at the edge of the woods that surrounded the Gray property. The two boys, brothers like himself and Drefus, became the playmates of Henry and Drefus. The pairs of brothers entered and left the kitchens of each other's homes with the simple naturalness of children. And the Hobson family had moved before that moment when, unaccountably, one or more of the boys would have become uncomfortable with the others, this maybe due to some word from one of their parents. But the Hobsons one day disappeared. And in what was like no time, the rough house collapsed in on itself, and the woods overtook it. Henry wondered about Jessie and Nathaniel. He wondered about The Faces of Man.

As winter approached, Henry couldn't resist it—his wool jacket was excellent concealment. He took the thick, fine-printed volume from the shelf. At home, he wrapped it in a pair of old overalls and hid it in various places. Behind the house and cornfield, in a sunny spot, a windbreak of briar bushes, Henry took his pleasure in delicious tranquility. His whereabouts became somewhat of a mystery to his family, who had a fine time teasing him about the "some little girl" he was visiting. Henry was happy to let it pass.

So he read. He finished Man. There were other things, of course, not as good as Man. There was Language, Law, such things as Leprosy and Mammoth; there was The Moon. Medicine was good. So was North America. But nothing else affected Henry like the section on Man. The second book that Henry permitted himself to borrow in this fashion, a much smaller one, had a simple title, *Natural History*. And this book was almost new. It make a cracking sound as Henry opened it, released a fresh, papery odor. "To Flossie, on Christmas Day, 1901." Flossie. She had a name, then, like anyone else. But Henry was too busy now to think about that. He had discovered wonders, unimaginable things like cells and cell walls; the whole world had become a wonderful bafflement of little tiny, invisible pieces. For a while, Henry tore things apart, certain that if he just tried hard enough, he could pick out one of them, a cell. He poked around a lot with a pin, before giving it up. But the Geological Time Table was almost as absorbing; and this, too, was hard to imagine. The world had been inhabited before. The world once, long ago, had been a strange, different world, wet, leafy, and silent. With huge, clumsy bodies crashing around, with brains not much better than a crawdad's. There were life forms, ancient life forms, still alive now, Henry read, in the sea. But Henry couldn't get to the sea. He and Drefus could always get to the Cahaba, a twisting and dangerous river. But further down, at the mouth of the Cahaba, the Alabama flowed—that would be like the sea. It was deep enough, wide enough. They said that in some places there were sunken ships. In some places you couldn't get to the bottom.

Henry almost jumped. "Here you go, now." Mrs. Gray walked out onto the back porch where Henry had been standing, with the stack of warm shirts in her hands. But she was not yet ready to release them. She had been thinking, as she ironed, and she had an additional word to say. "Now, you make her keep still in the wagon." Henry's mother, for some reason, never used Lillian's name. "You're gonna have to take a firm hand with that girl. A girl like that." Now Mrs. Gray overheard herself and reddened.

"Yes'm."

"You just be careful, now. Take the wagon slow."

"Yes'm." Yes'm! He was crazy to be off.

Their Thursday was a fine one, clear and sunny. It was not unusual for the spring bulbs to open in the first strong sun of February. Henry and Lillian had their lunch, a cold lunch after all, on a grassy spot above the landing. It was food that didn't satisfy. But the rest of it, the bright air and first warmth, the view of the river—those things satisfied. Henry liked to let his eyes trail over the slow, sun-shingled surface. It was hypnotic, the moving and breaking lines of light. The water looked placid. But Henry knew it was not a placid river. At the landing site, the opposite bank seemed far away, wild, a little-known country in itself.

They stayed at the library until closing time. And at the end of the day, they dutifully drove down Green Street, on the lookout for Drefus, who had a room at Strayer's boarding house. Henry's body had already tightened. He dreaded the odd animosity he'd become so acutely aware of—from Lillian toward Drefus. Drefus himself had animosity toward no one. It was the one shadow in his life with Lillian, this strain. The two of them were the people he loved most on earth. But neither Henry nor Lillian really expected to see Drefus that afternoon—who would have been immediately spotted on the porch of the sprawling gray building, which was always occupied with boarders and a small crowd. Henry was frankly relieved that his brother wasn't there. And beside him, Lillian was as much so. It was true that Drefus amused her, at times in spite of herself. She recognized his good nature. Yet she felt a dread associated with this brother. It didn't make sense. It was as if Drefus would inevitably cause something to happen. Not a little something of no consequence, like getting Henry tipsy. But something large and ominous that lay out before them, vague yet threatening. She tried to remind herself that she was a sensible person—she'd never felt anything of a disturbing nature about a person of her acquaintance. And the world at large loved Drefus. Possibly there was jealousy in the mix. Henry was hers in a way he was nobody else's. No one else knew the Henry she knew.

She put a hand over his. Self-consciousness made her solemn, as any deliberate lie was still, at that young age, a violation of her upbringing. She made her pronouncement very deliberately, "We'll tell your family how hard we looked for him."

The seriousness amused Henry. The generosity behind the falsehood touched him–as that trait of hers always had.

On the night Lillian lost the baby, the house was unnaturally quiet, once Dr. Harris made his departure. Henry heard the clock ticking inside the bedroom. He leaned against the bedroom door, doorknob in hand, then thought better of it. He waited to light a lamp until he got to the dining room. There he took down a bottle of brandy, a home brew, and a small glass. Lillian would sometimes take a little brandy. He went back to the bedroom and this time opened the door. Lillian lay facing the opposite wall. Her face in sleep looked untroubled. There would be time enough for her to remember, he thought. The loss pained him for her because he loved her. But there would be more babies. And he'd make things up to her somehow. He'd move her to Clanton. He could make his break from the hated mill, on the strength of that decision. He'd find work within a short distance from home, once they moved.

Henry left the door open, made a fire in the living room stove, all of this quiet enough not to wake her. The ticking of the clock jumped, resonated throughout the house. The small noise of it seemed out of place in the nighttime stillness. At this hour there were no other sounds. There was a passing train. Then its whistle faded out there, somewhere in all that straining darkness. He could hear her already, asking what she had done wrong, tormenting herself with some negligence that only she could imagine. He would not be able to comfort her. He put the bottle and glass down in front of him, absently but neatly pouring the liquor back into the bottle. Then he finished the bottle himself. He took an armchair in the parlor, to wait until she woke, he decided. Henry slept immediately, not stirring until the mill whistle sounded. A quick blast, followed by a longer one. The room was filled with murky, gray light. The filmy sounds of first morning muffled the clock. Then the mill whistle again, strange to his ears. The sound seemed to come from another world. He felt a sore weight moving under his forehead. He stood up to check on the fire, which was out.

Chapter 6

She saw it once, through crowds of branches—and she loved it at once: it was her house. Late in the afternoon, their sixth day of traveling, the wagon moved down a clay road, mostly shaded. This road Ralston knew, as Emma didn't, to be the lower south border of the farm property. The wagon listed toward a strip of woods which was part of the farm wood lot. There was a pecan orchard, not large—and overgrown. A graying farmhouse sat back beyond it. There was a good stand of oaks. One more such place in mile after mile of farm properties, the weathering houses and orchards. Emma had seen too many to notice—in the long days of travel, anticipation had slowly drained out of her. But here Ralston left the road and turned into a drive. The mules came to a stop.

"Well, Emmalie?" This little variation in her name—it was his one show of something like fondness. But Emma was preoccupied. She had been struggling with a can of sardines, which she had part way open. The fishy broth had leaked out onto her fingers. Ralston turned toward her, looking pleased. Now she had the can open. She sipped the juice herself, to be rid of it.

"Well?" he repeated. She was still busy. Then she caught on to something.

"Hmm?" He watched now with open amusement as Emma's eyes traveled over the house, darted to the orchard and fields, then returned to the house.

"Is this it?"

Ralston just sat, looking pleased with himself.

"Is this *it*?" Emma's tone had changed. It was no longer a question, just a collection of words. Emma made a noise and handed the can to Ralston. In her enthusiasm, she lost all sense of the strain she had been under. They were here. And the house was her own. It was bigger than she would have expected, solid and well built. Tall and squarish, sitting high up on its cellar. It was a handsome house in a sturdy kind of way. A porch ran along the front, with three columns. The sight of it delighted Emma, its neglect a detail too trivial for notice. They continued around to the back, where Emma spotted the pump, built right into the back porch. The Swann children had always had to run back and forth to get to the pump. Emma remembered having to run in the rain.

In her eagerness, the inclination to chatter returned to Emma. The house, empty except for the kitchen range and an ornate, fussy-looking stove in the parlor, had that strange feeling of vacancy about it. Across the back porch lay drifts of rain-pocked pollen, withered oak silk, and leaves. The prints of a pair of man's shoes led back and forth from the porch steps to the back door. But there was no trace of ownership left in those dim, hollow rooms. The house was theirs.

A ceiling. A room. It took Emma some moments to remember where they were. They had slept on a mattress laid down in the dusty front room. Ralston left the farm early. They made yet another breakfast that day on mush with a little sugar. It was a grim, unsatisfying meal. Ralston frowned as he ate. Emma too was not satisfied, hungry all the while she ate the mush. She found herself thinking, as she never had before, about food. The taste of new butter, fresh milk and buttermilk, the flavor of raw tomatoes, the sweet earthy taste of vegetables cooked with pork. But she was chatty and eager. She would start right away on her kitchen. The day was still wet and heavy with morning. By herself now, Emma swept and scrubbed down the floor. With the unpacked crates she made a makeshift arrangement of shelves and felt inventive about it. In her first flurry of work, she was content. But when she finished, an odd feeling came over her. For the first time in her life, Emma was entirely alone in a house. She had never, to her certain knowledge, been right by herself anywhere. Now she grew still and listened, for what she didn't know. In the house there was only silence. There were the bedrooms upstairs, which needed a good cleaning. But no. Wait. She didn't have to do it just yet. It would be hours before Ralston got back. She didn't have to do anything just yet. This idea made Emma pause with one foot on the stair landing. A look of secret excitement passed over her face. By nature Emma was obedient. She had all her life consistently—for the most part cheerfully—done as she was told. Now there was no one around to tell her. The small excitement increased. Why, she might just as well take a look around outside, first. She could make that decision.

As Emma walked out to the porch, she realized that it was no longer early morning. The day was brilliant with new-washed sun and alive with the noise of birds. She almost laughed out loud that the day was so fine, that she was here, where she stood: that it was her porch, her house, the property of her husband. Emma glanced up, shading her eyes with her hand. The sky moved rapidly above her—she seldom stopped to look at it. She'd just have a look at the outbuildings and orchard, what was left of the kitchen garden.

When Ralston returned that afternoon, the wagon was loaded with hardware and groceries. There was a cow trailing behind the wagon, a crate of old hens and a rooster. The two of them sat down right there, on the back steps, to eat the tomatoes, biting into them like pieces of fruit. They made supper that evening on Emma's flapjacks, stacks of small golden disks—between each she spread new butter and sprinkled sugar. There was a pitcher of fresh milk, the first they had tasted since the morning of their wedding. As she served Ralston, Emma kept up a running chatter about the food she put down before him. This would become her habit. It was a pleasure for her to serve food; her conversation was a way of increasing the pleasure of eating it. There was an eagerness in both of them then, not just for the food, but for the effort they were undertaking. This was their own place, to build up, to make prosperous with the steady progress of slow and demanding physical work. And for the present, that had a rightness to it; it was what both had been brought up to do. Everything formal, informal, that could be said to have been their education, the whole of their upbringing and training for life, had led them to this place, this business of making their lives. This, then, was to be their life. They were beginning it, with energies coiled like a spring.

When Ralston walked outside in the late light, Emma trotted after him. They stood together for a little, at the west fence, looking out over what had been the cornfields. Where Emma saw acres, Ralston saw neglect, even ruin. It was the best of soils, one hundred sixty-six rich Black Belt acres. A soil almost black, heavy in the hand and fragrant, not like the pale Wiregrass soil that fell through the fingers. Over the course of a single, sun-stricken summer, the acres of crops had reverted, were by this time thick masses of half wild vegetation. Emma knew a ruined field when she saw one—she could see that the state of things troubled him.

"Well," Ralston let his head fall between his shoulders and shook it, with something like a chuckle. "Looks like it's mine, now."

"I know you're proud of it." It was in Emma's nature to comfort. She gave a little stroke to his arm, and her hesitancy in touching him puzzled her. She felt a strong sympathy for him, then—she felt it often. She could have lavished him with affection at such times, if he had let her. Perhaps if she could have for once dropped that restraint, have been herself freely and convincingly with this man she had married, it may have made some small difference.

Ralston looked down at her curiously. He felt no need to reply, simply because a remark had been made.

Emma would have liked most to ask if he were happy.

She sat on the cellar steps, an unlikely spot for writing a letter. When she was discouraged, Emma hid. Or lonely: Emma hid. The hiding was compulsive in the empty house. She held a cheap writing tablet on her knees. With it she used a pencil that she kept sharpened with a paring knife. There was so much that she wanted to tell them! But Emma's letters to her family were much like theirs were to her: short profusions of affection, with a household detail or two added—they were, none of them, especially well lettered people. She wanted to tell them how it had been. She wrote, instead, a single sentence: "We have finished up with the harvest." The sentence said nothing at all. Now she wondered why nobody had warned her. Maybe nobody knew. They, Emma and the sisters, had never done much picking at home—they didn't grow cotton. They grew peanuts. And the men did the picking that had to be done. Maybe they wouldn't have even believed her.

She and Ralston worked together, that first week, then the second, another—Emma lost count. First, the ruined cornfields had to be dealt with. Ralston moved inside the rows, muttering profanities where the masses of weeds had already gone to seed. In places it was difficult for the two of them to spot the stunted ears, and a good number of the corn plants were barren. With the mules and wagon behind them, they pushed through the tangles, twisting and snapping the small ears where they found them. The tall grass tickled and tormented Emma. Her face splotched and broke out. It didn't take long for the continuous twisting of the hard, stringy ears to make blisters in the palms of their hands. The blisters would rise, break, and make sore places. Emma had to force her hands to work again—but she didn't try to beg off. She knew she could leave off before Ralston, to go inside for the cooking. The kitchen was strange and dark to her eyes, coming in from the fields. She built up her fire, to rewarm certain dishes, to begin others she would set aside for the next day. In her fatigue, she confused herself.

After the corn came the cotton. The bolls were small, under-sized like the corn, not easy to spot through the Jimsonweed and Johnson grass. The tiny bolls affected Emma like something delib-erately vicious. The hard, sharp hulls stabbed her fingers. Emma's cuts swelled and bled—and she knew she'd be stabbed again, in the same places. She wrapped her own fingers in strips of cloth, but Ralston wouldn't let her wrap his. The picking seemed to go on forever. Ralston swore. Emma wept. Salt water ran through her eyes. Perspiration or tears, she couldn't say—it didn't much matter. The plants caught and tugged at the bag that she pulled. The strong equinox sun hammered. With each other Ralston and Emma grew silent, bruised by their weariness. There were times during the picking when Emma cooked, served, ate beside Ralston without a word passing between them. Just to be still and be quiet—they needed that—though Emma less so than Ralston. After the corn and the cotton, the digging of the sweet potatoes, the lifting, cutting, and bundling of pea plants were gentle harvests, in comparison.

Now Emma was by herself. On the farm the couple's labor divided. Emma had no more part in the harvest, except for the daily gatherings of fallen pecans. She walked with her eyes on the ground, her feet making a dry, swishing noise in the leaves. It was comfortable work. It was lonesome. She didn't realize at first how lonesome—after the fieldwork, anything had seemed welcome. Now she lost sight of Ralston during the days. Until now they were working, pushing ahead, punishing themselves with work because there was a goal to keep moving toward—a great and final culmination. What had that been? Emma had lost the sense, now, of just what it was.

Ralston came in from the fields only to eat—he ate quickly—then went to the barn. She observed him as he ate—he was preoccupied. He seemed to have no need of her, beyond the food she set down before him. She had assumed it to be a fact of life—that need, until now satisfied, that she had for other people. People to touch, to tease and fuss over. She needed the chatter that made a day comfortable. Ralston felt no need for these things, it was obvious. By nature he tended to silence, just as Emma tended to chatter. Emma would come to learn that her husband was easy and talkative only in the company of men. Yet with his wife as the only audience available, at times he was driven to talk of the little daily matters that troubled him. This, then, would gradually become his habit: to depend on that audience. Emma answered in soothing non-sequiturs, little comments about his food or rest. His silences were no longer as disturbing to her as they once had been—she had learned to pace out the rhythm of Ralston's silences.

But the burden of her days bore down on her. Emma's longing for her family was like a physical illness. No one had told her it could be this way. Always, before, there had been company, the three other sets of hands, her mother's and sisters'—she had lived with the closeness of bodily contact. Now there was only Ralston's brief, nightly gratification of that need of men—there were no caresses, no fond touches—unlike her own family, Ralston was not fond of being touched. And with her own family there was always the jostling, the blandishments, as well as the kisses and pinches. The stroking. There was a thing that she wanted—Emma couldn't have attached a word to this feeling. She was nonetheless driven by it that night when she had come up to find Ralston sleeping. He lay curled on his side, facing away from the doorway. Emma sat down to unpin and re-braid her hair; and as her fingers worked, she watched him, not aware that her mind was also working. She was lonely—there had never been reason to give the feeling a name. The house was quiet. It was empty. The fields lying around it were empty. Silence—that mean, unaccustomed thing—filled the rooms of the night-swallowed house. Emma blew out the lamp and lay down behind Ralston. If only, if just—she didn't know what. Tentatively she touched his back, then withdrew her hand like she had touched something hot. It was not the sex act that she craved—Emma's body was not yet awakened. She knew nothing of sensual pleasure. In his sleep, Ralston twitched a shoulder, as he would have done to toss off an insect.

"We'll try going there, first." Emma nodded toward the building they were passing.

About three miles from the Griffen place, at a crossing of two farm roads, sat the Burnsville Baptist Church. It was a small, plain building of unpainted clapboard. But it had the potential to offer community, to provide some structure for their lives. Emma put an arm across Ralston's lap, to claim his attention. She had all the sanctions of upbringing behind her, here. And on this one issue, she was prepared to oppose him. But there was no opposition— Ralston was as aware of their isolation as she was.

On that first Sunday morning, the two of them sat, Ralston rested and aloof, Emma flushing and squirmy. The diversion provided by the appearance of the new young couple was agreeable to everybody. Emma felt the peculiar stillness of curiosity between hymns, as people sat again, settling into their seats. It was true that all eyes moved with careful interest over Ralston and Emma. And there was one pair of eyes that stayed on Emma, those of a Mrs. Sarah Hale. Mrs. Hale didn't entirely like what she saw; and Sister Hale saw everything from behind the little round spectacles she wore. No one knew her age exactly. She was a grandmother many times over, local midwife, consultant to the pastor and deacons, president of the Women's Missionary Union for as long as anyone could remember. Anyone unacquainted with Mrs. Hale may have said that she looked a little ferocious—anyone already acquainted with her could have verified the fact. Her personality was an odd composite of generosity and small tyranny.

Now Mrs. Hale analyzed the new couple, the details of their faces, their postures, their clothing. Ralston was ruddy and strong from his farm labor. Mrs. Hale didn't like the looks of the girl.

Who was pale. Whose eyes were circled. The smile she held on her face was wavery, at times outright painful to look at. But Mrs. Hale would have to see to the girl.

Neither Emma nor Ralston paid much attention to the words of the sermon that morning. Ralston was thinking back very pleasurably to the card game he'd discovered at Hendrix Feed and Harness, where he'd driven over one evening, to pick up a chunk of salt lick. Near the back of the store, next to a stove, a group of men sat around on chairs and upturned boxes, where a large crate, set on end, served as a table. The game was conducted in a companionable silence, each player being provided a comforting source of individual warmth. With the absentmindedness of habit, they passed a bottle around the circle. One of them noticed Ralston.

"Pass young Griffen a swig off that, will you, Willis."

Ralston stepped forward and smiled. "I thank you."

As they returned to the farm that Sunday afternoon, Emma was at her most chatty, with pleasure and relief. They had been welcomed all around. So that now, through the coming work week, she could think back. She could remember the faces at her leisure. She could plan. She would begin to imagine herself through their eyes. Ralston suffered her chatter with better than usual humor, his own loneliness comforted by the company of men.

Chapter 7

But Ralston took it too far.

At dusk, when she would have expected him to be finishing in the barn, Emma heard the sound of the wagon and harness, the team moving. Stepping out onto the back porch to investigate, she saw him bringing the wagon down the drive in the near dark. He sat stiffly—was, as Emma didn't suspect, already annoyed at the questioning he expected. He frowned as he drove. And he would not be stopped. The little noise of Emma's questions made his jaw muscles tighten. He was poised for flight. In a hurry. A man leaving the scene of a skirmish. For it was battle for Ralston. Once that first harvest was in, he warred with his land. It was a private struggle, one Emma had no notion of. Incompetence was a thing that puzzled Ralston—it brought him up against a barrier in his own understanding. But carelessness, negligence in a job, was another matter—it filled him with disgust. It made no difference to him that the fields that he worked had been left by an aging, possibly ailing, man. Ralston looked over the weed-strangled fields with a foul taste in his mouth that alternated between wild irritation, then sometimes with a sort of surprise. Contempt for the mess overwhelmed him. He cleared his throat and spat. The overgrowth made an ordeal of the plowing under that followed the harvest, but Ralston had prepared himself, so he thought, for that. It was angry work, this work of ripping up and pushing apart that resisting Black Belt soil, which was weighted with clay, netted with roots that drove deep, like knots of twine. He had worn out and replaced a plow point well before half of the rows were finished. Then had to go back over each foot of the fields with a harrow—between the furrows, the high grass had only been flattened, not pulled up. He began over the corn, matted with thick plants, like the sour Jimsonweed that grew up to his shoulders. The rows were crisscrossed with thin, tickly grasses, in places scattered with morning glory. Here the harrow was operational only for minutes at a time. Ralston drove twisted around on the seat, watching the trailing rakes mire down in snarls of soft vegetation. Again and again, he stopped to remove the mass that built up, with no choice but to throw it back into his rows. It disgusted him; he swore continuously. His father had always taken pride in having clean fields, Ralston remembered. Now he was driven. Over and over, he stopped and climbed down. He stopped again. His irritation boiled over. The debt of this negligence was his. And with this undertaking he had to succeed. His three older brothers had each taken land and had already started to prosper—especially Charles Junior. At the thought of that name, a shadow, like a wisp of blown smoke, flew across Ralston's mind. And now a flood of warm fury engulfed him. When he was annoyed, Ralston cursed and spoke out loud to himself, but when he was angry he became curiously silent. The anger fed on itself; he needed to spend it on some physical object. He needed to seize something fleshy, to wound it or tear at it. In his fit of fury, he grasped at a stalk of Jimsonweed and uprooted the plant, sending himself backward. Above him the sky, which had already paled over, grew bunched and dark with warning. Another delay. Another impingement. In his disgust, he kicked at the frame of the harrow, causing the near mule to start and step sideways. Not his wife, not anyone under that indifferent sky, knew Ralston's torment.

As he passed the porch, he spoke before Emma had a chance

to. "I got some business, Emma. I figure it'll take me a while." He didn't slow the wagon.

Emma had learned to read Ralston's posture. "Something the matter?"

He didn't turn, just clucked to the mules. "Nothing the matter. Just some business."

Emma couldn't imagine what it was he might have to do, out at night. She stood a moment, looking after him, but she was herself preoccupied. She had cut and basted a cover for the armchair they had purchased from railway salvage. The upholstery was split in a number of places, and the contents showed through like white scars. Emma had spent the early morning walking the front rooms of her house, assessing, taking stock. The floors of the rooms were rough. The wallpaper was graying. But this single, unsightly object, the armchair, seemed to her the most urgent business. As she fell into her work, her mind played back over her impressions of the church community. Emma passed several hours in this way, reasonably contented—though she had begun to listen for Ralston. Another hour passed, while she worked on the piping for the cover, close work that required her strict attention. Then she stopped. For Emma, the tiredness that signaled the end of her day was always sudden. She left a lamp burning for Ralston and went upstairs. Undressing, she was aware, as she never had been, of the darkness in the house. She stood in the pool of lamplight, listening. The quiet had become conspicuous. Something was wrong. He had had an accident. Something had happened to the wagon or one of the mules. She began to work on her hair, and the uneasiness veered toward fear. Emma sat on the edge of the bed, attempting to collect herself. She was in no immediate danger. She could always walk to the next farm along the front road—she had a speaking acquaintance with that family.

Then there were no more preparations for bed. She had

fallen into that sort of half sleep that imagines itself awake when Ralston came back. Emma could sense, almost smell, the unusual lateness—or earliness, by now—of the hour. He had waked her by jarring the bed. And Ralston, slightly intoxicated, was much relieved to see that Emma slept. His breath was all over the room. He'd been out most of the night. And he had been drinking. Now Emma was grateful for the dark.

There was no trace of sheepishness in Ralston's nature. And on the following morning, he considered himself fully prepared. He met Emma's face with belligerency, until he actually looked at her and saw her exhaustion; then, the belligerency receded a little. He went out to see to the animals while Emma cooked. That much was usual. But he ate far more quickly than usual, not looking up—anything to avoid an encounter with those tired eyes. Both of them knew that a confrontation was inevitable.

She went straight to the cellar steps, when he left. It was the first time in her life that she'd taken matters in hand in this way— it may well have been Emma's few moments as an adult. This was the man she had freely chosen. There was no point in weighing the fact—there were things that, once done, could not be un- done. There were things, too, that Emma didn't want to know. That the fair and faraway land of adulthood: her marriage, her life as a wife and mother—these things that from girlhood she'd lived for—had arrived. And this was all there was to it. She did realize that another sense of expectancy was with her now, at all times. She would be the mother of children. Emma consoled herself with this age-old and time-honored ambition. She would go on, she told herself, the best way she knew how. She would do what was expected of her—that was a point of personal honor. She had never been one to hold a grudge—to do so would have required deliberateness on her part. Until now he had not been unkind to her. He was a difficult person. Perhaps he was troubled. But she couldn't get near him. That was the end of the matter. Emma left the steps and resumed her day.

There were the ordinary sounds at midday: the rattling of equipment. Then the footsteps, the splashing at the back porch pump. But it was all right, just then. Because Emma was totally changed. She'd had a visitor. And briefly the world had fallen back into place—a place where people made visits, clucked tongues, and patted knees. Old Mrs. Hale was her visitor, and from that stolid but solacing presence Emma soaked up much comfort.

When she heard Ralston at the pump, Emma ran onto the porch with a face all lit up and smiling. For the time being, the night before was as good as forgotten.

"Mrs. Hale's come to visit!" Ralston was too self-possessed to draw back in surprise. What in the world—. "Look here what she brought us." Emma lifted the jars separately. There were canned tomatoes, string beans, young limas and field peas, sweet corn, okra, and peaches; berry and wild plum preserves.

"She brought us all that?" It must have been the old church matriarch.

"Uh-huh. And she wants us to go over on Christmas Day to be with the family."

Emma considered the visit entirely satisfactory. The two women had made a careful tour of the house, mainly for Mrs. Hale's approval and general information. From that first church appearance, Emma had called forth the woman's fierce protective feelings. So, from Mrs. Hale she elicited a kindness as sincere as it may have been curt. They had the comforting exchanges—if somewhat over-emphatic from Mrs. Hale—of an older woman and a younger one. Emma felt a deep, healing comfort in the fact that she was now known to someone—and in this way had both an ally and friend.

"That so?" Ralston relaxed a little. A calico kitten sprung, light as a leaf hopper, into the crate of jars, mewing. "And *that?*" he asked? He had a particular distaste for cats.

"Uh-huh." Emma grinned. Ralston noticed that her nose wrinkled.

That evening he stayed home.

Then he betrayed her—Emma thought of it as a betrayal. For her own part, she imagined that some sort of unspoken agreement had been made between them, when she'd been willing to let the matter go by: that they'd achieved reconciliation. At this dusk when she heard the noise of the wagon, she didn't bother to walk outside. Instead she paced the kitchen, working herself into an anger. And this time the departure wounded her. Emma fueled her anger with the image of her father, a fully domesticated and genial figure. She knew nothing else of masculine nature. Little or nothing of human nature at all, if the truth were told.

For a second night she slept almost not at all. And the next morning, dry-mouthed, she confronted him. The strain of the confrontation was already there, lying between them, like heat waves on an afternoon field. So that when Emma began, Ralston only stiffened—he was prepared. Emma paced. She knotted her hands. She possessed no tactics for psychological battle, as none had ever been necessary. She plunged in, in the only way immediately available to her: to fall back on the common notions of right and wrong.

"What you're doing. It's not right." Emma didn't look at Ralston when she spoke. "It's not right," she repeated. Now. Her point had been made. She had said it. She did—would always have—a strong feeling for simple right and wrong. And this was wrong—it had to be resisted and warred against.

"What's that?" Ralston pretended not to have heard her.

Which caught her off guard. "It's not right," Emma said again, but less assertively. She knew he had heard her.

Ralston pushed back from the table a little and crossed his legs, head cocked and appraising her. He allowed a few moments to pass before he answered. "What's not right, Emma?" His own voice was perfectly calm.

Emma must have looked desperate. She hadn't expected this tack. Why, they both knew! He knew exactly what she was talking about; but he was going to make her explain it. "This—. This business at night."

Ralston was coolly silent. He continued to sit cross-legged, inquisitive, jerking the foot of the crossed leg, eyes following Emma, head still inclined. All of this was deliberate. He waited. "What business?" It seemed to amuse him to toy with the conversation in this manner.

Emma's anger blinked and went out. She made an effort to get back her outrage, but it was no good. Defeat had already taken its place. The truth was that Ralston's coolness made her mind go blank. He had always intimidated her in this way. "Your leaving me alone at night, like you've done." Ralston let her stand there, twisting her hands.

"We got a little card game going."

"A card game?"

"Just a little card game. That's all."

Emma hesitated. She wasn't aware that she was pacing a small circle as she talked. Emma was not a large woman. Now she looked small, strained, and thin. Part of him felt an inclination to comfort her. But he couldn't do that—it would amount to surrender. Emma went on, attempting to make herself defiant. "Well, it's not right, leaving me here by myself. Something could happen. Why, my daddy—." But the look on his face stopped her—she remembered that look. And for Ralston, that last bit had set off something in him. Her getting pious on him like that stopped his sympathy cold.

He was suddenly galled. He stood up so quickly that his chair fell over behind him. He kicked it out of the way, shooting it backwards against the kitchen safe. For a moment Emma wondered if he might cross the room and hit her. But he didn't. He left his breakfast unfinished. And when he returned at noon, every move that he made was deliberate, over-noisy. But what seemed even louder was the unnatural silence between them, no simple matter of Ralston's usual lack of talk. For days the couple passed each other in the rooms and hallways of the house, ate together, lay beside one another at night, all in that same—to Emma, draining—silence. Ralston continued his nightly outings, moving around very emphatically now, with perfect composure. Emma didn't know, until now, that there could be a struggle like this between two people. The effort to withstand it bewildered, exhausted her. It was unnatural. It was Jacob wrestling the angel. That awful strain of the silence. Emma went through her usual business of cleaning, cooking, preparing the table. She was abjectly miserable. The force of Ralston's will was like a net of invisible wires. She wasn't equipped to endure it. She would have to give in.

Little tentative attempts at conversation signaled her surrender, and Ralston recognized her efforts for what they were. Now he watched her. As she moved about the kitchen, he studied her face. Emma, avoiding his eyes, had no idea of the sequence of emotions that followed, then, for him. First, there was the gratitude that she had let him go—she had released him. Almost, he thanked her. Almost, he reached for Emma, in the gratitude that he felt. But this he didn't know quite know how to do. Ralston had never taken a woman's hand in friendship or affection. And then there was his sense of shame at the unhappiness he knew he had caused her—Emma was not a tiresome woman. But his own need for himself was larger than any of these things. And the softer feelings were followed, close on, by annoyance at the whole complexity of the thing. But the struggle, for now at least, was over. They had come to a truce.

Emma joined the WMU, at Mrs. Hale's invitation. This was a handful-sized collection of women, larger near special church occasions. The group sewed with a verve, their hands working independent of their conversation. Their meetings were held at each other's homes. They had coffee or tea and refreshments. More importantly, they had long hours of comfortable talk. They discussed their own, other people's, children. Illnesses and remedies. They analyzed courtships, collectively clucked at any young persons' behavior they thought to be fast. They speculated about pregnancies; there was much general talk about pregnancy, to which Emma's ears anxiously clung.

In the spring, the meeting was held for the first time at Emma's, proud and gratified in this first formal offering of her home. The front rooms were by now fairly presentable, the floors waxed, the wallpaper scrubbed and brightened with a smelly, rubbery substance that Mrs. Hale had brought over. Emma had made a layer cake, and the pleasing traces of baking odors were trapped in the house. Emma was the youngest of the WMU members. Minnie Van Deusen, a couple of years older, was next. And on that basis Minnie claimed Emma as her special friend. Minnie was nervous, thin and birdlike, and tried over hard to please. In her eagerness she made blunders and said many wrong things. When Minnie announced that she and her husband were expecting "another one," the group observed the hunger on Emma's face. The girl had only the calico cat that Mrs. Sarah had given her. Minnie ought to have more feeling—she was crowing. Sudden irritabilities broke out against her. Whereas Emma, so transparent in her own feelings, was taken into the collective heart of the group.

A little more than a year from the night of the barn dance at the Watkins', from the proposal that had never been properly made, the long looked-for change in Emma's body came about. On a Sunday morning following church service, she seized Mrs. Hale and pulled her aside.

"I missed it!"

The older woman knew at once what she meant. "Now, you got to hold on. You can't be sure just yet. Been sick on your stomach?"

"No'm."

"Any nausea feelings?"

"No'm. Not none."

"You'll want to mind any soreness in your breasts." The two of them whispered together.

Emma wasn't able to wait. She went directly to the outhouse behind the building and carefully explored her breasts, was startled at the bruised-like tenderness she found there. Then she emerged triumphant. Now she could wait out the days with the quiet satisfaction of secret expectancy.

A sequence of mild and eventless weeks followed, as Emma waited out the slow passing of another lunar month. Then, on a morning in July, a morning already close with the hard heat that was to follow, she decided. Today. It would be today—it would be this very morning that she would tell him. Ralston came into the room in his usual preoccupied manner, already concerned with the day's business. The kitchen still held some of the feeling of night. He took a seat near a window just beginning to pale from the day. Emma was making flapjacks, his favorite breakfast. But she couldn't wait. She left the bowl and the griddle. She sat down at the table across from him.

"I got something to tell you." Emma sat on the edge of her chair, her hands pushed against her knees.

Right away Ralston caught the odd significance in her voice. He glanced up at her, but Emma didn't actually tell him. She grinned—that grin that made her nose wrinkle. Ralston studied her a moment before he began to understand. He leaned back in his chair. "Well?" Now Ralston, too, grinned. It had entered his mind that this was a thing that should be expected.

"Yeah!" Emma nodded.

"You sure?"

"I'm sure." It was not possible now for Emma to keep still in her chair.

"Now, ain't that something. Ain't that just something! When'll it be?"

"Close to April, I reckon."

"Close to April." Ralston looked at the floor briefly, taking in the information. "Guess we can put him to work at the planting." Both of them laughed.

August closed over Alabama that year like an itchy wool blanket. People and animals moved about sluggishly, stunned by the bright, enveloping heat. The air was stirred only by the rising and falling rattle of cicadas. Ralston moved around slowly inside the dim heat of the barn. His mules twitched irritably at the withers. But Emma responded to the heat with only the lightest surface of her mind. And on an afternoon following their noon meal, when Ralston drove off, his departure didn't register with her. It was laying-by time, a time of relative leisure on the farm. Ralston's comings and goings no longer made any impression on Emma. She was absorbed, now; she lived deeply inside her body. When later in the day he left for a second time, just after supper, she paid no special attention to the sound of the wagon. He returned in little more than an hour. Emma heard the noise of something heavy being unloaded on the back porch. Ralston, not seeing her through the doorway, put his head inside the kitchen and yelled. "Emmalie!" The screen door slammed. He was attempting to maneuver something large and clumsy between the back steps and the doorway. Then Emma saw it. It was a sewing machine! It wasn't new. But that didn't matter. How she had wanted one! And how had he possibly known? She beat a fist, in her impatience to get a look at it.

"How did you know!" Emma wasn't often surprised at her husband; but she was now.

He had studied her, then. There had been times when he had watched her, when she wasn't aware of it. She felt near overcome. She stepped forward to embrace him. And for both of them there was an awkwardness in the quick, unfamiliar gesture.

Chapter 8

On a workday morning in November of 1918, Henry drove the road to the sawmill, to one side of him disused pastureland, to the other stretches of skimpy woods. The morning air was humid, sounds of man-made activity trapped in the density of it. Henry enjoyed the drive at first morning. And from his distance, he could already hear Johnnie calling orders to the mules. There was the dull sound of logs being dropped, then a silence. Henry caught the first smell of cut wood, a smell a little like sweetened vinegar, and the traveling odor of sawdust. At this hour the men were already gathered, but only Johnnie was moving, with the mules. Simmons was sitting back on his heels at a distance, as usual. There was a murmur when the men saw the wagon approaching. The day had begun. Now partner and foreman at the Taylor sawmill outside Clanton, Henry had become the business associate of his father's old friend. He didn't know entirely how it had come about, this partnership. It amazed him, looking back, that he had gone along with the plan so obediently. Most likely because he had wanted to move Lillian into Clanton. The offer seemed to have popped up one day out of nowhere, surprising Henry—who was unaware of the long discussions that had been held between the two men, Mr. Taylor and his father. Who was, above all, unaware that he was a problem to be discussed—even if the discussions were conducted in an off-and-on, leisurely sort of fashion. Then one day there was this. "I've made a little investment, Joe." It was seven o'clock on an evening. Mr. Taylor leaned inside the doorway to the mill office, playing with a thin cigar that he seemed to be thinking about lighting.

"What now?" Mr. Gray's back was turned to his friend. He was stacking ledgers."Sawmill between here and Clanton." Mr. Gray nodded. He knew the place.

"Good little prospect." Mr. Taylor looked pleased. Now he moved the unlit cigar around in his mouth. "Need me a partner, somebody to manage the outfit. What do you think about Henry?"

Mr. Gray stopped his fidgeting. It took him a matter of seconds to process the idea. He smiled as his hands left the ledgers.

And so it had started, without Henry's knowing or being asked his say. It relieved Joe Gray, who no longer had any real peace of mind about Henry. Henry studied and worried overmuch about things. He didn't seem satisfied at the mill. And there was something else that was disturbing—a thing that Joe wouldn't mention to his friend. The crap games that went on in the wooded lot behind the building—for some reason, Henry couldn't seem to stay away from them. Craps. It was a habit that sneaked up on a man. Then opened up other habits. The stakes were trifling; the workers' wages small as they were. But it was true that Henry's eyes, along with the others', had come to fasten hypnotically on the dice. At his second round at the game, he had won a small sum, and from that point it became a habit. Joe Gray's uneasiness was growing. A weight seemed to lift from him at his old friend's proposal. This arrangement would set Henry up, right and square.

The road past the sawmill led nowhere, in the general direction of the river. A few families of Negroes lived along the road. And there was the one large house, whose owner passed back and forth from time to time on horseback. The sawmill was long and shallow and shed-like, built just deep enough to house the machinery, and surrounded by several acres of gashed and naked earth. Logs were piled unevenly around the property, like something dropped from a giant hand. The cubicle of Henry's office sat at the top of a set of steps near the conveyor. This makeshift room held only a tall stool pushed up against a writing shelf, behind which hung a gun rack and rifle.

The main structure opened west, catching the full brunt of the afternoon sun, allowing little or no distance from wind or rainy weather. In the full heat of the summer, the sun pricked like the points of hot needles. The mouths of the men tasted of wood dust. But here at least, Henry told himself, the space was open, the air not confined. There was no frenzy in the work. Just the slow, repetitive movements of mules and men. In the yards, at the pulleys, feeding and guiding the logs toward the large, single blade. All day long. Fetching and hauling, raising and pushing. Strenuous work.

Henry worked among the men without knowing them—and this was his first disappointment. He strung a tarp at one end of the building, and under it the men—all but Simmons—sat or hunkered for their noonday meal. It wouldn't have crossed Henry's mind not to join them—in the day's work, he lost any idea of himself as owner. But his presence among the men made them uneasy—it was a thing Henry could sense. Of the five Negroes, the large man named Johnnie seemed to be a kind of leader. He was huge-bodied, this Johnnie, his face one that wanted to laugh and talk, to sport around with this business of drudgery. But Henry's presence silenced him. Henry had eaten only one meal among the men. It was a silent meal. When he glanced at Johnnie, he saw the unnatural blankness on the man's face. Johnnie's eyes slid over a couple of times, meeting Henry's, only to be withdrawn again instantly. Beyond the group that was gathered under the tarp, Simmons kept his distance. Simmons was country, in the way of a shy and potentially fierce woods animal. He never spoke if he could avoid it, and the sound of his voice was reedy. While the Negroes ate under the tarp, Simmons, in his farmer's hat and faded overalls, withdrew to the edge of the woods, where he sat with his legs drawn up in front of him, facing out like an animal from a burrow. So Henry withdrew up the stairs to his cubicle, where he sat with the stool tilted back against the wall, high enough there to look out across the pastureland that sloped toward the river. In his absence, the other men relaxed. First came the bulging tumble of Johnnie's laughter, shaking loose from him in three notes. The answering laughter was softer; but after a time, the voices grew louder, the talk and the laughter regular and easy. So Henry left the men to their own company, Simmons to his place in the woods. He sat by himself—there was not much choice in the matter.

By early afternoon, not a person was left at the sawmill. Men had closed doors at businesses all over town. The armistice had been signed—the war was over! The whole town was out in the streets, the air working live with exhilaration. People shouted and laughed. There were dinner bells, cow bells, horns and whistles. Automobile horns were turned loose, in the general racket. A band had been put together. Speeches were being made. People joked over nothing, held conversations with perfect strangers, thronged deep, up and down Broad Street, as they were.

"Isn't it grand?" Smiling. This was Myra, Lillian's sister, at her most characteristic. Beside Henry the two of them laughed, like the others, at anything and nothing. Henry held his little girl, Elizabeth, up on his shoulders, her feet dangling down over his chest. He was relieved but sober. It would be the end, now, at last, of the fear; the long, windy arguments; the panic-fed speculations.

The end of his dread about Drefus, the only one of the Gray brothers not yet married—and so not exempt from the draft. But Drefus was safe. To the collective relief of the family, Drefus had settled into work with Southern Railroad, which employment was considered service in the national interest, so making him safe from the prospect of being abruptly drafted.

Beside Henry, the two sisters chattered. Both had taken the time necessary "to get themselves up"—they had that effect on each other, Henry observed. Myra approved, of course, of the move into Clanton, especially given that Lillian "wasn't strong"—this was the general conclusion of the McClinton family. Lillian was pregnant again, and to anybody's notice both happy and strong. Her eyes were never long off her daughter, now a toddler, whose legs she stroked, whose skirt she straightened, whose bonnet she was keeping an eye on. Behind the Grays, two women admired the little girl, who was, in fact, remarkable. Her hair caught the attention right away. It was the bright, red gold of new copper, soft and springy. And the skin that would have been expected with it, a bleached skin running to freckles, was tawny. Elizabeth's little features were less childlike than like some artist's conception. Henry looked at his daughter sometimes as any stranger might have done, just to pleasure himself. The two of them, Lillian and Elizabeth, gratified a vanity he didn't know that he had.

The two women standing behind them edged closer, expecting Henry to turn his daughter around, which he did. The Grays had grown accustomed to this sort of admiration of Elizabeth. And Lillian had grown complacent, finally, as a mother. At one point, Henry had wondered if she'd ever be the same. After the miscarriage, she passed whole days—weeks, it seemed—lying on her side, knees drawn up, facing away from the doorway. She cried openly at first. But after a while, the tears became secretive.

Henry and Lillian talked little, directly, of the loss. Affectionate joking was more in Henry's way. But his little sallies of foolishness were often silenced by the sight of Lillian's back—they embarrassed him, even. He took instead, after a while, to coming in to lie down behind her, fitting her curves. This seemed to suit her better.

At that moment, amid all the happy hubbub, Henry was preoccupied. Drefus. He had to see Drefus. Odd that being able to finally relax about his brother had set his worry loose, instead of calming it—the little nibbling worries he kept pushed down, that Drefus might lose his job, that he might, after all, join up or be drafted. With Drefus the fool for adventure, it could have happened. Between the sisters, on the other hand, Drefus was the ongoing problem topic. There was the issue of his effect on Henry, of his doing what Lillian considered "hauling Henry off" during his time away from the sawmill, of his general disruption to the household. Lillian was defined by and comforted, entirely suited, to her life as a small town wife and mother. It was evident that Drefus would not follow the course of the family man. That he would challenge every and anything. And to the sisters' minds, that made him the enemy of these ordinary traditions. Lillian relied on intuition in what she thought of as managing Henry. Drefus could not *be* managed. He unsettled her. There was the simple rudeness, among other things, to contend with. He, Drefus, appeared at any hour—apparently without a thought as to circumstances or to his welcome. There'd be a familiar knocking on the door, most often near bedtime. Drefus would be just back from a run.

"Hey! Where you been?" It was a common greeting between

the brothers. There'd be hearty hugs and back clapping. And the two men would settle in the living room or on the porch, where they'd talk and smoke, sometimes far into the night. One or the other would produce a bottle, Drefus from his pocket, or Henry from the closet. Henry brewed malt liquor at home, which he stored in the kitchen closet—the sound of the corks popping loose became familiar in the house. Then Drefus would elaborate in great earnest on the subject of where he had been. They laughed out loud in the talk. Both were long-bodied men; both tended to draw up a leg as they warmed to a subject. Drefus was in love with flight. He tantalized his brother with talk—now descriptions of cities—of Birmingham, Memphis, Mobile, New Orleans. Of train stations late at night, the goings and comings of strange, city people. His stories were the wonder and Henry the audience—it had always been that way. But the self-importance of each man was most warmed and gratified in the company of the other.

Much of the time, the brothers passed their time together in the simple pleasures of male camaraderie—nothing at all that even Lillian would have found blameworthy. They walked the woods and fields along the river between Clanton and Orville, sometimes shooting for squirrel, as they had done when they were boys, or for duck, dove, or quail. The squirrel shoots were products of whim, the playing of overgrown boys. The men needed the woods, the space of the fields, like they needed something essential for their bodies. Their senses fed on the separate sounds, the clean, flying light, the swilling of air that mixed all the good smells of dry grass and soil and leaf mold and water. As the winter moderated, they fished, this being the sport that each looked forward to most. And it was no more the pleasure of the sport that drew them than the great, flowing balm of the river. Taylor pastureland lay along the river near the mouth of the Cahaba.

From the main road to Orville, the men turned off on a narrow clay road. Here their landmarks were well laid out. At the dead oak, they opened a loose, barbed wire gate onto open pasture. A footpath veered off to the right. First, there was the Catalpa tree, then south, the roofline of the cabin, which was being used at that time for storing hay. Directly behind it, the boat was tied under the overhanging bank, where their climbing had hollowed out foot holds along root lines and rocks. The smell of the boat was familiar, old odors of soaked wood and fish and bait. Minutes would see Henry and Drefus out over the river, where they settled into the rhythm of the water, lulled by the strokes of light along the surface, at home in the muddy and ancient stink. They passed these long afternoons sometimes without talking, passing a bottle and cigarettes. Or sudden tensions, such as brothers have, could flare.

"What'd it *take*, to get you away from that mud pit, pal? To come on in with the railroad." Drefus' eyes narrowed as he gazed over the still line of the river. He couldn't for the life of him understand why Henry didn't see it. The times they could have. That feeling of being away, of being off somewhere else. The good rush of air on your face and body. The little lost, crossroad places nobody knew the names of. Then coming into the cities and towns. "It's good work. Time goes by in a hurry. Damned if it wouldn't make me crazy, Henry, that sawmill. All that racket. Same old go round, day after day." Now Drefus was growing incensed.

" 'S not the best place I can think of to spend a Saturday, that's for sure." Henry tried to tamp down the heat that was creeping into that familiar conversation.

"Why don't you come on in?"

"Don't reckon I can do that, Drefus." Henry squinted and jerked his rod.

"Why the hell not?"

"Bought in. That's why."

"Then sell back out!"

"I can't be off, leaving Lillian all the time. I'm a family man." Any hint of banter left Henry's voice then.

"I just don't *get* it with you, Henry! " The truth was the Henry didn't quite get it, himself—but he'd never let on as much to Drefus.

Henry lowered Elizabeth from his shoulders. Lillian and Myra were so busy enjoying themselves with the festivities that he was tempted to make off for Strayer's right then. As it turned out, he set off immediately after supper to walk over there. The November night was cooling, but people were still in the streets. The celebrations seemed to be re-gearing. At Strayer's all the lights were on, the porch crowded with men and women all talking at the same time. Drefus was there already, dressed like a dandy—he had always enjoyed a smart set of clothes. And he carried himself well. Henry chuckled as he spotted him, gesturing as he talked, apparently entertaining the couple who were standing in front of him—Henry suspected that the exertions were mostly for the woman. Henry took a seat in a rocker. He'd wait. In the excitement, everybody was generous; several flasks passed Henry's way, which he swigged from and duly passed on. Family suppers like his own were generally early. He knew that at any time most of the people on the porch would be off, somewhere, for their evening meal.

And he was right. The groups of people seemed to thin out within minutes of each other. Seated next to Henry was a plump woman with a cheerful face, her hair rolled in sausage curls beneath the rim of her hat. Henry thought that she seemed a little fluttery, and as Drefus approached, he understood why. Henry could see that his brother was aware of the woman—which Drefus was, very—by the trace of a change of expression, a slight swelling of the muscle beneath an eye. It was enough to get a message across. Drefus liked his women on the plump side, and the fluttery woman, who stood up now, suited his type to a T. Drefus, always flamboyant, bowed low, swooping his hat. Henry thought he heard a slight feminine noise of appreciation.

Then he dropped into the chair beside Henry, grasping his brother's knee, giving it a shake. "Well, how 'bout it, Brud? We can put our heads on our pillows at night, with no worries." He rocked forward, almost bringing the chair up with him. He was feeling expansive, and he continued, apropos of nothing. "Yeah," he began, as though he were answering himself, "I like my women soft and smooth and soothing. It's soothing you need from a woman, Henry, not rilement." Drefus spoke as if Henry had no woman—of course Lillian fell into another category.

Drefus went on, "There's this little woman, Henry, right outside Maplesville. Finest little woman."

"This one a widow, too?" Both men threw their heads back and laughed.

"Might as well be. Looks like a man would want to stay home with a woman like that. Myself, now, I'd stay home with her."

"About how long?" Henry baited his brother.

"Considerable time. I'd have to say considerable." Drefus made a poker face. Then they both laughed again. He was worked up. "Ah, the sweet flower that is woman!" Drefus sat back, elbows draped over the arms of the chair, looking about him, relishing of his own remark. He almost smacked his lips. He had been tippling since mid-morning.

"Feel like playing some cards?" He cut his eyes over at Henry. That last word managed to convey the idea of wild and mysterious goings-on with the cards.

Henry was used to Drefus' theatrics. "Brewed up some nice malt at home. We could sit a spell, first."

"Well, now, we could do that." It was never a matter of argument, only of what had the greater appeal. "This'n will only be for chips. " Drefus played for stakes as a rule. And often enough he won. Henry wondered if he might not ought to go home—there was something about a good card game that kept a man at it, long after he seriously intended to quit.

They left the porch together. The streets were full and noisy again. There were shouts directed to Henry and Drefus. The two men had a similar stride and similar height—Drefus may have been an inch or so taller. But it seemed at times to Henry that he still walked just below his brother's shoulder. The events of the day had made him emotional. His bond with this brother went back as far as memory could reach. Where Drefus went and what he did, Henry went and did. Sometimes Henry wondered why Drefus hadn't minded when they were boys—he was nearly four years older than Henry. Between them was Jay, the simple one. Jay was said to be touched—this from unkindly people. Jay talked to people that only he could see, chased imaginary playmates through cornfields. Jay never tagged along behind any living body. But Henry tagged along behind Drefus, even when he stood below the shoulder not just of Drefus but of all the others. Drefus had a way of crooking his arm and resting it against Henry's neck. It was a posture of defiance, giving the impression, as it was meant to, that Henry was under Drefus' protection. Drefus taught his little brother to fight—at least, he tried to. Henry wasn't much of a fighter by nature. And for that matter, for all his swagger, neither was Drefus. Henry had seen him really fighting mad only once, and the dispute had been over Henry. One of the other boys had muttered something about a snot-nosed brother—Henry hadn't realized that the remark was about himself until he saw Drefus, who just sort of walked into the fellow, fists working quick and hard, one right after the other.

Henry laughed a little into the air. He had remembered the time with the little Prichard girl. Drefus had always been big on the girls. And this one—Henry couldn't say, now, who she had married—had been beautiful, or was going to be, in that way that caused a certain stir among people, that made people uneasy. It was still clear to Henry, the memory of that morning, Drefus leaning against the patchy trunk of the sycamore tree. It was full summer. He was in knee pants, barefoot and brown, full of good health and too much energy, the energy all focused at that moment on Janey Prichard. The sycamore stood to a side of the Prichard lawn, where a play area was set up in the shade. Henry still saw it, the sandbox and a slide; a couple of younger children pushing toys around in the sand. The little girl, Janey— she was somewhere between his age and Drefus'—in a ruffled brown dress with tiny white flowers, leading, or trying to lead, a Dalmatian puppy attached to a leash. Janey had a self-important, pursed little mouth, eyes a flecked blue-gray, and an upturned nose. It was funny that the tilted nose was her prettiest feature. Right now it was red and a little scaly from sunburn. Her hair was a glossy brown and cut straight across, to fall a little above her shoulders, hair so thick that the cut edge of it made a kind of shape. Janey hadn't realized at first that she was being watched, and that the sight of her difficulty with the puppy was comical to the eyes doing the watching.

At Drefus' age, about fourteen, another boy might have minded being seen out in public in knee pants. But Drefus relied, as he always had, on the straightforward appeal of himself—which had yet to fail him. Girls were silly about Drefus. And although Henry was too young to have the curiosity at that time that he would have later, he sometimes wondered why. True, Drefus' features were straight enough, reasonably good, not especially handsome. But his young body was handsome. His lazy movements had a grace and a confidence about them. Drefus could lean against a tree, without moving, and somehow project a swagger at the same time. And that's how he was standing that day, just beyond Janey Prichard's notice. Then on one palm, he vaulted himself across the fence that surrounded the yard. Henry moved more slowly, climbing the fence. The boards were pickets. The climbing was tricky and annoying.

Henry thought he was witnessing a kind of war. The little girl seemed irked from the minute she saw Drefus. Her face got red. She became self-conscious, now, with her puppy. But Drefus was enjoying himself enormously. He grinned and asked questions that were pointless. Henry wondered at the odd behavior. Everything that Drefus said seemed to embarrass Janey, though the remarks were about nothing particularly embarrassing. It was the tone of voice—Drefus could still do it. He knew that his attention was making the little girl uneasy. He asked his questions and made his comments, each making Janey Prichard appear more and more self-conscious and fidgety. Her answers, which were perfectly all right, didn't sound quite right to herself. It would be years later that Henry would understand that he had watched not a war but a courtship. Drefus' grinning face flustered Janey, and her fluster increased his amusement.

The whole incident was unaccountable to Henry. If he had been in Drefus' place, he would have been the one feeling self-conscious. Because Janey Prichard was different. She lived in town, in Clanton with relatives during the school year, so that she could go to a private school there. She was only seen in Orville on weekends or some special occasion. All of the Prichards were different. They were big members of the church. Mrs. Prichard regularly hosted the women's group, which was nominally open to all female members of the congregation. Henry noticed that his mother spoke Mrs. Prichard's name in an odd sort of way, not like she said the names of her other women acquaintances. And she never attended the meetings.

"That your puppy?" Drefus paused a moment, then answered himself. "That's your puppy, and that's your little brother. And this is your house." His eyes moved slowly over the lawn, with an incongruous look, as though he were making fun of it all. "What's your puppy's name?"

Janey Prichard was gradually collecting herself, gathering her resources for the return volley. She had command of herself again. She dropped her eyelids, a thing she had already picked up—or never had to learn how to do.

"It's because of people like you that Mama sends me to school in town."

The sally delighted Drefus.

So he wouldn't take the bait. Janey's eyes widened. Her face had a scalded look—she was not used to being outdone. "You're stupid, Drefus Gray. That's what's really the matter with you. You're just stupid!" Again the eyelids dropped. Now the death dart: "My mama says that your mama doesn't even know how to read!"

Henry didn't look at Drefus. His chest filled all at once with a fiery liquid. There was a knot-like feeling in his throat, a whole convulsion of knots. Drefus—why, sometimes he hated Drefus, when Drefus bullied him or took his possessions. But no one besides himself had ever insulted Drefus, at least not in Henry's hearing. And their mother—there was something about their mother that needed defending. Henry sensed this, young as he was. He stared for some moments. He wasn't aware that his rage had grown murderous. Looking back, he knew that it wasn't a thing he planned out, when he picked up the little painted sand shovel and brought it down on Janey Prichard's head. The little girl's mouth opened, turned down suddenly. Her shoulders shook. She was a crier who didn't make any noise. Henry was glad that she cried—she had asked for it, all right. He saw the drop form along the thick edge of the dark, neatly cut hair, a drop of water that somehow turned red. Then another drop and another. Janey ran from the two of them.

Henry and Drefus stood for a few seconds on the lawn, not saying anything to each other, then slowly backing away. They said little or nothing to one another on the way home, and the stunned quiet continued into the family dinner. Meals at the Gray household were generally boisterous, always plenteous. In the Gray family, eating was a vigorous business. Henry and Drefus' appetites were unaffected by the afternoon's incident, but their unusual silence did not go unnoticed—at least by their mother. Joe, the youngest, was leading the general teasing of Olive, the oldest, whose young man had just recently asked for her hand. It had taken a few minutes for the sound of the motor car to penetrate the general din at the table.

Mr. Prichard was the only person in Orville to own a motor car, a funny-looking thing to most people's minds, which moved over the road with a sort of clackety sound. The sound of the approaching automobile had an effect on the faces of Henry and Drefus that their mother was quick to pick up. As the car stopped in front of the house, Mr. Gray stood up and walked outside. The two boys stopped eating.

"I think you two better get up from the table. Go out and wait in the kitchen." Annie Gray had no sure idea of what the trouble was, but she knew which two it had to do with. Henry and Drefus stood just out of sight inside the kitchen doorway. There was no need to look, but they each strained to listen. They could hear nothing of the conversation outside, although the family had gone dumb with curiosity. There was the sound of the automobile being cranked. The front door to the house slammed, as Mr. Gray came back inside. He was frowning. He was also a little red in the face. He said not a word to anybody at the table, but sat down to resume his meal. For Henry and Drefus, he raised his voice once. "When I get up from here, I want to know which one of you tried to break open little Janey Prichard's head! She had to have three stitches."

The two boys felt their pulses hammering at their temples. For reasons that Henry would never understand, Drefus, who was standing just behind him, grabbed Henry around the waist and twisted one of his arms up, high. "I'm the one!" he called out, answering his father. The pressure on Henry's arm was already painful, but when he tried to turn, to get a better look at Drefus, the hold became excruciating. Drefus' face had an expression that Henry knew well, the threat of physical torture. The matter was closed, and any attempt on Henry's part to protest only promised more and greater to come.

"Step out back." Mr. Gray's voice was more collected now.

And Drefus had taken the strapping that should have gone to Henry. He refused to talk about the incident involving Janey or his reasons for bringing the strapping on himself, and Henry knew that he had to drop the subject, or be pummeled and left alone. Later, even years later, when Henry mentioned it, Drefus still could get mad.

Chapter 9

They both remembered their first one. Even Ralston had been edgy—after all, it was his first, as well as Emma's. Though he couldn't have said with any certainty what the edginess was about. Ralston had never thought of his wife as a weak woman. The truth was that she wasn't weak. A little small, maybe—Emma stood just at Ralston's shoulder. But not weak or frail in the way of some women.

When Ralston entered the bedroom, she did appear small, lying there by herself in the bed. The little bundle was sleeping beside her. The women had raised the windows; but the smell of the birth was still in the room.

Emma looked drowsy. It surprised Ralston to see how deeply content she looked. Frankly pretty. She smiled a little, patting the bed beside her, for him to sit down. The gown she wore was short-sleeved. Ralston noticed the freckles on her arms. It hadn't occurred to him that the birth might injure Emma, that anything beyond the ordinary could have happened to her. For a passing second, then, it did occur to him, that she was fragile, at least, in that way. He felt a queer little tug in his middle. Ralston knew already, by then, that he had a daughter. He couldn't see that the "her" amounted to much of anything to look at. Emma pulled back the light covering from around the baby, a red little thing, all wrinkled up like a prune. A tiny sharp mouth and bump of a nose. Eyes of no color at all. It did have hair, though, dark, wet-looking hair.

"I'd like to call her Nettie." Emma looked down at the baby—as though the little red thing were an object of beauty.

"My mother was called Nettie." Emma's head swung up suddenly. She looked at Ralston with a curiosity he had never seen on her face. "Did you know?" It had never occurred to him, she thought, to ask anything about the life of her family.

The question struck Ralston as odd.

But Emma was just relaxed enough at that moment to ask it. She would have liked to talk, then, of her own childhood. To have talked of home. The place where they had both grown up. But they never had talked of such things. The birth made Emma miss home, her mother.

Ralston had no idea what Emma's mother was called. He didn't answer her question. It did occur to him that he should ask some sort of question of *her*, about any little thing he might be able to do for her. But the waddler was there, taking care of things. He could hear the waddler's voice through the walls. This was how Ralston referred, in his own mind, to old Mrs. Hale—he had noticed that the woman had an odd, shifting walk.

Emma covered the baby's face again, because Nettie was sleeping. She still had that dreamy smile on her face. The smile deepened. Ralston felt he should say some special words to his wife at that moment, but he couldn't think of exactly what they should be. He forced a breath intended to come out as a chuckle. "She'll be up and around before we know it."

The remark seemed to please Emma—that afternoon anything pleased Emma. "I expect she will."

"Well." It was Ralston's preparation to leave. But Emma's eyes held onto him. It was because of nothing special that she needed, he noted. But the look held him—asked something of him. Emma was relaxed and dreamy at that moment. The spell she seemed to be in left him somewhat at a loss.

But the spell was broken.

The house and yard were filled with the sounds of people. In addition to the other two, the old lady and her daughter, Minnie Van Deusen and her husband had come with yet more food, this William the sort of fellow that Ralston disliked on sight, quiet and docile beside the flutterings of his wife. Several of Ralston's own card buddies had come by, "to see young Griffen's boy." The men stood outside beneath an oak, exchanging stories and jokes, becoming uneasy with the delay. Nettie's birth had been long and drawn out. The old lady had been just before calling in the doctor, when the forces of nature picked up and righted themselves.

It seemed to Ralston that there had been some glee in the waddler's announcement. "Looks like you got yourself a girl baby." She grinned. From the first the two had been natural adversaries. At times the air between them was charged with the odor of warfare. And the little touch of malice wasn't lost on Ralston—she had to know that he'd wanted a boy.

But Emma proceeded to have boys, right enough, two of them, one after the other. And at each birth, Ralston had to put up with the women—he told himself that by now he should have been used to it.

"We'll be needing more wood in the box." It was the waddler to Ralston, who raised his wet face over the pump, making her request in the manner of someone expecting to be obeyed, and promptly. Ralston drew a hand across his dripping face, slinging the drops. They were back, the old lady and the poker face— Ralston's term for the daughter. This baby would be Emma's fourth, and by now the routine was predictable. Old Mrs. Hale was competent. She moved more slowly now than she once had, with a slight craning of the neck—a cataract on one eye made her incline her head. The daughter a woman in her thirties or thereabouts who had married late and had no children. Lou Anne was tall and straight, a calm and deliberate sort of person, often silent. But her silences were deceptive; Lou Anne had her opinions, strong ones, as well as her judgements. She stepped into Emma's kitchen quietly, as was her manner, complacently, taking over the management of it, of the household itself, as easily as if it had been her own. With Ralston she was matter-of-fact. He never grew accustomed to her slow—to his thinking, forward—drawling of his first name. She made constant demands on him—rightful demands, of course, in the women's opinion. But aside from their requests they ignored him. They took his presence for granted. Mother and daughter imposed their own routine on the household. The choices made from the garden or pantry shelves were theirs. Ralston had no quarrel with the idea of regular mealtimes—it had never occurred to him that the arrangement was made for anything but his own convenience. Now, if he were late, he'd find his three children and the women at the table ahead of him. And on top of that, things were different. The cornbread was different. There wasn't quite enough bacon cooked into the vegetables, to suit his taste. At times Ralston found himself outright hungry. Yet unable to ask. Unable, even, to explore his own kitchen.

In the evenings, the quiet sewing and murmured conversation of the women drove him to string a lantern in the barn. For Emma their presence was comfort—she enjoyed the sound of their voices in the house. She would have to be up and at work again soon—she knew that she wasn't ready. What a small joy, to give it over for just a little while to those others. Those other bodies weren't spent. Those other hands were strong and loving and capable. Emma held her own fairly ravaged hands just below her face and studied them, a thing she seldom did. Pushed her heels downward, flexing her feet. It was good to lie still and stretch, soothed by the coolness of the sheets. To lapse at will into the dark, curling comfort of sleep.

But Ralston was tormented. He didn't know what to say to the women—didn't, in fact, especially like married women, particularly that group Emma had taken to. The skinny one—he was thinking of Minnie—made him clear off as quickly as possible in some other direction. If he considered women in general—which would have been seldom—he'd have considered himself lucky. At least Emma knew how to stay out of a person's way. She could get a thing done on her own. With Mrs. Hale and Lou Anne there, Ralston moved through his house like a shadow. He took to the barn in the evenings and stayed there, cleaning, repairing, sharpening. He'd mucked the barn floor before it was really time. A combination of stubbornness, pride, and arrogance kept him at home, alone, in the evenings.

But his absence or presence made no real difference, for judgment had already been passed. And it was severe. His way with the children—the women didn't like the looks of it. He was remote. No affection at all that they could see. It wasn't natural. Nettie was now seven, an age where most little girls adored their fathers. But something wasn't right, in the way the little girl was shy of her father. Emma, too, had found Ralston wanting, as a parent. When Nettie was an infant, she had waited, watching Ralston, waiting for the change to take place. It was their own baby girl, her Nettie—Emma could have passed long hours, just gazing at her baby. But the change she looked for never came. She had hoped that they, she and Ralston, would come together when their family began. Her own parents had been friends; solid companions—odd, that Emma should understand that fact, now.

"Nettie's learning fast at school. She does her words and

numbers for Buddy. Now he knows them, too." There was coaxing in Emma's voice. Or: "Buddy'll be a little young for next year, but I thought I'd let him start. He wants to so bad." Nettie attended Public School No. 9, where the eight rows of desks seated the eight different grades, all of them instructed by a Miss Seay. Such pieces of news were met with a neutral noise, maybe. Sometimes with silence. Emma reverted still to that old wish that they would develop some friendship, some sense of common struggle, in their work, in their making of a family.

From the porch, after supper: "I'd like to buy him a little outfit for school." Buddy, her first son, was her favorite child, though Emma would have never admitted the fact. Her voice was tentative, in the near dark that filtered slowly those late summer evenings into the color of trees and fields. Against the wall of insect voices, there was no other sound but the slightly uneven rocking of the two chairs, the small twitterings of late birds. Night stirred in the branches. Nights made Ralston restless. He rolled a cigarette and smoked.

Ralston kept a foot up on the porch railing while he smoked. He had his hat on. Emma rocked. " 'S that all right? About his outfit?"

"That's all right"—"We'll see about it" was the more familiar answer.

"Maybe we could fit him up with something at Eagle's."

"We'll see." Ralston stopped, finished his cigarette, flicking the butt at a distance, a penciled arc of fire in the darkness.

Emma couldn't gauge his attitude toward the children. Was it simple indifference? The truth was that Ralston felt good will enough toward them. It was just that they didn't interest him. He didn't know what to do with small children. When he was feeling expansive, he might throw out a "Hey, there, little lady!" to Nettie, sometimes tugging her foot. With the second baby, Frank, it was pretty much the same—the "Hey there, little buddy" became the origin of Frank's family name. But he failed to note their differences. Where Nettie had been shy, the little boy, Buddy, bounced in his high chair and laughed at the sight of his father. If Ralston failed to greet him, he'd move up and down, with loud, baby noises; and the round eyes would follow Ralston. The third child, Ralph, now a toddler, was the one who favored Ralston, dark and clean-featured—the others were large-eyed and freckled.

"It's late, Daddy." Emma had slipped naturally into addressing Ralston in this manner, as she had always heard her mother do. "You're leaving?" She took it for granted that he would—the nightly absences were by now routine.

"Not just yet."

She wished, then, that he would stay. But he had in large part slipped from her world. "Well." Emma stood to go inside. The kitchen was dark. She stepped out for a moment onto the back porch. There was a feeling in her, one worn thin by this time: it was, none of it, what she'd expected. There was longing in Emma—she wondered if it were in everybody. Standing on the porch, she caught the strong, summery odor of soaked earth from the spot where her dish water had hit the kitchen garden an hour or so earlier. The fragrance of it followed her back into the house.

"Will he take us today, Mama?" It was Buddy. Ralston had fallen into the habit of taking the family into Clanton on Saturdays.

"I expect he will." Emma chuckled. She was changing Ned, the new one, as she spoke.

The children worked up a big excitement over the Saturday trips to town, so that the weekly trips into Clanton at least resembled a kind of family outing. Once all of them spent the day at a circus—they would never forget. For hours that day Ralston carried Ralph on his shoulder. This was a novelty—Ralston had never picked up one of his children for any reason but practicality—and Ralph's perch was the best method of simply getting one of them accounted for and out of the way. Ralph, his one lookalike child: Emma always wondered if he'd noticed. Did such things matter to him? If the occasion had been anything less than a circus, the sight of Ralph being carried would have been entertainment, in itself. At age five, Buddy already felt a certain responsibility for the others, including his older sister. His eyes moved upward to Ralph at moments out of something like caution, at other moments with a look more like envy—though Nettie for all the world would not have changed places with Ralph. But with the spectacle of the circus, concern or interest in Ralph was quickly lost. Emma walked or sat, gently bouncing Ned on her knee. That day the two of them, Ralston and Emma, enjoyed the acts—especially the elephants—the crowds, the odors of sawdust and cotton candy, as much as the children did. Once or twice Emma saw her husband laughing. She tried to catch his eye, but he wouldn't return her look. She would have liked to see him enjoying himself. Had he ever laughed? Had he ever been a child? His face relaxed for those few hours at the circus. He pointed out a thing or two from time to time. He was never jovial. His children would not have recognized Ralston jovial. And they had been used for as long as memory to the difference between their mother alone and their mother in Ralston's company—that was a fact of life.

"Nettie, that way, sugar." Emma leaned across Ralston and raised her little girl's head toward the trapeze artists—Nettie was still lost with the clowns just in front of the stands. "Buddy, don't miss the ponies!" The ponies were costumed and bangled; small dogs rode their backs. She made an attempt to catch Buddy's sleeve. Ralston frowned. The chatter and jostling—in his opinion—were nuisances. He gave her a look. And she realized that her husband's enjoyment in this event, as in all else, was a solitary thing. She had no idea of how great her own inhibition was in his company.

Emma gave herself to her children. In the early years it was Emma who watched Ralston, studying him, observing his habits and whims. Now Ralston watched Emma with the children, at times when she lost any awareness of him. Then she was someone he didn't know. He noticed that she laughed a lot—her nose wrinkled when she laughed with the children. What little things they found to laugh about, make so much over—he couldn't see it. Most likely a trifle, something silly—like that time years ago she hid under the bed, back when they'd had the farm for only a matter of months. Ralston had been on his way upstairs for the night and had found the room empty. Or so he thought, until he heard her laughing at the sight of his feet as he took off his socks. Her idea of a small practical joke. They spoke their own language, Emma and her brood, some kind of private lingo made up of jokes and little foolishnesses.

Emma feared for her children no more, she suspected, than most mothers. Summer in the Deep South was the time for the stealthy killer fevers. Her mother's last child, Emma's third sister, had died suddenly during a summer. Emma studied her children's faces, laid her palm on their foreheads, lifted their chins, to examine their mouths and eyes. Her own mother had done these things. She importuned God for the care of these children, and was comforted.

"When I was a little girl, we had storms that took the roofs off houses. Blew the chickens all the way out of the yard." On a particularly dark afternoon, it occurred to her to relate this incident for their entertainment. Toward evening cooking odors, the presence of Emma, drew her children one by one to the kitchen. And that was the beginning of it. "Mama, tell us about when you were a little girl." It became a small litany. And once Emma caught the drift of it, she developed an art. Emma remembered being a child, the little stray things that fascinated and stayed in the memory, a haunted house, a peculiar stranger, a certain dog run mad. Emma surprised herself at her own imagination. Now she had an audience. Eyes and voices, tugging little impatient hands.

Once she happened onto the phrase, "When my Daddy was little, just after the War—."

"Mama, what's a war?" from Buddy. "Before the war" and "after the war" were phrases they had heard all their lives—never referring to the war that ended the year Buddy was born. But to the South's war.

"Well," Emma thought about it, "a war is when lots of people start fighting each other."

"Like David fighting Goliath?"

"No, son. Not like that."

"Then how?"

"With guns."

"With guns? Do people get killed in a war?"

"Lots of people get killed in a war."

"They kill each other?"

"They have to, Buddy."

Here Buddy slipped off the arm of Emma's chair to go off by himself. He had to go over this new information, that people killed other people with guns. Squirrels and birds were killed with guns. The stiff, oddly heavy bodies fascinated Buddy, especially the squirrels. The little round eyes would be slightly open, covered with something like a thin skin. The squirrel was still there, the whole body, but hard—and different. Something was gone. But the idea that this could be a person and not a squirrel—it almost spoiled the story of David and Goliath. For a long time, Buddy asked no more questions on the subject of war. It was troubling. It was more fun to talk about things like the strange people who worked with the circus. For months afterward, the children were still talking about it. Mostly they just did church, instead of a wonderful thing like the circus. And church was boring.

Typically Ralston and Emma, like other farm families, relied on the church for their recreation. The dinners on the ground, the all-day singings, suppers, baptisms, revivals. Ralston went along with the family. But at the gatherings he stood off at a distance, in a clump with some of the other men. A man who was lonely in the company of his family. He was possessive of them, a little prideful, after his fashion. But apart.

He was openly proud of his acres. To be acknowledged a success by the other farmers was his main source of manly pride. It was true that Ralston had made his land produce, single-handedly and stubbornly. His yields generally met, occasionally exceeded, the county averages. But Ralston's tie to his farm was not affection for the land or satisfaction in the working of it, any more than his tie to his children was one of deep affection. It was struggle itself—that and pride—that bound Ralston to his home and to his land.

The land. He thought of it, still, as the enemy.

Chapter 10

The corn harvest was well under way the fall that Ralston brought home the Ford, that fall that would mark the change in all of their lives. The sky of October was the deep, humming blue of the equinox. The Griffens' fourth son, Billy, was just feeling confident about walking. Ralston had driven a good bargain for the truck, calculated on it and plotted for weeks, all the time moving through the routines of getting the corn in. All the family members had to put in an effort, in gathering the corn.

But for the moment Emma was doing, for all visible purposes, exactly nothing. It had been years since she held her counsel alone on the cellar steps—she had to be within hearing range of the children. And she should have been busy with the canning. But she had fled there again. As the truck was triumphantly hauled up the drive, Emma sequestered herself. She sat with her mouth drawn thin. Her eyes reddened off and on. He had hit Ralph again. He seemed to be always after Ralph, for one thing or another. Ralph, the one who favored him—Ralston never had seemed to notice. Ralph—the only one of them unable to hold his temper.

He had hit Buddy. Next, she knew that it would be Ned. If he had hit them on the bottom, it would have been different. The brief mental picture Emma had, then, of Ralph's little bottom made her eyes once again redden. For in her mind's eye, the eye of a mother, she didn't see the narrow backside of a six-year-old; she saw the plumped-out bottom of a toddler. The bottom or the legs—that was where it ought to have been. Not their faces. And never so hard. She knew he considered it discipline; but it just wasn't right. And what made it worse in some baffling way was that just a little while after such a scene, Emma would hear Buddy or Ralph laughing. Something about that didn't seem fair, that a child should have to pick up and go his way, to laugh as though nothing had happened. Or that *he* seemed to get away with it, when the children forgot all about it.

But Emma had her own ways of avenging herself, although Ralston, who thought he knew her, would have never imagined so. On that very morning he'd left to haul the truck into Clanton, Emma enjoyed her small revenge. He'd told her he'd be leaving for town early—he seldom included a reason for things like that. And as Buddy walked through the kitchen that morning on his way to the barn, Emma stopped him.

"You can go today, Buddy." Her nose wrinkled, like it did when she told a secret. Emma grinned—it was conspiratorial.

"But he said—."

"It's all right about what he said. "

Go where—that much Buddy didn't have to ask. "You mean just me?"

"All three of you can go, today." She laughed outright, then waved Buddy off with a flick of the hand. He'd expected to have to miss that day. He'd expected they'd all have to miss. Or at least Nettie.

The truth was that Emma did need her daughter. Around the kitchen sat baskets stacked with tomatoes, boxes of canning jars, Emma's racks and boilers. Billy would be into the tomatoes as soon as he woke up, and it would be up to four-year-old Ned, by himself, to keep Billy distracted. Ralston would allow the three oldest to go back to school only after the corn was in. It was a bad business, to Emma's thinking. And she would see to it that the three of them went that day—she could get away with it—*he* wouldn't be back. And she did mind the absences especially for Buddy, who was in second grade that year. Buddy had a special fondness for learning—Emma was aware of this, although, herself, she'd found nothing particularly interesting in school. But now Buddy entered a world each day that his mother could not enter. And returned each afternoon with the faraway pleasure of it. Emma encouraged the unusual attachment, realizing that for Buddy it was something private, precious even, a thing she would protect for him as much as possible. Emma quizzed him each day in the beginning, as she had done with Nettie, routinely asking him what he had learned. But she soon took on Buddy's wording. Now she asked him what he had "found out." Buddy learned his reading and figuring quickly, and with a certain impatience. What he really wanted to do was "find out." In those first six weeks, the sixth graders—all of whom sat in the same, one room—were finding out about crossing the Mississippi; and now the words "west of the Mississippi" resonated with long and noisy fantasies for Buddy. He talked to Emma about the Oregon Trail. The two sets of eyes were near duplicates, Buddy's round with excitement, Emma's amused, always looking two ways—her hands were busy.

"They walked, Mama. Some of them walked all the way to Oregon!"

"How'd you find that out?"

"There was a girl wrote it all down in a diary. Wrote about how she went to sleep walking." He looked off into his own imaginary picture. "They had to take the wagon right through a river, and the meal got all wet and spoiled. There were snakes in those rivers. Mama, do you know how many miles it *is* from here to Oregon?"

"Not rightly, son."

"It's more than two thousand miles, Mama. Some of them folks walked more than two thousand miles!"

"I see."

Buddy wanted to tell all of it, all over again, but he was wild with impatience to be outdoors. The best parts would come out again later. Buddy left the kitchen at a run. The back door banged.

It was around three o'clock when Ralston returned, hauling the inoperable Ford by wagon. It was a flatbed truck, dusty and dented, which belched oil and knocked in the engine. The truck was parked under one of the oaks near the front when the children came home from school that afternoon. Buddy was the first one to spot it, and started to run. When he reached the truck, he circled it—any vehicle was worth that much attention. But this one—it wasn't a truck that he knew. There was nothing unusual, in itself, in the sight of a rusty Ford truck parked under one of the oaks. But Ralston was nowhere in sight. Buddy scanned the yard—there was nobody, just the usual quiet of a mid-afternoon. He didn't stop to think about how he knew the difference—because there was no way to explain it. There was something different about this one, the way it sat all vacant, closed-up in the yard. He began to run again, now toward the kitchen, yelling. Emma stepped out onto the back porch. She had been waiting for him.

"What is it?" Buddy brought himself to a stop by taking hold of a railing and swinging.

"You know what it is." Emma grinned down at him.

"But I mean *whose* is it?"

"It's ours."

"Ours! It's *ours*? Where's Daddy?" He didn't wait for the answer but set off again, running. The far fields weren't yet cleared—it was easy to spot the wagon where the trampling left off. The team stood in that bored and listless way of mules, not even twitching when the ears of corn flew against the buckboard. Ralston would be somewhere deep in the rows. Through the tops of the rattling plants, Buddy made out the shape of his father's hat— knowing that he was expected to join him. Should have been there already, working along beside him. But this time there was no reprimand. Ralston frankly seemed eager to see Buddy that afternoon—Emma didn't know when she'd seen him so pleased. It hadn't registered with Ralston, even, that she'd sent the children off, behind his back.

"What are we gonna do with it? When can we take it out? Can we take it out after supper?" The words wouldn't come out fast enough.

"Hold up there a minute." Ralston didn't tantalize him. He stepped out of the row. "Can't do nothing with it, yet." Buddy twitched with impatience.

"Nothing! Why not?" In his excitement, Buddy stomped a foot.

" 'S got a rod knocking. Could spear the engine. Got to work on it some, first."

The explanation was lost on Buddy, but not the meaning. His face was falling. "Well, can I just take a look at it?"

"You can do all the looking at it you want to."

"Can I sit in it?"

"We'll see."

Then all of them moved in and out of it, jerking the lifeless steering wheel, trying out all of the knobs. But after that first time, the children were forbidden to open the doors of the truck. For the rest of the harvest, it sat there closed and useless. For a while the Ford became merely a fixture of the yard.

Buddy looked forward to telling the teacher, Miss Seay, by now a great friend of his. There was no trace of shyness in Buddy; but he wasn't pushy, either. He knew intuitively just how to take on the quiet good manners so pleasing to the female adult. In his first year, he became one of the students Miss Seay depended on. Buddy would be one of the special ones—it didn't take Miss Seay very long to figure out who these were. The ones whose eyes looked into hers so directly, whose faces would go quiet with the wonder she knew, that to this one, she could impart. Miss Seay was in her mid-thirties, had begun teaching before she was quite twenty years old. She had a mild face, a mouth permanently turned up at the corners from years of habitual smiling.

But Miss Seay had grown tired. What had started out for the young teacher as a fine and rare inspiration was by now worn down to a more settled commitment. But the spurts of inspiration always returned, the source of them unpredictable, often simple—as simple, perhaps, as a tadpole, small as a spinning, black seed. Miss Seay might place a jar on her desk one morning and say nothing about it. She would let the curiosity grow of itself. Then would begin the serious, daily inspections of the tadpole, especially critical on Mondays. And when it had grown legs, then arms, the body turned pale and fishlike, the ceremony would be planned for its liberation. There would be discussion, some disagreement, as to just the best spot to do this along the creek running behind the school. Finally as a group, with due ritual, the students would release it, with cheering and ardent well-wishing, all moved and gratified by what they had done.

And here, out-of-doors, the old inspiration might come to Miss Seay. She would talk. And Buddy was one who waited and listened to every word of such talk. Of places and people and far-off things, of the close-up, small puzzles of nature. Of stars, oceans, and insects. The human body and its invisible work. Near the meager strip of a creek, a topic such as the sea might suddenly come to Miss Seay. Something unlikely and unlovely, like the horseshoe crab—Buddy had once seen a picture of a horseshoe crab. Of the ancient intelligence that would drive that unearthly, disk-shaped animal to lay its eggs at the tide's edge, where it would be prey to the gulls. Of how it could not be dislodged by helpful hands and nudged back into the water, hands assuming in their human way that tomorrow's tide would do just as well. This was the way of all nature, its plan, Miss Seay intoned. On afternoons like these, the students stayed outdoors until the school day was over. On these afternoons Buddy walked home with the others in a kind of quiet, waking dream.

He'd been shocked to find that he would not be free again, once the corn harvest was done. That October he and Nettie were also required to pick up the sweet potatoes that Ralston had upturned and left to dry in the field. And in his outrage, Buddy forgot himself with his father. He didn't argue, even answer back—none of Ralston's children would have answered back. But he did allow himself one small display. He moved back from the table, giving his body a jerk, a single gesture of frustration finished by the stomp of a foot. Ralston was on his feet in an instant. He stepped across the room and hit Buddy hard against the face with the flat of his hand.

Buddy paused only long enough for the white hand print on his face to fill in with color. Nettie's fork fell on her plate. She lowered her head, and her eyelids moved strangely. Emma had not yet learned how to snap into the trance-like neutrality she would acquire later. She did have the straightforward common sense to keep quiet—to have stepped in would have only made matters worse. But the fact was that Ralston seldom hit the children. Seldom, because all of them were afraid of him. Seldom, because their psyches had become finely tuned instruments, more accurate than any barometer in registering the strange force of their father's moods. In the mornings the children were fresh and rested, full of that energy that breaks into talk. But with Ralston they were cautious, especially at breakfast. Each of them, without thinking about it, was at all moments conscious of Ralston— braced for the sudden alarm. If he were preoccupied—and he often was—they went ahead with their talk, paying no attention to him. At other times all of them knew to be silent. If they miscalculated, he had only to clear his throat. If Ralston was in fact seldom violent, a sort of quiet violence nonetheless seemed to be ready and waiting. And the children feared some unnamable thing in his anger more than they feared his hand.

Ned began to walk in his sleep.

"Mama." It was Nettie, standing by the bed. She touched Emma's shoulder. And knew not to say more—all of them knew not to wake up their father. Emma rose without a sound and walked into the hallway. "Mama, I got something to tell you," Nettie whispered—all her important communications began with these words. "Ned's doing something funny."

Already Emma was moving. Ned was on his feet, wedged into a niche between the wall and stair banister. Emma shook him a little—it wasn't enough. Then shook him harder, arousing him just enough for him to start in about the bees—the swarm of bees that were after him. He jerked, running a little in place. Pulled against Emma.

She would have to get Ralston. When Emma went back into the bedroom, she paused by single footfall. She had never had occasion to wake him during the night. Now she moved much like the children, who at times seemed to try to step without letting their feet touch the floor. Ralston could be easily startled, even from sleep. At Emma's touch, he leapt to his feet, standing with his fists clenched, looking much like a sleepwalker himself.

"Daddy, it's Ned." Ralston appeared to become aware only slowly that it was Emma. She started back out of the room. The gravity in her voice, no doubt, made him follow.

All of the others were awake by the time Emma got Ned settled and Ralston had finished with the hammering. He drove long nails into the banister and opposite wall, then strung lengths of rope between them. Ned woke up the following morning loud and full of energy, with no obvious recollection of anything out of the way. The family watched him, reassured a little by the ordinariness of his behavior. There were more nights of sleepwalking. And always there were the bees. Ned's sleepwalking spells would draw out for a period of years.

Since the big advent of the Ford, still parked and for all appearances useless, the family went into town without fail each Saturday. There was always something to do involving the truck, some part or tool to be found—Ralston's mind was occupied with the engine long before he could get his hands on it. And there was, too, the pleasure of companionable male debate concerning the overhaul. He spent much of these Saturdays at the repair garage on Water Avenue near the train station. Here he leaned over the open engines with the mechanics, blotting up oil and grease with his clothes, gesticulating, coming up with solutions—thoroughly enjoying himself. Men who came to the garage for business tended to linger. Emma noticed that there seemed to be no end to the enjoyment of a group of men discussing the repair of an automobile. Ralston was educating himself. And Emma and the children were happy to entertain themselves by walking over to Broad Street, to look through the Five and Dime.

Here they went directly down the long wooden aisle to the toy counter, where many partitions were filled with a different kind of toy, all of which had to be carefully examined. Emma's brood monopolized the counter. There was always a clamor of protest at the idea of departure, silenced only by the prospect of buying candy. Of this candy, the one certain purchase, the children would make a protracted pleasure, settling themselves on a bench near Broad and Water, almost brushed by the passing crowds of people.

Emma sat, now, within the stretch of blocks where she and Ralston first furnished and supplied the farm—she remembered having to trot after him, to keep up—occasionally losing sight of him altogether. Water Street, this side of Broad, was the old and original business district for Clanton, a jumble of lawyers' offices, a few private homes, hotels and restaurants, standing side-by-side with feed stores and warehouses. All of them housed in the fine, older buildings—with double balconies and grillwork, showy fa-cades mimicking architectures from countries that Emma didn't know existed. She and Ralston had once walked up Broad Street as far north as the Hotel Albert, a pompous sprawl of a build-ing, with rows of stone-trimmed windows and a recessed balcony. Neither of the Griffens would have known that this building was modeled on a Venetian palace; where Venice was—that there was, in fact, a Venice. Beyond that corner of Broad, Emma saw the church spires rising to the west. And she knew that there would lie the great houses, white and cool under their mantles of shade.

Seated comfortably in her everyday calico, Emma singled out the young matrons, making careful note of the details of their dress. Her eyes fastened onto the few short-haired women, whose skirt lengths were outright indecent. Unaware of the fact, Emma made occasional, just audible gasps. She scanned the faces of passersby for signs of disapproval and was duly rewarded. Here, surrounded by her children, Emma was anonymous. Solitary. On a Saturday in town, there were any number of such Emmas. Freckled farm women like herself.

For the children, the dime store candy involved close con-centration. No one just casually chewed. They chose mixed hard candies, so that there could be discussion and comparison, then inevitable squabbling. Now the last piece with the lavender wrap-ping was being disputed. Emma settled this argument as she usu-ally did, by taking the piece herself, to the combined outrage of her children, who watched as she unwrapped and placed the piece in her mouth, stating that it was the very best one. This statement had the intended effect of pronouncing the candy in question mediocre. And the children forgot it.

Once Ralston had the truck up on blocks and started the work, the trips to town on Saturday came to an end. Now men began to come by the house on Saturday mornings, one or two, at first. Word spread that Ralston planned to completely break down the engine. Then curiosity walked out from all corners. The actual progress was slow, for when the men came, the work was replaced by conversation that tended to length. Men circled the uncovered engine or squatted beneath the oaks. Buddy noticed that among the groups of men his father laughed out loud, made a lot of talking motions with his hands. From the windows or porch, Emma, too, looked on at the core of activity the yard had become. In the weeks to follow, some of the men would begin to stop by with their wives and families. The house and yard became a sort of gathering place. Emma loved having the house and yard full of company.

At last, when they were gone, it was the children's turn to investigate the working guts of this mysterious engine. All of them waited for some kind of signal from Buddy—that it was time to edge up to their father with the looking-on and the questions. Buddy himself watched Ralston from a distance, a little warily, like a woods creature may stop first, to test the air.

Chapter 11

When Henry left the house that morning, he was a cheerful man, a man with a pocketful of cheerful errands and a pocketful of found money. The money had been won shooting craps. It was a Saturday in early December. The morning air was still autumn-like. But there was an edge, the first thin lacings of winter. Henry lifted his head as he walked, enjoying the change. Relishing the infrequent break from routine—the crew expected him late. He walked down Water Avenue onto Alabama, then over to Arsenal Place, where he paused and crossed over an empty lot that looked out over the river—there was no reason to hurry. He saw that the river was up that morning. He gave himself the leisure of watching the slow, foam-flecked drift. The dawdling was intentional. Trifling domestic adventures like the one under way were among the few variations that marked Henry's days.

Some fifteen minutes later, he entered the Five and Dime, where he went right away to the toy counter, quickly locating the things he'd already decided on. A top, a small doll that nestled inside a bright yellow peanut, and a jointed tin monkey that moved up and down on a string. Henry was, by this time, the father of three daughters. Their second daughter, Mary, came into the world as her own, assertively unique self—totally unlike Elizabeth. Whereas Elizabeth had been beautiful, Mary was a comical baby. Her hair was dark, straight and scant. And she was fat. The chubby wrists and ankles looked like they were tied with string—double-jointed, as the colored folks called it. Henry found her greatly entertaining. Then, there was Betty Kate, their third—a towhead. The marked contrast among the three heads of hair was pleasing to Henry—he found it amusing that his three girls were so unalike.

His final purchase, on his way up the opposite aisle, was a bag of puffy, orange candy peanuts. Now he felt rich in small treasure and anticipation. It was just recently that he'd discovered the crap games that had provided the wherewithal for this fest, concealed inside a locust grove along the road he drove to the sawmill. And with circumstances as they were, he could avoid any reckoning with himself. It was so easy; he stopped for the game from time to time, how often he couldn't have said. Sometimes he stood by and watched. A tension, an urgency, rang through the circle of bodies. This time. It would be this time. Just this *one* last time! The small white pieces hit and broke apart again and again, settling in a crazing blur. And then the little maddening cubes lay still—somebody's pleasure, somebody's misfortune, how slight or large a misfortune most of them couldn't have said. Henry now carried a hip flask, one that Drefus had left lying in the boat. On occasion he lost track of time and misfortune altogether.

As he drew close to home again, Henry scanned the block ahead for any signs of his daughters, who, if he guessed correctly, would already be at their hopscotch game in the back yard of a neighbor. It was mid-morning. He heard only the tranquil sound of a broom being pushed along a sidewalk. He entered the house through the kitchen, letting the screen door slam behind him. There were no children's voices—he wished to surprise his little girls. Satisfied, he sat down at the kitchen table. Placing the large brown bag on the floor in front of him, he removed the objects one at a time, for the pleasure of looking over his gifts. The sound of the slamming back door brought Lillian, who paused in the kitchen doorway. He glanced at her, receiving a small, by now familiar shock—he still forgot she had bobbed her hair. His eyes moved, then returned to her face. Lillian's bob curled, and the softness of it set off her face in a way that surprised him. The change both pleased and pained Henry. Lillian's hair had never been cut until the bob; she had been able to sit on the ends of it. He had loved the feel of the hair in his hands. Once when he picked up a strand, the end wisp of one, something occurred to him. "This piece, here. You had that piece when you were a little, little thing." He glanced at Lillian, and his fingers moved up the strand, inventing something. "This piece, here, was your first day at school." He saw that the bit of foolishness pleased her. "And along about here was second grade. A fella named Henry thought you were stuck up and prissy." The fingers inched up. "Now about here, this fella Henry changed his mind. But his ears stuck out, and you wouldn't talk to him." Lillian laughed and swatted his hand. The hair was now carefully wrapped in tissue paper and put away in a drawer.

As she watched Henry, Lillian leaned against the doorway and crossed her arms, also crossing one smartly exposed length of calf over the other. A reprimand was coming. "That's what you had to 'pick up' in town?" She understood that he'd made a small windfall. It wasn't an especially serious reprimand, but Lillian did find the crap games common, not to mention wasteful—Henry saw no reason to hide the discovery from his wife. He boasted long and cheerfully of his occasional winnings, made no mention, of course, of his losses. Their eyes held just long enough for the unspoken question to be asked and answered. Henry chuckled as he reached into the bag for the candy.

"Henry, you have no business." Lillian emphasized each word—the meaning was perfectly clear to her husband. She kept her eyes on him long enough to make Henry raise his again, acknowledging her disapproval. It was the same way she scolded him when he'd had, in her words, too much joy juice. Her complaint met a volley of smiles—Henry was unaffected by the scolding. He held out the bag of candy. Lillian shut her eyes, gave a quick shake of the head. Then Henry reached over and pulled her against him.

"No, I don't have any business. But I won, jitterbug." This was the pet name that had occurred to him for his dainty wife. Henry attempted to take Lillian onto his knee, but she wouldn't have it—he was still under reprimand. But she did relent a little, leaning against him to look at the toys.

An explosion of noise came from the front hallway. It was Henry's towheaded daughter, three-year-old Beatrice—Betty Kate—having come in to use the bathroom. Betty Kate was given to urgent speed, but she would have paused at the sight of Henry even without spotting the wonderful array on the table. This third daughter was Henry's, in the same unaccountable way that Elizabeth seemed to belong to Lillian. Her whitish hair was so fine-textured that it floated, the tassel-like strands at times standing on end altogether. "Presents!" she shrieked, and threw herself over Henry's lap. Her eyes stopped on the monkey, as Henry had suspected they would. In her impatience to call the others, Betty Kate forgot about the bathroom. In a matter of minutes, there was a second burst of commotion, threefold. The girls all shouted at once, making eddies around the table, to get at the toys, knowing exactly whose object was whose. Now he brought out the little white bag of candy peanuts that he'd been holding under the table and put it in Betty Kate's hands. She cut her eyes at the two others. Of single mind, the girls raced back up the hall and onto the front porch. Such booty required privacy and leisure. Henry looked back at Lillian a little smugly. There was an appeal in the look, all the same. But the look, unfortunately, had just the opposite effect of what was intended. Lillian shut her eyes again and turned her head.

"Seems like there might have been something else." This purchase came from the stationer's. Henry made a staged investigation of the near-empty bag under the table. He pulled out a white, elongated box and placed it on the drain board of the sink. Lillian was able to resist picking it up for some seconds. When she did lift the cover, she saw a small magnifying glass, the handle enameled and decorated with roses. Her eyes loved it at once—she appreciated a dainty object, a little touch of unnecessary beauty. But she replaced the box top with no comment and left the kitchen. Their mutual pleasure in the giving and receiving of the gift would come later.

Occasions like that morning of gift buying, trifling as they were, marked time now for Henry. His workdays were identical—they seemed to move into each another, one day of the week so indistinguishable from the one before it that at times Henry lost track of just what week it was. The crew had settled into a pattern of working with each other. So that now Henry seldom worked with them. Again, as at the cotton mill, he looked on at the work, often walking beside the men to do so. At times he felt patently ridiculous. Drefus' talk of work with the railroad made Henry uneasy—because it frankly tempted him. How was a man to live the hours of his life shut up in a cubicle, tasting sawdust and watching other men work? Could he make himself do a thing like that, day after day and year after year? He would have held forth at length about it to Drefus, if there had not been that threat now coming between them–Drefus' constant attempts to lure Henry away from the sawmill.

Operations went smoothly. And there was one other loner.

At his breaks Simmons sat, as always, just inside the edge of the woods, but his face had a thoughtfulness at odd moments. So, even Simmons had his thoughts—the man's peculiarities interested Henry. Johnnie, the big one, was his most valuable worker. The man had come by once on a Sunday without telling Henry, to repair a spot worn to breaking in one of the harnesses. When Henry found out about it, he insisted on paying Johnnie for the job, asking the man to walk up to his office. Henry fiddled unnecessarily at his writing desk.

"Got a family, John?"

Johnnie's face changed immediately. "Why yes, sir, got me a wife and four children." Pleasure flashed out of his eyes, with the wide smiling mouth. Then the face shut down again, just as quickly. Johnnie ran a hand down the back of his head, self-consciously. He wouldn't talk. None of them would. Henry's position as owner isolated him from natural and easy conversation.

There were few interruptions at home, either, to Henry's routine. Drefus was in line for promotion to engineer, and his runs kept him away for weeks at a time. Henry's life became made up of small domestic occurrences. In the spring, Myra announced her engagement; and that was an occurrence. She would marry her young man Howard; they would move to Brown's Station. The engagement—no surprise—hit Lillian hard. She would lose her buddy, her chum in all the feminine adventures. How they had laughed when they raised the hems of their dresses—both careful not to go so far as to cut into the material. And without each other, it would have been no fun whatsoever to bob their hair.

"I suppose I should go ahead and write," Lillian began, with no further explanation. They sat together in a spot of sun that fell across the porch swing. And Henry knew what the seemingly vague comment referred to—a possible Christmas visit to

Mobile. Clanton was suddenly lonely for Lillian, without her sister. In Mobile, their mother lived with the oldest of the sisters. And from the first, the lady had taken a particular liking to Henry, which pleased and gratified the young couple—Lillian had feared that it might be awkward. Despite any image that their parents held onto, the girls knew that they couldn't expect not to marry at least somewhat beneath themselves. Yet Lillian had never seriously considered anyone but Henry. His every generosity comforted her. He was protective. He adored her in just the way that she expected to be adored.

"You go on ahead if you want to." Henry's answer was just possibly rhetorical, and it too was familiar.

Lillian didn't comment. Mobile was soft and balmy at Christmas. But they both knew that they'd end by deciding they'd rather make Christmas for the girls at home. For a while, both of them were silent, swinging with their thoughts. They had taken their wedding trip to Mobile, and neither of them had forgotten it. The old city worked a sort of spell on them, at times made them quiet together. They had spent their days walking, while something took hold of them that they could not have given words to: some combination of light and angle and odor and flavor, of a faraway place, with a salt tinge, a place long past them in time. The scaling port area touched off a kind of fever in Lillian and Henry that tantalized them like a thirst.

"Well, we can plan on it," Henry picked up.

Once or twice, he had wondered if Lillian might decide she wanted to move there, and had asked himself what he would have done, if she had. He supposed that, true enough, they would have moved. Henry would give Lillian her wish, because he would want to. It wasn't that Lillian brandished any power over Henry. She was gentle; she had a fragility, even—there was no taste for power in Lillian. But her power over Henry was a thing she couldn't have calculated, a power she would never use: that she could have, at any time, withdrawn her love from him. In that respect, her power was terrible.

For Lillian, too, little events in the lives of their children became markers of time. Henry would have denied that he had a favorite child, but his little girl, Betty Kate, had a favorite parent. She singled out Henry directly as her one most favorite person in all the world. Of the three girls, it was Betty Kate who clambered over Henry, hugged and kissed him with large slobbery kisses, pulled on his ears. Of the three daughters, Betty Kate was the one who physically favored Henry, something about the eyes and forehead. Henry didn't entertain his children, as another adult might have done—he outright played along with them. Their amusements were easy to come by. They built ungainly-looking, brown paper kites that got lost from sight on the wind. They flew bewildered June bugs from strings. Behind Lillian's back, Henry built an odd-looking, wooden contraption which drew groups of neighborhood children into the yard. He called it a flying jinny.

They made family outings onto the Taylor pastureland along the river, sometimes camping overnight on the bank, or pushing aside some of the hay in the old tenant cabin. Henry showed the girls a spring trickling out of the soapstone, where the Indians, he said, had scooped out the hollow that caught the water. He taught them all the names he knew for wildflowers, trees, and plants. He swam the brown, earth-flavored water with Betty Kate on his back. Henry fished for the supper when they camped, sometimes taking over the cooking of it himself, as he did on occasion at home. And as the day faded, he tippled from his flask and told his family ghost stories, stories that made the little girls jumpy and uneasy as they squatted for the last time before going into the tent.

There was one abrupt and unpleasant time marker: something

was wrong with Mary. To their amazement, she'd been held back in first grade—a puzzling event that required a conference with Mary's teacher. Mrs. Robb, who had also taught Elizabeth, had cousins in Orville. She knew Lillian's family, and had found in Elizabeth everything she would have expected in a McClinton child. But this other one, the quiet one, was another matter altogether. At the meeting held in the classroom, Henry despised the woman on sight. She was tiny and round. Her head was small and round; at the back of it she wore a small, round bun. Henry suspected that she had a round little brain, as well. It would have appalled the stuffy lady to know that in her diminutive roundness she was frankly cute.

"Won't you take a seat?"

Throughout the meeting, the little woman addressed herself exclusively to Lillian, not looking at Henry's face directly but at some point on his shirt front. But the woman felt the strength of his eyes, well enough. Who were the Grays, she wondered. She'd have to remember to ask.

Henry sat forward in his chair with his hat held on his knee. And he examined this Mrs. Robb—a dun-colored woman, of not much charm he suspected, this little self-important person who had found such fault with his child. He couldn't figure it. It was Henry's suspicion that, of the three of them, Mary was the brightest. This Mrs. Robb—Henry watched the little gray buttons of eyes that were fixed on Lillian, observed their flatness. He thought of the black, absorbent eyes of his daughter Mary. How she always wanted to know about things—anything, indoors or out—what the ocean was like, where rivers came from, how what Henry called the "innards" worked, when he took apart Lillian's snarled sewing machine. Mary was the one who listened to Henry's ghost tales with a look that cut right through them. It was his feeling that she knew he enjoyed himself, that she gave him permission to do it, but that the haint stories didn't really amuse her much. She was basically being generous. But the life cycle of the willow fly, on the other hand, that kind of thing made the dark eyes go black. Stories of her Uncle Jay—now, those got her interest. To Mary the sort of other-world eeriness of those stories was delectable. She would have wanted to talk to her uncle about those people he saw that nobody else could see.

"We're obliged for your time," Henry said out of nowhere, and to the surprise of the two women stood up, ending the conference. "We'll give Mary another year." He spoke as though he were the one to make that decision, not the little pin cushion of a woman. Something about his voice seemed to register then with Mrs. Robb. Now she looked at Henry directly for the first time. And she was surprised. Why, the gentleman—and he was a gentleman—had quite a dignity about him. He must have been educated, she guessed, somewhere out of state. Mrs. Robb's intelligence was of the most commonplace variety, but she had worked with people young and old long enough to recognize what she called presence in a person. She became cordial.

The old restlessness returned full force to Henry. In the evenings he'd find himself distracted, as if some invisible something plucked at his sleeve. He needed to move, but not for the ordinary pleasure to be had in a walk—there was no pleasure in the aimless walking Henry did on those evenings. He neglected to buy cigarettes on the way home from the sawmill. This was intentional, so that at night he'd give himself that errand, which would take him up Water Avenue to Pilcher's. The river was nearby. He'd walk over in that direction, lean for a while against a tree on the bank. There he stared out over the water, like someone who had forgotten something. He missed Drefus; he missed the talk. He felt none of that good fatigue that had always come to him in the evening, carrying him right off into sleep. At the end of his work-day, his mind would be numb—not from fatigue but monotony. Now he chafed and pushed the ground with the worrying tip of a shoe. He squared with himself: he wasn't satisfied. But he was long familiar with the feeling. He concluded that it was some-thing that would come to any man, young—but Henry no longer felt young. He took a pull or two from his hip flask. The liquid burned on his tongue and throat, a pleasing sensation. As for the old restlessness, he assumed that fault to be with himself.

The incident with Mary continued to hold his attention, still-ing the agitation for a while. As it turned out, in a routine visit from the health nurse, Mary was discovered to be in serious need of spectacles. Within a month of their fitting, she was promoted to second grade, where she fell short of exemplary conduct only by incessant reading at her seat. Henry's gratification was rich and long when Mary was then promoted not from second to third grade, but directly to fourth.

At home she discovered Dickens on the family bookshelf and was from that time lost to the world and her family. She chose to come up front in the evenings with Henry, while the other two did homework in the kitchen. From his armchair he watched her read. She sat on the floor in a strained-looking position, her legs stretched out in front of her in a "V." But Mary had no knowing contact with her legs—with the rest of her body, for that matter. Her senses roved the streets of Dickens' London. She must have felt Henry's eyes on her. Once she looked up, just long enough to make the announcement: "When I grow up, I'm going to live in London." The little tortoiseshell spectacles made her eyes look larger. Her head dropped back into the pages.

Lillian called the girls to bathe before supper. Henry laid aside his newspaper and picked up his magazines. As a rule he looked forward to his *Post* and *Collier's* but he didn't feel his usual pleasure in them that evening. He felt antsy, for no reason that he could think of. Mary had left her book lying face down on the living room floor. Henry picked it up, to see what she was reading; it was *Oliver Twist*—he wasn't acquainted with it. He turned some pages; he read over the opening. He backed up; he read the opening again. Then he relaxed, stretched, and began to read in earnest. When Lillian called him for supper, he was annoyed at the interruption.

"I'll be there directly. Put mine in the warmer."

He resettled himself and read. He didn't hear Mary come back into the room.

"Daddy?" She inclined her head and waited. "My book." Mary was patient. "My book, Daddy."

Henry looked up. "What's that? Oh, here it goes." And until every Dickens title was read, Henry and his daughter both daily entered that fictional world.

Why had old Miss Lewis never told them about books such as these, he wondered. Henry's life as a schoolboy seemed so long ago as to feel a little like something he had dreamed. But he would never forget that last day—his last day in eighth grade, his graduation. A mild day in May it had been—the very sun felt congenial. The graduation exercises had been rehearsed for that evening. All the others were jubilant. Old Miss Lewis herself was jubilant, inasmuch as her nature allowed. And Henry had expected to be. Instead, he had an odd, kind of hollow feeling. It perplexed him—he was outright unhappy, not jubilant. Something was wrong. He had it all figured out by the end of his walk home from school that afternoon. The Academy in town—it was no longer a private school; now Dallas Academy was part of the new Clanton school system. There was no longer a tuition.

He'd need the money to board in town—but he could find some sort of work for that easily enough. Now the pieces of Henry's fantasy moved into place. Damned if he hadn't come up with a way! He felt a little smug about it on the way home, imagining the pleased reaction of his family. But he hadn't followed his idea to its full conclusion, that the Academy—paid or not—was for students planning to enter university. He wasn't thinking that far ahead, rather problem solving in that dreamy way of chasing after a wish. He hadn't learned much of anything in grade school; that was the problem. Old One Blue eye had provided him with the *equipment* necessary for learning—he had to grant her that much. But he'd been offered little, or nothing, to learn.

From the beginning something was not quite right about the plan with his family—it was puzzling. He told his mother first, who had waited for Henry that afternoon. It was his own special day in the family, his graduation, and she'd made him a pan of gingerbread. Henry was excited, even agitated, telling his news. Mrs. Gray, a little damp from her cooking, just listened and smiled. She looked at Henry's jug ears fondly. She even touched his face, a thing she seldom did. Then her hands went back to her apron.

"Why, son." She laughed at him, indulgently. "The Academy's for those who plan to be doctors or lawyers and such." She patted him—again something rare. "The Academy's not for the likes of my Henry." Here she actually tugged on one of Henry's ears. "We're farm people." Her voice was cajoling, just short of caressing. But she didn't consider it a serious matter. Henry heard his mother and sisters talking in the kitchen, laughing about Henry's big idea. He was a one among many all right, that one! They called out to him. But Henry had left the house.

When he came in at dusk, to wash and dress for the evening, he saw that his father had been let in on the little joke. And his father had taken it differently. There was a strained expression on the older man's face. This was a matter that had no known precedent. No one in the family had ever taken a notion like that. After supper, Henry walked into his father and Drefus standing together just inside the barn. They went quiet. It was an embarrassed quiet, and Henry knew at once that he was the cause of it.

Mr. Gray cleared his throat, to establish the seriousness of what he was about to say. "It's like this, son. We're not people with that kind of income. Why, not a one of us has ever thought of going to university."

The subject had somehow been changed all around—it was no longer the Academy but the university. Henry wanted nothing so much now as to fall in with his mother and sisters, to pass the whole thing off as a joke. But his father and Drefus—they knew that the talk was no joke. The two of them just stood there, looking pained. Their mother, by contrast, had forgotten all about it. She was especially cheerful that evening, proud and possessive of Henry. He was an excellent student—no one had ever told her that. But she knew it. It would be like him.

Drefus didn't bring up the subject again—there was nothing more to bring up. But he watched Henry peculiarly. His own way would be more in the line of diversion.

"Think it's about time you made a discovery, little Brud. We'll call it an introduction."

Both boys stood in the bedroom—Drefus was no longer a boy, had to bend at the knees, in fact—knotting their ties in front of a piece of mirror glass. Which was difficult to do. The glass was too narrow for both to get a good view of themselves, standing there side by side.

"Yeah, I'd say it's about time." Drefus looked at Henry through the glass, nudging him. He would have pulled his brother over and kissed him, but that would have embarrassed both of them, may even have set off an argument. That night Henry had his first go at hard liquor. It must have been the way kerosene tasted, Henry thought, maybe worse. The stuff burned all the way down into his insides. But he had a second go, and another. It wasn't that bad, after all. He remembered laughing and laughing, almost flinging himself out of the wagon seat, backward. This was entertainment for the others with Drefus, who stood grouped beside the wagon. There was a girl, Eugenia, plump and giggly, with a space between her front teeth.

"He's a cutie, this one is. He's gonna be a sport." Eugenia brushed a strand of hair across Henry's forehead, but Drefus interrupted.

"Not yet, Genie. He's not that grown up, yet."

The evening lapsed into a pleasant blur.

Chapter 12

It was the keenest satisfaction he'd ever known. Ralston was oblivious to the noise, the rattling of the engine, the metal box of tools clattering along the floor of the truck bed—sweet, discordant music. Ralston was driving. For pleasure. He wouldn't have admitted, even to himself, that he drove only for pleasure. Would have cringed to be caught at it by anyone he knew. The road on which he started out was as familiar to him as his own fields. He knew without thinking about it when to turn off for the feed store, where he still took part in the card games. But at that first junction, if he kept going straight—he didn't know where that road went. The question intrigued him. The distance of it. What was out that way, he wondered now—then wondered, further, what that road would connect up to. Why, he bet he could make it all the way to Prattville, going just by the direction of the sun. Montgomery, even—Ralston had never been to Montgomery.

The roads were dusty by these last weeks of winter. The first rains hadn't yet started. Ralston found himself further enjoying the itchy dust smell raised by his tires. He watched woods and pasture and fields moving by him: the speed of it all! With the wagon, there was never much sense of movement. And in the wagon, he thought about anything besides what he was doing. Now he concentrated on operating the truck: the changing distance, the speed—which to him was enticing. He glanced over his shoulder. He was alone on the road. To his left were stripped winter cornfields. There'd be nobody out there. He pushed down on the narrow accelerator, harder than usual. The truck shifted roughly into a yet higher speed. Then the branches that flanked the road moved faster. More and more of them. Distance! Ralston himself had no idea how seldom he smiled. As he drove, his thin mouth made a bow.

In the beginning, Ralston thought he had failed. The truck moved forward slowly; it paused, jerked slightly. Then it gagged, sputtered, and died. He got out and re-cranked. He was alone on the farm that Sunday morning and was profoundly grateful that there was no one around to witness this particular humiliation. But Ralston's privacy was soon interrupted. Mr. Freeland's Chevrolet pulled into the drive. Ralston had never really liked the man, and this was no less than galling—to be caught like this, in his stark failure. He hadn't yet had time to think about the face he'd put on, given the embarrassment of it. The engines of the two vehicles came to a stop almost at the same instant, the Chevrolet smooth, the truck shuddering. Mr. Freeland stood half outside his car, one leg on the ground. He raised his hat. "You done it! Sure looks like you done it!" Now he walked over to Ralston, who was puzzled. He wouldn't have thought old man Freeland clever enough to make fun of him.

Ralston's face was a mask. "Not a very pretty performance," he muttered.

"Will be, soon's you get the valves cut." The other man still had a smirk—what Ralston took to be a smirk—on his face. But the reaction, after all, was sincere.

Others arrived during the day, and Mr. Freeland hailed them all with the same outburst. "He done it! Sure looks like he done it!" Ralston was set upon to crank the engine, which he did with disguised reluctance. But the demonstration was cheered and congratulated. No one minded the coughing and sputtering—seemed to take much notice of it, in fact. It had cranked. He had done it! Arrangements were made for hauling the engine into town. And in this last piece of business, the process of Ralston's education was completed: the finished job required a machinist—it never would have been possible for him to have done it alone. By mid-afternoon, the engine block was once again removed and loaded onto a wagon, to be pulled into Clanton on the following morning. He was consoled. And in any event, with things as they were, Ralston knew that he couldn't have covered up a true failure. The interruptions to his work on the engine were routinely caused by someone's coming by. Or a whole clump of somebodies.

The Griffen farm had become a regular hub on Saturdays and Sundays. Emma grew to expect it—soon fell into the routine of baking on Saturday, so as to have something to offer the wives who came along with their husbands. For her, it was a pleasurable business, those family calls. She moved by habit back and forth from the kitchen to dining room, peering out windows, to check on who might be arriving. And she would have now just possibly been more content than at any time in her marriage. Except that she *knew,* without understanding what it was that she knew. Something was going to happen. Something was not as it should be in her household. Her children were troubled. Were they all of them troubled, she wondered. A sort of menace hovered just at her elbow, just out of view—some dark thing shadowing them. Emma tried to will it from her mind.

These days Ralston only hitched the team for the farm work. Everything else was done in the truck. There was always something to fetch at Hendrix Feed & Harness. Occasionally Ralston drove all the way into Clanton on a weekday, for some mechanical part that he needed. Throughout the harvest the truck had been up on blocks. Even then he'd made time to look at it occasionally, to make comparisons between his engine and the ones he helped break down on Saturdays at the garage in town. He'd begun work right after the plowing under and winter sowing were done, and then by stages—the work was always interrupted. First, he'd pulled off the engine head and drained out the ropy black oil into a bucket. The children stood by in line to watch this process, all of them fairly peering. Where did all the thick, black stuff come from, and what was the stuff, they wanted to ask—but none of them did. It was Buddy who'd been the lucky one—he'd had to help. *Had* to. His father couldn't have done it all, without another pair of hands. From under the truck, Ralston knocked each piston up through the top of the engine. Buddy's job was to pick up and move each one of the cup-like, metal objects. And Ralston had warned him of the danger of dropping a piston or letting it come into contact with grit or dirt. Buddy carried each of the four pieces without fumbling, a silent "please, God" circling through his mind. He'd never been asked to do something really important for his father. That night at supper and for a day or so afterwards, the others sneaked looks at Buddy. Of admiration and envy.

Then Ralston began on the rings and rods, and this was work that required undisturbed concentration. The January light was strong and clear. Even under the leafless branches of the oak, it was a good light to work by. When he worked, Ralston's face had that contentment of a man who was taking pleasure in the job he was doing. Not that pleasure was necessary in a job, even much to be expected. Ralston had been raised to a work ethic which was strong by any standard. And his own conscientiousness—pride, maybe—went further even than that, pushed him at times to a kind of hard perfectionism. Ralston had disciplined himself with his farm; now he could look on the fruits of that discipline with satisfaction. His fields were plowed under and sown to lespedeza. His machinery was cleaned, greased, and stored for the winter. The fences were tight. The rotting north wall of the chicken house had been replaced. He had earned this present satisfaction, the margin of time it had brought him, and he looked forward to it, alone. The single-mindedness that would allow him an unhurried involvement in the work. On Saturdays and Sundays there was always the company, which of course slowed down his progress—although the avidity with which his opinions were now sought was deeply gratifying to Ralston. This from others who newly owned an automobile, who owned a troublesome automobile, or who had considered the owning of an automobile; and that included just about every farmer and resident in the Burnsville area. It was an agreeable thing, this deference to his opinion, although it was no more than Ralston privately considered he'd always been due. But his opinions had never been asked. There had always been the others. There had always been Charles.

From a little distance on the road, Ralston heard the voices of the children coming home from school, lighthearted voices that answered, interrupted, clashed with each other. The work beneath the oak had given him an uncalculated opportunity to make observations about his children. He noticed that their disagreements were direct and simple, usually quickly concluded, even when blows or physical torment were involved. There were no obvious grudges, no particular jealousies that he could detect. Even now, parenthood puzzled Ralston. His children grew up around him—something that had nothing to do with himself. He knew his crops better than he knew his children. Their lives took place with no effort on his part. If the truth were known, he was a little afraid of them. They were Emma's. Emma knew how to deal with them—this mild-mannered woman, whose main mode of discipline was to threaten to break a switch. It was her ultimate tactic, this threat. And it was usually rhetorical.

The five children clustered around the kitchen table, their heads, of varying heights, drawn together in a huddle. It must have been a family characteristic—all of them stood on one foot, with the second foot resting across the top of the other. All of the feet at this time of morning were bare, but in shoes they continued the habit. It brought no end of scolding from Emma—each child had a single shoe that stayed dirty or scuffed white. The center of interest for the group this morning was the collection of dimes, five separate dimes, a rare and wonderful treat. Emma had given each of them spending money for town. This was the first Saturday morning that the truck was up and running.

There were deliberations under way.

"No. You're the one gettin' the marbles."

"I thought Ned was gettin' the marbles."

"Ned's gettin' the men."

"Look. It don't really matter who gets what. We stop by the hardware and somebody gets the firecrackers. Then, somebody else buys the men and the marbles. Then, the last person buys the candy. It don't matter who it is." All of this was from Buddy, who patiently outlined the plan, listing the points on a finger.

"What about Nettie? What'll she put in?"

Buddy glanced over at Nettie, who, although part of the group, was not taking part in negotiations as usual. She was in a quandary that was causing her annoyance, even unhappiness, certainly much frustration. One of her great wishes would have to be paid for dearly or abandoned altogether. She could no longer pool with the group as she once did, for her wants had become different, had become decidedly feminine. What Nettie really wanted—oh badly, fervently wanted—was a little heart-shaped blue bottle of toilet water. *Evening in Paris*, it was called. It would require her whole dime. She could, of course, buy a set of ball and jacks instead, and still have Crackerjack money. But the little blue bottle—she wanted it, and to have it would mean going hungry, deprived of sweet stuff on a Saturday. She was tormented by the choice.

Ralston walked into the kitchen, and Billy swung around with a grin that fairly startled his father. If he hadn't been shy with Ralston, he would have run up to him then. Instead, Billy wrapped his arms around himself and ducked up and down, in anticipation. Ralston realized that something was afoot—that something was expected of him. And when Emma came down with her shopping bags, he understood. The family had worked themselves into a swivet of excitement over a trip to town in the truck. Emma had never been inside it. The five children had only once bunched together in the front seat, for a ride around the farm property. Now, each of the other faces stole a separate look at Ralston. Excuses passed rapidly through his mind, none of them sound enough to have satisfied that line of staring faces. He supposed he could have outright refused. Instead, something prompted Ralston to go out to the barn and load a layer of straw into the truck bed. On his way outside, Ralston had an odd recollection. His own father, although himself a farmer, had preserved a certain uncommon gentility, changing from work clothes into his meeting or visiting clothes when he came in, in the evenings. Ralston had an image, then, of one crossed leg and a well-polished shoe. When Charles Junior was little, the boy was invited to ride the jerking leg up and down, like a hobby horse. None of the others had ever been invited to do that. His father had always been ready to please Charles Junior.

The five children were like a gaggle of biddies in the straw-covered bed. For them, the trip into town had all the excitement of a carnival ride. The roads were familiar. On the road to the farm, they knew every bump and dip. But the difference in speed between the truck and the wagon turned those same bumpy places into a wild joy ride. They were jostled and pitched, thrown against each other, shrieking and tangling. Bits of straw flew from the bed. Emma sat rigidly in her seat, one hand against her chest, clutching her handbag. With the other hand, she held just as tightly onto the door handle. Her face was grim. The unusual speed unnerved her.

Ralston laughed out loud. "Emmalie, it's not gonna kill you."

Emma looked ahead. She had no sense of humor about it. "Well, I reckon it's all right." She got through the drive into town on the strength of sheer stoicism. When she got out of the truck, her legs were stiff. But she thought she'd do better the second time. But that second time, the trip back to the farm, would be Emma's last for a good while to come. There would be only the rarest of such hay-scattered joy rides. Ralston had no intention of using the truck for the purpose of family outings. He couldn't get his mind off it—he was captive, now, to the strange lure of speed and distance. And he still wondered where that road went and where it connected, if he didn't keep on going in his usual way to Hendrix Feed & Harness.

Chapter 13

It wasn't as though this were the first time it had happened—
that he'd stayed away overnight. The first time had been on a
Sunday. And on that following morning, Ralston walked in with
the casualness of someone returning from an errand. At one time
the look on his face, his very posture, would have challenged
Emma. That morning he glanced her way with no more concern than if he'd just walked inside from the fields. "Been up to
Birmingham with young Hendrix. Settled him in. He's on at a
factory up there," Ralston explained in an everyday voice.

"I wish you'd have said so before, so I wouldn't have worried."
Emma was above all a practical soul. Confrontations only made
things worse.

But this particular time: Emma asked herself later if from
the beginning there'd been anything different in that day. His
work clothes hung on their hook on the bedroom door—this was
usual. Without any thought-out intention to follow his father's
example, Ralston had taken to changing into more presentable
clothes when he left the house. His work boots were carefully
placed against each other on the back porch downstairs.

Generally, Emma asked no questions concerning his whereabouts. And she knew virtually nothing of that new inner world
her husband inhabited. But she had come to feel a marked curiosity: what made him do the things that he did? He wasn't
a bad man at heart, for all his peculiarities. He wasn't directly
unkind to her—or to any of them. But he was different from

other people. Things troubled him. Maybe from way back, she reasoned, something had troubled him. Men were altogether different from women, on any account. She knew that Mrs. Hale's daughter Lou Anne understood this difference, just as she did. Emma wouldn't speak of such private matters, however. Though she had moments of temptation—or what she considered a wicked temptation. What she wanted to do was complain, in full detail and at length, to someone who would listen and sympathize. Someone who would *really* listen. And she knew that this person was Lou Anne—a good gripe session would have a distinct appeal for Lou Anne. But here Emma came across an obstacle, a certain code of behavior she didn't know she had, or when or where she had learned it. A code that wouldn't permit her this comforting outlet. There were some things you just didn't talk about—or if you simply had to, only with blood kin.

She thought of an afternoon when there'd been just the four of them, Emma and her three best and dearest. Of the three, Minnie was fond of gossip. Old Mrs. Hale was fond of opinion—mostly her own. Lou Anne preferred thinking. And reading romance novels—which she did secretly, though she didn't try to conceal them from Emma. She often carried a book in her skirt pocket. Through the window the women could see the men grouped under the oak, leaning over the truck. Emma watched Ralston holding forth and gesticulating. He had a good audience, and that included Lou Anne's husband, Foley. Lou Anne squinted. "What he's doing," she drawled, looking at Ralston, "he's playing with it. He's outright playing with that thing. Making a toy of it." Although her eyes were on Ralston, Emma noticed that from time to time they moved over to Foley. Lou Anne seemed to enjoy watching Foley, homely enough little man though he was.

Minnie giggled in her nervous way, appreciating the remark. "Ain't it funny, the way men do?" she added, without imagination.

Mrs. Hales eyes jumped. She had cataracts on both eyes, now; and the heavy lenses she wore magnified her eyes to caricature. "Sure, they're a-playin', just like the young ones out back are playing with that ball."

Lou Anne went on, "The world is different for them than it is for us. They don't understand us. They only understand each other. We understand them better than they understand us."

Until that comment, Emma had paid only light attention to the rhythm of idle female talk. Lou Anne's statement made her think of Buddy. She could watch Buddy doing just about anything—eating, sitting still even—and kind of move into him, with her feelings. She understood how it *felt* to be Buddy. With Ralston it was guesswork. Early on, she'd realized that she could never feel what it was really like to be Ralston. She'd learned his little habits and preferences in daily things. She knew what displeased him. That was the sum of it. Later that evening, Emma sat on the stairs for a good while, her head propped on her hands, contemplating this insight.

Neither could she imagine that other part of his life, beyond his work there on the farm. And he didn't talk about any of it—the card playing, the truck. When something was on Ralston's mind, he simply brooded in silence.

Even with the limitations of her sense of him, Emma knew when something was worrying her husband. "Something troubling you, Daddy?" There was no reply to this question. Emma watched him push the gravy around his plate with a piece of biscuit. It was the last of the Sunday ham, and she'd set it aside for him. He wore a set of denim overalls, very faded, and the shirt he wore must have been one of his oldest. The arms were too short, drawn up from washing; the sleeves of his underwear showed at the wrist by an inch. Ralston's wrists were strong and brown, like his face was even now, in late winter. She remembered that her father's wrists had been thick, the hands large and homely; freckled. Ralston's hands were slim-fingered. In his early prime, he was a fine-looking man—a fact Emma was covertly proud of.

Her little essays of sympathy were habitual, if seldom gratified. She would have liked, at times, to rub Ralston's neck or shoulders when he was tired or obviously worried, but he didn't take to that sort of thing. Emma considered repeating her question—but it would only annoy him. What preoccupied Ralston at present was a critical matter. Buddy alone would have been aware of it, if he'd in fact been paying attention as he stood by one afternoon, overhearing snatches of a conversation that didn't really interest him. What Buddy wanted was a closer look at the shotgun the man that talked to his father was carrying. Ralston looked at the ground, pushing a foot as he talked.

"Give it up, huh?"

"Yeah, that's what I heard."

"Think there's anything to it?"

" 'S what he told Hendrix. Says it's all of it up for sale, herd, equipment, everything."

It was a nearby dairy farmer who had decided to sell out, and Ralston was considering the purchase of the milk farm, himself. It would have been a profitable move, but somehow he couldn't make himself do it. It wasn't just that the work might be too much for him, though he would have no doubt had to hire on. But he couldn't make himself *want* to do it, and this reluctance puzzled him in himself. To let a chance like that go by—it was not a thing that a successful man, like his brother Charles Jr., say, would have done.

Late that afternoon Ralston walked his fence lines—he already knew they were tight—for almost an hour, and by dusk had once and for all put aside the idea of expanding. He sometimes wished he could put all of it—farm, crops, the whole works—aside. It weighed on him. The March dusk was mild that evening; there was a sweet taste to the wind. Ralston lagged. His land was mostly flat, but there was one small rise, and from where he stood on it now he could look down on the farmhouse. Its windows were faintly yellow. He could imagine the comings and goings in the kitchen—too busy for his liking. Too noisy. He could picture Emma. She fussed and carried on at the children, laughing most of the time. She seemed to enjoy teasing them. Ralston came to and went from that house; it was necessary shelter. It belonged, really, to Emma. The children were Emma's. All of it, Emma's. He fed them, clothed them, and housed them—all of this working singly—as well as any man could have, better even than some, he told himself with pride. But it was, none of it, his. Only the heavy black soil was his, to war against, he felt like. Ralston looked down on the house with a regret that had no knowledge of itself.

Emma realized now that she was by herself again in the kitchen, although the children had ducked in and were already back outside for the afternoon. Her attention was on the biscuit dough she was making. The day was still bright outside. At the moment she didn't hear their voices. She cut in the lard, dribbled water over the dough, pushing the moist mass of it around with her knuckles. That was when it came to her, the sudden intuition that made her wipe her hands clean. She went upstairs to the bedroom and dropped down to look under the bed. It was just as she'd realized, standing there at her worktable. The suitcase was gone. Emma crouched for a few moments, looking into the empty place, taking it in, then went quickly around the room. She went to the chest of drawers. Everything had been taken out but his work clothes or anything worn enough to soon fall into that category. She didn't know when he had carried the suitcase out of the house.

Emma put herself through a process of reasoning, all of it mechanical. Ralston had never visited his family. He must have decided to make a visit, now that he had the truck. It'd be like him, to take off that way, unannounced. She'd write a letter to Charles. She'd be clever about it. She'd send some small message for "when Ralston gets there." Emma returned to her biscuit dough.

When the children were in bed, she didn't undress. She forgot, even, to think about it. She sat instead by the window, in the rocker she had used with each of her children. It was a clear night. The moon was full. Emma looked down on the whitened yard, taking in the shapes of various objects, the sharp moon shadows. She went downstairs. She might have stayed and paced the kitchen, but her footsteps made too much noise in the house. She went onto the back porch; even there she couldn't be still. She walked out into the moon-flooded yard, around the edge of her garden, then toward the barn. But there she was distinctly uncomfortable. There was something of Ralston there near the barn—she didn't feel private. But Emma wasn't completely alone. The house cat skirted the edge of the barnyard, following her at a distance, one of the kittens from Mrs. Hale's old calico. Emma changed her direction and walked down the drive. Here she stepped over a ditch and continued down the open road that ran past the farm. Her arms were folded tightly against her body. The little ghost shape, tail erect, slipped along the road behind her like a scrap of blown cloud. The farm was an unfamiliar landscape of moon white and shadow. The night was wide and alive and breathing. Emma walked as if she could walk clear of herself. But it was no good. He had left her. Left all of them. He was gone.

When she turned back again, she drew her own shadow along the hard clay.

Chapter 14

At not quite 6:30 on a Sunday morning, the sound of the telephone woke Henry. The ringing was strange to his ears, and he lay for some time resisting it, sleep-soaked and perspiring. Night had brought no relief from the early heat spell that had lasted for more than a week. He and Lillian had tangled themselves in the bed sheets, which felt damp to the touch.

"Henry?"

By now Henry was sitting up in the bed. The ringing was shrill.

"It's got to be something important, at this hour of the morning." Lillian's voice was already apprehensive.

She stood next to Henry in the kitchen, her head below his shoulder, listening to the conversation. Which wasn't difficult to do. Mr. Taylor shouted into the receiver—it was a habit. Why this call should have taken place at that particular hour or why Henry should be asked to go out right away was not clear. But no one asked for an explanation. People nearby had got word to the Taylors. The sawmill had burned to the ground. It had happened some time during the night.

"I'll be on out, soon's I can get dressed," Henry hung up, and he and Lillian stood for a moment, exchanging looks, then looking past each another. They were stunned. *To the ground.* That meant gone. All of it.

"Do you want me to go with you?" Lillian asked, in that solemn voice reserved for emergencies. It was like her to offer to help, and offer it sincerely, when there was not a thing in the world of a practical nature that she could do.

"Expect I'd better go on out alone."

"I'll make you some breakfast." Lillian managed bacon and eggs fairly well. She never failed to scorch the toast. She herself didn't eat, and neither of them said very much. It wasn't possible yet to take in what had happened.

The morning was filmy when Henry cranked the automobile. The sky was a spongy gray mass, like the sun had dropped into it and dissolved. Henry drove slowly out of Clanton in the direction of Orville, shifting down more often than was necessary. There was still only foot traffic at that hour. His speed didn't change as the car crept out through the edges of town, past the Live Oak Cemetery, past Bloch Park, until there was no more town, only pasture and borders of woods. He was stalling. His eyes trailed over sagging gray buildings or stray clumps of cedars standing in the fields. If the sawmill was burned to the ground, there wasn't much use in going out to look at it, he told himself now. It was gone; that was all there was to it. When Henry turned off the main road, he brought the car to a stop for no reason and sat there with the engine idling.

But as it turned out, the destroyed sawmill, its roof collapsed over it like a lid, was not even a particularly dramatic sight. Only ugly. As Henry approached the property, the desolation of the place stood out at him. A ragged and scarred piece of earth, made useless now by the fire. Close up, he saw that the debris was a tangle: splinters of charred wood standing out at odd angles, whips of blistered rubber. The steps going up to Henry's office were still standing, fragile looking as a wasps' nest. The sun had burned through the first cover of morning. Now a powder floated up from the rubble, making slow flakes of light, just as Henry's mind had first slowed, then stopped. But he knew he had to set it to work again. The thing must be thought through well and carefully—trouble was that he didn't know where to start. It was Henry's curse—or his blessing—that he never had seemed to feel the way most people did about money. He used money as it was intended to be used, then forgot it—it had no more importance for him, then. But money was, of course, the main issue for the family. Yet in some strange way, for Henry that wasn't the worst of it. Standing there looking over the scene in front of him, Henry would have been hard put to say what the worst of it was. The waste. Was it that? All the hours. The days. Now the reality of it began to break through. He had come to this place, to spend the long and slow hours of his life. And day after day those hours had been sucked out of him. The hours had made days. Which had slipped into years. Years he had given no thought to.

He was suddenly wild. Pictures moved through his mind, at first slowly, then racing. Wild, without reason. Faces and voices and smells and sounds. Old Miss Lewis fanning herself. The drop on the tip of her nose that all of them watched—she didn't know it was there. The sniggering they had tried to swallow. The job he'd had at the merchandise store, running odd coal orders on Saturday mornings. That time he'd turned over the wheelbarrow and spilled the coal all over the ground and had tried to scoop it up again in his hands, dirt and everything. The matchbox, then the candy box, where he kept his little bits of pay—not even Drefus knew about it—pushed way up under the bed. He didn't know why he had hidden it. He could just as well have shared it. The teller at the bank in Clanton, a man with a little raisin-like face. The tight wads of bills, the little bundles of coins wrapped in newspaper. His father waiting outside in the wagon–the patient humility on his face. The time Eloise choked at the mill and couldn't stop coughing—they'd sent her home, at Henry's insistence. Johnnie. Johnnie's little girl, that day she had walked over to the sawmill—from somewhere, Henry couldn't imagine. And stood on the road, her head ducked, waiting. She wouldn't ask for Johnnie. Just waited. Simmons had seen her but didn't say anything.

The hours. All of it. Years. Henry had been proud of himself back in the beginning, but even then it wasn't because of the money. He had nothing to spend money on, really. Until Lillian. Then the sawmill. His quarter share of the sawmill had taken it all. Each tight little homemade bundle of coins was a bundle of hours. The ticking away of his life. And this was what he had done with it; this was what he had to say for himself as a man. The older folks, Mr. Taylor especially, had thought of his effort as quite an accomplishment. And so it came to seem an accomplishment, too, to him. This was what he had done: what he had paid for with himself, Henry.

Henry jerked back from the black heap lying in front of him. Now the sawmill was gone, like some sum swiftly lost in a crap game. He wasn't aware that he hadn't moved during all of the time he stood there thinking. It seemed to him as if his feelings had flung him this way and that. He stood for some time longer, with a foot propped on the whitened stair steps, no longer registering the ruin. His mind was quiet now. Blank. The morning was quiet. From the pasture across the road, the single sound of a meadowlark flew over the air—it was a sound Henry particularly loved, a clean, sweet sound that fell like an arc. It caught his attention. He looked up that way. When he glanced down again, he gave a push with his foot, and the stair steps collapsed into pieces. It was at that stray moment that it came to Henry that he wasn't sorry—he wasn't sorry that the sawmill had burned. The admission of it, once it was out, oddly enough didn't amaze him. Now he stepped across the road and walked a little. He stood before a line of sagging barbed wire that ran along the stretch of pasture.

The old pasture hummed with sun motes and the heat waves that stood in the distance. At the far end of the field was a single, moss-hung oak, smoky green against the line of woods. Henry's eyes fastened on the shape of the tree, taking in something he needed from it—there was a kind of knowingness about old trees. He heard the sound of the bird again, somewhere off where he couldn't see it. Now Henry knew for a fact that he wasn't sorry. And once past that point, it was difficult all of a sudden not to be glad. He hadn't let himself actually think of the place as a trap; or if he had, he'd grown too used to the weight of it to take much notice. Now the whole of it dropped away from him, like a sheer pane of water. Already he began to lose touch with the feel of its having happened at all.

Henry was no longer alone when he crossed back over the road. Two of the Negro men he knew by name only were there. They said nothing to Henry. The sight of the ruin made a person quiet. Then all of them seemed to arrive at the same time—all the others. It was the idea of it, the curiosity, that drew them—they had already been paid on Saturday morning. Henry heard the sound of an automobile. In a matter of minutes there was Mr. Taylor, then Simmons, along with some others. But Simmons, for once, wasn't quiet at all. With his companions he talked constantly, a low-pitched, reedy murmur. Then there was Johnnie, by himself. Mr. Taylor was dressed for church, wearing a suit and hat, pushing his jacket back from a protruding middle sheathed in starched cotton. Like Henry and the others, he stood and looked. Then grimaced and broke the silence.

"Had t've been somebody's cigarette, Henry. 'S all it could've been."

"Expect so."

Both of the men looked ahead of them, with a foot moving over the ground. "Wind picked up overnight. That one stub could've smoked half the afternoon, yesterday. Heat didn't help, either."

"Expect so," Henry repeated. The truth was that he didn't feel much like talking about it. The speculation was pointless.

"Son, I don't know what to say." Mr. Taylor shook his head. "Just don't—. I'm awfully sorry, Henry." He continued, "Well, we've got some reserves put by." That was the first Henry had heard of any reserves. "There's that policy on the machinery. Course, I'll buy back your piece of ground."

"Yessir."

"See if I can't find some wage work for your white fellow yonder."

Henry glanced up at Simmons, not until that instant realizing that he'd come to dislike the little weasely man. He'd felt like firing Simmons that day Johnnie's little girl had stood in the road, waiting. "I wish you'd look out for something for John."

John. That would have been one of Henry's darkies. For a moment the older man looked not at a business partner, but at Joe Gray's boy. He might have smiled, if a person could feel like smiling. It was just like the boy, he was thinking, to look out for one of his colored.

"Well, I'll be off. Come on by the house in the morning."

"Yessir."

Mr. Taylor went back to his automobile. Henry's eyes met Johnnie's, and the two of them walked over to each other. Johnnie's face looked tight and hard.

"What'll you do now, John?"

"Don' know, sir. Just don' know at all." Then his head swung up. He looked directly at Henry. "What you aim to do, Mr. Henry?"

Henry chuckled. "Looks like I don't know, either, John."

By the time Mr. Taylor had cranked and begun his drive into Clanton, both families in Orville knew what had happened. Drefus, working over in the next county, had been informed by a sort of grapevine as rapid, itself, as the rails. By early afternoon, Myra and Howard came in, both carrying baskets whose savory fragrance left its wake in the heat laden air of the porch and hallway. Howard hung back, deferentially allowing this private moment to his wife. They found Lillian sitting alone at the kitchen worktable. The porch was too hot, throwing off its day's worth of heat in strong, woody waves. The porch was too public.

"Where's Henry?" It was Myra, her voice somewhat dubious, in spite of the bravest intentions. For an answer, Lillian only raised her head and looked into her sister's eyes. It was enough. Something further still had happened, Myra understood.

"Well." Myra attempted that little light feminine laugh of dismissal that the sisters shared. She began to chat almost gaily. Howard, by contrast, made not a sound.

Henry couldn't have said any more than the rest of them why the day turned out like it did. As the men stood at the site of the fire that morning, Mrs. Taylor was already on the telephone to Lillian with reassurances, a gesture that Henry expected. He knew that he would be made offers of work as soon as word of the accident spread. He had no immediate fear for the welfare of his family. He wanted some time, he told himself. He wanted the easy companionship of men. He would go by Ed's fish camp— his breakfast had thinned down to nothing. He'd have a morning meal of fried fish and hush puppies, the two standing items on Ed's menu. He'd stand around with the men for the talk and wisecracking. He'd watch the catches coming in. By mid-morning, news of the fire would be general knowledge. He'd be offered condolences, sincere ones, followed up by a joke and a laugh.

By the time Henry got back to his car, his mind was already on something else. He'd have to stop off first at the way station, as they called it—the shinney was sometimes bought up by midday on a Sunday. Henry drove back out to the main road, to turn off again at a road of rutted clay, half hidden by cornfields, at the end of which a Negro woman named Beulah operated a still in her kitchen. She was an odd one, Beulah, strictly business. Henry had tried jollying her, but she ignored him. She handled the bootleg in the same deliberate way she would have handled a hoe or a harness. The supply that he bought was a relatively small amount, for somebody planning to be in company. Only Henry knew that a mouthful or two went ringing through his blood system: that there was that difference between himself and other drinkers. Because of it, he would have been observed to drink fairly little.

There had been the expected condolences. He had been served a hot and heaping plate, on the house. Later, he'd been loaned a rod and taken out with the men for some fishing. They stayed on the water until late afternoon. They joked. They tippled and shared. More than one person took note that for a man who was ruined, Henry seemed on top of the world. Fine wires of exhilaration shot through his body. He felt richly jovial. When they returned, the men stood Henry to a second meal. There were additional rounds of pocket flasks. By evening, the building was dense with smoke and bodies and voices.

"You gonna make it, old man?" Someone referred to Henry. There was general laughter.

Henry made a brushing motion with his hand. "See y' in the mornin'," he sang out, incongruously.

As soon as his car began to move, Henry realized that he had to urinate—badly. He cleared the open car door just seconds before the automobile rolled backward and came to a stop against a tree root. Henry relieved himself, splattering himself in the process. It seemed to him that he drove at the usual speed, but the fact was that he rolled home at the pace of a wagon. At his driveway, he told himself he was too tired to bother putting the car into the garage. He brought the car to a stop at an odd angle across the driveway. When he left it, the headlights were still burning. The engine choked down by itself. Henry didn't notice that the lights were also on inside the house. Inside the kitchen, Lillian, Drefus, Myra, and Howard stood or sat. At the sound of the car, Drefus came up front to let Henry in. No one else made a move. They were a grim, unconversational group, and they had been there, in the kitchen, for hours. Lillian made coffee and passed around a store-bought coffee ring. They drank the coffee, pots of it, from need rather than pleasure. In the hallway Henry was jovial again and noisy, but Drefus answered in a low, coaxing voice. Drefus himself was ashamed. He felt in some way responsible. He had passed the time there, waiting with the others, in miserable self-consciousness. Had left the house only long enough that afternoon to make certain arrangements. Without knowing it, Henry had already been made an offer of work—which Drefus had solicited and accepted for him—to start right away, at a good rate, house painting for a local contractor.

"I think I may lie down a while." Howard chose those few moments to disappear up front into the living room. Drefus left again, through the back door, torn between the desire to say something and to escape. Whatever the something was that he should have said, he hadn't quite worked out. And while Henry slept, while Howard slept, while the three children slept, the two women sat by themselves in the night-swallowed kitchen, facing one another across the table, both of them quiet. Neither woman had as much as given a thought to sleep. The two faces had a family resemblance, most noticeable about the eyes, which were large and round, especially when the faces were solemn, as both were now. Myra filled both their cups with fresh coffee, added cream and sugar to her own, tasted it for the first time that night with real enjoyment, before looking up again at Lillian, whose cup wasn't touched. Lillian sat with her palms pushed against her eyes, and the sight of it was unbearable to Myra. She moved quickly to the other side of the table and pulled Lillian over, stroking her sister's head with her cheek.

"Now, everything will work out all right, Lillian. He had a shock. That's all."

"That's not all."

"Why, baby, you've got to look on the bright side. It was awful about the sawmill. But Drefus already has a job lined up for Henry. Things will work out."

Now Lillian jerked her head away. "He drinks, Myra."

Myra laughed and rubbed her sister's shoulder. "They all do."

"This is different. He drinks all the time."

Now Myra reacted to something in Lillian's voice. "I don't think I know what you mean."

Lillian sighed, uncrossed and recrossed her legs, which trickled with perspiration. "It's just that he's always drinking. That's what I mean. All the time. Even out with the children and me. He carries a flask."

"A flask." Myra crossed back over to the other side again and sat down. Among the sisters she was the mild one, a gentle presence on this earth—as simple of heart as any well-behaved child. The complexities of what Lillian was telling her were frankly beyond her capacities of reason or experience. "But does he drink to get drunk?" She had heard that question asked.

"That's just what I don't know." And here Lillian's face went crooked. "It's so hard to tell with Henry. It's never much. Just a little all along. But all the time. All of the time." Her voice rose and collapsed on the words.

Myra understood—it *was* hard to say with Henry. Whether he was cheerful when he drank due to his own good nature—or cheerful because of the drink. Herself, she would have said almost anything at that moment to comfort Lillian. "Henry does have a cheerful nature."

"Cheerful. I know. Oh, I know." There was a pause. "I'm scared." Lillian had never said that to anyone.

"Scared," Myra echoed. "Have you decided what to do about it?"

"I don't know what I *can* do about it!" Anger edged into Lillian's voice.

"Have you talked to him?"

"I don't think he realizes it, himself."

"What about Drefus?"

"I think it all started with Drefus."

Myra considered. "You're tired." The weak comment dropped off into the silence of the house, a murk of syrupy darkness. Now waves of alarm passed back and forth between the two sisters, these small, round-eyed women who were almost extensions of each another. Even Myra understood that liquor poisoned a man. Poisoned his family. Their very lives.

"Have you thought about talking to the doctor?"

"I've thought about it." Lillian sighed again. It was a last resort, possibly—she had considered it. "Maybe I'll do that."

Now Lillian wanted to drop the conversation—just to be by herself, so she could think. Her head was wooden with fatigue and alarm. She wasn't sure that she would be *able* to think. Then possibly, she told herself, she could pray.

The night outside was loud with the sound of crickets. A

stirring of air filled the curtains at Lillian's back. It wasn't cool air, but it seemed cool, compared to the air inside the kitchen. It brought a grass-like odor in, that mingled with the scent of over-cooked coffee. Now Lillian felt the drops of water glide down her crossed leg. The two women had forgotten the heat, had put time aside altogether.

Myra stood up finally. "Well, let me wake up Howard."

Chapter 15

In the beginning Emma panicked, her mind careening off in a fear that made her fairly sick to her stomach. She couldn't do it alone. It was man's work, the farm. There wasn't the strength in her body to do it. For days after finding the empty drawers, Emma moved through time with no order, aside from the necessary routines of taking care of the children. She got up as usual, to make breakfast and pack the children's pails. But when they were gone, she walked the house compulsively, like someone caught in the urgency of a task. She'd forget what she was doing, find herself midway into a room with no idea of why she'd come into it. She slept for hours on each of those mornings. For as long as the moon was full enough to see by, Emma sat or walked late into the night. She walked the pale, unreal-looking yard; she walked the road, the rustling edges of fields and garden. The nights were crowded with sound, the insect noise almost strident. The sound seemed to pass right through Emma. Her mind raced and veered—she didn't know how to quiet it. She argued with herself, pled her own case against nobody. Against Ralston. Against the world. She had demanded so little of him. In her way, she had tried to be a friend to him. It had seemed the most she could do.

She had moments of candor, now, that she had never allowed herself. She would not choose this man, if she had it to do over again. There were men who were worse—that much she knew. He was respectable enough in the mind of the community. In public, Ralston observed the proprieties. Emma knew that it was wearying and lonesome work that he did. But would she have willingly done it over? No. She would not have. But then wait: without Ralston there would not have been Buddy or Nettie, without whom her life would not be recognizable—her very self again, these two were. Their eyes, voices, and hands. Their every thought and pleasure. After all, no—she could never have chosen to undo this life she had made, given that it held her own children, whose unique selves could never recur. As she walked, Emma thought too of her house. She knew she was going to lose it. She didn't know when or under what circumstances she would lose it. But she carried the dread of that loss around with her now, like a weight. From outside, Emma's eyes came back to her house, the dark, sitting bulk of it. Inside the walls of that house, she had given birth to her children. It had housed them, their lives and hers. Her five children slept comfortably, now, within the shelter of that house, which was changed, in some way, by night. Inside the dark kitchen, there was that strange quiet that followed their clamor, the used odors of cooking, the smell of children's bodies close together in a room. The house had absorbed them; at night, the creaking wood of it breathed them out again. Even Ralston. He was a lonely man, an unhappy man. This was a passing intuition on Emma's part. She thought—a rare thought, for her—of the fact that the same moon that looked down on her rooftop, herself, also looked down somewhere over him.

On the following day, Emma came to herself. She slept again that morning, after the children left the house. Because there was no one to cook for at midday, she had given no thought to cooking a meal. The sudden hunger caught her offguard. She stoked a fire in the stove and fell automatically into making the quickest meal she could think of. She made a pot of mush cooked with milk, and stirred a few teaspoons of sugar into the bowl. It had been years since Emma had eaten a bowl of mush, and in her hunger she distinguished the separate, bland flavors of it. Its goodness surprised her. It was the simple food of her childhood. It gave her heart. She would do what necessity demanded. She would make a plan—there was some comfort, at least, in making a plan.

But this solitude was hard. The house was quiet. The yard was quiet. Emma strained for a sound. There was none. Her children could not be made privy to her fear—they must be sheltered. They were troubled, she knew. She wondered now if they always had been. Ned still had the spells of sleepwalking. Always, he brushed at the air and complained that the bees were after him. And there was that strange scene with Ralph, which had taken place just before Ralston left. On a certain wet Monday, the already belligerent Ralph had gone too far. Had bloodied the nose of a schoolmate nobody liked. But that fact didn't alter matters.

"Where's Ralph?" It had to happen.

"He had to stay after."

"Stay after? For what?" Buddy gave a quick lift of the shoulders and fled from the kitchen like a rabbit.

The others slid around the house and yard silently that gray afternoon, in the drawn-out suspense of waiting for Ralph to come home. And in due time, he walked up the drive, bouncing his lunch pail against his legs. There was something different about the way Ralph was holding his head. Ducked. Emma noticed it right away. He let the kitchen door slam behind him, walked inside a few feet, then let books and belongings fall to the floor, any old way they may. There was none of the usual pouting. He seemed resigned to the punishment that would follow. Ralph was switched or made to stand in corners because these correctives were customary, not because they did any good. Now his lower lip did come out; but it also quivered. The four others had drawn silently toward the kitchen, from various spots; and all of them were as surprised as Emma when Ralph burst into tears. Just stood there, limply, and cried. None of them—nobody—had ever seen Ralph cry. Emma noticed that Ralph's skin didn't blotch when he cried, like the others'. She made a move toward him, a move Ralph took to be the commencement of his punishment. Now he started to yell. Emotion worked over his body.

"Why son—." Emma put out a hand.

"He teased Nettie about her freckles! About her *freckles*! He said they were ugly!" Ralph paused to draw an arm across his face, then began all over again. His sense of justice was outraged; the world of fair and just, for Ralph, stood on its end.

All of them were grouped now in the kitchen. Emma took a quick look at Nettie, to get a sense of her daughter's feelings about the incident. "Freckles are pretty," she answered. But there wasn't time—her attention was for Ralph.

"Now son—." This child was physically so much like Ralston, the resemblance startled her. It was like being given a look backward in time. Nettie stepped up, moved by Ralph's loyalty, intending to pat her little brother, if he would let her. And as she did so, she caught sight through the window of the Ford.

"Here comes Daddy!"

The effect was instantaneous. Everyone in the room scattered in different directions, including Ralph. Within moments, Emma was the only person left downstairs; and her face was a mask. Had he walked in on that scene, a situation that was already upsetting enough would have become a full-scale, family catastrophe. Ralston employed a single disciplinary measure: a brief but strong belting. Set against this, Emma's threat to break a switch was laughable.

Why had they feared their father like that? Emma asked herself now. They were good children—there were few enough incidences of such parental discipline in the family. But the question was no good—a ridiculous question, even. They feared him exactly as she did. Their father was an unknowable. He didn't behave like other people. And his total absence from the farm was by now conspicuous. With this absence, everything in their lives abruptly changed. When the three oldest were asked to muck the barn floor, they didn't argue with each other—although the heat had turned the usual shadowy barn into a reeking inferno. Buddy and Nettie were given an additional morning chore. In the earliest light, each was sent to the barn, to fill the planter with corn kernels. This meant stepping on and off of the frame of the planter, over and over, transferring lard cans of corn into the holding containers. Emma would spend most of the day on the planter, seated behind the mules, as she had done all that week and the one before it. When they returned from school, Nettie would be responsible for most—or all—of the family supper. The remaining chores had been rearranged. Everything had changed.

Could they have missed him, or was it only the need to be sure, Emma wondered. Ned had asked. Billy had asked. There were strange little silences in mealtime conversation, the faint buzzing of curiosity. Billy asked the most often.

"Where's Daddy?" Again. They were seated at supper. Billy stabbed limas with his fork as he asked the question.

But she couldn't be sure it was the right time. "Everybody needs to see their folks some time or another, don't they?" Emma absently pushed the dish of new limas and bacon toward Billy, who needed none.

To Emma's knowledge, Ralston's only contact with his family was the yearly Christmas letter, his father's composition, a formal letter written out in a fine, flowery hand, relating news of the family health and prosperity, as well as the one, unvarying phrase, "Your mother is well."

Emma continued, to divert Billy, "What do you think your

granddaddy looks like?" It was a contrived question that met with no special curiosity.

"I bet he's mean," Nettie answered suddenly, and her eyes widened in surprise at herself. She exchanged a slightly startled look with Emma. She knew she had said something she ought not to have said.

Buddy knew. The two of them, mother and son, understood one another by a kind of telepathy. Emma felt certain that he'd gone to his parents' room and confirmed what he too must have guessed—just as she had. They didn't yet talk directly about it. But when they were alone together, their voices had the hushed and worried quality that they may have used in a sickroom.

But the tension broke loose one afternoon, during an unusual stint of farm chores, when the heat was relentless and everybody was feeling irritable. Emma and the three oldest were each lugging an armful of wood from the woodpile into the kitchen. The sun had a wicked bite that afternoon. The wood bark was rough, and pressed sharply against the skin. Nettie's left arm was being cruelly pinched. The others properly dropped their loads into the wood box. But Nettie let hers bang at her feet, in a display of temper.

"What's this some kind of 'business' Daddy has?" They were told, at this time, that Ralston had business.

"I don't know what business it is, Nettie. I expect there's not any business. Your daddy's gone. And I don't look for him to be back." Emma spoke in a level voice. It was out, now. She understood that it was time.

Buddy and Ralph vanished like spooks. And Nettie just sort of went quiet. Emma took her daughter by the shoulders and turned her. "Why don't you go have a look through the scrap box? You might just find something pretty. Make a little something for yourself." It took a few moments for the suggestion to have its effect. Nettie had seen her mother do wonderful things with odd scraps of material. To be given access to the scrap box was unprecedented. To provide a diversion was all that Emma knew to do.

She watched Nettie leave the room. The bare feet didn't make any sound. Nettie's ankles were almost twig-like. Emma didn't stop to cross-examine herself, as other women might have done. She didn't have the time—she had lost too much time already. It was May, and she was just finishing getting in the corn. It had taken her almost four weeks to do it, twice as long as she had allowed for. Emma looked into the empty doorway, while other, more pressing thoughts crowded into her mind. She had calculated that she could manage no more than half Ralston's usual acreage in corn. She'd let the cotton and sorghum fields go fallow; the pea and sweet potato plots were laid out that spring just large enough for the family's use. Even with two Negro men hired to turn the ground for a share, the planting developed into a sad and discouraging business. It took all the strength that she had, both of body and mind.

Did you love him? Why did she keep hearing the question, like the annoying words to some silly tune.

Lou Anne had known, it seemed, from the beginning. Common sense dictated, then, that others knew. But here Emma defied common sense. She told herself that her predicament was not, in fact, common knowledge. She had been schooled in an inviolable privacy concerning personal matters. Public knowledge— even her family's knowledge, at this particular time—would have been torture. She had attended a single church service; it was an agony—it was here that Emma maintained her most significant public face. She felt bare. Exposed. The print handkerchief she carried was reduced to a sodden ball in her hands. She hoped that the congregation was preoccupied—on that morning the hot spell was in full force, the temperature inside the church near insufferable. Odors of perspiring bodies mingled with those of scented talc, inexpensive perfume, and laundry starch. No one asked where Ralston was, but *how* he was—these were a kindly folk. Still, Emma knew that each person in the room must have, at one time or another, secretly examined her face. People knew. They would have had to know. At least Mrs. Hale didn't—she had remarked only that Emma was looking peaked—though even with the lenses, she could scarcely see Emma. Had she known the truth, Emma was certain, there would have been an indignant scene.

But like Ralston, Lou Anne was different from other people. This, in an agreeable way, for the most part. She had none of the typical restraint.

"Ralston's gone."

Emma had already heard the sound of the automobile on the drive—Lou Anne was the only one of her woman friends who could drive an automobile. Emma had stepped out onto the back porch and sat down on the top step, to wait for what was coming. Lou Anne walked in long, purposeful strides. She dropped onto the step next to Emma.

"He's gone, isn't he?" It wasn't a question.

"Well—."

"Don't *well* me now, Emma!" Both women were slightly shocked by the anger in Lou Anne's voice. She laid a hand over Emma's lap. "I'm sorry." The anger was at Ralston.

"How'd you find out?"

"Floyd Hendrix told Foley." Lou Anne dropped her forehead against a palm.

Emma just sat. There wasn't really a whole lot to say about it.

"Does your Mama—?"

"No. Nobody'd tell her." Lou Anne looked out across the yard, which was burning, squinting at nothing in particular. "Do you have any idea where he is?"

"I don't. I tried writing to one of the family." Emma's voice trailed off.

"What'll you do by yourself with the children?"

"I'll stay. As long as I'm able."

"But how on earth can you do that, Emma? You can't run a farm!" She shielded her eyes and looked directly at Emma, who had prepared herself to tell only the tiniest fraction of the truth, even to this, her best friend.

"Well, you know Nate Thomas," Emma began. She referred to a Negro family who farmed a few acres near Burnsville. "He's got grown sons," she continued. "I figured to have a couple of them work the fields, for a share." Emma would have the men do the turning, only; but she didn't add that. "Maybe Foley could go over to talk to them for me." Always there was this dependency, in matters of the outside world, on the mediation of men.

"Of course he will." Lou Anne searched Emma's face as she answered. She, Lou Anne, was a forceful person, a strong person. She wondered, now, if Emma had such force. A woman farming alone. With children, all of them young. It couldn't last long.

"Do you have a mortgage?"

"A what?"

"Does Ralston owe money on the farm?"

"He don't owe money." Emma looked at Lou Anne with a blank face. She knew nothing of mortgages. She knew nothing of managing money—even in what manner or where Ralston had kept theirs. None of this had been thought necessary in Emma's preparation for life.

"Emma, do you have any money?" It was a delicate question

to ask. Lou Anne handled it with none of the usual deference.

"Oh, I've got a good bit put by. A right good bit." Emma was surprised at the ease of the lie, although she had planned and calculated it. "And my folks will help out, along." Emma's family knew nothing at that moment of her predicament.

Lou Anne felt a little relief. Emma had no long-term plan—that was obvious. But the immediate present seemed manageable. She leaned back now on her elbows and relaxed a little. Her face took on the wondering look that was well known to Emma. "He was a funny one all right, Ralston. What was he like, Emma?"

"Ralston?" Emma was prepared, after a fashion, for questions about herself. But about him? What he was *like*? For a fact, it wasn't the kind of thing people generally asked. She studied a moment, making an effort to consider Ralston as another person might have seen him. "He was a hard enough worker. You could say that about him. He did right by us that way." She stopped there, knowing how much more there was that she could have said. The answer sounded inadequate, even to Emma—Lou Anne was her true friend. "I don't rightly know how to say what he was like. He kept to himself a lot, I reckon. I think maybe things troubled him." Emma was hedging on the question, and surprisingly—or out of sympathy—Lou Anne accepted the hedge. Both of them knew that less had been said than withheld.

"Did you love him?" Now, this was worse. None of them had talked of their marriages in that way.

"Love him?"

Lou Anne leaned over now on her arm. "Yes, Em, love him, for heaven's sake. Did you *love* him?" Lou Anne realized that she had never thought much of Emma in this particular way: as a woman. She looked on her somewhat as a child. Her love for Emma was deeply protective.

The two women searched each other's faces, then looked out

ahead again. Emma was aware that she and Lou Anne meant different things by this word, love. Lou Anne read passages to Emma from her romance novels, from time to time. There were burning kisses and losing herself in his arms. Swooning, and dot dot dot. For Emma, it may have been more a matter of taking care of. But she surrendered. "You know, Lou, I can't say as I thought much about it, back then. It wasn't like you and Foley, if that's what you mean." She didn't know herself what it was like for Lou Anne and Foley, only that it was not something she had experienced. She knew that Lou Anne had a very special feeling for Foley.

"I was only seventeen when I married," she went on. Lou Anne had been almost thirty. "I thought about other kinds of things, I reckon. I thought he'd be a good provider. I knew he'd been raised right." It sounded like a list that Emma might have gone over at some time to herself. Then, to the surprise of both of them, Emma laughed. "I thought he was mighty good-looking. I guess I thought he was kinda shy, not being talkative and all."

"Ralston, *shy*? Shy like a rattler." Now Lou Anne laughed a good belly laugh. Emma herself didn't laugh, but Lou Anne didn't seem to notice. The comment displeased her—came close to angering Emma, though she didn't know why. Lou Anne resettled herself on her elbows, still squinting against the sun. Again with that wondering expression.

"I love Foley." Foley. It was his surname; but everyone, including Lou Anne, used it as a given name. The name had a friendliness about it. "I'm glad I waited." It was uncharacteristic of Lou Anne not to consider how that comment may have sounded— that the statement may have been unintentionally cruel. Lou Anne shaded her eyes again from the burning glare, to look at Emma. Emma felt a funny, heat-like sensation crawling up toward her collarbone. "I might have done better to have waited." She was moving dangerously, here—it was territory that Emma had never skirted the edge of. And she refused to move into it, now. She intentionally put an end to the subject. "I've just done the best I know how." And she may have stood, at that point.

But at that moment the women were interrupted by all five of the Griffen children, who had come to the porch to splash themselves at the pump. The boys dropped on their backs on the porch, concentrating on the cool trickles that slid in different directions beneath their clothing. But Nettie sat close to Lou Anne, her "Aunt Lou Anne," and snuggled, hot as it was. Now Emma and Lou Anne were compelled to speak of trivial matters.

Lou Anne stood to leave, and Emma stood with her. And they talked again, with their eyes. Emma could feel herself getting emotional, which was no more than Lou Anne had expected. Emma looked up at the house, her skin splotched all of a sudden. "I expected to live out my whole life in this house."

There was no shallow reassurance to offer.

"Taxes, Lou. I won't be able to make the taxes." This was the worst of it, Emma knew. This was how it was going to happen. Ralston had always complained about taxes, so that for Emma the word itself assumed all the proportions of calamity.

Lou Anne's mind cast around for some kind of encouragement. Taxes. "We'll see if we can't get them put off, somehow or another. I'll talk to Foley about it."

Emma looked at Lou Anne with a slight suggestion of relief, as Lou Anne started to back away, their hands joined so tightly that the nails of each cut into the palms of the other. Lou Anne began toward the automobile, then a few feet away from it she stopped. She had never liked Ralston, never had trusted him. Now she hated him in a delicious, rousing way—she knew it was un-Christian. She turned. She was a tall woman. At times her body seemed to waver a little when she stood. She pressed her lips together, then said exactly what she wanted to say. "He's not worthy to kiss your foot." The soft drawl had all the impact of a hiss.

Emma listened to the automobile pulling away, until the sound of it grew indistinct in the afternoon heat. She sat for a while on the steps, listening to that last statement, hearing it circle through her mind. But when she stood again, she dismissed it. It dropped from her memory.

Chapter 16

She had known all along that they would be hungry. And it was her fault. Because of pride. These were Emma's judgments against herself. She had grown introspective, after a fashion. It began with the first quiet cold of approaching winter. She'd done things wrong; she'd done everything wrong. She hadn't thought it through well enough—any of it. If only she'd held back this little bit here, been more careful there. Emma moved from her chair to the stove, her apron held pouch-like in one hand, and in a single motion with the other, opened the fire box and laid in a wedge of limb. She'd been picking pecans through the morning, the leftovers, those that were crushed or broken in the wrong places. She had to dig and stab for the nutmeat inside; certain pieces she examined first, like a jeweler looking into a watch. The pecans had saved them, that final, windfall crop from a random orchard. But this year it had been different with the pecans, which had always before been a casual crop. Emma stalked the orchard that fall, watching, waiting for the first signs of the developing pods. This year they had beaten the branches with cane poles. And this year she'd let the children climb into the lower limbs. The crop had been good. And the kitchen was again supplied with meal, lard, the usual staples. For a little while, they had eaten fairly well again—and for the first time, with food not produced by their own hands. Emma bought a coat for Buddy—she realized now that she should never have done it. With the cash money from the pecans, she'd even paid an installment on the taxes. Now at least that bill was owing, not delinquent. But by now Emma had learned—it required such painful error, to learn. There was a little put back. Only a little. It was inviolable. And it was not enough.

As Emma picked the nuts, her mouth jerked slightly, as though she were counting. In a way, she was always counting. Amounts of this or that. Her mistakes. At times she thought she might think herself crazy. Silence floated through the house like slow particles of winter sun. It was a gray afternoon. There was the sound of a trapped horsefly knocking against a windowpane, like a single drop of rain or a dull popping from inside the stove. Emma had taken to sending Billy to school with the others. He was a full year younger than Buddy and Ralph had been when they started. But Miss Seay knew Emma's predicament. She let Billy fall in—he fell in happily—with the others; his attendance was never recorded. His absence in the house was a relief, even if the quiet seemed unnatural. Emma wished for some distant, neighborly sound, some familiar sound, like a dog barking. At times she had to concentrate fully on the oily bits of nutmeat. Mostly, her mind strained ahead and plunged backward. Strained against everything.

At first her thinking operated as it always had—she couldn't think now what had been the *matter* with her! The winter before Ralston left, the sow had been bred, and by May there were piglets. When Emma sold two of them, she felt that elation that comes with a distinct triumph over adversity. The children would have to have shoes, good shoes, for the opening of the school year. And for Nettie there'd have to be a couple of dresses. All of Nettie's classmates had dresses with faded lines around the skirt bottoms, where the hems had been let out, or wore older dresses that were makeovers. But along with these would always be a couple of dresses that were new. The choosing of material, the planning, and sewing had always been domestic adventures, things over which Emma and her daughter made a great and pleasurable fuss. Nettie would *have* her dresses, Emma determined; she went through the motions with a cheerless obstinacy that made her little girl uneasy.

And there was no playfulness in the house—that house that had fairly rattled at times with jokes and teasing. While Emma sewed in the dining room, Nettie did the cooking. There was a time when Emma would have amused herself wonderfully at Nettie's expense. She sat close enough to the door to be able to look into the kitchen, by leaning back in her chair. Once she would have talked through the wall to her daughter, advising her, taunting her.

"Now I know just what you're about to do. And you'll make a soggy mess of it. Hold on to the chicken 'til the grease gets hot."

This would have caused Nettie to smile and step back in a hurry, just at the instant that she was about to drop in the first piece. Emma would sense the hesitation, then lean back to look in.

"Caught y', didn't I?" It might have provoked a botched wink, a skill that Emma had never been able to master.

Throughout the summer, Emma counted on the corn crop—still, she hadn't yet understood. Now she looked back and castigated herself. She hadn't thought to dole out the special things that the children loved, the thick berry jams with the crunchy seeds, the tart tomato chow-chow that had always been set out on the table. All at once, it seemed, by mid-August, the store of these things was used up. The canning shelves were stripped clean; and the garden had little at all left for putting by. Emma walked through the plundered kitchen garden like someone assessing the site of a ruin. It had of necessity been a child's garden; and it had yielded a child's results.

Her corn crop had been trifling, the final yield hardly more than she needed for seed and the animals, after the Thomas boys were given their share. Emma wondered, at odd times, at the skill, the sheer stamina, that Ralston must have had in him. She didn't know, as the Thomas sons did, that Ralston's furrows were laid so straight, the earth seemed to roll over from the plow blade—or that his soil, green-manured with lespedeza, was crumbly and responsive to the touch.

Once the ground was turned, Emma planted by herself. She had learned how to deal with a mule. You used the tail ends of the reins—you had to know how to bully a mule. She made it the children's job to take care of the kitchen garden and pea crop. She sent them out with pieces of sweet potato, once she herself got the holes ready. She couldn't stop to oversee the work. And so had no knowledge of the tears and squabbling, the carelessly dropped pieces, the missed places, the overlooked weeds or thirsty patches of soil. There'd been no time that summer or fall for the wild harvests that they'd always enjoyed together, the plum and berry gatherings. The children missed their leisure, the long Saturdays of baseball, train watching, the lengthy hikes to the places that were good to fish or swim. But more than these things they missed their mother. Nettie, especially. In the past, among themselves, they had joked about Emma's carrying-on, all the little nonsense things—and the teasing. They didn't understand that they relied on these things. There was no joy now in Emma. And, for the children, everyday life had thinned down into something gray and flavorless. When Emma tried to force the old humor, it was worse, somehow. The children felt the strain.

But no one else seemed aware of it. This was due to sheer force of will. This was due to her pride and conniving, Emma later accused herself. The WMU group made its rounds to Emma's, as usual. The members were tactful, silent on any subject that might approach a certain delicate matter. Emma made a jam cake, then a pecan cake, both made with lard, not butter; but no one appeared to have noticed. And Emma's mind crept back now, worried over the mean hoarding that had gone into making these efforts, a secret, cramping effort that drained and exhausted her. She made Christmas gifts of shelled pecans, as she had done before on occasion. She should not have spared those pecans. And she gave herself the leisure for making gift bags, little cloth bags, elaborately decorated—it was time that should have been spent on the household mending. The pecans were gifts, it was true. But the gifts were also one more gesture made for the sake of appearance—that false and prideful appearance that all was sufficient within the household.

Christmas had been the worst. When she tormented herself over the stockings: just a few pieces of candy, an orange apiece. But she had not given in. By then she was learning. She hung the stockings empty. And on Christmas day, she went over early to the Hale farm, to help with the cooking. Old Mrs. Hale lived, now, in the innocent twilight world of the elderly. The house was swollen with people, doors slamming constantly with the movements of both children and adults. Emma knew that her own would pass all day long in and out of the front rooms, which were food-laden to holiday excess. The family returned home with gifts, most of them edible. They came home well-fed.

They came back to a house without safety or comfort.

The children convened from time to time, in a dispirited and aimless sort of way. The conferences typically started out as private conversations between Buddy and Nettie. But the younger children were alert for such conversations. When Buddy and Nettie talked privately, it was serious business. Everyone wanted to be in on the serious business. Once Buddy came across Nettie on the front steps by herself.

"I hate him," she started in. She didn't glance at Buddy—Nettie knew who was there. The pronouns "he" or "him," when said in a certain manner, referred to only one person.

Nettie went on, "I hate him, and I hope he dies!" Her voice inched up a key or so.

Buddy sighed. Nettie was saying an awful thing—Nettie'd say anything. "You ought not to say a thing like that, Nettie." It was a mild enough censure, said automatically, but it had the effect of inflaming Nettie.

Now Nettie turned on him. "And why not, I'd like to know?" Her anger flew loose. "Just why not?" Nettie was fairly vibrating. She tore at the lace of a shoe, no longer looking at Buddy. The laces were catching it. They were cotton, and one of them broke.

"He didn't love us, Buddy. He never did." Nettie's face flooded with color. "He didn't love Mama." Nettie's lips now started an odd sort of traveling from one side of her mouth to the other. Buddy knew that any attempt on his part to soothe her would only cause her anger to turn on him. His own silences were deceptive, Buddy being a child whom feelings entered, never finding an exit.

Turnip greens were on the table almost daily, following the harvest. And would be until all the leaves were pulled, after which the dishes of plain diced turnips followed. Those and dried limas—it was always limas.

"Mama, what are we having?" It routinely began by mid-afternoon.

"I can't tell you."

"Come on, Mama! What are we having?" A foot stomped; the twitches of a grin.

"Reckon I don't know."

"*Mama*—!" A final jerk and stomp against the lit and mocking face.

It had been a game of Emma's, one that she enjoyed more than the children did. But the questioning stopped, little by little at first, then altogether. There was not much to do about the bland, repetitive meals that left the children vaguely angry and unsatisfied. Emma made brown tomato gravy, until the children complained at the sight of it. Then she stewed the canned tomatoes, the only thing that yielded enough to be put up that fall. The slight bite of cooked tomato cut against the dull taste of pone and dried limas.

Billy stood in the kitchen next to Buddy. Again the question. But outraged this time, and meant to provoke. "Mama, what are we *having*?" Emma didn't answer. "*Mama!*" It was a final, open challenge. Buddy permitted himself one sharp stroke up the back of Billy's head, which Emma let pass for that once.

As she sat by herself with the pecans or the endless limas, Emma's eyes trailed at times toward the shotgun, propped, as he'd left it, between the wall and the pie safe. A puzzling thing, the fact that he'd left it—she'd only recently noticed, by chance. Emma found herself looking more often at it—at first, she only gazed at it absently. Then she remembered the boxes of shells which were stacked against the wall. She put down the bowl in her lap, filled an apron pocket with shells and took up the gun, stepping out into a late Fall day ringing with empty blue sky. She walked toward the stand of oaks in front of the house. And waited a little.

She lifted the gun, tried its weight against her shoulder, lining up the sight on still objects, then training it on the halting and starting movements of squirrels. It was for no more than a matter of seconds. A ripple, a movement. The laughing voice of her father. The answering titter of girlish voices. Yes, he had taught them well, with their shotguns in hand. In her first rounds, Emma missed some shots; then she didn't miss anymore.

"I can't keep it up over the winter." It wasn't a statement made out loud but part of her incessant argument with herself. Emma sat at her machine—she wasn't sewing. It was here that she had the habit of pausing by herself during a morning, usually for a cup of coffee. Which she didn't drink now—there was none in the house. She looked over the colorless, winter-fading fields, not seeing them.

"It'd give us some time," she continued. She could sell some things off—the house was comfortably furnished.

"Everybody will know." At the price of full public disclosure. Emma had kept up the appearance of being able to manage without stopping to wonder at her own secrecy. To conceal the worst truth was as strong a compulsion as common decency. Shrewd as she was, even Lou Anne failed to suspect that Emma had lied. Because Emma didn't lie—at least that much was simple.

"I've got to do it. –but what about Buddy?" The farm belonged to the children. Buddy's or Ralph's—or any one of theirs who wanted it. "It's ours. I can't leave it." But she would have to. And when the time came, she'd go home to the Wiregrass. To the Swann farm. She would lock the doors to her house and leave it. And then pray for its safety against the wind and the weather. Her life here would be over.

The wedge of limb that Emma had laid in the stove split, with a quiet explosion. Over a couple of hours, she had filled several good-sized bowls with pecan pieces, to be roasted when the children came in. The broken shells were heaped into a bucket that sat beside her. Emma reached down to pick up the bucket. She heard a sound, like a kind of whistling. She listened. The sound seemed to be coming nearer. Before her mind had time to relay the action, she was moving toward the gun. She ran, now, frantic and clumsy, collecting the cartridges. She plunged toward the back door, crashing against the bucket. The screen door stood open behind her. Emma didn't pause to look at the ground. She ran toward the whistling, the black mass that moved between her and the sky. Wait, she told herself. She would have to wait. Until they were just over the kitchen garden. She didn't take a true aim but fired into the mass again and again, as long as the birds were within range. She heard the soft sounds of dropping bodies between her shots. She was panting like someone who had run a distance. There was an unfamiliar, whining noise that she didn't recognize as coming from herself. Emma lowered the gun. With the exploding shot, she had brought down twenty-three of them. They lay scattered now, all quiet, across the yard and garden. She stood up straight, still panting, leaning against the shovel. She could rest soon. She went to the barn and came out again with a fruit basket, into which she gathered the limp, glistening bodies. With this load, she walked out to the back fence and dug unhurriedly, pausing often in her relief. When the hole was ready, she took up each blackbird, driving her thumb into a spot just below the breastbone and popping out the breast area, clean. She paused for a final time, one foot resting on the shovel rim, and leaning. She had left the house in a cotton dress and a sweater, and all at once she was aware of the cold. She had done her work well. She could make the meat go a long way. Billy, maybe Ralph, would ask. What kind of bird was it? She would brag then about the game birds she had brought down. That was it—she would say they were game birds.

Chapter 17

He came back, as abruptly as he left.

A little past midday on a Saturday, Emma sent the children off to the wood lot, to start on one of the trees they had managed to bring down over the summer. The children's job was to remove the smaller limbs and stack them into the wheelbarrow. As they moved across the back yard in an uproar of dissension, an inspiration came to her.

"Now, don't let Billy or Ned try to fool with the saw. They're too little."

The five children went abruptly silent. Buddy saw through the maneuver at once, but Ralph looked suddenly thoughtful. All at once the five of them moved again—again with a clamor of voices. Emma smiled at her success. They'd bicker and compete with each other, now, for the privilege of doing the sawing. It was a cold day, but bright with sun. And as she looked across the chilly, sun-flooded yard, she realized she would have liked to go with them. But her mending basket was full. It was always full.

The sound of a car on the drive struck her as odd—she wasn't expecting company. A traveling salesman, most likely. She'd offer a glass of water and send the man on his way. As she stepped toward the door, Emma saw Ralston walking across the yard, with his head down. He wore a business suit and a felt hat that concealed the upper part of his face. She moved back quickly. There was no time to think or prepare herself, although Ralston walked with no special hurry. It seemed a long time that he stood just outside the door. Then he knocked, as any stranger would have done. There was no way to avoid answering—no way to compose herself as she'd have liked to. When she opened the door, she was frowning. Emma looked at a place just below the knot of his tie, the color leaving and coming back to her face. Neither of them looked directly at the other.

"Come in." Emma heard her own voice—it wasn't quite right. But Ralston was already crossing into the room. He too was frowning. He removed his hat and walked over to a clear space in front of the windows. Then held the hat by the brim and turned it. Twirled it. Emma took a seat and waited, she didn't know for what. There was not a sound in the house or yard.

When he looked at her, it was not quite at her face but in her general direction. His voice was uncharacteristically quiet.

"I wouldn't have expected to find you here. Had some business to settle with Hendrix."

There was no reply for Emma to make. He cleared his throat and continued, "I was on my way home to Malvern. I thought to find you and the children there."

To find her. On his way to—. Still, there was nothing for Emma to say. And if there had been, she may not have said it. Emma's tongue was trapped—because her mind was trapped. A spot in her chest was burning.

He had come back, it was true, to seek her out. And although Ralston had gone over the prospect of this hoped-for reunion again and again in his mind, it hadn't occurred to him to prepare what to say. Nor had it occurred to him that there would be any special awkwardness—that when the moment came, he might not know what to do. Now the difficulty of it overcame him. He turned, let out a breath, moved a foot across the floor. He didn't know how he'd expected to manage the situation. So he said, simply, "Emma, I've come back."

Come back. He had come back. Still, there was nothing to say. Emma didn't move in her chair. But her feelings, now jarred loose, careened in opposing directions. The children. Safe. They would be safe again. They would no longer be hungry. But he had deserted them, left them to get by any old way that they could. His own blood—wife and family. There was also anger in the wild rush of feeling. And the shame of it. Bruising. She would never get over it. Emma's emotions were crazy, in their sudden release. For so long it had been there: the dread that tugged at her mind like a tiny, malicious bite. Fear of the hunger. The cold. The mortgage money. The crops. All of it. But it was over, now. He had come back. For a few moments the welter of relief and long overdue anger jammed inside Emma. Then she was overcome by it all. She raised her apron to her face and wept, just as she would have done if she had been alone, without a trace of self-consciousness. She was no longer thinking at all. She didn't know how long she wept; nor did she know that Ralston was watching her.

"I'm sorry, Emma."

It was such a quiet voice, Emma didn't know how she had heard it. And his voice brought a halt to the weeping. For all her confusion, Emma felt a sudden curiosity. Ralston's voice was different. There was something she had never heard in his voice. She looked at him directly then for the first time. And the sight of his face answered her curiosity. It was as if his face had been made out of clay that had gotten wet, softened, and slipped out of shape—Ralston's face had a crumpled look about it. He realized that Emma was studying him, and that he would have to endure her scrutiny. He swallowed—hard enough that the movement in his throat jerked his chin sideways just slightly. It was obvious to Emma, astounding to her, even, that he was miserable under her eyes. By all rights she should have made him suffer—she should exact that much from him. But an unexpected thought came to

Emma then, as much a surprise as the sight of his face. He had hurt her and the children, it was true. Was it possible that he had also hurt *himself?* Emma didn't know if she watched Ralston's face for a long or a short time, didn't know that at the same time she was looking into herself. A shutter in her mind opened, startled her, closed again. She loved him. All along she had loved him.

The rush of feelings closed back in on her, locking her mind and her speech in place. She was as silent as if Ralston had not been there with her in the room. Now he began to pace, not knowing what to make of Emma's reaction—the weeping, then the silence. But she had opened the door to him. Hadn't turned him out again. And she hadn't ranted or raved. At last he broke in.

"You're all right? You—." He paused. "You and the children. You're, all of you, all right?"

"We are." Emma's voice took on an assertiveness now—her pride began to take over. Her mouth made a line. "We've held on. Things are low just now, but we've held on." She knew that Ralston would have noticed the scarcity in the kitchen. She stopped herself midway to the stove—it was a habit—to pick up the coffeepot. There was no coffee to warm.

"The children are out in the wood lot. I'd call them in, but I don't expect they could hear me."

Ralston had not yet released the breath he didn't know he was holding. If he was not mistaken, the words he just heard hinted that she might accept him.

"I've got some things to bring in from the car." He said this in a tentative voice, one that asked her permission. The little gifts he had with him, all ready, the one preparation he had made for his reunion with Emma and the children. He had expected to travel all the way to the Wiregrass to find them—had never dreamed of finding her here. This pale woman with the tired eyes—it was the first time that he had looked at her with any real interest in years. One of the few times, in fact, in their lives together. His admiration for her took him off guard. He wouldn't have imagined a will like that in Emma. Now Emma no longer dropped her eyes. For behind them rushed impulses, intuitions, that were new and strange to her. Then again, they may have only been forgotten.

She was mistaken about the children. They were well back within range of the sound of her voice. They stood together at a distance, with the half-loaded wheelbarrow, watching Ralston go into the house and walk out again.

"It's Daddy."

There was a long silence.

"He's got a new car." A weak little remark from Billy.

For once, there was no discussion. Each child retreated into his and her own secret, inside self. They watched Ralston enter the house for a second time. One of them made a move forward, Buddy or Ralph. Inspired by Emma, Ralph had set up a rivalry for who got to push the wheelbarrow—but this abruptly subsided. They pushed the load to the woodpile and unloaded each sawed up piece of limb. They didn't hurry—they were none of them prepared. Inside the barn, Buddy went through his motions with special care. Hung up the bucksaw. Rolled the wheelbarrow to its proper place. Then all but Buddy would have waited a little longer. But he started out. Just as Ralston had done, Buddy dropped his head, squinting, and crossed the yard. Emma had been tense, straining for some sound of their return. And as Buddy's foot fell on the steps, she was on her feet and opening the door.

"Come on in and speak to your Daddy." Emma didn't smile, but her voice encouraged them into the kitchen.

"Nettie."

"Hey, sir."

"Buddy."

"Sir."

Likely Emma didn't realize that she called the children's names in their birth order. The gifts were there on the table, gifts from their father, obviously—but it was Emma's job to present them. There was a factory-made slingshot and several bags of marbles for the boys. For Nettie there was a small Bible, bound in white leather. Ralston had given Emma a white lace handkerchief, the only one she had ever owned. She hadn't yet picked it up. She was intrigued by the choice of the Bible.

The family was never to know how it had happened, that during his absence from them, Ralston had gotten religion, the harsh religion of the Nazarenes, one that suited his temperament exactly.

Ralston greeted each of his children with a nod. There was a little tight smile on his face. He looked at a point just above the line of their faces, aware that all of them were studying his. Especially Buddy. Buddy was waiting for something. And the gifts, novelty though they were, were not what it was. But whatever it was, Buddy knew it was not going to come. Emma touched his arm, as a prompt. "Thank you, sir." Now the other thank you's followed. The five of them stood uneasily, looking to Emma for the cue that they were dismissed. But Ralston got up again, muttering about doing some shopping. Emma knew that he meant to supply the empty kitchen.

The silence following Ralston's departure filled every room in the house. Only when they heard the sound of the automobile pulling away did the children come quietly downstairs again, still moving a little unnaturally—they didn't know why. And, for some reason, they skirted the kitchen. Only Nettie paused, tilted her head—Buddy knew that obstinate tilt—and started to enter the room with Emma. Buddy jerked her back. There was a curious quietness about their mother, a quiet that they were, for the first time, not invited to enter. Their mother had never, by word or gesture, demanded secrecy or privacy for herself. But something in the way she kept her back turned informed them of her right to it, now.

That afternoon Emma didn't cook dried limas. They had thick slices of ham with rich, red gravy. They had tiny sweet pickles and canned cut corn. Emma made rice and biscuits. There was butter on the table. And bowls of canned rice pudding. It was a feast that each child could have created in fantasy, on a hungry late morning or afternoon. But for all of its goodness, it was not a comfortable meal. Emma prodded each child for some little token of conversation. She asked, as she never had to, about school. The children each responded with some offering that they hoped might suffice. Ralston was at his most affable. "That so?" "Well, now." All the time he had that little tight, unfamiliar smile. The children sidled away from the table, well-fed but needing their retreat, and Emma finished up in the kitchen.

It was dark outside when she came to the front room, but Ralston hadn't lit a lamp. He sat in a chair which he had turned to face the windows; he hadn't moved as the late light faded to dark blue, like drops of ink dissolved in water. Now the long window shapes were black. When Emma came in with her work basket, she held a match to one of the lamps and sat down near Ralston, who picked up the newspaper beside him and rattled it. It was just now that she noticed he hadn't smoked.

"Where'd you go?" It was the only time she would ask him.

"Oh, I went upstate." He turned a page and folded the newspaper back elaborately, so that it rattled again. "Went upstate."

Emma knew Ralston. She hadn't really hoped for a reply more explicit than that one. A familiar silence settled between them.

Ralston held the paper in front of him, not seeing it. There were many things that he wanted Emma to know, but he didn't know how to say them. It was true that he'd been upstate. The entire time he had been in Birmingham, where Floyd Hendrix, Jr. helped him locate a room in a boarding house, supplied him with useful information, where to buy liquor or locate women. Had spoken for him when Ralston applied for a job—which he located fairly easily. He found work as an automotive mechanic; and inside the first week, it became obvious that he had a considerable skill. He worked long hours. He had no quarrel with overtime, as long as the repair work interested him. Soon, customers began to ask for him by name.

All these were things that he could have predicted. What he hadn't expected was any change in himself. But there had been a change. Ralston became a brooder. He found that he wanted to be alone. Little by little Floyd Hendrix quit asking him out for card games or evenings at nearby speakeasies. Finally, he left Ralston alone altogether. And although Ralston was fond of young Hendrix, he was glad of it. At the garage, he was talkative enough, joking along with his co-workers. He was liked by the others. But once he left work, Ralston was silent. His personal life was almost totally silent. The other boarders were familiar with the silent type; they eventually left off their attempts to make conversation with him. Ralston grew to like sitting, just simply sitting, outside on the porch by himself. Not even taking a newspaper outside. He rocked, while the evening darkened around him. And he brooded. He thought back over each part of his life, selecting, concentrating on different periods of it, like someone drawing cards from a file box. He thought often now of his boyhood. There had been so many of them—Ralston had twelve siblings, in all. He had been somewhere in the middle, indistinguishable among the rest, so it seemed to him. His mother he dreaded as a boy; he cringed at the shrill lashings of her tongue, and was glad then for the presence of the others. In their number there was protection. Yet he studied her at times, from a distance. Mrs. Griffen had an aversion to cats. He stood by, once, with some of the others, silently looking on as his mother, in a fit of pique, hung a stray cat from a tree at the back of the house. The sight of it made the children shudder. She didn't look very often at Ralston in particular, and he was grateful for that. For maternal comfort he relied on his sisters. Ralston hadn't dreaded his father—there was nothing to dread. As a toddler, he had watched him, followed after him, vied, at times, for his attention. His father, Charles Senior, was at least predictable, and there was safety in that. In contrast to his wife, he was a person of striking calm. An aloof sort of dignity. He had fathered thirteen children. He seemed to have affection, attention enough, for one, his oldest son, Charles Junior.

Ralston was aware of his failure with his own family—he didn't try to excuse it in himself. But in Birmingham he tried to avoid thinking of them, once he had worked out an explanation for their welfare that satisfied him. He was not a family man, by nature; but it had been expected of him. Nor was he, by nature, gratified in the work of a farmer; but that, too, all along had been expected. He had attempted these things, because he had been taught to expect them of himself. But he had failed—there was no use in taking the idea further. He thought of his abandoned family with genuine remorse. But here he had drawn up a scenario that largely relieved his mind. Emma would sell the farm; she would return home with the children. And his mind stopped there.

He hadn't expected to dwell much beyond that point on Emma and the children. But he found that he did think about them—increasingly, with time. Emma. There was a restfulness about Emma. And his son, Buddy. Buddy was not yet ten, yet Ralston could see in him, already, the makings of fine manhood.

He didn't brood on the question of their safety, because he assumed that they would be well. That the scenario which he envisioned might be false never once occurred to him.

Ralston porch sat then in all weathers. Even when the storms of late summer drove rain whipping across the porch, he would take a chair from the line turned against the wall of the house. On Sundays he watched the members of a certain church congregation come and go. The church, which stood almost directly across the street from the boarding house, was a long building of red brick, ugly and squat. The shallow yard in front of it was trampled bare. Above the door on a wooden plaque, the words were painted, Church of the Nazarene. It was on a mild Sunday morning in November that Ralston sat on the porch in shirt sleeves. He wore a dress shirt and pants but no jacket or tie. His attention was caught by the sight of a woman in a yellow dress. It wasn't a startling yellow. The members of this congregation were, for the most part, drably dressed. So it was not just the pale note of color that caught his eye—it was the woman's walk that caught his attention. He saw her only from the back. The body inside the dress was like liquid. There was happiness in the way she moved. He heard her laugh and call out to someone she knew. He stood abruptly and walked across the street. This without hesitation— he gave no thought to how he was dressed. He had later forgotten the woman and the whim that brought him across the sidewalk and into the building. He wasn't sure, now, that he had ever seen her face. His redemption; his return. These were the great dramas of Ralston's existence. And it would be as close to a sense of humor as he would ever come to reflect—chuckle to himself, from time to time—that he had been led to God by the swish of a yellow dress.

Emma grew tired quickly in the evenings—Ralston remembered. He recognized the little habitual movements that marked the end of her day. She set her work down. She rattled some things in the kitchen. The January night was perfectly quiet. She would go up any moment to the bed that they had slept in together. And for this Emma knew she wasn't ready. But for this one contingency, Ralston was prepared. He made clear his intention to sleep downstairs, and when Emma went up for a pillow and blankets he thought he detected a certain relief. The front room was almost totally dark. Only the small lamp that Emma carried up and down stairs was burning. Ralston made no move to touch his wife, not even her hand; nor would he, for months to follow. Still, there were those things that he wanted to say to her. He collected himself, to make the effort. Ralston's personality was too long fixed, now, for change. His conversion would not change him in small ways—he would never be a talkative man. If anything, he would become more silent, in a way that could come across as evil-tempered. Emma knew that he wanted to say something to her. She thought, even, that she understood his difficulty. He cleared his throat.

"Emma. Things will be different." It was the most that he could manage.

It was enough, for the moment. As natural and easy as Ralston was fumbling, Emma ran the back of her hand lightly down the side of his face. "I expect they will." She turned to pick up the lamp. And she went up, taking the light with her.

Chapter 18

Griffen Motor Company was opened for business in spring of 'twenty-eight. Ralston leased a building just off the business end of Water Avenue, with more floor space than he'd need, to start out with. The building had been a wholesale grocery and had double front doors, with loading doors at the back. The windows were sealed with paint and grime, but with the doors open, fresh air moved through the work area. Ralston's calculations were as detailed and thorough as planning could make them. His priorities had an order. First, the machinery. Ralston would never forget— it seemed a long time ago, now—that time with the truck, all the to-do of hauling in the vehicle for the valve job. Machinery; then tools. After signing a lease on the property, those were his priorities. Ralston added to his tools with deliberation. Some of those he had now were old, used even before he'd acquired them, the first tools he'd used for work on the truck. He still liked the feel of those old ones in his hands. He'd done nothing to the building but clear and sweep it out. As yet he didn't even have a business sign. But on that first morning, a Monday, Chuck Wilkins, on his way to the repair garage on Water Avenue, had spotted Ralston, had come in full of fellow feeling and loud congratulations. He glanced around the high old building and, unable to make any special remark on it, congratulated Ralston again.

"Good to have you close by."

Ralston nodded.

And then Chuck Wilkins, who was late for work that morning,

tried to call attention away from that fact with his news. That
young fella with the truck had opened up, just around the corner. The other mechanics as well as the owner, Carty Frazier, had
been interested enough in this information that Chuck had pretty
much gotten by with being late. Although they all knew Ralston's
name, the men wouldn't use it at first; it would be a token of ac-
ceptance when they began, as they would shortly, to refer to him
simply as Griffen.

Carty Frazier was in a bad mood that Monday morning.
Customers were flocking in, demanding service, expecting immediate service on demand. Mondays were like that. Frazier's sched-
ule was full. And people got rude when told no, no matter how
politely you put it. It rubbed against Frazier. This morning his
heartburn also bothered him, that and the bad air of the building.
He worked with a light bulb hanging close to his face. The odors
of grit and old motor oil were just warming to a stink.

" 'S a fella here needs an oil change. Engine's running rough."

Carty had been leaning over an uncovered engine. He stood
up to swear, but he had an idea. "Hey. Send him around the corner, would you. That fella with the truck."

So, Ralston had customers the first day his business opened
its doors. That was how it began, with the overflow business from
Carty Fraizier. Ralston worked without an assistant, alone with
his by now well-honed skill. Slowly, it developed that those businesses that had sent customers to Ralston began to take the overflow back from him.

Ralston had promised Emma that things would be different.
And she thought mainly of domestic difference—which was in
fact what Ralston intended. But that there would be changes of
the magnitude of this one—his having taken religion, to begin
with—no one could have guessed except Ralston. Right away the
children were aware of a certain difference in their parents. It was

not just the fact—in itself, now unaccustomed—of their father's being there in the house again. There was a climate change in the house, some subtle thing that puzzled them; they weren't able to pin it down well enough to put it in words. They sensed a kind of unity, something new, between Emma and Ralston. And the response was simple jealousy, which they would not have understood by that name. Nettie fell into the habit now of going off by herself, to brood. Her location of choice was always the front porch steps. Buddy looked out that way whenever he wanted to find her. And he knew his sister well enough to know that when he did find her there, there would most likely be something on her mind. Sometimes he avoided her. Nettie had a way of speaking out about things—anything. Buddy handled matters differently. And once, she had upset them both, in a way that wasn't easy for either one of them to shake off. As he approached her on the step that afternoon, he could tell that she was about to come out with something contrary.

"Are we glad Daddy's back?"

Buddy had been about to sit, but then he stood again. The two of them looked at each other. As the words left her mouth, Nettie realized she had made a mistake. It wasn't a topic that she wanted to talk about, after all. She raised her arms and bounded off, and Buddy walked off, frowning, in the other direction. It was one of those times when he should have left her alone.

But their mother was cheerful again, although the children were slow, at first, in adjusting to this new cheerfulness. Gradually the tension relaxed. But there were surprises, little new things that caught them off guard. The pie safe in the kitchen had always been fair game in the afternoons. Now Emma might just as well listen from another room when they went near it.

"Don't touch that piece of pie. It's for Daddy."

This was new, and it rankled. It seemed especially to rankle

Nettie. She and Buddy left the kitchen with a couple of leftover biscuits.

"Daddy's pie. The pie's for *Daddy*." Nettie made a face with the mimic, wagging her head from side to side. It made Buddy laugh. He gave her a thump on the upper arm, hard, then ducked and ran off.

"I'll get you, Buddy!"

"I'll get you, Buddy," he repeated, safely outside her range. He did love Nettie! There was only one thing he could think of that was wrong with his sister. She talked too much.

For Emma, the puzzling thing was Ralston's insistence on driving into Clanton on Sunday mornings, to attend services at the Church of the Nazarene. In a general way, Emma supposed that it was a positive sign, but she wondered at his choice. Herself, she saw nothing attractive about this particular church or congregation. The clapboard building was nothing more than one large room, like any country church. There was no tower. The church itself was well kept up, but Emma noticed the lack of shrubbery, the absence of plants or flowers. In her own church, the pulpit area was decorated each Sunday by offerings from various gardens. That congregation entered cheerfully, sobered appropriately for the sermon and prayers, then broke up again, as genially as they had entered. The Nazarenes were a different sort. Religion was a dire business. There was little friendly chatter. Even the singing seemed dutiful, at times laborious.

Ralston did no work now on Sundays. And he wanted the children quiet. He read his newspaper. Once Emma had seen him reading the Bible. For the most part, he simply sat. Emma's curiosity, already intense, mounted—she wondered no end at this change.

"You'll be wanting to go in on Sundays, from now on?" She took a seat.

"Think so. Yeah." He cleared his throat.

Emma reflected. She could still go to her own Wednesday night prayer meetings. And she could contribute again now to the weekly suppers—it would be such a pleasure

"You've found God." Emma raised this question in the form of a statement. It was a well-worn phrase of religious rhetoric, but coming from Emma, it was startlingly intimate, even invasive. Ralston was profoundly embarrassed. The words scalded him. He moved his neck around inside his collar, swallowed a couple of times, as if he might have been meaning to speak, then abruptly stood up and left the room.

On all other days of the week, Ralston was industrious with a fervor. He made repairs to all the outbuildings. He even worked on the house and the porches. He replaced some of the back steps and repainted them. Although he no longer left the family at night, he did have the occasional business call. A Mr. Quarles had called on them one night at suppertime. After the meal, the men walked around the property—they were outside together a long time. It began to get dark. Emma looked out at them with curiosity, as they stood close together, discussing something that seemed to interest both of them a great deal. Ralston gesticulated, moving his arm in a sweeping motion.

And then the announcement: the farm had been sold. They were moving into town.

Emma met the news with a peculiar blankness. Somewhere, in some secret place, the earth tilted. Ralston himself was so pleased with his scheme that his family's opinion hadn't factored in. No one thing had gratified him in this way since he had first found the farm property, nearly fifteen years ago. When he smiled, his mouth turned up, bowlike, at the corners. The force of the announcement in itself pried Emma's mind loose; caused her own, immediate reaction to jump its track and catapult ahead. The children would go to city schools. And that would be an advantage. Her husband would be a businessman, not a farmer. Both of these things were advantages. It would be another start, and a better start, for her family. She told herself that in all ways it would be better: best. In the days that followed, she began to move, if a little absently. Her hands worked. The children were all set to work. And unlike Emma, the children did talk, grouped and regrouped, to try on the idea and air it together. The group verdict after all this discussion was that they were excited and pleased. They encouraged this opinion from one another. They were, it was true, excited, even if something didn't feel exactly right. Each of them pushed aside the strange little something.

"We'll be able to walk to the picture show!"

"Nah. Daddy won't let us."

"We won't ask Daddy, stupid. We'll ask Mama. Mama'll let us go."

There was a pause.

"That old church we have to go to. I don't like it. The Sunday school teacher said that going to picture shows is a sin."

"It ain't no such a thing!"

"It surely ain't!"

Nettie took control of the conversation and changed the subject. "We can walk to the dime store any time we want to." Again the group considered.

"We'll have to go to a new school."

And at this idea, all five of them went silent. Nettie looked at Billy thoughtfully. "Billy won't get to have Miss Seay."

Now the others looked at Billy in sympathy. Billy realized suddenly that he was the focus of attention. Nettie's words penetrated, and his reaction was violent. He shook his head, "But I *did* have Miss Seay!"

"Yeah, but you didn't *really* have Miss Seay," Nettie explained.

"I did, too! I did! Buddy, *tell* her. I did, too, have Miss Seay!" It took a while to calm him.

In the farmhouse, all the rooms were set on end. The family began on the move right away. The house that Ralston had chosen for them in town was large, well-built, and graceless, recently painted a mustard yellow. By contrast, the farmhouse looked worn and faded. They had waited several years after taking the farm to paint the house, and that coat of paint had long ago weathered to fine streaks in the grain of the wood. It was a gray house. Without thinking about it, Emma had come to accept it that way, even to love the color, especially in summer, when the soft, rosy masses of crape myrtle stood against each side of it. Now she didn't look at her house; she no longer saw it. Every detail of the day centered around the move, which was accomplished with amazing speed, due to the help of her WMU group. It seemed, all of a sudden, that everyone was there, all day, each day. Ralston's men friends helped with the hauling. Emma's friends almost took the effort away from her. The idea of the family's being reunited appealed to their sentimentality. Even Lou Anne tried, with uncertain success, to work up some friendly feeling for Ralston. There were suddenly so many capable hands. The women arrived in the mornings, bringing food from their own kitchens. The house was a din of activity. And in the hubbub, Lou Anne was a calming influence; Minnie flustered and caused confusion. Old Mrs. Hale sat looking on at all the to-do. Emma was going on a trip. Emma was having the walls re-papered. Thoughts blew gently through her mind, rested briefly, like stray scraps caught by a twig and lifted away again.

Then it was time. There was nothing left to do but take the

last of the clothing, a few kitchen things, the mattresses and bedding. Emma went about, preoccupied. On the night before the last trip, it crossed her mind to wonder if she would sleep. And that night she did have some difficulty. Ralston slept soundly. But she turned repeatedly. Then she realized that the moon was in her face. The curtains were no longer hanging. She turned again, and the quiet laps of sleep washed over her. In her mind there were no traces. Or so she thought.

Everyone promised to visit. Emma promised to visit. On the morning of the Griffens' departure, assurances were passed back and forth. It wouldn't be a real parting; they wouldn't think of it that way. A basket on the front seat of the car was loaded with food—everyone had cooked. And Ralston had borrowed a truck. Mr. Quarles was driving the family vehicle, with Emma and the children. Now the goodbyes became clamorous. Everything that had been said was repeated.

They said they would come, and they meant it. And they would come, on rare occasion. It was scarcely twelve miles. It was the whole earth away.

The last ones to leave the house were the children. Emma could see that they were bickering over something. Billy was crying and running along beside the others. She'd have to take him up front, on her lap. All of them were shouting at once, and Billy was yelling into the noise.

"I did, too, have Miss Seay! I did! I did, *too*!"

Chapter 19

Elizabeth did, too—have everything in her own small domain under control, that is. Henry's oldest girl, this little honey-tinged fruit of a daughter, seemed to have not a need in the world. Elizabeth chose the kitchen table for her homework area, for her own use, exclusively. It was quiet back there. And this was all the same with Mary. Mary did no homework; in the evenings she simply continued to read, preferring, anyway, to be up front near Henry, who often as not was there reading, himself. Betty Kate had no real homework to do—she made hers up. And now she was complaining about something or another. The girls' bickering had always struck Henry as comical—a fact he was wise enough to conceal. But it was different with Elizabeth, who was now in sixth grade. In some way, just about everything was different with Elizabeth, who'd refused for some time to bathe three to a bathtub; who refused to change into her nightgown until she was ready for bed. It wasn't seemly, she pronounced. Henry had to bite the insides of his cheeks at this—his sense of humor at times annoyed Lillian. Elizabeth dealt with her father in the same faultless, polite manner she reserved for other adults. She thanked him for his offers of help—with parsing sentences or memorizing dates. She shuffled papers or rearranged something on the table, with a tight smile silently dismissing him.

With his present sense of satisfaction, he could afford a certain indifference to such slights. His employment as house painter had an almost recreational value for Henry, so different was it from the old confinement. He could take the girls by the drugstore for an ice cream in the afternoons, if he took the notion. For a matter of weeks, he'd worked directly next door to his home, making the neighboring house a mustard yellow. He was released, at last, into the everyday world of people. His routine took him directly into the daily life of the town. And how good it was to be out! The dusty blanks of his days at the sawmill had sucked his senses dry. Now they absorbed small detail, like shrunken plant cells would moisture. Back alleys had always lured Henry—were tantalizing places, especially in the old areas of town. Henry stalked the old alleys as a schoolboy would do, senses alert for small discoveries. He passed carriage houses converted to garages, some with fraying buggies, discarded toy wagons or hobby horses that had once belonged to children as old, now, or older than he. He caught all the cooking smells from breakfasts and dinners, the sweetish stink of garbage, the sunny odors of soapsuds and warm grass, newly watered. He listened to the carryings-on of cooks and delivery men, the shrieks of children unsupervised behind houses. He occasionally overheard quarrels from anonymous upstairs windows. These were the smells and sounds of days going by, simple days in the everyday lives of people.

Sometimes he did a bit of finishing up on a Sunday. There was a gravity, a serenity, about Sundays in these long-settled neighborhoods, a kind of sure and safe satisfaction in living. A well-being that could be overheard in voices. Henry relished the early Sunday quiet of the town. For commercial jobs, he worked all over Clanton, often in the older business sections, on the old riverfront buildings, some of which had been for years neglected. In the first stages of the work, the rooms would have a musty, long unused smell. They would have to be cleared of old objects and rubbish. The jammed windows would have to be knocked loose and opened, and the sight and smell of the river would rush in.

Henry felt a little like a prowler, at times, alone in one of these rooms, wondering who had last touched these odd things, the discarded ledgers, stationery objects and papers—and when. It brought him that good kind of faraway feeling that he'd once had sitting in the library reserve room, reading anything of history he could lay hands on.

He laughed more easily these days. And he didn't mind the work, in itself. There was a steadying, a soothing, quality about repairing and painting. Henry had built up a reputation as a good worker. He never drank on the job. But he often ended his days with a stop at the Bluebird, a cafe on the untended block of Church Street near the river. Here, customers discreetly brought out the flasks from their laps, beneath the cups and saucers. Hundreds of cups of coffee were ordered at the Bluebird during the course of a business day.

But Henry had a worry, one that most of the time he could nudge back into a corner of his mind, where it ceased to prickle: the income he provided for his family was adequate, but not as high as it had been at the sawmill. When the worry edged its way out into the open, he told himself that he should look for better work, some sort of supervisory position. He knew exactly where he could have gone. His father was ready, at any time now, to retire from managing the cotton mill—he, Henry, could have stepped right into the job. He could not—he couldn't make himself do it. He couldn't shut himself up again inside those humid walls of noise and lint dust. But then, he felt that he *ought* to do it. Most of the time Henry held the idea at a distance; but when it did work loose, it preyed on him. Then he sought relief by allowing himself to waste time—this being a commodity he could have hugely squandered, if he let himself. Those four little boys in the yellow house next door, for example—somebody ought to take those boys fishing. A farm family had moved in, shortly after

Henry had completed the job on that house. Henry noticed that they were big churchgoers, sometimes disappearing all day on a Sunday. But to the best he could observe, he didn't think that the fellow ever took his boys anywhere else. And that was a downright shame. There was something peculiar about that family—Henry knew that farm families could be peculiar. Shy of strangers, especially town folk. But the new owner, a farmer turned mechanic, had something frankly wrong with him, to Henry's thinking. If the two men caught one another's eye, Ralston glared at Henry. It must be that he had some sort of disposition problem, Henry chuckled to Lillian. It would have astounded him to know the truth: that the Griffen family was forbidden to have anything to do with the neighbors next door. Ralston didn't want the boys—or Nettie, either—having anything to do with those three little girls. Mr. Gray was a drunk. More than a drunk, he was a gambler. He had a brother that was talked about all over the state.

Henry would have paid the boys all sorts of attention, if the family hadn't been such a queer lot. A shed, a long building also painted the same mustard yellow, stood between the two back yards. And the far side of this shed was the boys' hiding place, the only place on the property where they could not be spotted by Emma. They loitered and convened there daily. Once Henry had come upon them unexpectedly, and the boys jumped, the four of them at once forming a line, all solemn-faced. The solemn faces amused Henry; but he held back the laughter. They stared. He stared. Henry couldn't have known that each boy was poised for a flight of survival. That each boy was asking himself the same, urgent question. They were looking directly at the drunk. And what did a drunk *do*, exactly, they asked themselves now. They knew that drunks beat their wives and children. But what might a drunk do to *them*? Instead of cracking a grin, Henry put his palms together, then slid them in opposite directions, letting the two middle fingers protrude, one up, one dangling. It was an old hand trick that Drefus had taught him in school. Buddy and Ralph kept straight faces; but the little ones grinned. Henry laughed out loud as he walked away, hearing the giggling that broke out behind him. Already the four of them had huddled, to argue about how to do what the drunk had done. That night after supper, when Emma asked, "Where'd you pick that up from?"—it was a trick that she also remembered from school—Billy blurted, "the drunk—." Until Ned jabbed him. Ralston was reading his newspaper and overheard nothing. Emma had understood Billy perfectly well; but she too chose to overhear nothing.

Emma herself frankly spied on the Gray family—that is, she watched Lillian. This she did from one of the upstairs windows. A young maple tree blocked her view from downstairs. Back in Burnsville, Emma's women friends, along with her children, had been the deep and steady comfort of her existence. They were women too much like herself to cause her any real curiosity. But Emma was intensely curious about this little woman next door, who was just in time that spring to deadhead her hydrangeas. Already, the twisted red leaf buds were creeping along the old stems. Emma noticed that the woman worked without gloves or a sun hat. Such a tiny thing she was. And so dainty. She was always dressed up, it seemed to Emma, to go out making calls. Continued observation made clear that this was how the little woman routinely dressed. It was just plain odd. And for the first time, Emma thought critically of her own everyday print dresses.

Emma wasn't aware of any particular insularity in herself. She didn't reflect that in the country, the world had come to her. She had only to make the opening gesture; then, that surrounding world claimed her. Here in Clanton there had been a single visitor from the church, a Miss Bell, who became Emma's fast friend at once, her single—and critical—source of womanly camaraderie.

As far as the family next door, Emma would have blithely ignored Ralston's edict—at least during the day, when she could get away with it—except that something made her shy of that other woman. Her being so proper and ladylike, not just in the way that she dressed but in how she moved, how Emma overheard her speaking to people. And what *would* make a woman like that, in her sad situation no less, hold her head up just so, Emma wondered. Already Emma admired Lillian. And despite the dire goings-on that she would have imagined in that household, given what she was told, to Emma all appeared to be well.

But all was not well.

Do you love me? It was a question the two of them had always passed back and forth, a little private exchange of affection.

Something was wrong. Even when they were most cordial, something was wrong. Something lurking like a child's bogeyman standing in a corner. A demon with teeth, to cut into the soft flesh of their hearts—though they didn't know that, yet. It *couldn't* be, each of them thought—not for them. They joked together. They told themselves they imagined it.

"Do you love me?" They had stopped at a landscaped area above the river, where the high bank was fenced off. They stood against the grillwork, watching the dusk settling into a luminous dark. The surface of the river was a dull white. The witching hour, Henry called it. He took Lillian's hand in a way that seemed casual.

Tears dropped from Lillian's eyes to the front of her dress. What? How could her eyes have made tears that quickly? Lillian dropped her face into her hands and frankly sobbed. She turned away from Henry, who turned her right back, with a gentle hand on each shoulder. She would not look up at him. "I'm just so unhappy." What? Then, it was worse than he thought, all the household changes.

"I'll always love you." The delayed answer—it came out like a dirge. What was *this*? She looked like someone about to be slaughtered. The answer, far from comforting, alarmed Henry more than anything else could have done. Why was she so solemn about it? And why the awful crying—when just minutes ago, they'd been a laughing family, out strolling to buy ice cream cones. "What's the matter? *Jitterbug*?" This little sentimental effort was pathetic, at that moment.

"What's the matter?" Henry repeated.

She didn't answer. Feeling helpless, Henry looked out over the river, pulling his flask from his hip pocket. But before he had loosened the top, Lillian yanked the flask from his hand and threw it. They didn't hear it hit the bank or the surface of the water. "What'd you want to go and do a thing like that for?" Henry's shock was genuine.

"Because I don't love *that*! That's why!" She walked a few feet away, heaving with emotion. And they stood watching each other. Almost with hostility.

It was worse, then, than he thought.

Now Lillian became wild—it wasn't like her. "I hate it! Do you hear me? I *hate* it? It will ruin all of our lives!"

"You're talking about the flask?"

"I'm talking about the liquor." Now she stopped, challenging him.

Henry's face was a blank. The puzzlement was genuine. "Lillian, a man needs a little drink, along."

A little. Along. *They all do.* Lillian still heard Myra's words that awful night of sitting up in the kitchen. For another two people, the exchange there on the bank may have been a trifle, forgotten in a matter of hours. But for these two—they who had loved one another even as children—for them the incident was soiling. Each knew that something was wrong in a way they didn't know how to make right. And each of them secretly wondered if they would ever again be happy. It felt total, this sudden halt to their easy fond feeling.

"We're going home." Lillian dropped his arm and moved away so quickly that he couldn't stop her, to surround herself with the girls, and thus barricade Henry from further talk.

Henry walked behind his family, confounded by the scene with Lillian. Trying to reason it out, to figure out what he himself had done wrong. But he came up with nothing. Could it have been something about Elizabeth? He realized that Lillian was especially protective of this oldest one—had not a doubt that for Elizabeth's sake Lillian would have been fierce. A subtle change had come now to their eldest daughter. In some way difficult to define, she was womanlike. When she walked, Elizabeth fluffed the back of her hair. The hand was very conscious of, busy with, the hair. No, he couldn't think of anything that could have set off Lillian about her. The household economies, he told himself, were nothing especially burdensome since his change of work. True, the family no longer had regular domestic help. They had eggs less frequently for breakfast, fewer and smaller pot roasts. Henry continued to lose negligible sums—as he thought of them—shooting craps, but he passed the locust grove only occasionally. He was fond, as always, of bringing home presents, but now they were gifts of found objects. He picked anything blooming in indifferent corners. He'd bring home a bird's nest, sometimes an unusual feather or stone. Once he brought Betty Kate an oyster shell from a heap in an alley. The shell was an iridescent, coral-pink on the inside. But nothing of that sort would have suited Elizabeth.

Was it what he had done to the automobile? He'd made it over for use as a truck. Had taken out the back seat, and in its place his paints and materials were loaded in haphazardly. Between jobs, stepladders were tied onto the top of the car, where they slid perilously by degrees toward the rear. Even Henry knew that the automobile was disgraceful.

But as it turned out, Lillian's efforts at household economy were not unmanageable. Like any Southerner of that period, she had been taught to take pride in being able to manage. Each morning she continued to dress herself as carefully as if she were paying visits or shopping in town. She did her housework, her sweeping and dusting, in low-heeled shoes and silk stockings. Henry caught sight of her once with a mop and pail, a sight that he wasn't used to. He promptly took them from her, passing over the floors in little more time than it would have taken Lillian to think about it, the bucket and mop like children's things in his hands.

No one knew Lillian's feelings. She would not have said that she was an unhappy woman. It was a person's duty to be happy. But at times, in the privacy of her sewing room, she suffered painful attacks of dismay at her inadequacies. As she saw it, the problem was that she had not been given a talent. Lillian was sincerely Christian; and she believed that God had given each person a special talent. But she couldn't imagine what hers might be—she didn't feel that she *had* a talent. Grace and poise in a certain way that people seemed to admire—she had that. She also had a way that made people, men especially, enjoy performing little services for her. Little services. That was what Lillian did—she wouldn't have considered kindness or gentleness a talent. She was regularly asked to make church visits. She was never asked to sing with the choir. Lillian didn't sing—she bleated, in little flat sounds that wobbled off key. Her inability as a cook embarrassed her.

Fortunately, she had an odd knack for making mayonnaise; her WMU group always looked forward to Lillian's fruit salad, served with mayonnaise and crackers. It was considered sophisticated.

Each mid-morning, she sat down before her sewing machine, composing herself in the manner of someone stoically facing a disagreeable duty. Sewing was her personal purgatory, yet she had determined to let the dressmaker go. For her two younger daughters, the dresses Lillian made were a source of secret hilarity. Which was fortunate. Something was always, one way or another, just off, somehow, about the dresses: one sash longer than the other, one sleeve more tightly gathered, a waistline that seemed to creep or slip to one side. All this despite the fact that Lillian wore spectacles now for sewing, tiny, rimless spectacles that flattered her eyes, magnifying them just slightly. Her personal daintiness had, for some reason, a touching quality about it. If it had not been for a suggestion of pug to her nose, she would have been a remarkably beautiful woman.

As the family walked back home up Water Avenue that evening, there were greetings called back and forth. They were again, Henry thought, for all appearances a group returning from the most tranquil of domestic outings. Of course there were no greetings called from the yellow house next door to the Grays. Someone had hauled a tractor into the farmer-mechanic's yard— people said that the man could do anything. Henry didn't know but what he detested that sort of fellow—a feeling heightened by the fact that Ralston glanced up from the engine and glared at him, before making a curt little nod to Lillian.

Between themselves, it was as though they had made an unspoken agreement—both Lillian and Henry had been shaken.

The incident overlooking the river was never again referred to. Henry courted his wife with jokes and teasing. His little acts of courtesy increased. They were both for a while especially solicitous to each other. And there were again those times when Lillian was so much like she had always been that Henry was sure he'd only been imagining most of it. Yet when he was almost content, that idea—and with it the hot prickly sensation—returned to him. The cotton mill. Yes, that—the shadow of it would not move. But there was time, he told himself. He could consider it all, in good time. It was summer of 1929, a good time. Life was full. He could take it at his leisure.

"Has anything happened?"

"Just more about the stock market." Henry brought his newspaper with him to the kitchen table, frowning as he read. Lillian removed a plate from the warmer and walked over to him. He'd worked later than usual at a papering job that afternoon and still wore his paint-crusty smock over his clothes. To place the plate in front of him, she had to tap on the newspaper. Henry scarcely glanced at the plate. It was beef stew with carrots.

The crash had happened, but most of Clanton didn't know it—it was just another newspaper headline. To most of the population, the words "stocks" or "Wall Street" were of that vague, impersonal language heard on radio broadcasts or spotted on front pages—if unsettling at all, distantly so, in that way of incomprehensible events beyond anybody's control. Not to say that there wasn't some talk. But it was said that the situation would not become serious. Business appeared in Clanton, at first, to go on as usual.

By March Henry had the Sisk job—one that would provide

him with rich material for storytelling. He'd come across the job—or, invented it—in his Sunday strolling, which had at this time become a full professional undertaking. For these occasions he put on a good suit and tie, shaved very carefully, and removed the stray flecks of paint from the eyeglasses he now wore on a continuous basis. From a drawer in the dining room, he took a handful of the business cards he'd once had printed but seldom used. Then Henry strolled the neighborhoods of Clanton. The activity of walking, in itself, brought out the geniality of his nature. The first daffodils and spring bulbs were already at their peak. And the matrons in the downtown neighborhoods were out of doors by afternoon, tending or supervising.

Mrs. Sisk was out alone that afternoon, standing toward the front of the yard, just a few feet from the front fence—and suitably dressed for a Sunday afternoon. Henry had for some time been eyeing the house, which was enormous, turreted, part fish-scaled, with balconies and a drapery of fretwork around the porch. The house was scaling just noticeably. He stopped on the sidewalk and began to survey the house, very obviously. Mrs. Sisk had noticed him but pretended not to—she was not a woman to be solicited. Henry greeted her, said a word or so of introduction, dropped the most impressive of the names he had worked for, for jobs both large and small. The trickery was in the wording. He began with the phrase, "When you decide what to do about the house--." Said, of course, with the greatest courtesy. "When." Apparently, she observed, there was that which required correcting, in his opinion. He wedged a card into a tight place in the grillwork of the fence. Mrs. Sisk ignored him. Henry touched his hat.

Mrs. Sisk didn't pick up the card. She continued her search for the signs of swollen buds on her roses. But now she also glanced at the house. For the next half hour or so, she continued to move about her garden, a bony woman with slow, studied movements.

And her eyes returned, to trail over the house. On her way back inside, she took the card.

Henry called at the house later that week. Behind the door panes, which were of patterned glass, he could hear footsteps approaching that were obviously not Mrs. Sisk's. Heavy footsteps, with a bounce. A Negro woman dressed in uniform answered the door. She nodded pleasantly and lifted her chin, waiting.

Henry placed another of the business cards in her hand. "I've come to inquire about the work on the house." Matilda had not been made aware that anyone would be coming to the house about work. A little frown flickered, as she opened the door into a wide, central hall that rose up into a stairway. There was a single piece of furniture in it, a large pier glass on legs, which reached almost to the ceiling. Mrs. Sisk had stepped quietly into the doorway opposite the mirror and stood watching Henry. He was fully aware of her presence. He was also immediately aware of the existence of a certain protocol.

The servant, Matilda, had been coached down to the last syllable. She smiled, lifting her chin again. "Whom shall I say is calling?"

Now Henry caught the spirit of it—it amused him. "You can tell Mrs. Sisk that it's Henry Gray, come to inquire about the work on the house."

As Henry said this, Mrs. Sisk openly watched him. She was a thin woman, but lanky, not fragile. And she didn't lean against the doorway. She stood very erect, her hands clasped in front of her. Gray-haired, with an aquiline nose, her eyes so deeply lidded as to resemble slits. She didn't sniff, but she managed to give that impression.

Matilda turned to Mrs. Sisk. "There's a gentleman here come to inquire about work on the house."

Mrs. Sisk's eyes looked directly into Henry's. "Tell him that

I'll expect a detailed, written estimate."

"You'll need to write it all down, sir." Matilda turned to Henry. "What grade of—."

Henry was interrupted. "Tell Mr. Gray that I use only the best quality materials." Matilda let this statement carry itself; but Henry continued to directly address her, not Mrs. Sisk.

"Would there be a color change?" Henry looked at Matilda.

"I see no need for any change of that sort." There was almost a sniff. Mrs. Sisk's heavy lids fell like a drapery. It was her signal for having closed a conversation, and Matilda knew the signal. Mrs. Sisk turned and went back into her sitting room.

Henry laughed all the way home, a long, running chuckle. He realized he'd walked into the best of luck, to have pulled off the job. He didn't know yet *how* lucky—that far more than luck, it was like the hand of God moving.

With all the scraping and fancy work he had to do, Henry worked on the house well into the summer. Coming and going, he noticed that the people next door in the yellow house were obviously taking precautionary measures. The woman had turned nearly the whole back lot into a vegetable farm, it looked like. There were farm people, Henry knew, who went at work like it was recreation. But Emma worked from no particular sense of hardship; Ralston never mentioned the word "depression." And Emma's friend, Miss Bell, would not have comprehended such a thing. Henry frankly admired Emma's industry; but himself, he didn't like seeing a woman at work with a hoe.

Henry called out to her. "What are you putting in now? A cotton crop?"

The woman stood up. She was wearing an old-fashioned sun

hat with strings. Now he walked over—a transgression somehow, he sensed. But he did it, anyway.

"Corn'll sure keep a person busy, till it gets high."

Emma gave a tight little smile. Privately she wondered if she hadn't gone too far, putting in the sweet corn. Everything, weed or otherwise, wanted to grow in that rich, bottomland garden. "I see you've got melons." Henry had always thought of having a melon patch.

Again the tight little smile—he assumed it was from shyness. "Oh, they're easy." You didn't have to do anything much to a patch of melons.

Now he noticed the sturdy zinnias that grew along the edges of the garden. Emma saw his look. "It's the bugs that like them. They keep the bugs off the other things," she allowed herself to explain.

"My mother used to do that." He never had understood why his mother planted zinnias in her garden.

As Emma spoke, she made a little sweeping motion with her hand. At which point Henry took the hoe, and without saying a word began on one of the rows himself. She noticed how rapidly he did it, wishing that she could have worked that fast, the swift strokes of the hoe loosening the summery scent of the soil. She stood by at a loss. It was awkward—embarrassing—watching the man do her work. She should say some polite little something.

Henry was alert to the shyness, as he assumed it to be. So he helped her along. "Don't you think a thing about it. Hadn't had a hoe in my hand since I was a boy. Feels right good, it does."

Henry, himself, was at anything but a loss in talking to neighbors. "That's a fine lot of boys you have."

Now Emma smiled outright—she couldn't help it, when someone gave a compliment to her children. And the children were, in fact, getting along well. After a short time, they had been indifferently accepted, then liked, finally admired among certain of their schoolmates.

Then Henry saw that the woman's smile was replaced by a frown. He suspected she was thinking of Ralph, who was sporting an outstanding shiner.

"Now don't you worry about that one who likes to fight."

Emma blushed at having her mind read. It was already established that no one but an idiot bothered the Griffen boys.

Henry kept up his rapid hoeing. He was moving quickly down the row. Emma edged along beside him, not knowing what else to do. Then he began on a second row.

"Yeah. Boys like to fight," Henry continued. " 'S perfectly natural." He said this, feeling sure it was so, although himself, he'd never been especially fond of fighting.

"Well." It was a polite acknowledgment of his remark. Emma was struck that he seemed like a perfectly nice person, this man reputed to be a drunk.

She felt she should return the compliment about her boys. "Your little girls are awfully pretty, especially that one with all the curly red hair."

Henry nodded. "She's a bit prissy these days."

Why, he did seem like a nice man. She wondered if Ralston were not mistaken. And she could no longer restrain herself— Emma enjoyed a good conversation. "Girls will be like that. My Nettie is," she volunteered. Nettie, now in her first year of junior high, wore *Evening in Paris* to school each morning, one careful dab behind each ear, unaware that the cheap scent was a subject of ridicule among the popular girls at school. Next door, the scent would not have been allowed into the house. But Emma and Henry were, both of them, innocents in such matters.

Henry chuckled, then looked up directly at Emma. "Expect you miss the country, don't you?"

He was the one person to have said that to her. The remark impressed her as especially kindly. "That I do," she answered him. "That I do," she repeated more softly, to herself.

At odd times when he was certain the old man wasn't home, Henry walked into the next yard and picked up the hoe, which stood against the wall of the back porch. It gave him pleasure to have a few minutes of work with the soil—and the woman could use the help, he felt sure. He always carefully put the hoe back just as he found it. One Sunday, when he knew they were all at church, Henry worked the whole corn plot. Emma spotted the clean rows and knew right away who had done it.

When he finished the Sisk house and all its trim, Henry was contracted to do the kitchen—a separate building—the cook's house, the carriage house, and the gazebo. Then she had him start on the plaster and woodwork inside. He re-papered all the downstairs rooms, scraped down and re-painted window trim and baseboards. He completed the work with care and skill.

It was the last regular job that he had.

There were suddenly no commercial jobs available; work on private residences was even harder to come by. Henry lowered his rates. He began doing odd jobs, when he could find them. And the household economy did suffer, for the first time. Stores all over Clanton began to mark down and keep perishables that would have once been discarded.

"Mama, those peaches are rotten." Outside the store entrance, Elizabeth corrected her mother. She picked up a few rosy peaches from another bin and dropped them into Lillian's basket, then moved away, satisfied, without noticing that Lillian put back the fragrant, whole fruit. From that point, Lillian did her shopping during the day. And a little furtively. The women who knew one another all moved furtively around the arrays of wrinkled carrots sprouting fine roots or the green-tinged potatoes, the day-old bread.

The Gray family began to eat soup in the evenings. Each evening, now, supper consisted of bread and soup, the soups being unfamiliar concoctions put together from whatever Lillian could find cheap and available. She made biscuits, at first because being absentminded as a cook, she didn't stop to think that corn muffins would have been better with soup. Then she stopped buying meal. Biscuits were cheaper to make.

"Why do we have to have soup all the time?" It was Elizabeth.

"Soup's good for you."

The girls knew from long experience that when something was "good for" them, it was useless to protest. Mary ate by making a lot of unnecessary, dipping motions with her spoon, as though the soup were nasty. Betty Kate squirmed in her chair. "When things get better," she began. Henry and Lillian were startled. Where had the child picked up that phrase? Her full question was: "When things get better, can we have pineapple puddin'?"

"Yeah. Pineapple puddin'." Then Mary changed her mind. "No. We can have spice and nut cake."

"No. Chicken and dressing!"

The conversation was all about food. But Betty Kate grew quiet. She had said something wrong, she knew, and it confused her. It was just pineapple puddin'—that was all she had said. But her mother had looked at her, a long look, such a funny kind of look that the idea of pineapple pudding suddenly made her sad. Henry and Lillian ate until the soup was gone, knowing that no amount of it would satisfy them.

"Henry, we've got to sit down and do some planning."

They were alone now in the kitchen.

Henry knew that this moment had to come—and knew as well how much he had dreaded it. They made no move to leave the table; Lillian paid no attention to the dishes. He planted his feet in front of him, leaning forward to rest his arms against his thighs. Lillian knew the posture well—it was his worry posture. But she would *not* be put off. She pulled her chair over directly in front of him. And she waited. Henry could see both of her hands, turned upward, lying together in her lap. They were tiny, childish-looking hands. When he looked at them, he thought of a little stray incident with the hands, a time when a bird, almost grown, had fallen from its nest near the porch. The hands made a picture in Henry's memory, one under, one over the body of the little bleating round thing. Lillian had put it back into the nest, anxiously, afraid that the mother bird would not accept it; but the bird did.

Henry opened the conversation, after a fashion, shaking his head, not looking at Lillian. "Don't know, Lillian. I just don't know what we can do."

She replied a little fiercely, "We'll do exactly what everybody else is doing. We'll just have to get by on our savings, until things get better."

Then there was the silence. It lengthened. It lay between them like a spreading pool of water. Lillian's hands did not change position. But as the two of them sat together this way, she realized. She suddenly knew. Henry looked up, finally, and his face confirmed it all. He had already cashed in his life insurance policy; he had thirty-two dollars left in the bank. Somewhere in his mind Henry must have held onto the notion that calamity was not a possibility—because calamity had already happened. He and Lillian were born during decades of hardship. Then there had been the Great War. The burned sawmill. These things would have put an end to calamity. He made no further provision for it.

It was closing in on them, again: the ugly menace, the lurking bogeyman—they both knew the feel of it. They had told themselves that by forgetting, they had willed it away. For Lillian, Henry had been her cherished friend, her mainstay, for so long that she could scarcely remember not having him there, or having his constancy to depend on. Now, it was this same person—this dearly loved one—who had become the focus of dread in her life. She could put together what had happened, and the understanding struck a blow to her middle. She no longer looked at Henry—there was no use—but sat abstractedly, her eyes averted. So that he could watch her face now without fear of confrontation. The small lips, so perfectly shaped. The sadness of them. The simple sweetness of her face hurt his heart.

The hands in front of him disappeared in a quick motion. Lillian stood up then, but she waited for him to look at her. Which he did. And he was sick with shame.

"Great God!" She turned to go out of the room, leaving Henry. It was not language she ordinarily used.

The bundle of green beans that Emma had Buddy take over were intended as no more than a simple thank you; Emma had not forgotten Henry's kindness to her with the hoeing. It was an ordinary enough thing to make a gift of surpluses from a kitchen garden. And Emma herself was seldom out on the street. Ralston bought their staples in bulk, somewhere on the other side of town. Emma was not, then, one of those women who would have known what her neighbors might have been—or not been—buying for groceries. She did know that a change had come to Lillian; it was a thing Emma could see in her face. And there had been an occasion that left Emma thinking about that other woman for the rest of the day. Lillian left the house to shop, as she always did now, by herself. Emma noticed how nice she looked in the two-piece dress she was wearing, and reflected, as she had done before, on what a slight little thing she was—hardly big enough, it seemed, to manage a house and a family. But Emma saw something else about Lillian, and it shocked her. She saw unhappiness on that other woman's face. Lillian's head was held high, as always; but her whole face had changed. Emma herself was no stranger to pain and worry; and she understood now that she was looking at someone else who knew these things, too.

Ralston came in that same evening with a face full of thunderclouds—his face so tight that his jaw muscles flexed. Business must have been troubling him, Emma assumed—although Ralston's garage doors were wide open. People needed the skills that Ralston had; he was not only a mechanic but a machinist, a decision that went all the way back to Mr. Freeland's hailing him that morning with the stalling truck engine. Ralston had the needed machinery to keep an old vehicle operable. So his dark mood that evening had nothing to do with business—had its origin, rather, in an innocent politeness on Lillian's part. She had asked him to thank his wife for the beans. And Ralston had looked at her so hard and long that his eyes traveled back and forth between the two of hers. Henry was right, Lillian said to herself. Something was definitely wrong with the man.

Supper that evening at the Griffen household was a virtually silent meal. Ralston cleared his throat a bit more frequently than usual and frowned as he ate. When their father was like that, the children disappeared to their rooms after a meal. Later, Emma was moving around in the entrance hallway, rearranging some of the scattered shoes and school things the children had left there. From the living room Ralston rattled his newspaper so sharply that the sound made a snap. In the extreme quiet of the house, the sound was startling.

"I *told* you not to have anything to do with those people!"

Emma thought it best not to answer. She was thinking that next time she'd send over sweet potatoes—sweet potatoes were nourishing. She had been piecing together certain facts since she saw Lillian's face that morning. Emma knew that men were out of work all over town. And Mr. Gray's car was no longer leaving his driveway. She was afraid it had happened to him, too.

Chapter 21

Mary was winning at Parcheesi. And that may have been why Betty Kate decided that they had to have music. They were grouped on the front porch, just in front of the window where the radio stood—or had stood—in a handsome oak case. She let the front door slam behind her and charged into the living room. But Betty Kate stopped abruptly. There was nothing there, in that space. The radio was gone.

"Mama!" She began where she stood, although Lillian was back in the kitchen. Betty Kate continued up the hallway, yelling all the way.

"Where's the music? What happened to my music!" Lillian was trimming apples, this bunch as much soft spot as apple. She didn't turn at first. She didn't look forward to this moment.

"Where'd you put the radio?"

She tried to be casual about it. "It's broken." Some part of Lillian's mind reprimanded her—it wasn't right to tell a lie to a child.

"It wasn't broken this morning." The news broadcast had been on before Henry left—before, without the girls seeing him, he carried the radio outside and put it into the car.

"But where *is* it?" Now Betty Kate was frantic. Something wasn't right. Mary also trailed back to the kitchen. Elizabeth stood just inside the doorway.

"I told you. It's broken."

"It's *not* broken! I want my music!"

"The radio's gone." More severely. Lillian was willing to take the subterfuge just so far.

"Gone? How can it be gone?" Betty Kate was attempting to talk and get up a wail at the same time. She couldn't do both. But the wailing was half-hearted. She didn't believe it about the radio. So she started again.

"Where is my music?"

Anyone could have seen Lillian's mind working visibly on her face, in the effort to come up with a fabrication. Then she gave it up and leveled the straightforward truth at Betty Kate.

"We sold it." Now. It was out and done with.

The answer, which she recognized as the real and final one, had an unusual effect on Betty Kate. It silenced her. She let herself be pulled outside through the back door by Mary, who thought it best to lead Betty Kate all the way around the house, rather than on a path any closer to their mother.

The radio was not the first thing to disappear in this manner—just the first thing that the girls had missed. Lillian forgot not an item of what had been sold, not even the things that no longer counted. There were stacks of packed boxes along the walls of the bedroom. The Grays were doing no more than other families all over Clanton were doing, in the secrecy of their own homes—sorting through their possessions, deciding what could be sold off or pawned. That morning Lillian was sorting her own things. She pulled her drawers out one at a time, kneeling for a while in front of each one, her hands at first working slowly. There were plenty of things she could do away with. She considered herself composed—she didn't realize that her hands and mouth were angry. Certain items, now, she almost tore at. Lillian stood up, to work on the top drawer, which held her underthings, hosiery, and handkerchiefs, all carefully folded and laid in rows. Inside the rows Lillian had tucked an occasional bar of soap, Yardley's

English Lavender. It was a thing her Aunt Nancy had taught her to do. She looked over the rows of delicate, lace-edged handkerchiefs—Lillian had been taught to never be without a "really good" handkerchief. The sight of the handkerchiefs irritated her now, for some reason. She removed them all. She fairly dumped them, her hands no longer methodical but fierce and impatient. But there was one thing. Lillian picked up a tiny red and black speckled box, with a gold snap and hinges, and a satin lining. In it lay a filigree pin, designed a little like a triangle that had been pulled out of shape. Over the filigree lay a sprig of leaves and a flower, these of platinum. In the heart of the flower was a good-sized, beautifully cut diamond. The pin had been given to Lillian by a great aunt, and looking at it, her hand went to her throat. She had the habit of absently touching her pearls. But Lillian's strand of pearls was one of the first things that had been pawned. Lillian removed the filigree pin from its box and fastened it inside the pocket of an old apron, which she then folded tightly and put away with her everyday things.

Now they followed each other in rapid succession, efforts such as these: the separate, fear-driven measures. Lillian already had the Leghorns that Myra and Howard had brought in from the country. The hens lay prolifically, but the family ate few of the eggs—the eggs were bought just about as quickly as they were laid. The girls took to the hens as they would have to a number of identical pets, naming all eighteen of them—there was always dissension over who was who. The only certain identification was Xanthippe, a brooder, a hen who would not willingly part with her eggs. Removing them required the use of a stick. Xanthippe had to be pried.

Lillian had grown used to the discrepant sound of the hens, clucking or flapping around in the yard. For a moment she thought that she heard something else. Something like a faint little knock at the back door. And it was a knock: Ralph, who had begged off school that day with a—possibly imaginary—toothache. The boy held a bag in his arms, so fully loaded that the tips of the sweet potatoes showed over the top. He looked at Lillian for a moment, frowning, trying to remember what to say—Ralph had been given his line before he walked over. And now he'd forgotten it.

"Mama said to tell you—." He looked puzzled. "Mama said—." He looked a second or two at Lillian, then gave up and shrugged his shoulders.

It was the closest to smiling that Lillian had come that morning. "How kind of your mother. Just put them down and wait a moment."

She went back to the scene of her struggle with the boxes and came out with one of the bars of Yardley soap, still wrapped. "Please give this to your mother for me. And tell her how much I appreciate the vegetables."

On his way down the steps, Ralph remembered his line and snapped a finger. "Oh. Mama says—they're more than she knows what to do with!" He looked pleased with himself.

Lillian laughed out loud.

At her kitchen worktable Emma sat looking at the bar of Yardley—it gave her much pleasure just to smell it, then set it down and looked at it again. The soap that Ralston brought home with their household staples was a dark yellow, medicinal-smelling substance, cut into sharp, irregular bars. Emma didn't think she'd ever come across scented soap. And the package was as nice as the soap was—far too pretty to just tear up and throw away. Soft tissue paper, pleated like cloth. On the paper band that held the wrapping together was a picture of a woman and two children, dressed in old-fashioned clothes, somewhere on an old-fashioned street. No, she couldn't destroy the wrapping. And she couldn't think of an occasion important enough for using the soap—she frankly didn't know what to do with it. She put it away in the drawer with her underthings, having no idea that in doing so she was using it for the very purpose Lillian intended.

Emma had seen Henry the morning he left with the radio. And she knew exactly what that family was doing. Of course there were Nazarenes who maintained that a radio shouldn't be owned, in the first place—listening to dance music was a sin. There were some of the church members, Emma thought uncharacteristically, who could make a sin out of just about anything. Now a true sin, she reasoned, would have been knowing that those people's children were hungry—that those two people had to live knowing that, and were themselves hungry—yet do nothing about it. She still remembered the sight of Lillian's face as she walked down the street that certain morning. And since that time, she had seen the look again. Emma remembered it in herself—she would always remember.

And as for Mr. Gray, Emma continued to herself, in some kind of imaginary argument—no matter what anyone said, she knew a perfectly nice man when she came across one. The thing about the liquor: she'd heard it said that some people just couldn't help it. That it was a thing in the blood. Mr. Gray was a man who would have never harmed a living soul—she knew that. And she knew, too, that she was going to help those people in whatever small way that she could.

It was the Leghorns that provided her a way. Now that Lillian had the hens, Emma could go over to buy eggs, like any of the neighbors. She had watched Lillian so long by this time that she had almost gotten over most of her shyness. She felt that she knew the other woman. She would be pleased, she thought, to talk to her.

She stepped up to the back steps and called.

Lillian walked onto the porch, smiling very graciously. "How do you do, Mrs. Griffen?"

Emma, too, smiled. "Do you have a half dozen?"

"I'm sure that I do. If you could wait just a little—," Lillian hesitated. It would mean having to deal with the birds, herself.

Emma read her mind easily—it wasn't quite possible to picture the little woman putting her hand up under a hen. "Chickens can be a nuisance. You can have one of your girls walk them over this afternoon." Then there was a slight frown. "If it could be by around four o'clock, I'd appreciate it."

Lillian assumed that she wanted to bake—when the truth was, of course, that Ralston didn't want to see one of the girls in his yard.

Then Emma paused—this would be the difficult part. "Ma'am, I'd like to pay you with something besides money, if you don't mind."

That was a common request these days. Lillian often bartered for a certain amount of this or that. But the lack of cash money was not Emma's problem. The problem was how to get the help to Lillian, without embarrassing her, making the other woman feel shamed and exposed.

"Of course. What did you have in mind?"

At her side Emma was holding two large jars wrapped in a dishcloth. They were some of her Fordhook limas, put up green. Emma knew that the exchange was by now customary—Ralston too was often paid by barter. At the time of her canning, he'd been paid with a side of cured pork. There was as much ham, almost, in the jars as there were limas. The woman would only have to make bread that evening, Emma thought. She was giving the family a meal. Emma unwrapped the jars.

"I couldn't possibly accept those, Mrs. Griffen."

"I'd take it kindly if you would." The green eyes looked directly into Lillian's. Lillian noticed that the woman had remarkably still, intent eyes.

"Well, one of them at least, then." From Emma.

Now Lillian paused. Maybe the woman did need the eggs instead of the vegetables—which she could see at a glance had large pieces of meat cooked with them. Emma handed a jar up to Lillian, who stood on the porch, feeling awkward.

"I do appreciate it," Emma said, as she backed away. Then she gave Lillian a smile that was almost verbal, set the second jar down quickly on the bottom step, and walked off.

That night, just as Emma imagined, the limas and ham—and Lillian's puffy white biscuits—made up the Grays' meal. Lillian was grateful in a way that all but hurt her. Where her children were concerned, pride could not interfere with what she did.

The farm woman came again—Lillian didn't yet think of her as Emma. And again. Exchanging warm bundles of corn muffins, once a bottle of milk, always substantial and nourishing things, for a handful of eggs that by now Lillian knew she didn't really need. Emma gave half of the eggs away to her friend, Bobbie Bell.

"Please do call me Lillian."

"Lillian." Emma blushed a little. "I'm Emma."

"Won't you come in, Emma?"

"Oh, I couldn't do that. I've got something on the stove."

She always said she had something on the stove.

So they stood out-of-doors. Stood together like two conspirators in something. Stood feeling the flow of confidentiality and goodwill pass between them, as palpable almost as something against the skin of their hands.

Henry found work for a couple of weeks through a contact of Drefus', on a new building start, which was without explanation suddenly stopped. On his second day at the job, the van arrived, and the parlor set, only partly paid for, was repossessed. The van made a number of stops on Water Avenue that afternoon. Panic thumped through the neighborhood like a pulse. Lillian stood for a moment against the living room doorjamb, surveying what was left of it—loose books, a lamp, scattered papers. The room had a stripped, vandalized look, to her eyes. She shut the door on the room. It ceased to be part of the house.

As for Henry, he wondered why she was always so silent when they were alone. Of course there was all the trouble. But he and Lillian had always talked over such things at length. And why was there none of that old sense of humor? Lillian's humor was to Henry's thinking innocent. She had always enjoyed small mischiefs. But shouldn't the two of them at least try to keep these things up, for the children? Again there was a distance between Henry and Lillian, grown far past the point of anything he could tell himself he imagined. Throughout the years of their marriage, it was often Lillian who came to Henry at night. Here she had a code of behavior to abide by, so that this was done with a certain coyness, often playfully. She stroked his back. She tickled a certain spot behind his ears. Sometimes she giggled—it was girlish. She'd been girlish then. Now she was matronly. Henry's worst suspicion was that now she merely tolerated him. He knew Lillian; and he knew that, by her own lights, she would have tried to do what was right and fair. And this he honored. But right and fair was not tenderness or laughter. There was a place, now, where he wasn't allowed. Because she would no longer allow him. He stood outside in the dark.

His sense of shame was like a poison turned loose in his belly. What was happening was the natural result of fault: *his* fault. He had been irresponsible. What he also knew somewhere else in his mind was that not a hammer was flying all over Clanton, at least not one that he could lay hands to. There was no work now, it seemed, that didn't go to a family friend or some distant cousin. In November when the leaves fell, Henry raked leaves for anyone willing to pay for it. Again, he walked the streets, stalked through the neighborhoods, surveying the yards. He was at back doors when cooks arrived in the morning. Once he'd been at a back stoop when a cook arrived with her brother, also carrying a rake, also counting on having the job. Henry and the young man had surprised each other sufficiently to have caused the Negro to forget to drop his eyes. Both of them knew that Henry could have claimed the job, just by being there. The Negro looked quickly at his sister, turning to go. But Henry had left, instead.

It was no longer tolerable to Henry to be in the house with Lillian during the day. Herself without blame. Herself going about the innocent pattern of her days. His eyes strayed often to Lillian's mouth; it was blameless. There was the perfect sameness of it, the little arched upper lip. It was no one other person's mouth, anywhere in the world. Then, unaccountably, he was angry, when he'd never been more, at most, than occasionally annoyed at Lillian. It unsettled him. He had unsettling images. He had a fleeting picture, so fleeting that he didn't have to make himself own it, of the little mouth being struck—anything to destroy that perfect blamelessness of it.

He spent whole days walking. He knew what he needed to do. But he couldn't bring himself to—at least not yet. Until this time, he had avoided the bare, broken-down neighborhoods of East Clanton, with the packed black dirt, the rows of sad shotgun houses, gone soft with rot. But the time had come for some move—Henry knew they couldn't hold on to the house. There was no other choice but East Clanton. When he walked like this, restlessly, for the one purpose of moving, he gravitated always toward the river, the space of still sky and water. There were spots in town where men collected, to talk and to worry; there was the endless killing of time with talk. But Henry avoided the talkers.

Afterward, he thought about the odd job he'd walked away from, the yard of unraked leaves, the small change it would have brought. Something almost too trifling to regret. The afternoon had been bright earlier, but had faded. Now it darkened. Ragged clumps of cloud moved into the place where the sun had been, blotting the light. All the town seemed shabby and spent. Henry darted a glance toward the Bluebird Cafe. But he couldn't be still. There was a plucking in his brain, in his legs and arms. His head was charged and buzzing. When he reached the shadows of the bank, he pulled out the pocket flask he had replaced. He thought at the same time of Lillian. What did she know? What could she understand, she who had been as carefully taken care of as a child? That, at least, he could blame—he could blame her for blaming *him*. Henry was at last realizing that he was up against something he had no power to change. There was nothing that he, Henry, could cause to happen, just by willing or wanting it to happen. It was no longer a question of error. Error he could have undone. He took his liquor in slow, deliberate sips. He stood by himself in the half-dark for some time, propped against a tree trunk. His mind wouldn't go quiet. The resentment wouldn't let go. So he coddled it.

Chapter 22

Henry heard Drefus' footsteps on the porch before the familiar knocking began. Lillian heard the sound, too, from another part of the house. She took herself into her sewing room and closed the door.

"What you say, old man?" Drefus laughed. He stood just outside the front door, dressed in a heavy wool coat and wool hat with earflaps. The night air was fragrant but biting cold. Drefus had pulled on the hat carelessly, and the earflaps, one doubled under, one standing straight out, gave him a comical appearance. The hat and coat were issue of Southern Railroad, but Drefus was no longer employed. He was riding the rails all over the state and into Tennessee and Georgia. And to Henry's mind—he couldn't deny it—the "runs" held an air of adventure, mystery, about them. The lure of strange places. It was true that the other places were sometimes not much to speak of, in terms of distance. But there would have been a difference, Henry suspected, just the same, in the town blocks, streets, and pool halls, the porches where people talked in the dark. And any place would suit Drefus, when the urge to be off again was on him. Drefus entered the front hall more quietly than he would have done usually and glanced toward the living room, to which the door was closed. There was no gleam of light beneath the doorway. Mr. Panichas, the Grays' roomer, was already sleeping, then. The men passed through the dining room, instead. The scent of night lingered in Drefus' clothing and moved with him into the house.

In the kitchen, too, the men had to lower their voices, because of the girls. The Grays used the cooking stove to warm the back rooms. If wood was plentiful, it wasn't exactly convenient to come by. In the afternoons Henry climbed over the fence that separated the Grays' lot from the wooded area that fell to the river. There he had to fight his way through brush and tangles. The ground was treacherous with low places and gullies disguised by the brush. It would have been an easy matter to break a leg or an ankle.

"Want me to lay some sticks in?"

"Nah." Drefus was pulling off his boots and settling into a rocker that was pulled into the kitchen.

"Been to the folks'?"

"No. Came straight here." Drefus stretched and relaxed more comfortably into the chair. When he crossed his legs, the foot of the crossed leg reached almost to the floor. Drefus would become increasingly gaunt-bodied as he aged. He nodded and dropped his chin to his chest, frowning a little. And staring. Henry knew the look—Drefus had something to talk about, and Henry knew what the something would be. It was ground that the brothers had already covered and couldn't agree on, but Drefus had never been one to give up.

Henry hadn't bothered to close the curtains. The night was a dark one. A lamp burned on the table—there was no longer electricity in the house. "Need a wash? I can just—." He moved toward the back door, but Drefus made a negative noise that interrupted him. The city had turned off the water. But each night Henry went outside and lifted the street plate, and with a wrench turned it on again.

"Well, we'll get you set up here, with some blankets. Got to check on the Place"—Henry used the word like a proper noun—"first thing in the morning. Got a trotline out."

Drefus flung his head back and made a mouth. "A trotline?

You got *a* trotline out? We're gonna put trotlines all up and down the river, pal." This was the first that Henry had heard of any such plan, but Drefus had evidently done some thinking. "Need to build us a box"—he referred to a double box for keeping ice. "Figure we can start with the stores down around Five Points and work our way in, from there."

"Umm." Henry assented. It wasn't a bad idea at all.

Drefus went on. "Got to get a hold of those traps of Daddy's. Mink and beaver's going good. Even muskrat."

Along these lines the brothers agreed easily. The more spirited conversation could have started there, which would have invariably grown louder. Drefus had a bottle hidden under the dry bunches of Lillian's hydrangeas, and he walked out to the porch from time to time, to refresh himself, as did Henry. Drefus' long hands dangled over the arms of the chair as he sat. Now he raised one, cutting the air with a palm. Henry knew this gesture—a pronouncement was coming.

"Things are looking bad, Henry. Looking bad. Looks bad just about everywhere you go." He shook his head and made a noise, for emphasis. Then he took another tact. "You know, Henry, I got a mind to see Joe." Joe, who lived in Texas, was the oldest of the Gray brothers; but Henry knew why Drefus was edging the talk toward Texas. Each of them read the mind of the other, and both knew that it was too late at night to start in on the argument. Drefus intended to get Henry out on the rails and away from Clanton, as soon as they could get Lillian and the children settled. And though he knew they'd have to wait, he did permit himself the one comment, made in simple human frustration. "Hell, Henry, there's oranges ready in Texas, right now!" Drefus didn't know himself how realistic the idea was, that he and Henry would be better off following the rails for work, but he didn't dwell overlong on the specifics. He was crazy for movement, the open miles and empty spaces. The gathering places and camps. There the far-fetched talk made him restless, foolhardy.

Henry didn't take the bait. "Got to be up before day, Drefus. Truck's not even loaded." The Gray family no longer had a car. Henry had traded it for an old flatbed truck, just marginally operable.

Henry and Drefus had been gone for hours by the time Lillian and the girls were stirring—the fish would sell as quickly as they were caught. The children were loud from the time they woke up, and Lillian felt sorry for Mr. Panichas, enough that at times she agonized for the man. It wasn't the noise that was the problem—Mr. Panichas was sure to have already been awake. It was the matter of privacy. The man was painfully shy. He didn't board with the Grays, just rented the one room up front. But the fact that there was a single bathroom was problematic for Mr. Panichas. He fairly cringed when he walked, as if drawing himself in might make him less visible. He was small, neat, a little prissy, or so the girls described him. His occupancy at the Grays' was the result of happenstance—and outright deception, on Lillian's part. It had been one morning following service at the First Methodist, that Mr. Panichas stood as he often did with his family, grinning a little uncomfortably, as was his habit. When somebody mentioned that John was looking for a room—his hours at the telephone company had been cut back—Lillian was at her most gracious. She touched Mr. Panichas' arm.

"Well, that's convenient. We have a room. And you could bring in your own things. It's empty."

Mr. Panichas smiled and batted his eyelids, as his sister answered for him. He'd love to have a look at the room.

"We'd be happy to have you look at it—this afternoon, if you'd like to."

No one had thought of taking a roomer. The room Lillian spoke of was not empty, not even swept out or dusted. Henry's old easy chair was still in it, along with piles of boxes, these filled with the contents of drawers. The Grays' dinner had been hurried that Sunday. They'd had to rush around, clearing and cleaning the room, then opening the windows to air it. But when Mr. Panichas arrived, Lillian was the soul of composure. John Panichas returned after dark that evening, bringing with him very little, only a suitcase, a folding army cot and bedding, and an empty bucket, for coal—there was a fireplace in the living room. The girls would have been happy to make a family member of him, but his embarrassment embarrassed them. He suffered; and Lillian, characteristically, suffered along with him. He was relieved, that morning, that the men had already left. The strong masculinity of their presence made him all the more uncomfortable.

But by the time Mr. Panichas made his cringing way down the hallway, Henry and Drefus were already out on the water. They walked Taylor pastureland to the cabin site in daylight so new that they couldn't entirely see where they put their feet. Memory and habit took over for them. They cleared the trotline—each hook was taken—just as the first brightness leaked in above the bank. The surface of the water was a pearly gray. A mist lay across the river, which moved aside as the boat cut through it. The cold air was damp, settling into their clothes like moisture. In the quiet there was the occasional sound of an animal body entering or leaving the water. The line had mostly cat and mullet. There was an eel on one of the hooks. Henry took hold of the flailing, snake-like body and jerked the hook free. There was a time when he would have tossed it back in, but now he dropped it into the washtub, along with the rest of the catch. He wouldn't take money for an eel, but he would give it away. The men drove through the back roads, the cotton roads, where most of the population were Negro sharecroppers; and little more than an hour later, Henry found a taker for the eel.

Once the business of selling the fish was done, Henry and Drefus went through the motions of a morning that they once would have pursued for pleasure, a pattern established for years. They made a quick stop at Orville's general store for crackers and cheese, and large single hooks. Then they made for the woods, for the low spots of water, where even in winter crawdads could be found. The old truck, reliable when settled into gear, crept over rounded clay roads, dry, now, in this season. They drove into low areas where the sun had not yet lined the lakes of branches. They were headed toward the bridge. And it didn't cross the minds of either of them that they had never, as adults, approached the bridge together in an automobile—had not approached it at all. The bridge was part of the landscape of their boyhoods. A place of evil doings. Henry slowed the truck. The water beneath the bridge would have been good for trawling, but neither man had ever considered going into that water. It was said to be used for balling and chaining, a way of backwoodsmen for taking the law onto themselves, as it applied to their darker brethren.

"This place here's not much to my liking."

"Well, mine neither." Drefus sounded put out. "Let's move on." Now he looked down at the water and continued, "What went on, here, Henry—we won't ever know what went on, here. Could have been murder. Could have been nothing at all. Talk." He considered, "We don't know a thing about this world, Henry, you and I. Not a thing." This last with a tone of distinct reprimand. Typically, Drefus made this sort of comment for the purpose of conversational argument. But now he went quiet. Then: "Maybe we ought to've just enlisted." And that was a statement of disgust.

Henry protested. "But you've been to *New Orleans!*" Henry had taken a notion that he wanted to see New Orleans, a place name that for him symbolized all things faraway and exotic. Drefus had talked of the old streets filled with people and music. There were always crowds, he said. There was a wild time called Mardi Gras. There were pale-eyed women who were not really white. Drefus said that New Orleans was like being in another country—that it affected you that way. His dreamy meanderings had affected his brother more than Henry allowed him to know.

"So, what's New Orleans?"

Then, that was the mood Drefus was in. Henry decided to drop the subject.

But Drefus went on, " 'S not even out of the *South*!" Irritably. "They say folks are pretty much the same, everywhere you go. Only, think I'd like to be able to find that out for myself. Women, now, " he began, on another tact.

"Expect they're all about the same everywhere?" This question, coming from Henry, gave both of them a needed laugh.

Drefus' mood began to rally. "You take crawdads. In New Orleans, you know, they eat crawdads? Call 'em crayfish."

"Naw."

"Sure do. The Cajuns down there—they're half French. You know, some of those Creoles don't even speak English." He paused. "With the French, it's worse than crawdads. Say those people eat snails."

"Now, I don't believe a thing like that."

The brothers shook off the mood of contention. Now with their bait and equipment, they returned to the cabin site, which by this time Henry had made into a full working camp: the Place. The morning was at full height, the air bright and thin. They pulled the boat out below the cliff, where it dried in the sun that was strong on the bank. Henry and Drefus forgot their work, then, as a commercial occupation—it had always been sport. And both men loved the high place. On that morning the air had a brittleness that brought to mind things like the smell of leaf fires or the taste of windfall apples. They had a still set up, hidden within the line of trees on the cliff, where they helped themselves, using fruit jars.

The peace of the place didn't make Drefus quiet. It didn't, for that matter, have a quieting effect on Henry. The contention was building again between them. Had they been the sort, it may have been better to just slug it out, Henry thought. While he tacked a hide to the cabin wall, Drefus sat against a tree, for a smoke. No one had raised the idea yet, but the subject was open and ready.

Drefus started—obliquely, he likely imagined. "There's dams, Henry, pipelines, roads. We'd just have to keep the jump on 'em. Money's already there for those things. There'd be pay."

Henry kept up with the hammer, frowning, trying not to be drawn into the argument.

Drefus kept at it. "Look. The work's not here. We got to follow the work, Brud. Work's not gonna follow around after us."

Now Henry did stop, lowered the tacks and the hammer. "I got a family, Drefus, in case you hadn't noticed." When he began again, he just missed his thumb. And by now Henry too was peeved—an annoyance that seemed to grow with each strike of the hammer. Suddenly he flung it down, ripping the skin from the wall. "I've had enough of here for one day." They had scarcely arrived. Dreyfus had been rolling a cigarette, and his look of puzzlement made Henry madder. "Which way you headed?" Abruptly. It wasn't a question, but Henry's way of letting his brother know he was through with him for the day. And coming from him, the words were a fair blast of anger.

Dreyfus got the message. He whistled and raised his hands in mock surrender, one of them wrapped around his jar of shine. It was obviously not a time to fool around with his brother. Each man knew the other's limit of tolerance.

"Now listen here, Dreyfus, I won't leave my family without a roof." He had already won the argument—at least for the time being, but he continued.

Dreyfus looked back at this middle-aged man with spectacles, who had once walked at his shoulder but who now stood him down. "Well then Brud, that's just what we'll do. We'll find them a roof."

And they parted again, Drefus for the home place, where he chafed, paced, against the quiet line of gray woods and spent winter fields. Henry for the gritty streets, which seemed to burn with impatience. Urgency. A fear altogether different from what people knew and took for granted. He'd seen families turned out, a couple, even, right there on Water Avenue, people gathered in front of their homes looking bewildered, their belongings an unsightly heap on the sidewalk. Like any kindly person, Henry averted his eyes. Men who had worked all their lives were on the streets, crisscrossing Clanton, pausing from time to time, not giving up; there would have to be an odd job, somewhere—just have to keep looking. In Henry's line, there was nothing to be had; and there was nothing at all in the way of new construction. For a couple of days, he worked to replace a stock boy who was sick in bed—for a few hours, only, in the evening. He stocked shelves and checked lists and dusted. He had been paid with cash, but would have worked as willingly for groceries. If house payments were provided for—the Grays had made no payments of any sort for months—Henry reasoned that he could at least feed his family. And there was Drefus, now, to help him. Henry had started to fish commercially already, before Drefus came back. For poor man's food—sold his catches of poor man's food, mainly to Negroes, to feed his own family, in return, with poor man's food of another kind. Once, when Myra and Howard brought in a full milk can from the country, Lillian seemed to have lost her reason, had gone, by herself, to the henhouse, then sent the girls down the street, to buy a can of pineapple and a few cents' worth of sugar.

Later, Henry would realize that he had Dreyfus and his contentiousness to thank—it had goaded him into the thing he'd been most avoiding.

Broad Street cut Clanton into east and west. And although the commercial heart of the town had once belonged in East Clanton, now East Clanton was the wrong side. The further east, the further wrong. Henry began to walk. He walked Water Avenue across Broad Street. He walked the blocks of old riverfront buildings. He continued east, past the city landing and toward the railway depot. Then past the cotton compress, where he cut over into the residential section of East Alabama Avenue. Here there were pleasant blocks of clapboard houses, none of them especially large. The yards were shaded, the sidewalks swept. Then the cross streets of little shotguns began—two rooms with a kitchen. First was St. Ann, which he surveyed to begin with. Here the houses stood very close together, but a few of them were painted. There was the occasional small patch of lawn, sometimes fence. On these first streets, the little houses had a settled air, mean though they were. He had hoped to be able to find something on one of those streets, but there was nothing vacant.

Then there was Range Street, which began at the railroad yard. Henry hesitated before he crossed the tracks, frowning—he didn't quite look himself—staring out across the lines of tracks, a block's worth, at least. There was no vegetation on Range Street, a chinaberry tree or two, maybe. The rows of shotgun houses, never painted, were worn to a bleached gray that blackened when it rained. Range was the last cross street in East Clanton, a street running the length of the backside of town. It was the end, could be felt to be the end, of something. There was no real difference to the eye in the houses and rotting privies, in the dirt yards, from any of the colored neighborhoods in Clanton. But there was another kind of difference, and it was this: in their own sections of town, the colored population lived where they always had lived. Neighborhoods were made, bare yards swept clean, plants potted in lard cans and set out on porches, discarded tires or stones whitewashed, for decoration. For here was all of home and safety and caring, just as it had always been, in the only way it was allowed to be. But on Range Street, home and safety stopped. It was a place of more than one kind of poverty.

Henry crossed the railroad yard only part of the way. By then he had seen what he needed to see. On the edge of the yard, where an old line of tracks fanned out and stopped, there was a house that was evidently vacant. Its front windows were boarded, the side windows blank. A gray and rattly thing—it was a shack. It would have to do, at least until they could find something better. Henry saw no children. For him the idea of poverty had always brought to mind the faces of children. He had seen them all his life, in the schoolrooms for scant periods; in the back woods; later, in the mill. Pale faces; little slack mouths. Where had they disappeared to and how had all of them grown up, he sometimes wondered. His own family had been poor in the way that just about everybody else was. But poverty was something different. People didn't like to use that word. They used another word: country. Simmons was country. Simmons would have been one of those children. And now Henry was entering their country, to take his own children, the little girls whom Lillian had raised so carefully by the rules of what was or was not ladylike. Lillian. He had to stop at the idea of Lillian—he had to stop somewhere. He would go through the motions; he would walk through it all without thinking about it, like he'd have had to do with some physical injury or a death in the house. Later, he could think about Lillian.

Henry turned to pick his way back along the tracks. The air was gritty. There was a high wind that he didn't notice. Cloud shadows moved across the rails, a pattern like the rippling of grass. He didn't notice. He had his sights on what he was doing.

Chapter 23

At home on Water Avenue, Betty Kate peered up under the house into a spot below the kitchen. At age eight, she was no longer a towhead. The whitish hair had darkened to amber, its inclination to stand on end at last given way. Though she stared intently, she wasn't looking for anything in particular. Maybe it was a sort of last rite.

"Mary, come here a minute!"

"What is it?"

"The fairy ring."

Mary frowned. All of them were edgy that morning. Mary, too, had been looking for something, she imagined, with a troubling uncertainty as to just what that thing was. They had both outgrown the fairy ring, but Mary joined her. For years it had been a favorite pastime, a small pool of standing water that dripped from the icebox through the floor of the kitchen. When they had owned an icebox, the little pool was permanent, ringed by traces of salt from the water. They had lined it with rocks and planted things there—amazingly, some of them had taken root—made loans of special objects or left permanent offerings for the fairies. There was nothing left to the fairy ring, now, just a little dry hollow in the sandy soil beneath the house. There was nothing to do there, anymore.

There was really nothing to do anywhere that morning. It was a March day, neither warm nor cold, and without sun—clouds, either—a sort of blank, indifferent day. It was the day they were moving. Their Daddy and Uncle Drefus were gone again in the truck, to take a load of things over to the new house. Of course Betty Kate and Mary had wanted to go, but their mother wouldn't let them. All three noticed that she was being funny about the house. And she had that way about her that warned the girls not to cross her. Lillian had spoken to all three of them one night after supper. They were moving into a neighborhood that wasn't nice, she explained. They, the girls, were not going to like it. The move wouldn't be permanent. They would only have to be there until things got better—the phrase was now a household byword. It was a terse little lecture that Lillian gave. The girls could tell when their mother didn't want a lot of questions on a subject, so they didn't ask many.

Lillian and Elizabeth sat on the steps of the back porch. Everyone was waiting. Lillian had insisted on waiting. Henry had already paid the twelve dollar rent on the house on Range Street. But the Grays had said that they would vacate Water Avenue on the fifteenth. And though that date fell on a Saturday, which meant having the girls underfoot, Lillian intended to stay until the very last minute. She wouldn't budge—she knew what the house in East Clanton would be like. She sat with her knees drawn up, Elizabeth leaning against her. The fact was that Lillian and all three girls had fallen into the torpor that follows an emotional scene. There'd been an uproar. It all started with talk of Sue Wilkinson, a friend of Elizabeth's from Sunday school and her authority in all matters. It was her duty as a friend to warn Elizabeth, Sue Wilkinson explained. No nice person lived in East Clanton, and Range Street was the worst street of them all. The houses were just like colored houses, she said, all falling down and unpainted, with rats running around inside. Elizabeth had come first, privately and tearfully, to Lillian with this information. Next, she had turned on her sisters with it, as a best weapon in an argument. The younger ones never paused to question the veracity of what Elizabeth told them. Betty Kate started to wail, and Mary had gone off somewhere by herself. All three of them remembered the terse little lecture, and sudden misery inflamed young tempers.

"Sister's been telling things." Some final volley had provoked Betty Kate into coming to Lillian.

"What kind of things?"

"That we're gonna live in a house for colored people."

"Oh, Elizabeth." Lillian inclined her head, sighing.

"Sue said—."

"You've told me all about what Sue said."

There were other families that had moved; pupils had dropped out of school without explanation. But the girls didn't know anyone who had moved to Range Street. The Grays' final decision to move had not been especially timely.

"But Sue—."

"I've heard all I want to hear about Sue."

Elizabeth glowered at her mother. Lillian was still seated on the back steps—she'd stopped using the front porch now, for some time. There was no porch furniture left, not even the swing. Elizabeth, usually defiant to the last in an argument, just sort of for once wilted. She sat down again beside Lillian and leaned against her. It was a terrible day. Nothing was right. Even arguments didn't come out on her side, like they usually did.

While Lillian and the girls bided their time on the back steps, two goodly souls, Emma and her friend Bobbie Bell, were fretting and scheming next door. They had discussed the Grays at length—and with true feeling, neither of them being artful or spiteful enough for smugness or self-satisfaction.

What to do about it now, the sight of a family having to leave their home like that, with nothing but a few sticks and a crate of hens. They had to do something. But what? They worried and frowned. They reached agreements and discarded them, unsure of themselves—it was as close as the two friends would ever come to an outright spat.

Well, whatever it was, it couldn't be made to look like charity. It would have to be more like a gift. A housewarming gift.

The two women looked at each other meaningfully, at the image those words called up. They didn't know if the Grays *had* a house to go to. There was additional discussion.

What the family needed was staples.

But that would never do. Staples would for sure look like charity.

Then fancy goods of some sort, such as Emma might happen to have in the pantry, although it was not a time for the Griffens—for anyone—of anything fancy.

The jars of new onions might pass. The chow-chow and jam and such.

Yes. That would be more the thing. And of course something baked.

But there was no time to do any baking.

Emma had made a custard earlier that morning. But a custard would be messy. Well, not if they left it in the pan. Which they decided to do, wrapping the warm pie in a dish cloth.

It was obvious to both of the women that they didn't have much time. They had seen the loaded truck leaving. Emma picked up a wicker basket, and they walked into the pantry closet together, loading. Bobbie selected the things they'd agreed on, after all the deliberations. Emma nestled more commonplace items in between. Bobbie looked at her friend a little quizzically; but

Emma looked back with a face that clearly warned Bobbie not to utter so much as a word.

They put what was more in the way of fancy goods on the top layer of the basket, then added the pie. The wicker basket was no more than medium-sized. But loaded as it was with canned items, it made an unwieldy load—it was about as much, to tell the truth, as the two women could manage between them, without spilling it. On Bobbie's side the wicker rim had a sharp protruding stick, which tore a hole in her cotton stocking. Well, never mind that, now. They started out the back door and across the yard together, waddling slightly with their load.

All five of the Griffen children were at home that morning—and all five aware of some unusual activity in the kitchen. By the time Emma and Bobbie were making their cumbersome way across the yard, curiosity had drawn Nettie and the boys from their various corners. They trailed along quietly behind the women, knowing somehow that it was not the moment to ask any questions. Knowing, too, that the rules were abruptly broken: they could go into that other family's yard, because their mother was going. They could even talk to those little girls, they suspected, with their mother standing right there.

The two women arrived at the porch, puffing and agitated. Emma couldn't disguise her face—she looked stricken. She attempted to pull her mouth into what might pass for a smile. "Just a bit of a housewarming." She knew it didn't sound right. But she had to say something.

"Oh, how thoughtful. How very—." Lillian too knew that her mouth wasn't working right. She was afraid she would lose control. She saw the hole in that other woman's stocking and knew exactly how it had happened. Emma and Lillian's eyes held for some seconds, saying everything that the little spoken parodies left out.

"You've been so kind," Lillian said directly to Emma—the sum total words she could manage.

It took some effort even on Buddy's and Ralph's part to get the basket into the kitchen and its contents unloaded. Relieved, now, that the undertaking had been accomplished, the group of them stood in the yard next to the porch. Lillian had come back outside. She knew she should come up with some token of conversation, but for the moment she was at an unusual loss. The effort, mercifully, was spared her. The novelty of the situation made the children voluble—all of them were suddenly talkative. Emma and Bobbie stood by, smiling a little unnaturally.

"What's *that?*" This was from Ned, pointing to the flying jinny, which had long ago lost its neighborhood popularity.

"I'll show you!" Betty Kate jumped up off the steps.

"Not now." Emma spoke very quietly to her group; but all obeyed at once—it was one of those rare times when obedience was a reflex action.

The hens were making an irritable racket, all eighteen of them packed into a slated crate, like cotton balls inside a jar.

At a brief lull in the general conversation, Betty Kate claimed the audience for herself. "Xanthippe won't get off her nest," she volunteered, for some reason, to Emma.

"Now, which one would be Zantippy?" Emma asked.

"She's right there."

"No, she's not. She's right *there!*"

Lillian stepped back into the kitchen and cried.

They heard the rattling of the truck before it pulled into the driveway. Drefus entered the back yard walking on his hands—it never failed to produce gales of laughter from the girls. But Henry wasn't quite up to the mood of it that morning, gloomy in a way that was unlike him. The whole burden of relieving the shock of the move for the children had fallen to Drefus, who went out of his way. He had hitched into town early, bringing the makings for a kite, which would take the girls' minds off of things that afternoon. Drefus routinely tormented his nieces, if he happened by early enough to catch them sleeping. He sometimes sang to them. At other times he quoted poetry. It was always the same poem, the one about "gather ye rosebuds"—Drefus thought the poem was funny. Henry suspected that it might have been the one thing his brother remembered from school.

The shenanigans had yet to fail, so far; and when Drefus approached the porch on his hands, all three girls, to his great relief, were instantly hilarious, Lillian's face still and sad. What she didn't know was how much effort Henry and Drefus had already put into the house. It was a typical shotgun, two front rooms with a kitchen at the back, a simple rectangle. The men began by prying the planks loose from the front windows, surprised that someone else hadn't already pulled them off for firewood. The windows were small. The house was murky when they walked into it. There was a mildewy, rotted sort of smell in the rooms. The men's footsteps shook the rickety floorboards, habitation itself being the one fabric that had held the place together. There was nothing of any value in the two front rooms, just a scattering of empty cans and a filthy fireplace. The kitchen had a small cook stove, an old Avondale, heavily spattered with grease. The surfaces of the house were furry with a dampish black dust. They were not going to be able to get much furniture into the house, but, then, the Grays no longer had much furniture.

"Don't see why people would go off and leave a place unfit for the next person to live in." They stood just inside the doorway.

"We'll get it fit, pal, before we bring Lillian into it. Fit as we can make it." Dreyfus snorted and brought out a flask.

The liquor didn't slow down either man. They cleared and scrubbed down the rooms, the stove and kitchen, using brushes and Octagon soap, until the boards were soaked and softened—both men's hands were red through the following day. The yard had more trash, not a scrap of it usable, and a foul privy, which Henry also scrubbed down and filled with ash from the fireplace and stove. It was the most, then, that they could do.

And there was nothing to do now but put together the last, odd load and be on their way. Drefus was making a big to-do with the girls, provoking the Leghorns. Henry thought that Drefus was overdoing it a little with the hens; at the same time he was grateful. All of them had overdone it, when the crate came ajar and some of the Leghorns got loose. Betty Kate was holding the wildly squirming kitten, a little white, fluffy thing that a neighbor had given them as a going-away present. With the chase after the hens, everybody was laughing. They all laughed too hard and too long.

The quiet that followed was awful. The wild laughter had tripped over into other emotions. The silence continued as the truck moved out the east end of Water Avenue past weedy warehouse lots, then turned at the last street, across the span of railroad yard. From that distance, the house was a gray, odd-looking object, a box. As they pulled up beside it, not Elizabeth or Mary or Betty Kate—no one said a word. And at this juncture the family was denied their privacy. On the front porch of the next house, a woman leaned against the wall near her door. Her body was plank-like under the cotton dress and skimpy sweater. She held a stick in her mouth, slowly moving a ball of snuff along her lip. She stared in that silent way that country people stared, fairly aggressive with curiosity. Her eyes fastened on Lillian. Henry attempted to stare the woman down, but she was paying no attention to

Henry. Then Henry forgot her—he, too, focused on Lillian. Now everything changed. The resentment that he'd secretly nursed against Lillian dissolved. He took her elbow in one hand, as she stepped down from the truck, closing the door behind her clumsily with the other, not letting go of her, not taking his eyes off her face. He moved like an awkward man courting. Lillian didn't seem to be aware of Henry or of the woman—of the house itself, much, for that matter.

Drefus took the girls off—Henry never knew what he and the girls did that afternoon. He knew only that he wanted to be with Lillian—to make things up to her in some little way, though he knew it wasn't possible. He'd never seen her so silent. Moving around trance-like, in motion from the minute she walked through the door. Keeping Lillian in sight, he pushed beds and chests of drawers into place—there was little enough that needed arranging. Then he stood inside the second room and watched her, quiet and orderly about the work of unloading boxes. Lillian seemed to have made up her mind to go through this ordeal without flinching, and Henry admired her. He had always admired her. And now he felt like telling Lillian that he had noticed—that he had always noticed—all the little things, the little things about her that were kind, that were touching. But he said none of that.

He said instead, "Tell me what it is I ought to be doing," as he stepped inside the kitchen. "You can't do any of this—you don't know where anything goes."

So Henry sat. Lillian was busy now around the stove. She stopped and looked down at him. "We're not the only people this is happening to." She was surprisingly calm—it was obvious to Henry that she was making an effort to comfort him. This was unanticipated—the behavior threw him off. He dropped his elbows onto his knees with his hands in front of him. They felt clumsy to him, all of a sudden, heavy and useless.

"I didn't do anything right."

"No." Lillian was moving. "You didn't manage things well. But there are people who have, and it didn't make that much difference, in the long run." She continued with what she was doing.

Lillian's hair had grown out again. She'd done it up that morning in a bun, and a spirally piece had come loose along her face. She wore an old dress that Henry was familiar with, once a fairly smart street dress, one that the hem had been shortened on, then let down again so soon that there was scarcely a line. The fashion fuss had been a lot of silliness, after all, Lillian decided.

At this unlikely moment, with all his sense of shame and clumsiness, Henry wanted his wife. He wanted to say a lot of fond, foolish things to flatter and delight her, to make her feel pleased with herself. To stroke and comfort her, hear her laughing. But with things as they were, he said nothing. The disgrace of it silenced him. He watched Lillian's hands touching things—he'd always liked watching her hands. He saw her lay an object aside, a lemon, slightly shriveled. Lillian glanced at him.

"It was a present from Myra."

Henry looked puzzled.

"For Elizabeth's hair."

Henry nodded. He knew that lemon juice had something to do with hair.

"Jitterbug?"

Lillian stopped. He had asked a question with that word. But he didn't know what the question was. And if there was an answer, neither of them knew that, either.

Henry left the house with a couple of biscuits in his hand and several more in his pocket. The biscuits were puffy, low on shortening, and they were left over from the night before. Lillian would be just getting up to wake the girls, Henry thought, as he walked across the yard. The traps attached to his belt jangled as he walked, circular metal jaws connected to a chain. He was headed toward the river from the east side of town, and as he crossed the span of tracks, the morning light spread palely over the neighborhood, making the roof shapes steely, half-real. Henry didn't look backward toward the street—he never did that—but ahead, in the direction of morning. The neighborhood stopped, for Henry, at the fan of tracks. Beyond that point, his surroundings became routine workday surroundings. There was a section of colored houses between the house and Mulberry Creek. Once there at the creek, the river and woods were easily accessible. They'd tied a boat there, he and Drefus; and while Henry worked the wooded bottom land east of Clanton, Drefus was doing the same thing near Orville. The truck, which was parked over near the stockyards, Henry used as little as possible, in order to save gasoline—used it, in fact, for the one purpose of taking his catches to market. To get to the creek, he'd have to cross the fields behind the slaughterhouse, fields deep with winter sedge grass, which was soaked in the mornings. The grass swished against him, drenching him to the knees. As Henry walked, he kept his mind on what he was doing—it didn't do to dwell too much ahead these days. He had more than a dozen trotlines out, as well as baskets made from willow wood and netting. From the river and woods, he could feed his family.

As the morning brightened his senses were pleasured in little ways. Spring was beginning out of that dead March. There was the smell of soil and new growing things, little slivers of new green here and there. Henry thought of his daughters. The girls had picked up and gone to their new school the very morning following the move, as though no great event had taken place in their lives. Lillian was being firm with the family. She wouldn't allow the girls to complain. She wouldn't allow them to associate with the neighborhood children, unless this or that child had been personally introduced to her. She'd permitted a single question— it came from Mary. Permitted it, possibly, because the question was so straightforward. They were at the kitchen table. They were quiet with their biscuits.

"How long are we going to have to live here?" So quietly. The whole space of the room squeezed in, to listen.

"I don't know the answer to that."

Betty Kate tried to steal an opportunity. "We're poor now, aren't we?"

This question Lillian ignored, and after a few moments, Mary offered Betty Kate a single syllable, which wasn't sufficiently gratifying. So Betty Kate talked to herself, "Yeah. We're poor, now. We're real poor."

Only one thing about the house was unexpectedly fortunate: being at the edge of the yards. A railroad yard wasn't a neighborhood—across the rail yard there were no curious eyes. Everyone came and went from the back side of the house, next to the yards. And at the back of the house was a chinaberry tree—a rare enough thing on the street—which screened the two adjacent back porches. Kudzu, mile-a-minute vine, grew along the chicken wire fence and crept up the trunk of the chinaberry. These were little details that were critical. Lillian clung to the privacy of that corner, never thinking of introducing herself to the neighbors. This was not an ordinary situation; the ordinary rules did not apply.

Everybody ate biscuits in the morning, cooked in a Dutch oven, and carried off more biscuits for midday. The sight of the white, puffy biscuits, dark on the bottom, became distasteful to Lillian. She had little appetite for them. She had never had much appetite for fish, less, even, for the gamey, tight-textured meat of squirrel—one of which two the family ate now at each nightly meal. Lillian's constant battle was with the stove, which was small and choked down quickly with ash. She emptied the ash bucket into the privy, the spot from which she was most likely to catch sight of a neighbor. Lillian had been raised with a certain idea of herself; and if it had been in her nature to nurse her wounds, the idea would have been bitterly amusing to her, now. She was a lady: the idea that she was a lady. The granddaughter of an Urquhart and an Easley. Gentle, ladylike admonitions had nudged Lillian and her sisters this way all of their lives; they took it for granted. When they were scolded, when behavior of any puzzling sort was urged on them, the explanation was always the same: the behavior was, or was not, ladylike. That was the end of the matter. It had been decades—long before Lillian's childhood—since the McClintons had owned land or assets, to speak of. But the daughters were admonished, exhorted, daily and constantly, to remember above all that they were ladies. It was the credo of their girlhood.

Chapter 24

*R*iding the rails. Fragments came back to Henry, pieces of memory that didn't come together whole. Night. He seemed mostly to remember night. Maybe they slept during the daytime, between points. The whole thing seemed at times like something Henry had dreamed. He and Drefus did a lot of drinking—they drank just about all of the time. Henry let himself go—into the drink, into the dark, where he troubled and dreamed.

They waited no more than a block off Broad Street, in the heart of the colored section. The lines of rails gleamed faintly. Across the rails came the sound of dance music, pleasing noises of a colored honkytonk. It seemed to Henry that he always remembered it there, a funny-looking, two-story building with a top porch, all going lopsided, like it was about to slide over. There was the odor of hot grease in the air—fish frying. There were the yellow rectangles of light, then the train, which blotted out the light shapes, and which threw off a bitter, metallic odor. Cold wind rushed against Henry's face. Then a squeal; the cars began to slow. Drefus said that a boxcar or two would be left empty. They would sleep until Birmingham. There were others, now, silently walking out from between buildings or dark niches. Henry thought it was risky being so close to Broad, but Drefus said there'd be nobody watching—Drefus, who was by that time spectacularly drunk. They'd been waiting for close to two hours, and this was a cold January. Cold, with sharp, bright chunks and pinpoints of stars. It was Henry's malt brew that they drank. No use to leave it behind at the house.

*Hours—it had been just short hours ago that they'd all been to-
gether in that little shotgun kitchen, watching the girls' white cat,
Snowball, dancing around in paper boots. They laughed then, all of
them, like there would be no other moment in the world but that one
right then. A kitten skipping around with tissue paper tied to its feet.
Snowball, enticed by the odor of the malt, had drunk a couple of laps
before it jerked its head back and made a sneezing sound, a disgusted
little sniff. Then it slept. The boots, oddly enough, were Lillian's idea.
There was no paper. But Mama's hatbox! The girls begged for a little
paper from Lillian's hatbox.*

*The other figures moved farther out, stealthily, with the caution of
night creatures, until the cars slowed.*

"Now!"

*They were running. The cold bars were a shock to Henry's hands.
A whip-like feeling, hot, passed through his body, a signal of danger—
Henry didn't know that he'd been afraid. There were others already
there. Inside the enclosure of the car, the cold air seemed damp from
the exhalation of bodies. A weak starlight fell just inside the doors.*

*Drefus slept with nothing under his head. Henry watched his
head moving rhythmically against the metal wall. He'd done a lot of
singing that day, Drefus had. He'd waked the girls early with "Tiptoe
Through the Tulips." But he didn't pull back the bed covers that
morning, like he sometimes did, to tease them.*

*They had to take in the lines and haul up the baskets. The two
little ones wanted to go along—Elizabeth had walked into town
with Lillian. The girls were bundled; it looked like they had all their
clothes on under their overalls, then sweaters on top, and matching
caps, little earflaps and strings. The wool was worn and nubby, not
new. Henry hadn't seen the sweaters or caps before, didn't know where
they'd come from. Betty Kate's nose was red from a cold.*

*Drefus had overdone it again, making a to-do about every little
thing. They'd made dough balls with flour and lard and soap, so the*

girls could play at pole fishing while the two men worked. They hid the boat, then walked back over ground soft with dry grass, winter-bleached, wheat-colored. Underneath the soft matting was water. Cold—it soaked quickly into their shoes.

Drefus slept through Maplesville, directly across from the open doors, through all the halting and clanking of the train stop. Now there were more of them packed inside. The dark made everybody silent. The sound of the stick made everybody draw back from the doors. But the uniformed agent walked looking at the ground. Drefus was right—the man didn't care. He hit the night stick against the cars, so that anybody would know he was coming. He didn't look inside the open doors to the boxcar. He didn't, even, walk back as far as the coal cars, where figures moved like moon shadows.

Henry didn't think of sleep. He concentrated on the trail of the warm liquid that moved directly to his stomach and then dissolved there, making his legs and arms feel comfortable and loose. Must have been he was the only one that felt much like talking. The two boys beside him looked scared and self-conscious—they were young ones, Henry thought. They stood between Henry and the open door. He remembered being the age of those boys.

"Where you boys going?" The noise of the wheels made his question private. The young one—taller, but Henry thought he looked younger—wouldn't talk. Henry could see his eyes, very round, beneath the brim of the cap. The stocky one didn't seem to mind talking, to answer a question.

"We got folks up above Birmingham."

Henry didn't think before he brought out the packet of biscuits, which had grown gummy and tough. The stocky boy shook his head. Henry replaced the biscuits.

"Near Birmingham, huh?" Henry offered him the bottle, and the stocky one drank. The tall one just looked nervous. Henry saw the tilted peak of his nose, which looked a little girlish. All three of them

stood, swaying with the rhythm of the car. They could have just as well sat.

"Yep." Stocky swallowed and breathed out an explosion. "Aim to make a new start, we do."

A new start. When their lives had not even begun. A new start, in that poor, pine waste above Birmingham.

The tall one moved his head impatiently, like he wished his buddy would shut up. Henry had the sudden suspicion that the tall one was a girl. He imagined Lillian then, back at the house, at some little chore. She and Elizabeth would be in the kitchen by themselves, the other two on their beds, reading most likely. Lillian's eyes would not be on what she was doing, but looking through it—off somewhere, like a person listening to something.

A new start. Henry considered it. In that cold stretch of night, there was no one new thing in the world. Just something old and unseeing, like the dark, itself.

He decided to sleep.

Chapter 25

In the heart of town, Mrs. Hooper parked her Buick at one of the places marked for hospital staff, although the parking area was almost vacant. The Vaughn Memorial had been steadily reducing staff since '31. Sally's workday was officially over; and at that time of afternoon, about five-thirty, she could get down the basement steps below the back entrance to the huge hospital building without being delayed by anyone. Mrs. Hooper was one of two remaining public health nurses, herself assigned to work with the whites; a Mrs. Vinson worked with the colored. The dusk was already thick. If Sally had been inside with the lights on, the ground level windows would have been rectangles of solid night. Her cook was prompt with dinner, but dinner could wait the ten or so minutes required for Mrs. Hooper to get some idea of the day's donations. She opened the door to a certain empty, basement room—empty of anything but cardboard boxes and scattered, loose heaps of clothing. The entire room smelled like the dampish contents of a laundry hamper—that and aging material, a slight hint of decay. Tomorrow morning, early, she would have to sort through the clothing. For now she wanted only a quick tally. Sally knelt. Her hand touched something so soft, it was almost like touching liquid. Angora. Mrs. Hooper had put her hand on an angora sweater. She stood up with it, now. She was a tall woman, and the weight she had put on at middle age finally relieved what had always been Sally Rawls Hooper's gawkiness. She paused beneath the overhead light long enough to examine the sweater. Perfect condition. A little soiled at the sleeves. A pale yellow, angora pullover. It would be beautiful on Elizabeth Gray. Then she noticed the spot, barbecue sauce, ketchup, or something. A little vinegar and water would take care of that. Her long hands were folding the sweater, even before she raised the question of whether or not Lillian may have vinegar in the house. She had to stop this, she told herself, half dropping the sweater, then just as hurriedly refolding it. Her work was all the time with her, now. Before the Depression, Sally had worked three days a week. Now she worked full-time, overtime, for the same pay. And whereas before, her tasks had been well defined, now she was asked to do—and did—just about anything that needed doing. Distributing food items and used clothing was the most pressing of her job duties. Sally Hooper had never seen need, close up—certainly less, seen hunger. And she was troubled, enough so that it was affecting her sleep. Mr. Hooper now complained that Mrs. Hooper talked in her sleep almost nightly; and for the first time in their married life, Mrs. Hooper had become aware of how loudly her husband snored.

Well, Lillian would have the sweater for Elizabeth, and she, Mrs. Hooper, would remove the stain. She tucked the folded sweater under her arm, pulled the chain on the overhead light so hard that it swung, and left the room. She would see Lillian at church on Sunday morning. Mrs. Hooper wondered, as she walked back out to her car, what it was about Lillian Gray that made her feel this protectiveness. She wasn't aware that a number of others felt the same way. Lillian's landlord, Mr. Minter, was also a member of the congregation, but he had never before this time rented to anybody who belonged to the church—his properties were not of that sort. The situation with Lillian Gray embarrassed him acutely. And what was more embarrassing was that Lillian had several times defaulted on the rent. Mr. Minter ignored the missed payments, dismissed them as a business loss—he didn't know what else to do. He didn't send his rent collector over to Range Street to see Lillian. He called on her, himself. Lillian received him with a combination of cordiality and gratitude. Aside from the missed rent payments, she was just managing to get by. There were the milk and vegetables that Howard and Myra brought in from the country. There was the occasional money order from her mother, in Mobile. Henry converted his haphazard pay into money orders and promptly sent it home. Lillian didn't know that the amounts she received were the whole of Henry's wages—it was Drefus' money that fed the two men. The first money orders from Henry arrived with no message. Then Henry got the idea of writing on the inside of the envelopes, which he purchased at the post office. Right away Lillian noticed the heavy impression of pencil marks from the underside. The messages were brief. "On to Los Fresnos. The weather is good." "Not such a good crop here. Too many pickers."

Lillian spoke of her circumstances very naturally—she was one of those people who could have made just about anything into polite conversation. Henry was, as Lillian put it, traveling for work. Drefus had gone over the plan with her in detail, to make it sound convincing. There were the citrus and strawberry crops in South Texas first, then the early spring radishes, carrots, onions—Lillian would not have used the term, "picking." Then they might move on to the oil fields; to the pipeline camps. There was always, Drefus insisted, work to be had on road projects, sewers, dams. They'd follow the work, wherever it took them.

Of the four at home, only Lillian and Elizabeth owned presentable church clothes; and only Lillian and Elizabeth went regularly to church. Elizabeth had become Lillian's appendage, a smiling, polite little appendage. People looked at Elizabeth and nodded to themselves in approval. Elizabeth felt the interest, but not the approval.

"We can't keep going to church each Sunday morning, dressed in the same old clothes!" Elizabeth cried easily these days.

Lillian was patient. "It's perfectly acceptable to wear the same outfit, if the outfit is suitable. We're not the only ones, Elizabeth, wearing the same clothes."

But it was different. Other people still lived in real houses. Other people didn't walk from blocks and blocks away, to get to church. Elizabeth had heard the words "perfectly acceptable" until she was sick and tired of them. And this thing, the Depression—that word she heard constantly. It was supposed to explain everything that was embarrassing, or wrong. And everything was wrong.

Lillian went by herself on a Saturday morning, to get the flour. It was the Red Cross that acted first, using the local school buildings. Lillian walked the few blocks to Francis Thomas School and stood in line with the others. There was a filmy sunshine that morning, but it was cold. No one in the line made conversation; they stood and shuffled. An empty classroom had been set up as a distribution office for the commodities, as they were called: meal and oleomargarine in a block, that had to be mixed with coloring; dress material; the lace-up oxfords in cheap, papery-looking leather that were so stiff and uncomfortable. Mary and Betty Kate hated the shoes, but many of the students at Francis Thomas wore them, attempting at first to hide them, by propping their feet on their tips, then forgetting about them as the stiffness gave way. Lillian went back, alone, each time, for the commodities. For the clothes she crossed Clanton to the Vaughn Memorial—alone, when the girls were at school. She walked down Alabama Avenue toward Water—not remembering. Not allowing herself to remember. When she took the group of them to Bloch Park, they purposely walked some blocks north of the old neighborhood.

The worst problem was clothes for Elizabeth. The clothes that the younger girls wore were donated from Byrd School or Dallas Academy—Mary or Betty Kate didn't have to worry about running into the previous owners. But in junior high, Elizabeth did. She refused to wear the donated clothing. Lillian nudged her along, a little at a time. A simple white blouse. Anybody could own a simple white blouse—nobody in the world would ever recognize it. Elizabeth's clothes became conspicuous, if anything, for their lack of conspicuousness.

"Now tie this in a bow under your collar." A dangly, bright plaid ribbon. Lillian made herself smile. She coaxed. "Go on. The first thing you know, all the other girls will be doing it. Be proud of yourself, Elizabeth. Be a lady." Lillian rearranged the bow that Elizabeth had made, drawing out the ends of the ribbon. For a while in Elizabeth's class, ribbons tied under the collar became popular among the girls.

The February days were gray, now, and chilly. It wasn't that it rained continuously, as much as that it seemed always about to rain. Lillian and the girls had made a habit of walking all the way across town to spend the day at Bloch Park. They stopped first at the library, where they exchanged stacks of books for different ones. They carried stacks of books; they carried bundles of biscuits. At the park the girls did all the running around that they weren't allowed to do at home. But with the weather chilly and wet, all of them were cooped up. The girls became omnivorous bookworms, so much that Lillian had to forbid books at the table during meals. Mealtimes were, to say the least, not happy times— were the worst reminders. That evening the Grays had the one dish, dried black-eyed peas cooked with a piece of pork. There were always the white, puffy biscuits.

Elizabeth walked into the kitchen with a book under her arm, but Lillian stopped her with a look.

"Put the book away, before you sit down." Elizabeth wouldn't quite give up.

"Sister's got a test." Mary interceded for her. The book was *A Tale of Two Cities*.

"That makes no difference. No books are allowed at the table."

Elizabeth slipped the book into her lap. She'd read it a couple of years ago, anyway; but she reviewed it in her head as she ate, not paying much attention to her plate—black-eyed peas didn't require much attention. She pushed a biscuit into her pea gravy and remembered something. "The poor people in Paris mopped up the wine spilled on the cobblestones with rags and handkerchiefs. Then they squeezed it out into their mouths."

Betty Kate perceived this to be an interesting tidbit.

"What's a cobblestone?"

"In France the streets are paved with round stones instead of brick." Lillian passed a plate with the three remaining biscuits.

"Oh. *Oh!* You mean they put something off the street into their mouths?"

"They were starving," Mary informed her, importantly.

"Well, I wouldn't put something right off the street into my mouth."

Betty Kate was prattling, and nobody was paying attention. Mary had eaten her last biscuit; now she idly pushed her finger around in the trail of pea gravy left on the plate. She licked the finger and returned it to the gravy. Mary became aware that Lillian was watching her—although Lillian said nothing. Their eyes met. Both pairs of eyes were quickly withdrawn, then trailed back to each other, bouncing away again.

Not a word was spoken; but both of them heard it. *A lady always leaves something on her plate.*

Mrs. Hooper's first visit to Lillian was a little awkward for the two women. Sally Hooper argued with herself about whether or not to go by Lillian's, at all. But Lillian was just minutes away from Francis Thomas. And there were weevils in the beans. It was another embarrassment, in a situation that was already embarrassing—she'd have to warn Lillian personally about the beans. But then Lillian had laughed about it, making a little brushing motion with her hand. She should have counted all along, Mrs. Hooper told herself, on Lillian's way of easing a situation; and afterward she was glad she decided to call. Lillian came to look forward to the occasional visits that followed—they were never long visits. When the weather was mild, the women sat outside on the front porch. Once Sally had seen and entered the house, Lillian put her shame about it aside.

On a May afternoon, Lillian and Mrs. Hooper sat on the porch with their tea. Lillian could offer her friend tea that afternoon. She could even offer milk and sugar—the few tea bags and the little handmade packet of sugar having been brought in with the milk, on Howard's farm wagon. Sally looked like she needed the tea. Lillian noticed that there were pink rings under her eyes. Lillian admired the work Sally Hooper did and had told her so, on more than one occasion. The idea surprised her—that it was work that she, herself, would have liked to do. It gave Lillian pleasure to nurse a sick person, although members of her own family were seldom sick—Henry never. Before all the changes, Lillian routinely dosed her girls with castor oil, quinine, and sulphur mixed in blackstrap molasses. With more display than was necessary, she nursed them through the common childhood illnesses. Lillian and Mrs. Hooper sometimes talked of nursing.

Later, Henry told himself that he should have stopped when he saw the automobile in front of the house, the bulk of which blocked his view of Lillian and Mrs. Hooper. Where the lines of rails fanned out and crossed beside the house, old freight cars had been standing for years—now Henry doubted that they were empty. He and Drefus had jumped off on Water Avenue, and Drefus had gone right off to Strayer's, where he was given a cot on the back porch. Henry stopped long enough to walk up Washington Street to a variety store patronized by colored, to buy three of what the girls called balloon boxes, boxes of wrapped taffy with a prize inside, almost always a balloon. These he carried rolled up in the bundle of his coat. He had only small change left in his pockets. As he walked, he was aware of the grit in his shoes. It was unusual weather for May, too dry. Beyond the street, where the fields began, the green of the trees had darkened to the leaves of full summer. The afternoon was fading. It would be about suppertime, Henry supposed. He didn't feel especially hungry, but he hadn't slept much, to speak of. Maybe that was why he didn't stop to think about what he was doing.

Mrs. Hooper would have been gone a matter of minutes later, if Henry had waited. Already she and Lillian were standing when Henry walked into the yard. Henry knew he was filthy, his clothes stiff with sweat and grime. In these same clothes, he'd also been filthy with drink—sick with it, even. Henry hadn't drunk alcohol for a matter of hours, but his breath threw off the stale odor of liquor. Neither of the men had shaved for months—there was no point and little opportunity. Henry's beard, not a neat one, grew out in dirty-looking streaks. He was a sight that a person would want to avoid, but at that moment there was no avoiding him. The women stopped their talk and stared. Lillian's face didn't change. She may have meant to greet Henry, may even have thought that she did. She turned to Mrs. Hooper.

"Mrs. Hooper, this is my husband, Henry."

Sally Hooper had little experience with socially awkward situations. And she had no natural flair. It was Henry who stepped forward and offered his hand.

"Pleased."

Sally Hooper didn't realize that she failed to say anything at all. Lillian's face was scorching.

Betty Kate and Mary burst through the door. "It's Daddy. Mary, it's Daddy!" Mrs. Hooper made her leave during the commotion.

"Balloon boxes! Get Sister."

Henry's and Lillian's eyes met over the heads of the girls. Henry was laughing. It was like him to laugh. Mortified though she was, already Lillian was telling herself that it could have been worse— boys from school now came by fairly often, to see Elizabeth. Lillian walked in behind Henry, the girls, and their racket.

"Everybody okay?" Henry turned toward her.

"All okay."

"Well, this one doesn't look okay." Henry laughed again and held out his arm for Elizabeth.

"I have final exams tomorrow." Elizabeth sniffed a little. Something was not okay, but it had nothing to do with exams. Elizabeth had held it in for weeks, but it had come out just a few hours earlier: she had loaned Lillian's carefully wrapped, cut hair to Sue Wilkinson, and Sue Wilkinson had lost it. Elizabeth quarreled bitterly with her friend, but it was useless; the beautiful hair was gone. It was an incident for once so serious that neither Mary nor Betty Kate made a comment. Elizabeth was miserable; she didn't pay much attention to the appearance of her father, except to notice that the beard was awful.

"Now what ails her?"

"Not a thing." Lillian had her back to them now. Two pots cooked on the burners, one of greens, one of rice. Lillian had some difficulty deciding which one to put the square of fat pork into. She finally decided on the greens.

"Where's Drefus?"

"Strayer's."

"Aren't you hungry, Henry?" Lillian didn't turn, and she hadn't smiled. But the room was busy with girls and the contents of balloon boxes.

"Not now. Just need to lie down for a little." Henry lay down on the bed in his foul clothes and slept the whole clock around.

Later that evening, when the girls were asleep, Lillian drew a chair up to the bed beside Henry. She didn't feel like she could sleep. She could see that Henry lay on his stomach with one arm thrown out. His head was turned in the other direction—she would have liked to be able to see his face. Lillian had missed her husband, missed him with her heart and her body. She had pored over the little scribbled messages on the envelopes, trying to get everything out of them, even what was not there. When at first she missed Henry, it came to Lillian that she had never been without him—she didn't know what to do about missing Henry. The tenderness she felt then was lavished on his shirts, socks, any little thing that needed attention. She'd made an effort to darn the socks—she never seemed to get a darning stitch right. But working on the shirts had given her satisfaction. Once, Lillian took the stack of shirts from the drawer, she told herself, for a final check-over, but had sat with them in her lap instead. She lost track of the time, holding the shirts.

In her imagination, it was possible to forgive Henry the embarrassment he had caused her. And she knew that with time she would, in fact, forgive him. But about this other thing, the awful drinking: he would *have* to be made to realize. Henry was, always had been, a happy sort, happy-go-lucky. He was a drinking man, that was true. But he was not—God help them—a drunk. A man could stop drinking; a man could do just about anything he wanted to—Lillian told herself this. And she would force him, if it came to that—Lillian knew that in the end she would have to force him. She picked up the arm and moved it over. It was flung over her side of the bed.

Henry and Drefus tried to pick up where they had left off. And they were lucky in the time of year. The willow flies were out—the fish would bite at just about anything. Before returning to the trot lines at dusk, the men would fish without stopping directly from the boat, and the catch would be good. As seldom happened, they took little enjoyment from their work that day, and there was little conversation between them. It was Drefus' opinion that they shouldn't have come back to Clanton, should have kept on into South Carolina and Virginia for the tobacco crop, then made a swing into West Virginia, for the apples. There'd be a peach crop upstate and in Georgia. But Henry insisted on seeing his family, though he wondered, now, if Drefus' idea wouldn't have been better. They were pretty much in the same way at home with him here, fishing and trapping, as with him traveling and sending back pay. But being at home was worse, in a way that he hadn't expected.

Things weren't right in the house. Henry didn't remember the girls bickering constantly; now Elizabeth and Betty Kate, especially, stayed after each other. Betty Kate seemed to be threatening Elizabeth with something, but Elizabeth could still terrify her sister with a look. At the supper table, there was no telling of stories, not a lot of conversation of any sort. Lillian avoided looking at Henry. At night the small front room was stuffy. Lillian lay with her back to Henry, but he could always tell when she wasn't sleeping. In the vagueness he could just make out the peak of her shoulder, the line of her back, these shapes he had known so well, and for so long. Once he would have moved up behind her, tickled her or bitten her. She would have laughed and turned around, or swatted at Henry. Lillian had left him, in her feelings. This Henry knew. He also knew that he still had a trace of her esteem—that he would have lost even that last trace if he had touched the line of that little back.

They were apart.

Henry wanted—yet didn't want—to go home in the evenings. A feeling of dread was with him at all times, now—he couldn't shake it off. He attempted to drink it off, and that helped a little. Lillian had taken to being sickly, something Henry didn't recall from before. He watched Mary moving around the kitchen with a spirits of ammonia bottle and a glass of water. The odor of the ammonia made him sit back, when Mary opened the top.

"Mrs. Hooper brought it over."

Henry had no grasp of the details, here.

Mary poured ammonia into a teaspoon and stirred it into the water. "Mama's got the vapors." She didn't smile at her own remark. She walked up front with the glass, and Henry sat in the kitchen—he wouldn't have entered the front room then. The time was past when he felt at ease with his wife—he wondered if it would ever be back. Lillian. She had always been there; when Henry thought about it, the time in their lives when they hadn't been together seemed so small that it hardly counted. And it had come to this between them: come to the point that once he left in the mornings, he didn't go back to the house at all during the day. There was no place to go when he avoided the house, except to the empty warehouses. The company of unwashed men who camped by the tracks or the river.

Henry had known since morning that the river was falling. No use to bait up that day—the fish wouldn't bite when the water dropped. So he had ventured it—maybe he was making the problem into more than it was. He would go home. He walked with a bunch of squirrels tied together with twine. He had already stopped to clean and skin them. And his hands being familiar with their work, he'd deftly avoided the mess of blood on his clothes. But his hands were bloody. Henry walked up to the back stoop to drop the squirrels, then went directly to the hydrant to take care of his hands.

She was there. Already she had stepped to the door and seen the squirrels—she had come to hate the sight of the stiff, red bodies. They were ugly, almost indecent looking. The sight of the legs cooking, especially, the little ends of bones like matchsticks, were hateful to Lillian. And the smell of squirrel meat cooking stayed trapped in the house.

"Is anything the matter?"

"River's falling." She nodded. So he walked into the kitchen and sat. Inside the kitchen he felt suddenly unclean. He remembered, too, that he hadn't shaved that morning.

"Any coffee left?" Henry rolled a cigarette, scattering grains of tobacco.

"No. We drank it all." Lillian looked at his hands, noticed the black lines of squirrel blood under his fingernails. She looked away. She dipped the few dishes and moved toward the door, to empty the pan. She wasn't used, anymore, to having Henry in the kitchen. His knees seemed to fill all the space between the table and door.

"Let me do that." Henry moved clumsily, sending a couple of potatoes and a carrot to the floor. These and an onion were special finds. Lillian could make something a little like beef stew, with the squirrel.

Lillian stooped to gather up the vegetables as Henry tossed the water. They moved past each other without touching. Before, Henry would have reached for Lillian. *Can I have a little sugar?* Which would have been their old love language. Now he would have been rewarded—content—just to be talking to her. Simple talk, in the way that once had been so easy.

" 'S Elizabeth seen any more of that friend of hers?" This was an indirect reference to the hair. The whole story had come out during Elizabeth's and Betty Kate's squabbling.

"We're just going to have to let that matter drop." Lillian stood at a work shelf with her back to Henry. The mention of the hair unsettled her. She lowered her hands, as if to beat them at her sides, but again picked up the onion. The hair incident had strangely upset Henry—he remembered the feel of the hair in his hands.

"She's having a hard enough time, as it is," Lillian continued about Elizabeth.

"What kind of hard time?"

Lillian turned around. Fiercely. "What do you *mean*, what kind of hard time!"

Henry dropped his chin. He had made a mistake. Still, he wanted to hear Lillian talking. Any little thing would be enough. There was no point, he realized, in talking about the situation they were in. No one talked about recovery these days: only relief. Henry knew that Lillian went regularly for the commodities.

"Well, the little ones—they don't seem to mind the school too much."

"They depend a lot on each other." With that tone of voice that terminated a conversation. But she was calmer now. She wiped her face with the back of an arm. It was the onion.

Henry's mind had split in opposing directions. It was too much for him, here, alone with Lillian. He wanted to be with her, he also wanted the easy refuge of the warehouse.

"Anything around here I can do?"

"Nothing I can think of." There was wood in the box, more stacked on the porch. "Well." Henry made a move to stand up, but he didn't stand. He was waiting. And as Lillian moved to the table for the last of the vegetables, he reached for her hand. Only one word of it came out. "Sugar?" Lillian ignored the word. She knew that Henry's eyes would not be quite focused, would be looking at some point just above her face.

She quickly drew back her hand. "Henry, you've been drinking."

There was no answer for that. Now Henry did stand. He had to take care of the squirrels. He ought to walk into town and check on Drefus. Whatever he did, he had to leave that house. His head was buzzing. He couldn't be still. He didn't know that Lillian stood at the window and watched him walk away. That her eyes passed over his shoulders—she loved the shape of them, such good shoulders they were. His back was still narrow and strong. In her imagination Lillian stroked the shoulders, lightly, then harder, working the strength of her hands down through the skin, soothing, encouraging. But she couldn't do that, couldn't be soft with him just now. He could do what was necessary—she still told herself that. The drinking was a matter of resolve, pure and simple. He would have to be made to *see*, that was all. With her help. And if she was firm with him. She could only help him, Lillian reasoned, if she were firm with him—if she held herself back from that temptation to stroke and comfort.

Henry walked out over the fan of rails. There was no sun that day, just a strong, dry wind. He stopped behind one of the cars, not for a windbreak, but to take something—his half pint—out of his back pocket. A gritty wind came in gusts, scooping up leaves and twigs and blowing the dark bits around, like sparrows flying. It gave him a last, desperate idea. If the wind kept up, it'd be strong enough for a kite. For a third time that day, he went back into the woods, this time to look for dogfennel, for the kite frame. Would Lillian have burned them, or would she have kept aside the kite makings, the flattened brown paper, little torn strips of cloth, like she always had, in her sewing box? Henry wondered.

"It's my turn!"

"It's not your turn."

"It is." Betty Kate made snatching motions at Mary, who held the kite behind her back.

"It's Sister's turn."

The remark stopped Betty Kate, for this once. She was ashamed; she knew she had told on her sister.

"Okay, now. Run!"

All of them laughed, running and jiggling the kite. The kite snapped in the wind, inched up in the gusts, then made a fishlike nosedive for the ground.

"Everybody gets a turn, first. Then I'll have a go at it." Henry watched each of the girls take her turn.

"Daddy, you try." Henry's effort was usually needed to get the kite off the ground. He held his cigarette in his mouth, squinting against the smoke. At a rough spot, he almost lost his footing. Mary took the kite from him.

"No, me. I can do it." From Elizabeth. She ran again. "You

have to let it out a little at a time." The others yelled and coaxed. "Keep your eye on the string!"

The kite did a crazy series of loops to the ground. The two girls were panting.

"Okay, Betty Kate."

"I don't want it."

"It's your turn."

"I don't *want* my turn."

Now the others stopped. There was something wrong with Betty Kate. She was frowning. Her lower lip was poked out. And she wouldn't look at her sisters. Instead, she watched Henry, who had been looking on from a distance. He'd had a nip or two as he stood in the field. Indecision held Betty Kate for a moment, while all of them watched her. Waiting

"This kite's no good. It won't fly." She began to walk.

"What?"

She turned. "Something's wrong with the kite!" Their father had always made a fine kite.

She walked up to Henry and took his hand, turning him. "Come on, Daddy."

Henry had drifted away from himself, standing at his distance in the pasture. He didn't think of not obeying—his child wasn't asking a question. The only thing to do was to lead her daddy home. She didn't pause for the others to follow.

Chapter 26

*P*ieces of time. Scraps, lifted this way and that. Mornings in places nobody knew. Climbing out of the boxcar, legs cramped, eyes smarting with sun. The smell of morning, strong and new. Smell of metal and oil, wheel metal burning against the metal of rails. There were the rail jungles, rugged men themselves faded like scraps, little spotty patches of fire rings and junk shelter, cook pots and crates, bits of mirror glass attached to tree trunks.

It was Henry's turn to do the walk into town. It was begging—there was no other word to call it by. Drefus had walked in the first several times, by himself. It didn't seem to bother Drefus like it did Henry. There was one time, a late morning in some little town, a line of sunny back yards open on an alleyway. It was still surprising for Henry, the sense of distances passed in the night. Not knowing where they would be in the morning. These other places—in most ways, they were all the same, really, except for those first few minutes, the astonishment of somewhere new, some place where every day went along in its own way, as it had always done back in Clanton or Orville. Neither world had any notion that the other world existed. But the little differences, in the main streets, general stores, in the string of back yards, were enough to make a place somewhere else. For the first time in his life, Henry was somewhere else.

Henry walked up the alleyway, looking into the yards. It was still early in the day, not yet dinner time. The sun was everywhere that morning, new spring sun that looked a little like water spilling along the corners and shapes of things. The air felt clean and cleansing.

How to make a choice, one yard or another—Henry didn't know. He walked into one of them. There was an old tree near the alley with a rope swing moving a little, empty. He walked across short grass, still pale with winter. He could hear sounds of activity inside the kitchen. There was a small back porch. Henry didn't call out. He stood there and waited. And she saw him soon enough, the woman—the woman Henry still recalled an impression of, although he didn't look into her face directly. Young, neat, with dark, wavy hair and thin-plucked eyebrows. In a dress and a flowered apron. Cleanly-looking, and fresh. Safe from the world.

He would have never imagined himself doing a thing like this. Henry didn't take off his hat, but touched it, then lowered his face, like he could hide it under the brim. He knew that the calm eyes would be looking him over. He was only another bum. And he was a dirty one.

"My brother and I are traveling." Henry didn't realize that he stepped backwards as he spoke. "I wonder if—." He hadn't planned out what to say—he should have. He didn't finish his question. He fixed his eyes at a point on the ground.

"Just wait out there under the tree. I'll get you something."

Whether the wait had been a long or a short one, Henry couldn't remember. The woman walked back out to the porch, with a brown bag and a jar of water. Henry walked up and took them.

"I do thank you, ma'am." Henry thought that she smiled and nodded.

"You don't have to trouble about the jar."

"Yes'm."

She couldn't be expected to know the difference: that he wasn't a tramp but a family man. A person of respectability.

Henry walked quickly out of the yard and into the alley, but only so far as the next lot. There he leaned against a garage, in a patch of sunlight and grass. Now he investigated the contents of the bag.

Two sandwiches wrapped in waxed paper. The food odors rose up to him, mayonnaise and mustard, bologna, the slices of bologna two to each sandwich. A clean piece of lettuce, a red slab of tomato. Henry rewrapped one of the sandwiches, put it back in the bag, and slid the whole thing into his coat pocket, for Drefus. Then he squatted to eat. The bread was fresh. He loved each of the flavors, anticipated each separate one. He smelled the tomato as he bit into the sandwich; jets of saliva jumped to the roof of his mouth. His jaws ached slightly. The tomato was the most delectable of the flavors. It seemed that no one other thing had ever been as delicious as that bite of tomato. It tasted of sun and soil and wild-growing things, like hot dandelion flowers. It tasted of memories.

It took Henry minutes, only, to eat the sandwich, but he would remember those few minutes for as long as he lived. He remembered squatting, looking out over a kitchen garden, fresh turned, across the alley way behind the houses. When he finished eating, he waited, for the few moments that he could still taste the flavors of the food in his mouth. For some unaccountable reason, he felt like weeping. He rubbed his chin, waiting for the feeling to pass. Over a sandwich. No. From gratitude. No. From something else. He didn't know. He didn't know himself very well at that moment.

The 'shine made the dread go away. The dread waited for him now—he had to watch out for it. A burning spot in the center of his chest that got bigger and bigger.

When the weather warmed up, they rode on top of the cars. From up high the world was wide open. For Henry mornings were good— morning had always been the best time. The land lay empty, sun- filled, quiet of everything but a kind of rustling, like insects. There were days, then, of driving heat. Drefus burned until water blisters stood out on his nose. Henry could see the sun burning red, right through his closed eyelids. Sometimes, during the very worst of the heat, the sky would get thick and pale over. Shapes of trees swelled, became smoky-looking. Then the rain would come. Henry laughed into the noisy sky, rain pelting his face, sliding into his collar. He remembered the taste of salt and rain.

The little runnels of dread were gone, for now. He was easy. Easy. Drefus was moving down the catwalk, halfway upright. He squatted at Henry's head. Henry could feel Drefus unbuckling his belt, then refastening the belt to the rails of the catwalk. Henry lay on the rails with his coat bunched under his head.

There were nights when he rode on top all night long. Moon-white nights. Moon drunk. Moon blind. Henry was sick all over himself. Sick, and Drefus had him belted to the catwalk. There were nights when he could see the cloud shapes moving along with the car. Inside, the sound of the wheels was like a knocking, a vibration from deep under water. On top, the sounds were light. Faint clacking sounds. Henry liked them, liked the rhythm. The cars swayed as they clacked. Sometimes he and Drefus crept up toward the engine, where they were covered with grit and cinders. Henry squinted, watched the lines of tracks swallowed up under the train. Miles. How many miles. The whistle flew back over the top in the smoke, blasts from an old organ.

Pictures moved by like cards dropped into the slots of a viewer. There were the farmsteads, all laid out, safe and secure, places to come home to. There were the little crossroads towns, dark at night, huddling, they seemed to be. They jumped the car before the cities and the railroad police. Henry had wanted to see the cities, but they circled through the country, instead. There were miles and miles of empty track, miles of no landscape. Just brown miles of earth moving past. Long brown miles of nowhere.

Henry couldn't remember the number of the road, county road something or another. But it didn't matter; the one that started behind the fire station. It was too dark to see much; but the road made a whitish path.

"You go on out that road there, say about three miles. Come to a filling station sits on the right."

"Take it, there?"

"No. You're gonna have to keep on going till the road forks. Go left and on up about a mile. See a big old house, sits on the left. Empty."

"Take it, there?"

"No. You're gonna have to keep going——."

They waited at the spot, an intersection of two county roads, an open space in the middle of fields. Henry and Drefus had done their walking at night—they had to be early enough to get on with the first pickers. There were too many wanting to pick in those parts. The truck should come by near daylight. Henry and Drefus were there long before daylight, but they were not the first to arrive. A couple of men squatted in the open, near a tree, not even visible until they stood up. They stood up to establish position. A car that seemed to have a family inside it was parked near the road. From that direction there was the sound of a baby crying. That group would be second. Henry and Drefus were third.

It was chilly during the night, and damp, the ground all wet. And nothing to do but pace, wait, walk out into the bushes when you needed to. The others gathered, a little at a time, a good-sized group, but not yet too many. Dawn was gray, then white, then sunlit. Finally hard, brilliant sun. The truck had not come. They'd had a false lead. They would spend that day walking, maybe finding something; maybe not. There were still crops that needed picking; and it was all stoop labor. Rough, mean work—no pleasure in anything about it. They stooped for onions. The heat came then. The onion tops would get slippery. Henry knocked the soil from the bulbs—some flew out of his hand. He forgot, wiped his eyes. His hands stank of onion. His eyes smarted and filled. There was a line, like a pencil line, across his shoulders and back, where the stinging followed the line of the muscle. Carrots were worse than the onions, hard to get out of the ground. Had to dig the soil away sometimes with your fingers, finger-nails. But there'd be nothing today, unless they walked. Drefus pulled back when Henry reached out for his coat pocket.

"Not yet. We don't have much of it."

"Well, just a little bit, then."

"Not yet." Drefus took a step sideways. "You'd drink up every bit of it, Brud, in one swallow. Don't know as we'll eat today, either. Need this." He clamped a hand over the bottle.

And they didn't eat that day. They had walked—Henry felt like he'd sleepwalked. That night the fish were there for the first time. Henry had a case of the shakes. Drefus had been watching him, ready to dole out the liquor a little at a time, if Henry needed it for medication. But Drefus had miscalculated, waited a little too late. Henry sweated. He would have been sick, but there was nothing to bring up. The fish were everywhere, then, sliding around and behind the others. Fish bodies flipped, eel-like, then glided slow, through the murky gray-green. It was the heads that were worst. Fish heads. Fish bones. The faces slid apart and back, into other bony faces. Dissolved again. Some with thick, sharp jaws. Prehistoric. Henry flailed from side to side. Drefus sat across his stomach, offering the bottle, now. But most of it spilled. When it was empty, others stepped up, to offer their own bottles.

"Just a bit at a time. Here, now. Else he'll throw an arm or leg outa socket."

The others looked down.

The train moved through the night with its miles-long blasts, its round beam of light searching over the tracks.

Chapter 27

In the yellow house on Water Avenue, Bobbie Bell moved in and out as comfortably as a family member. When Emma was not in sight, her entries were sometimes preceded by a little sing-song whoop, a familiar "yoo-hoo." Any of the Griffens would have recognized the sound, anywhere in town. Emma was not in the kitchen at present, but the smile of greeting lingered on Bobbie's face. She removed her everyday hat, a flat, cylindrical object of some indeterminate color. Bobbie Bell was by nature a contented person, a spinster who lived inconspicuously with her sister's family. People may have sometimes wondered at the contentment, if they wondered at all. Bobbie Bell was not just a plain woman. The truth was that she was outright ugly, ugly in a way that bothered the eyes, guiltily disturbing the person who looked at her. After all, it wasn't Bobbie's fault. She was, as everyone said, as good as gold.

Her hat and handbag deposited, Bobbie glanced around the kitchen, to see what she could do for Emma. On the work table, a heap of turnip greens lay on a sheet of newspaper. These were the first spring greens from Emma's garden, frost-planted seeds. In the pantry hung an extra apron, which Bobbie tied around herself. She then set to work sorting the greens.

"Hey, Miz Bell."

"Hey, Miz Bell."

A door slammed.

"Hey there, boys. How are you?"

"Fine." In unison. It was Buddy and Ralph, who were together most of the time. Although younger, Ralph was the taller of the two, but not as muscular as Buddy. And while Ralph was naturally tawny, Buddy was tanned, the freckles on his arms and face darkened a shade. The two of them moved with the casual ease and energy of healthy adolescence. Both boys were handsome, very different from one another—there was no family resemblance, to speak of. But they were allies. When younger, both the boys had been over-quick to take part in a fight—Ralph still was. Both were excellent students, naturally and casually, as were the others.

At three o'clock, their sister's appearances were generally unpredictable. Nettie had girlfriends with whom she walked Broad Street, talking, window shopping, critically commenting on other groups of girls who were doing the same things. But all that had changed, now, with Nettie. And about *the problem*—of which all the family was aware—Emma was distressed and worried. She'd have to talk it over again with Bobbie. Yet she trusted her children. None of them were questioned about their whereabouts, when their time was their own. But the two older boys had little, if any, afternoon time of their own; and about this fact they nursed a private resentment. They had the routine jobs of changing oil and tires or repairing flats. After a quick stop at home, they were expected at the shop. Buddy and Ralph moved about, prowling the kitchen and pantry—neither surprised to see Miss Bell by herself, busy in the kitchen. And they had years ago ceased to wonder at their mother's choice of a friend. At first they'd made fun of her—Bobbie's appearance provoked that reaction from children. Her nose bulbed in several places. She was short and stocky, with an uneven middle. But Bobbie Bell had a special talent, one not detectable on casual observation. She was a loving and devoted friend—she had a special gift for friendship.

Buddy was in a bad mood that afternoon. He banged the doors to the pie safe and whistled through his teeth. Both boys grabbed what they wanted and slammed up the stairs, muttering and grumbling when they passed Emma in the upstairs hallway. Ralph swore. At an early age, he had developed an unexpected fondness for girls. His imagination roved off to all sorts of places that afternoon other than the family business. And because Buddy had begun school early, at fifteen he was in his first year of high school. He'd played football that first fall. And although he was short, he was fast and agile enough to be considered a valuable player. Though not a gifted one—Ned would be the gifted one. One after-school activity seemed to encourage another. Buddy had wanted to run track. He'd been urged by his classmates to run for student council. But these activities were prohibited; Buddy and Ralph were due at the shop.

Inside the room that they shared, the boys kept up their complaining. The conversation got nasty. In his agitation, Buddy forgot that his mother was nearby—was, in fact, moving a dust mop along the hallway just outside the door. Emma overheard a phrase or two of the griping. Both boys were changing clothes, moving around jerkily as they spoke. But Ralph was interested in more than griping. What he wanted to know was if Buddy had ever done anything really *serious* with girls. So he answered offhandedly. "Just tell him you won't do it."

"Tell him I won't do it—yeah, and pick myself up off the floor." Buddy's face darkened.

"Just tell him you want to run track in the afternoons." The little Gilman girl's chest was developing, Ralph had observed.

"That I *want* to? Yeah. I want to. It's not a rat's ass to Daddy what I want." Buddy slung his school shoes into a corner. "Nothing's a rat's ass to Daddy."

Emma jerked upright with a gasp that was just short of

audible. She stood with the dust mop planted in her hands. Her son's language had shocked her, but his meaning was worse. It was not Emma's habit to react immediately. She would take her feelings off with her privately, to work over, first. She would have to have a serious talk with Buddy about his father.

But then Ralph remembered. "Mama, Miz Bell's downstairs."

The friendship of Bobbie Bell—it had been that one, incidental factor in the family's move from the farm that had made all the difference for Emma. For her, the change had come so abruptly that action was the sole course to follow. On sight, she accepted the ungainly yellow house matter-of-factly; she had no special argument with it. It was commodious. Working in it was easy enough. Claiming it as home was another matter. The huge sprawl of a house—it was ugly to Emma—a stranger's house, with no warmth, no trace of those it had housed and sheltered. There was no sign of attachment left behind in the unbeautiful, over-large rooms. She called the house Old Yellow—at times she almost hated it. But with a garage shed on one side of the back lot, and a dense, untended hedge on the other, she had at least some sense of privacy. Her yard was one of the older city lots, cut long and deep, and by now almost totally under cultivation. On her back porch, beyond which the river glinted in winter, she enjoyed the illusion of not being in town. This porch became her dwelling place.

Somehow, Bobbie had known on that first—now distant—time to come around to the back of the house. And on her initial call, something happened between the two women. They could not have said what it was—some intuition, some indefinable thing in the face of the other, made both women start to laugh. And the laughter had never stopped. Bobbie called regularly, sometimes daily. At the sight of each other, they laughed. They laughed at anything and everything—any little trifle would do. From that somber congregation to which they belonged, they created comedy and melodrama, and frothy, delicious gossip. But there were times when they worried and grieved together. Thirty-one and -two were years of sad, unlaughable histories. After those years, people began to say that the worst of it was behind them. Emma still wondered where the Gray family had gone, and whatever had happened to them.

As she walked into the kitchen, Emma scolded her friend insincerely. "Now, Bobbie, you leave those alone." She referred to the greens. "I didn't know you were here." Both women laughed a little, at the sight of the other. "I'll make us a cup." This was Bobbie's invitation out to the back porch, where there were rockers. And the day was the sort to call a person out, the sky clear and still, the air spiced with the odor of growing things. From a basket on the porch rose the peppery smell of tomatoes, just picked green, and still warm. "I want you to take some of those." Emma inclined her head toward the basket.

"Where's Nettie?" Bobbie made a jump in the conversation, in a way that she and Emma had together. She had no interest in Nettie's whereabouts. Her question concerned *the problem*.

"I *am* worried, Bobbie. I'd say she's likely to be with Farrington."

Both women paused to raise and lower their cups, in preparation for this discussion. "I can't seem to do a thing with her about it," Emma went on.

It was a credit to Bobbie as a friend that she didn't offer advice she had no faith in; and there was no subject on which Bobbie Bell felt less confident than that of romantic attraction. The main point against Farrington Whyte was that he was not a Nazarene— but all this had been previously discussed. She put down her cup and saucer—Bobbie had formed an opinion. "Well, I've thought about it. You know, it might not be so bad, after all. The boy's not to blame for his family. He seems a nice enough boy"—Bobbie was generous by nature—"and he's got his whole life ahead of him."

"Ralston's dead set against it." Now that was another matter altogether.

At the time of this conversation, Nettie was already close to home. She was alone—she had just left Farrington—and she was smiling. On the fourth finger of her right hand—the left would be reserved for the day, itself—she wore a thin gold band. She and Farrington had been to the pawn shop, and the ring, set with diamonds so tiny as to be nearly opaque and worn to a break at the back, was a cheap one—she would have another one, later on. Nettie stopped, to remove the ring. She folded it into a hand-kerchief, which she pushed deep into her purse. From her school notebook, she took out a piece of used paper, tore off a corner, and wiped the lipstick from her mouth. This she did several times— the lipstick was a deep red—and the paper burned her lips. She folded the paper and pushed it, too, down into her handbag. She was content. Farrington—the sound of the name moving through Nettie's mind caused her to flush with pleasure. He was a tall young man, very slim, in coloring similar to Ralston. When he wasn't looking, Nettie devoured Farrington with her eyes. The sight of the back muscles moving beneath his cotton shirt made a rush of heat move down between her thighs. They had little more than six weeks to wait until Nettie's graduation. But they wouldn't wait—they just couldn't. They reasoned that it made no difference, really, if they married right away. Nettie could breeze through the final weeks of high school without opening a book, if she had to.

Now Nettie walked into the yard. Her greetings were expansive and affectionate. Miss Bell she called Aunt Bobbie, and it touched the woman in a way that no one knew but herself. Nettie looked especially cheerful that afternoon. She had what Emma thought of as that Farrington look about her. She went into the kitchen, then rejoined the women, with her moon and stars in her hand. And as Nettie sat and talked, she stitched. She was covering some cardboard cut-outs with gold cloth and sequins. She said that the things were pieces of scenery for the school play. It was true that the scraps and sequins had been given to Nettie from a box of discards from old school costumes. But there was no school play.

Emma expected the usual quiet of a Sunday morning that day. She rose unnecessarily early—it was the habit of a lifetime. But she looked forward to her solitude, on this one day of the week. Her first task would be to look over Ralston's clothing. It was a habit she'd acquired, that each morning since they'd come to Clanton, she carefully chose his clothing for the day, which she then laid out for him. After all, her husband was a business-man. He had to be properly dressed. The fact that on workdays Ralston would change the clothes Emma chose for coveralls made no difference to her. On Sundays she was especially particular, and sometimes she scolded him. Until the novelty wore off, the scoldings amused the children. Ralston meekly submitted when Emma jerked the necktie from under his collar, muttering at him. "Now, you got that all Key West and crooked." She might slap at his back and shoulders. "I'd be ashamed to be seen out in public like that!"

These Sunday mornings by herself were Emma's thoughtful times. What she felt most often these days was gratitude: that the business had stayed open, that they were well and had somehow managed to have enough. Satisfied with her selection of clothing for Ralston, Emma went next to the kitchen. As there were no chores for them on a Sunday, she let the children sleep. Nettie had taken to coming down last. She often sat up late at night, mooning, as Emma put it, over Farrington. She sewed. Emma would stir in her sleep, overhearing the whirring noise that the treadle made, from across the hall. But she needed Nettie this morning and would have gone upstairs to get her, if Ned hadn't come down instead. He had waked up hungry. This beautiful one of Emma's—his face was still soft and childish from sleep, as perfect to Emma as an angel head. She gave him a shake, then she sent him upstairs for Nettie.

But Nettie wasn't there. Nettie was nowhere in the house to be found. And the whole family was aware of it well before Ralston was. All of them waited, dreading the moment of truth, yet strangely excited. Emma chose to let the breakfast proceed until Ralston noticed Nettie's absence, which he didn't do right away.

Then the question came. "Where's Nettie?"

All movement stopped, except the movement of eyes toward Ralston, whose own eyes moved around the circle of staring faces. He knew immediately. "Where *is* she?"

"Well, Daddy—."

"She's not here in the house?"

"No, she ain't."

The faces gave it away. Ralston rose from his chair, then sat down again, slinging aside his napkin. His face tightened. He pushed back his plate, frowned, and cleared his throat.

"Buddy!"

"Sir."

"Get on over there to the Whyte's. Find out where Farrington is."

"Yessir."

Buddy and Ralph stood up at the same time. And they had not quite cleared the block before they heard the sound of bare feet running behind them. The young ones were coming, too.

It was near mid-week before Nettie made an appearance. She came into the kitchen a little after one o'clock, when she knew that Ralston would have left again for the shop. She was innocently beaming. "Mama, look at my ring!" She held out her hand.

Emma didn't walk toward her. "Nettie! All of us have been worried half to death!" And she wouldn't embrace her daughter. Emma dropped into a chair, lifting the edge of her apron and resting her face on it. She would have her own private moment of censure. Nettie sat down at the table across from her, making an effort to look contrite.

"You shouldn't have done it that way, Nettie. Not that way. It wasn't right."

"I had to, Mama."

"Why'd you have to?" It was a sincere question.

"Because Daddy would have never let me marry Farrington. You know that."

There was no argument for that, so Emma said nothing. Still, she leaned against her hand, herself contriving a face of disapproval. She was enormously relieved to see Nettie.

"And oh, Mama!" Now Nettie reached across the table. "I love him so much. You just don't know!" She squeezed Emma's hand. Her nose wrinkled.

Emma wouldn't relent. Not yet. Nettie went on—she couldn't contain herself. "It'll all work out, Mama. You'll see. The family's so nice to me. You know that little house behind the Whyte's? Well, Farrington and I have that, just to ourselves." It was a very small building with windows, something between a cook's house and a storage shed, located in the Whyte's back yard. Nettie went on, "I'll get it fixed up so cute! I can't wait to get it fixed up. I've already made curtains and a bedspread to match." Nettie stopped for a moment. What she didn't say was that on the ceiling above their bed were tacked the moon and stars she had covered with gold cloth and sequins. This was a detail that Emma would never be aware of. But if she had seen the ceiling, it wouldn't have embarrassed her. Nothing about Nettie would have embarrassed her. She would have looked a minute or so, maybe come out with something like "Well, I sewanee." But by herself—and later—she would have wondered about this wondrous thing that her daughter experienced.

Emma couldn't hold on to her annoyance at Nettie. There was a truth that the past several days had revealed to her: that she could not imagine having lived her life without having this daughter in it. Now she listened, still withholding enthusiasm, as Nettie gushed and went on. Emma stood up to stir the apples that cooked on the stove. The makings for pie crusts were set out on the table. Nettie fell into making the crusts without thinking about it, and in her exuberance elaborately fluted the edges. It was the first small smile that Emma permitted herself.

"Now ain't those pretty? You can't leave them that way, though. Daddy'll know." She was abruptly solemn. "You're gonna have to give me some time, Nettie, to get things fixed with your Daddy."

"I know." Nettie pushed the edges of the crusts back down and pressed a fork against them.

And Emma knew she could fix it. She could settle him down again, once he'd had his outburst. He'd grumble and frown. He'd never say a word to agree with her. But she could manage him. This change had come about so gradually, she would not have said, at any one point, that the change had happened at all. That she was no longer afraid of Ralston. That she could at last influence him, even impose her own will on occasions.

A mirror hung in the dining room. Now Nettie caught a glimpse of herself in it, and the image pleased her. At this time, her femininity had to be satisfied with the cheapest grade cotton, material that would quickly fade. Nettie knew that the fabric was poor, but it didn't diminish her pleasure in the effect she'd created. Out of the dress material she had also sewn little strips, which she tied into bows for her hair. Nettie's hair was auburn. Its thick, spongy waviness was at that time enviable among the girls her age.

Emma felt a sudden uneasiness. The boys would be through the door any minute. "Nettie, the boys. You'd best let me—."

"Yes'm." Nettie understood, but she didn't move with any special hurry. She stood directly in front of the mirror now, to examine her face. She hadn't wiped off the lipstick, and Emma made no comment about it. Nettie's face had grown pretty. She had tiny, pointed lips and luxurious eyelashes. She turned her face to one side, then to the other, smiling. Emma stood behind her, watching, also approving Nettie's appearance. Pleased in all respects with her daughter. Standing there, watching Nettie, she had the sudden understanding that life moved through her. She was more than herself, Emma. She lived in Frank and Nettie and the others. The strength of herself had formed the bond for them all.

Arranging her puffed sleeves, Nettie glanced at her freckles and remarked with less than usual conviction, "I hate my freckles."

"Freckles are pretty," Emma answered, as she always had.

Chapter 28

In the fall of 1932, Elizabeth Gray entered high school, a three-storied, showy building of red brick, with relief sculpture over the broad entrance doorways. Here, things happened to Elizabeth—not exactly things that could be called events, as such. But encounters. People reacted to Elizabeth, often without her knowing it. She walked into the orbits of other lives. She was an intruder. But she didn't know that, either.

Elizabeth's teachers noticed her. When Elizabeth walked into a room, people stared. Even her sisters at times found themselves staring at her, with simple, somewhat disapproving curiosity. Elizabeth's hair was now auburn, and coppery. Her eyes were hazel, but they often appeared the same color as the hair. Elizabeth walked everywhere, so that her skin was a little bronzed. She looked healthy and scrubbed. Something rosy and gilt. She put a person in mind of some blooming thing. Or something edible, a peach or a pear, maybe. It was obvious to anyone that Elizabeth was an innocent; but her beauty was not merely prettiness. And there was no innocence about that. It made people edgy, self-conscious around her—they didn't know what to do with their eyes. Lillian had taught her to always keep a pleasant expression on her face; but Elizabeth reserved her smile, and that only increased curiosity. People examined her oddly, as though looking for some sort of explanation. The typical explanation would have been family. But Elizabeth Gray had no family, as far as most of those who looked at her were concerned. A generation ago in Orville, her mother Lillian had had family. The McClintons were Family. But Elizabeth Gray had "people." Everybody in East Clanton had people, from one place or another.

Mrs. Reid, the elderly science teacher, had years ago ceased to actually hear the furor in the hallways. At present she thought of the fruit flies, of which there were a great many jars. Mrs. Reid lived for the experiments, which went back as far as memory. So that she didn't notice when Marian Adams and Suzanne Walker slipped out of class—it was easy to do when Mrs. Reid was involved with the fruit flies. Their own minds, however, were anywhere but on the experiments. They had Glee Club next period, and some of the senior boys were in that class. Each girl wanted to check on her hair and face before the next bell rang. The basement restrooms were dim, so that the girls had to stand close to the mirrors.

Marian had a pimple. She had been taught to keep her hands off her face, for her complexion's sake; but she could not take her eyes off the pimple, which was right in the middle of her cheek. She pushed the cheek out with her tongue for a better inspection.

Suzanne's mind was only briefly on her hair, because it was hair that didn't require much attention. Pulling a comb through it accomplished no more than settling it back into place. Suzanne's mind was on gossip. "Who's this Elizabeth person we've been hearing so much about?"

The pimple would get even redder before it started to go away. "What?"

"This Elizabeth person."

The girls considered themselves happily alone. But they were not. Elizabeth herself was in the last stall, in the corner. She had been preparing to flush, but now she waited.

"Oh." At the moment Marian wasn't as interested as her friend. Her own hair was thin, with not an ounce of curl to it.

"You know, I hear Bob doesn't even call up Faye at night, anymore."

"I know."

"You've heard about it, then."

"Yeah. From what I hear, Faye might as well look around for somebody else." Marian held up a pocket mirror and examined her profile. Before they left the restroom, each girl would reapply her lipstick, whether or not it was necessary.

"And she's got it bad, you know," Suzanne Walker went on. "But now Bob has just dropped her, flat."

"I know."

"Well, so who is this Elizabeth person?"

There was nothing more Marian could do about her hair or the pimple. Now some energy came into the conversation. "Well, that's just what's so awful about it for Faye. She's *nobody*. Just nobody at all. Some little freshman from over in East Clanton."

"East Clanton. I don't believe it."

"Yeah. Really. That's what's so embarrassing about it."

Nobody had pulled up her undies and rearranged her skirt. Now she sat down again on the seat of the unflushed toilet. The bell rang.

"Well, I'll have to see her, myself."

"Oh, I'll point her out to you at lunch sometime." Breathily. Casualness was part of the cruelty.

The household on Range Street had become a household of women. The iron sat permanently under the cook stove, ready for use. Elizabeth had so few clothes that Lillian had to spot them between washings. She routinely suspended things over the stove in the evenings, to be ironed dry the following morning. There were mornings when Elizabeth walked to school in clothes that were slightly damp. She tormented herself then with embarrassing fantasies. But she needn't have. Her hair, which was always beautifully groomed, her coloring—these things by themselves outfitted Elizabeth. All of her life adults had noticed her. But it was the approval of friends her own gender that mattered. Elizabeth dressed for the other girls of her age. Her best friend was still Sue Wilkinson, who was protective of Elizabeth—the hair incident was history. If Sue approved of her, the others did— at least those who attended the Methodist Church.

That particular Saturday was warm and muggy, would be too warm by afternoon to make a fire in the stove for heating water or ironing.

"Now, you've waited too late, Elizabeth, for a bath." Lillian stood in the doorway, inclining her head against the doorframe.

"Well I've got to have a bath, anyway. I've got to wash my hair." Elizabeth washed her hair almost daily.

Lillian noticed the kettle and a boiler already heating on the stove. "You know the whole house will heat up." It seemed that October would never turn cool that year.

"I can't help it."

There was only the one water bucket. Elizabeth picked it up again, to walk back out to the hydrant. But Lillian stopped her. She gave in. "I'll help you with that. Get your things ready."

That meant stripping in the next room. There was only a towel to be gotten ready. A bar of Lifebuoy and a bottle of Halo sat on the kitchen windowsill. The hair washing was a ritual that Lillian and Elizabeth both generally enjoyed, but Lillian's clothes would be soaked. The whole kitchen would get wet. The rough floorboards drank in the puddles. Elizabeth sat down in the galvanized washtub and drew her legs up, wrapping her arms around them—it was a tight fit, it was no fit at all—while Lillian scooped and poured the water. Elizabeth sat with her eyes squeezed shut, and Lillian knelt to work the lather, pushing Elizabeth's head back and forth with her fingers. There was more scooping and pouring. The floor was drenched for a second time, when Elizabeth stepped out to re-warm the water. The stove hissed as she lifted the kettle.

Nobody paid any attention to the sound of the roadster. No one visited the house in an automobile except Mrs. Hooper, whose huge black Buick was silent. The Gray women had their privacy, or so they assumed. No one entered the house from the back steps except family. But Bill Banks and Preston McLaughlin had pulled their car around to the back, to avoid blocking the street. As they parked, the two boys were discussing Elizabeth. They had discussed Elizabeth for some time and at some length. It wasn't just that she was pretty—they had carefully analyzed this. Elizabeth Gray had something; they decided that it was poise. Neither boy had ever used that word aloud—they had more or less grabbed it out of the air. But each knew that it fit—that Elizabeth Gray had what they would have to call poise. And they were pleased with themselves for having decided to make the visit—no one else they knew would have visited that part of town. They looked forward to taking Elizabeth for a ride.

Force of habit caused Lillian to overlook the sounds at the side of the house. And the water was noisy. As the boys shut the car doors behind them, both looked at the house with some uncertainty—they weren't sure it was the right one. But neither boy was uncertain of himself. Both knew themselves to easily be the most popular boys in the senior class. If anyone could get away with taking out a girl from East Clanton, they could. Bill's hair was still wet from combing. He was primed. It was all decided—he was the one most seriously interested in Elizabeth. He smelled of clean, wet skin and shaving lotion. And he was full of anticipation. The boys strode across the uneven yard.

It was due to the kindness of accident, only, that Lillian walked out just then to the back stoop, to shake out a blouse for Elizabeth. So that Elizabeth had time to hear the voices, to understand what was happening. Lillian spoke first, pinning the blouse. She raised her voice cordially. "How do you do?" It was a voice of welcome, not the voice of avoidance that she should have used, according to Elizabeth.

Bill ducked his head in a way that was mannerly. "Are you Mrs. Gray, Elizabeth's mother?"

"I am."

It couldn't be happening. Anyone in the yard could have heard Elizabeth stand up in the tub, which was small enough to make a sucking sound against her body. She went through the bedroom door and closed it without taking time for the towel, which fell part way into the water. Now she leaned against the closed door, dripping. Her mother would send the boys away.

But Lillian didn't send the boys away—she knew better. She did, in fact, just the opposite. Elizabeth couldn't believe what she was hearing.

"Well, do, please, come in."

"Thank you, ma'am." Near unison.

Then the sounds of footsteps. Hundreds of them. Right at the door.

"Have a seat, boys."

The water had only that minute settled in the tub. It was gray and filmy, a little clabbered-looking with soap curd. Lillian ignored it. The boys ignored it. Both were well-mannered enough not to stare at the room.

"I'm so sorry. Elizabeth isn't well." Lillian said this with such pleasantness that it may as well have been any conversational comment.

There were polite murmurs.

"Won't you both have a seat?"

Mary and Betty Kate were also on the other side of the door. But it was one of those times in which not a word was spoken. Nobody made a sound. Elizabeth was hot all over. She no longer noticed that she was wet. She pulled a cotton housecoat, Lillian's, from a hook on the door, then huddled behind it. She raised her eyes to the doorknob, although she knew that it wouldn't open. She was safe. But astounded at her mother. All three of the sisters listened as one person. And they began to relax a little. Each of them picked up any behavioral cue from Lillian—their mother wasn't the least bit uncomfortable.

"Can I get you anything?"

It couldn't be possible.

Lillian was seated, now, and smiling. It was entirely possible. Because Lillian was in her element. At first sight of the boys, she knew them—not those boys personally, but the type of young men that they were. She could rely on their good manners.

"Oh, no ma'am." It was almost simultaneous. Lillian had made her offer in the perfect confidence that it wouldn't be accepted. There was not a thing in the house to offer. But she was sure enough, even, to repeat herself. "Are you sure that there's nothing I can offer you?"

Elizabeth relaxed on the floor. Mary and Betty Kate sat close behind her. All three pairs of eyes were round. Their mother didn't hurry the boys. In fact, her behavior did everything to encourage them to stay. She continued to ignore, so that they ignored, even forgot, the tub of filmy water, the soaking towel.

"You boys would be a little older, now, than Elizabeth."

"Yes, ma'am. We're seniors."

"Well how wonderful. What are your plans?"

"Pre-med." Again, almost simultaneously.

Bill tilted his head toward his friend. "Preston's going to Auburn"—he stressed the last word. "My family goes to Alabama."

"I see. What made you decide to go into medicine?"

Lillian liked the two boys right away—the friendliness was genuine. And the boys were delighted to talk about themselves. There was a good bit of polite, comfortable laughter. Elizabeth's hair was drying by the time they left the kitchen.

"Well, do come to see us again. Elizabeth will be so sorry to have missed you." She spoke as though Elizabeth herself were far out of earshot.

The scene that followed was terrible. There were arguments, tears, protests. Elizabeth would not go to school on Monday. No one could make her. She would never again go back to school.

But Lillian was at her calmest, her most emphatic. "You will indeed go to school on Monday. And you'll act perfectly natural. Do you hear me? Perfectly natural. You'll be your very best, most agreeable self. Do you understand?"

Elizabeth didn't reply, only looked at Lillian oddly. Her mind was working. And on Monday morning she did behave exactly as she'd been coached. Elizabeth was engaging, cheerful—at what the boys would have called her most poised. Both of them asked how she was feeling. Neither one made any mention of the visit, itself. Only the one remark.

"You sure do have a nice mother."

"Yeah, you sure do."

Both of the remarks were sincere.

But the incident wounded Lillian. And she would not forget.

That afternoon Sally Hooper drove out of her way across town to Range Street. And she was smiling. She felt gratified by an unusual sense of accomplishment. She felt—she would have had to put it—frankly elevated. There was a phrase that for years had lived secretly in Sally's mind. To be of use. She had wished her life to be of use. But she couldn't feel with any certainty that it had been that sort of life. Half-formed, unsettling questions lived alongside the inspiring phrase. But she could reward herself with this: she had been of use to Lillian. When a nurse's aide at the hospital quit, to be married, Sally stepped in at once. No one need trouble—she had the perfect replacement. Sally hadn't stopped there. She had pinned Mr. Minter, the proprietor, to the telephone on Sunday afternoon. Lillian had to be moved right away out of that house to another, more suitable of Mr. Minter's properties. But there were no suitable properties, Mr. Minter protested. The conversation had gone along, tug-of-war fashion, until Mr. Minter thought of Mrs. Philpot, a great aunt. Her roomy old raised cottage sat off the ground on brick arches, beneath which was a full, groundlevel floor. And in which Mrs. Philpot had had an apartment built that was not yet rented—that was not yet fully painted. People were doing that sort of thing these days, the old lady justified herself. The fact was that Mrs. Philpot was afraid by herself in the house. The house sat on Alabama Avenue, catty-cornered to the many-columned Vaughn Memorial Hospital.

Now, while Sally was fighting the wheel of the car, Lillian was fighting her cook stove, peering into it with a stick that she used as a poker. The wood wouldn't catch. She jammed the pieces around in the stove, saw the angry edges of the kindling flare. But Lillian wasn't occupied by the struggle that afternoon. Her mind was on other things. She sat back on her heels. She had made up her mind. Her thoughts still dwelled painfully on her daughter. It wouldn't happen again. Because she wouldn't allow it. No; not again. Not ever.

"Tell you the truth, I don't care if I never look at another apple."

Henry said this as he and Drefus stood, heads together, looking into a piece of mirror glass they'd propped. It was chilly and damp on the glassed-in back porch of Strayer's. Both men wore their coats. They stood just under the bulb, over a dishpan that Drefus had taken from the kitchen. It was around five o'clock in the morning. Rosalie Strayer would be coming into the kitchen at any moment. Her kitchen help would be arriving.

Drefus dipped his razor. "You've got some paper in your pockets for a change, don't y'?"

Henry made a reluctant noise. They'd been back in Clanton for only a matter of hours, had walked together to Strayer's, come in through the back door and slept there for a while on the porch. They heard the wooden sound of footsteps moving through the sleeping house. The swinging door to the kitchen came open.

"Who's there?" The voice was unruffled.

Drefus put his head around the pantry doorway, his face lathered. "It's only me, darlin'."

Rosalie gave a little snort of a greeting. It was still very early. "Where'd you come in from?"

"Been all the way up into Pennsylvania this time."

"Doin' what, all the way up there?"

"Apples. Had to go after the crop to one place and another."

"Who's that you got with you?"

Now Henry stepped around the doorway and nodded. Drefus spoke for both of them. " 'S just my brother, here, wanted to spruce up a bit before he goes home. Said he like to've scared his wife plumb off the porch last time we showed up."

Rosalie laughed a full daytime-like laugh. Now the sudden business of pots and skillets banging grated on Henry. His head hurt a little. He hadn't quite come to himself.

"Open your eyes?" Between them they carried one bottle, kept in Drefus' possession.

Henry took it. "Need to brush my teeth before I leave."

"You don't mind if we just step into the hall bath a minute or two, do you, Rosalie?"

Now she was too busy for them. "You go on ahead."

Henry brushed his teeth, hard, rinsed and gargled with the water. By the time he walked over to Range Street, Lillian would be awake and up. He set out alone. He needed the walk—it'd do him good, he told himself. The morning light was no more than a stain, the air full of cold, floating moisture. The town blocks were swallowed. What Henry could see looked strange to him. He'd noticed that, as he and Drefus walked the night streets—that familiar things, buildings, all looked smaller than he remembered, all of them different, somehow. He didn't walk directly east but downtown toward the river. He still didn't feel quite himself. He needed some time—he'd take a look at the water. He stood a little while, next to the bridge tender's house, which was dark. He sucked the wet, heavy air into his mouth and throat, tasting it. And waiting. He was waiting to get that feeling of morning, that feel of the day being new. Morning always had a feeling of promise to it, any morning, anywhere. But he couldn't get it. Maybe the walk would bring him around. And it did, a little. As Henry walked, he thought of his daughters. *Having a hard enough time, as it is*—he hadn't forgotten. He felt the need to do something, make some kind of gesture. Gardiner's Island. Now there was a thought. He'd see to the truck first. Then they'd load in the camping gear. Funny, he could get back the moldy, nose-prickling smell of the tent canvas—it was a bad smell, but he liked it.

It brought to mind all their nights and mornings along the river. On a camping trip, everybody had always laughed a lot, at no particular thing, made games out of nothing. And nights were good. Things were different outside in the open at night—tree shapes, clouds, sky. He was pleased with the idea—and feeling better, remembering how Betty Kate used to carry on whenever he said they were going. "Can we go? Can we go?" Tugging on him. "He already *said* we could go." Elizabeth would roll her eyes at her sister.

And Lillian. He told himself that things would be better with Lillian. He told himself that he would explain—he didn't know exactly how he'd explain. Henry knew that he was drinking too much. But he could cut down. It was the crazy work. It was the trouble. But things would look up, sooner or later; it would all be different. He saw the little house from a distance—it, too, look-ing smaller: grayer looking, like a shut wooden box. From across the rail yard, Henry could see that the lights were not yet on. Maybe Lillian was feeling poorly—he'd offer to make the break-fast. As he walked closer, the yard, the house looked yet stranger to his eyes. Not quite right—there was something missing. Lillian hadn't kept the hens for a long time, now. But that wasn't it. The back stoop was swept clean, like a wind had blown over it. There was no wood stacked. The clothesline was taken down. Henry knew before he let himself know. Before he touched it, the back door came ajar, by itself. Everything was swept clean. He could see straight through to the front room. All of it clean and emp-ty—he couldn't take in all of the empty. There was one object, a cardboard box, which sat in the second room, out in the mid-dle—he guessed so that he could see it. He walked inside and ex-amined the box, not from curiosity, but because he knew that he was meant to. His clothes were clean, mended, and neatly folded. An old pair of glasses, in their case, sat on top of the clothes. She must have thought he would need them. There was half a bar of soap, folded in paper, and a pair of shoes, also wrapped. There was no note. As Henry rifled through the things, lifted a few, he could visualize the hands, Lillian's hands—he could see the fingers moving over the different objects, arranging and rearranging them. He didn't know how it was that Lillian's feeling, her caring and worrying, came across from the way she had so carefully tucked in the things. *In sickness and in health.* Henry stood up. He wouldn't ask himself all the questions right now. He would take the box and go. He lifted it to his hip—it seemed to have no weight at all. He looked around the rooms. There might be something here for him to do, some last little detail. But there was nothing. *From this day forth.* His free hand went automatically to his pocket. He rattled something—the key. Not knowing what to do with it, he left it in the door.

Chapter 29

Betty Kate and Mary grew into young womanhood in the safety of West Clanton, but that buffer, relief though it was, compensated the three girls less than it did Lillian. To Betty Kate the thought of that other time wasn't any less real, just because it was at a safe remove. It, the memories: the hard times. The hungry, terrible times. The worst days in the cramped and mildewy shotgun house on Range Street. "It" sat in her memory at a distance, now, it was true. But in another way it was always right there next to her, some secret thing unnoticed by others, like a safety pin hidden beneath her clothes. An invisible small badge. Yes, they had crossed into safety. But there would always be East Clanton.

Betty Kate was walking home at that moment up Alabama Avenue, one of the oldest residential blocks in town. The street was brick-paved, lined by oaks, heavy and moss-hung. At the far end was the enormous Vaughn Memorial Hospital. Handsome properties sat in between. All of them lived in and mellowed by an indestructible gentility. Against the dark tree splotches the Philpot house gleamed faintly, even from a distance—old Mrs. Philpot kept all the lights burning in the evening. The broad, white house sat luminous and heavy—but gracefully designed on its understory of brick arches. There had never been lack of safety here. And they had come from the bare, packed dirt yards of East Clanton to this unexpected place of refuge. Of course there were limitations, things that Lillian taught the girls to ignore and accept, by steadfastly doing so herself. The Gray women entered their home through a back door, into what had once been the basement of the house. In their own living area, the arrangement of rooms was a little odd, to say the least. There had been a single, immovable object, around which the whole apartment had to be designed, this being an outsized, claw-foot bathtub about a century old, they figured. Around it, the newer and undersized fixtures looked silly and improbable. And of course there was the oddity of what they called the parlor, one long, shallow space running almost the width of the house, with the back wall broken up by a fireplace once used for cooking. Now it was merely an elaborate wall of brick, set in a fan-like pattern—the whole layout, in itself, furnishing the room somewhat, with its fussiness. Which was fortunate, since the room held a sole piece of furniture. The explanation that she would be doing Mrs. Philpot a favor to "store" the Victorian settee had been made with effusive apologies. If Lillian could "find room" for the thing: a fine old piece, whose rose-colored brocade had faded to near white. The whole maneuver contrived by Sally Hooper, who had taken the piece of furniture out of the home of one of her own relatives. The settee stood in front of the filled in fireplace, facing the windows. Alone. There was not a single additional thing in that, the most public, of rooms. And there were no apologies. No explanations. Far better to have simply done nothing than to have attempted something ineffective or tacky. So that it was in this odd parlor that Elizabeth had been charmed and won by the planter's son, George Yeager. And in this parlor the Grays received any and all of their visitors. Possibly it was unconscious courtesy: someone— Lillian herself, or one of the young men who had stopped by—always stood, excusing themselves politely.

As Betty Kate entered the back yard, she realized that she would have some time to herself. Lillian frequently stayed past her hours at the hospital. Now only Betty Kate and Lillian lived in the basement apartment. And there were fewer visitors, although Betty Kate by herself was no small attraction. Mary worked for a government office in Montgomery. Elizabeth was occupied learning to be a Yeager, aided by her mother-in-law, Millie. By herself with the others in the Philpot house, Elizabeth complained. There were so many things that a Yeager woman did or did not do. Yeager women, for instance, did not wash dishes—although that in itself was no problem. At a bridal shower, Elizabeth had been given a set of dish towels; and Lillian, who sat beside her offering polite comments about each gift, made the remark that Elizabeth would enjoy the towels when drying her dishes. "Yeager women do not *do* dishes." Millie's chill declaration. Millie Yeager would never see the basement apartment on Alabama Avenue. She was aware only that the Gray women lived in the Philpot house, which in itself was perfectly acceptable.

There were fewer visitors, too, at this time, because of Frank "Buddy" Griffen. He was there every weekend. He was there almost each evening. Sometimes he stopped in on returning directly from work, before going home to the yellow house on Water Avenue. It had taken some time and effort, on Betty Kate's part, to rid the house of the other callers. Betty Kate was overly kind. Boys wouldn't fail to embarrass themselves—she felt sorry for them. Boys had no sense. The most homely didn't fail to go after an especially pretty or popular girl. That poor Ingraham fellow, for example, who looked like a freckled rabbit—yes, most especially in those cases it was necessary to be kind. But happiness itself made the unpleasant task easier. Betty Kate was in love with herself. Not being able to help it, she imagined her every small move through Frank's eyes—she refused to call him "Buddy." And she was charmed by herself. She was well used to conquests, but this one she wouldn't have expected—if for no other reason, because he was five years older than she was. And yet it was she he had singled out. In this light she imagined herself and was delighted. But there was more than just that. Frank "Buddy" Griffen made her feel something that until now Betty Kate had attached no word to, in connection with another person: he made her feel safe. There was a sureness, a safety in him that she hadn't come across in anyone else, something she knew to be completely dependable. His confidence in himself—that, too, delighted her. Buddy's self-assurance was a quiet sort of thing, but obvious, all the same. He was sure of her absolutely, because he was sure of himself. This Betty Kate was aware of, and with someone else it might have bothered her. But for now, she was lost in small ecstasies. His mouth, alone; the dimples. She knew she was being foolish—it had never happened to her before. She touched his ears with her fingertip—Buddy didn't know the effect on her of his small, shell-shaped ears. He had unusual coloring. The dark hair and pale eyes were Irish. Emma's coloring. She had more or less forgotten the farm woman who was his mother.

That afternoon she'd have some time to correct her hair and make-up—only lipstick and a quick splotch of face powder—in case Frank should stop by before dinner. Perhaps they could sit out on the porch that evening. It was the first week of March—neither spring nor winter, one of those Alabama spells of seasonlessness. Betty Kate preferred the porch, not in any connection with weather, but because she and Frank could be alone. The front porch of the house, in fact, served as a parlor much of the time, in all but the coldest months of the year—Mrs. Philpot encouraged it.

The old lady was not merely gracious about the Grays' use of the porch, but insistent. Privately, she considered herself extremely lucky to be renting to people like the Grays. Lillian Gray was, of course, a fine person. And the girls had been perfectly well brought up. But there was that other, unfortunate situation, she sighed to herself. There was, in a word, Henry. Even old Mrs. Philpot's elderly ears picked up on the sound of his arrival, from as far as several houses away. He drove an old Model A, and the car moved along with that swinging, guttural sound of a much-abused muffler. Inside the car were additional noises, the sharp clanking of empty bottles rolling against each other. Henry had taken to drinking beer. Because it was cheap. The taste appealed to him. And because the relatively low alcohol content sufficed for the crazy chemistry of Henry's body in the way that only the hard stuff would have, for another man. He reeked foully of beer, both stale and fresh. So that the two younger girls, much later, without thinking about why, would find that particular odor and taste disagreeable.

In the first, strange months of their being a family without him, Lillian and the girls didn't speak of him often—this by some unspoken assent. But there were those moments when they'd catch themselves looking at each other in a certain way. All of them knew, then, what the others were thinking. Where was he? Was he well or ill? It hurt Lillian most to wonder if he were hungry. In the beginning he wasn't allowed to visit. Then he began coming by at birthdays, holidays, times that provided some pretext. At each of these times Henry made himself as presentable as circumstances allowed. He braced himself with cups of coffee. As reliably as if they had discussed it as a detailed plan, the girls conspired to crowd their parents, protecting the one or the other from each other. Preventing their being alone. Some awful, sad thing happened when the two parents were together with no one else in the room, although neither Henry nor Lillian said a word at such times. As far as the girls had noticed, they didn't even look at each other. Henry sat with his elbows propped against his knees, dropping his head down into his shoulders. And the girls wondered how it was that in this way, without saying anything, he seemed to be pleading. And that their mother—herself without words—was saying no. There was something in the way she held her head, in the way that she moved, even, that said no to Henry. The silence between their parents was terrible, something in it too powerful for understanding. Henry always left money at the close of a visit. Often the bills were heavily soiled, and worn to the softness of cloth. And often, after Henry left, Lillian took to the room that she shared with Elizabeth, closing the door behind her. Betty Kate took to the back yard, where she ducked behind a large camellia bush, sat back on her heels as she had as a child, and cried.

Once Lillian had come out of the house and startled her. "This is foolishness. Now get up from there and come back inside the house." A little ferociously. She was chastising them both—they had, after all, to be sensible. Lillian had become more sure of herself. She no longer had spells of what Mary once called "the vapors." Her occupation suited her exactly. The uniform she wore was gray, not white—a detail, only, to Lillian's thinking. She considered herself fully a nurse. And even if her salary was small, Lillian's sense of herself was satisfied.

Frank "Buddy" Griffen's sense of himself, too, was satisfied. He worked as an electrician, a field crew chief, at Craig Air Field—and made a good salary. He paid his mother board money, a fact that appeared to amuse her. His car was a '39 Hudson—only a year old, as good virtually as new. The black paint he kept polished to mirror brightness. The brothers were not allowed to eat or drink in that car; but they did plenty of joy riding in it. It was the kind of car that made a person feel good to be seen in. All in all, Buddy's circumstances suited him to a T. He had a good job, an excellent car—and now he had a spectacular girl. In the collective mind of Buddy's young and fairly intolerant world, there was this clear distinction: the natural winners and the losers. Buddy Griffen was a winner. He never questioned whether or not he could do a thing. He had that kind of ability, he knew, that was given out less generously to most other people.

The four brothers were pals—always, they had stuck together. For all his sternness, Ralston was not a watchful parent. And as long as his sons did nothing in particular to attract his attention, he let them be, with no questions asked. They crawled along through the back roads, singing. *Soooo, you can have her. I don't want her. She's too fat for me.* Rounds and rounds of it. They amused themselves grandly—until all hours of the night and morning. That is, all of them did, except Billy, whom the others over-protected. It was unjust. Unjust because the brotherly caution was due to the accident of size. At seventeen, Billy looked three or four years younger. He was therefore not allowed to drink beer with the others. And at some cruelly early hour, when the fun was just cranking into full gear, Billy was quietly deposited at the head of the driveway, to slip into the house through the back door. The truth was that he could have come into the house making all the noise that he pleased. Ralston was a sound sleeper. He snored loudly and pleasurably—all of them wondered how their mother lived through it.

For all the nightly hoopla, the brothers understood that Buddy was also fond of being out alone. As he drove, Buddy did all his ruminating—much of it, at present, about Betty Kate. The Gray girls had always been very much noticed. There was a fellow or two, even, who said that each one was the prettiest girl in her class. That kind of opinion was of course debatable, and the Griffen brothers enjoyed debate of this sort. The oldest one, for sure, had some legs on her. This observation was made by Ralph, who was a leg man—and who had admired Betty Kate's, until that point when Buddy let him know in no uncertain terms that no further commentary was permissible. Ned went in for a nice behind—which asset Betty Kate also possessed. For Buddy, it had always been faces, first—the other things fell in line after. The redhead was a beauty, no doubt about it. But there was something in Betty Kate's face that the redhead didn't have. From the time he spotted her that evening outside the Wilby Theatre, Buddy had given great thought as to just what this difference was. Was it that the face was young? No—that wasn't quite it. Betty Kate didn't yet fully comprehend her own power. Still, that face was no face of a child. Finally he thought that he understood it: she could be hurt—that was what made the face different. How he understood this thing Buddy couldn't have said: that she could be hurt. It angered, unsettled, him—the power of his own feeling unsettled him. But there was a simple sweetness of heart about her. He trusted her entirely.

Buddy's thoughts were not always so lofty. He had his own, private language for parts of Betty Kate's body. Her rounded bottom he thought of as a June apple. And true, she was a leggy girl—at times he found himself thinking of her fondly as "shanks." But her breasts he couldn't make light of in this way. Her breasts were perfect. Buddy went dumb with wonder at the most secret, physical presence of her.

Sitting next to Betty Kate on the front porch swing, he could smell her hair. It was almost no smell at all. Something as clean and indefinite as trapped sun. He had noticed for some time that she was always wearing the same skirt and sweater. The sweater was thin and nubby, almost worn through in spots. It was too tight across the bustline, and this embarrassed Betty Kate. So that she pulled at it savagely when it was wet, trying to stretch it, and succeeded only in making a small rip under the arm. Buddy noticed that the woolen material of her plaid skirt was cheap—and worn so thin that he wondered if it could be seen through when she stood up. The sleeves on her sweater were short. Was she chilly? Outright cold? He felt an odd little nudge inside him, something like anger, at the thought of her being cold. Already he loved her. And she would never again be cold. She would never again want for anything. It would not have been possible for him to believe that there was someone else—Betty Kate's old man, that old reprobate—who wanted that certainty for her, just as much as he did, himself.

It was a fortunate thing that they sat so often out on the swing, out of hearing from anyone else. For their talk at times was the prattle of two children. Love nonsense, it essentially was. "Do you remember me from back then?"

"You were the one with the white hair that stood up like goose down," he may have answered. This line of banter was one of their favorites. The chitchat was inconsequential. Much of their conversation was still in their eyes, each one taking the other deep into him and herself, learning each other; memorizing.

"Get down! It's Daddy." They had been sitting inside on the settee, happily lost, so that Betty Kate didn't notice the noise, the growl of the old Model A, which she and Lillian subliminally listened for. All at once, she stood up, pulled Buddy around to the back of the settee, and crouched.

"He's been drinking." It was a remark she could have made at pretty much any time, these days. Henry's continuous tippling had given way to days-long binges of fearful drunkenness. At such times he would appear, fumble against the door a while, finally turn and go away again. Betty Kate lowered her head. "I can't stand to see him like this," she added.

Buddy had obeyed her moves without asking a question. But he did edge over just enough to bring the doorway into view. It was unnecessary on that occasion to conceal himself—Henry couldn't have seen them, at any rate. He wore his usual felt hat; but he had misplaced or lost his glasses. He stood for a while, frowning and squinting, tried the door again, then gave it up and left. Betty Kate and Frank crouched behind the settee, not talking, until they heard the sound of the engine. Then she simply sat and stared, as if there were no one else in the room. Buddy had never seen her face so still, or so plainly beautiful—it hurt him, almost, to look at. She sat with her hands resting in her lap, palms up. Somehow Buddy knew that he should leave at that moment. But he had to make some gesture. He took her hand and squeezed it a little. He had an urge to turn it over and kiss the palm.

They should have the old fellow locked up—Buddy told himself that he should have called the police. Or at the least advised Betty Kate to do so. He was shaken; at the same time he was thoughtful. They would be together for life. Yet he was learning that there were places, small worlds, in this person he loved that he could not know or touch. It was on the following evening that he asked her to marry him. Afterward, they rocked together on the porch long hours into the night, held in a solemn reverie by this thing that was larger than they were. This other country they had entered.

Returning home, Buddy parked his car on the street, toward the far corner of the house lot, not understanding why he did this. Only that something momentous had happened; something was forever changed. He wanted to come across no one. On this end of the block, the houses were large, but plain. Country houses that had somehow made it to town. The yards, so still in the dark, had a trance-like quality about them. Now, as Buddy walked up the driveway, everything seemed transformed. The same, over-familiar back yard was different. Because *he* was. And because it mattered now that she had once been there; meaning nothing to him, then. Now he looked into that other yard, knowing that he couldn't have back the years they had missed. All along it was going to be she, little towheaded Betty Kate, and he hadn't known it. His eyes searched that other yard, remembering. She had this unusual effect on him—made him want not just herself but something he couldn't determine, and so could not have. His feeling for Betty Kate: when he was most in love, ready to split with the joy of it, strangely it hurt him. It was curious. The familiar back yard was dark. The leafless March branches made the space of the sky seem larger. So empty and still that the soft night noises were like the sound of the earth breathing right through him. There was presence here, some sort of immensity. Buddy understood just for a moment that this night sky was flung out all over the continents—farther even than that. And that it still held the years, his and hers, in a way that he could not comprehend.

He broke into a smile—he would have liked to whistle. To think of it: that he, Frank Griffen, would be the head of a family. His own. That there would be children. A boy of his own, most especially: himself, made over and started out new. He could imagine his boy. A smiling baby with dimples in its knees and a single front tooth. He'd be a pal to his boy. And as soon as the boy was past diapers, Frank would put this son up on his shoulder and carry him forward into the world.

His eyes adjusted gradually to the dark. There was a bright, white spot, his mother's sun hat, carelessly dropped in the rows of spring onions where she had been working. His mother: could she have understood what he was feeling? Was there anyone else at all who could have felt anything this rare and fine? His own father: Buddy felt not a doubt that in his lifetime Ralston had loved exactly nothing, would have known not a moment of this sweet and fine thing that Buddy knew. And the old man—her old man: had he ever felt a rare and good thing in his life? Buddy thought he knew the answer to that, too.

Chapter 30

Bryce Hospital
Tuscaloosa, Alabama

In the fourteen years since that spring night in 1940, there had been many phone calls of the sort that Buddy wished Betty Kate to make.

Behind Henry's wing of the hospital, the grounds were long and deep, and lined by thin woods. Then beyond that, pasture-land. Just ordinary pasture. And although it was dim under the trees, the early sun already lay bright over those stretches of open field. A herd grazed beyond the creek that bordered the grounds. Henry could sometimes hear the push of the working mouths cropping over the grass. At dusk, one old broad white cow carried the last light around with her, gleaming on her flanks. The stretch of pasture was homey and quiet in its everyday business, while some seventy-five yards behind it, the world was cut off. Henry had stopped seeing the chain-link metal—he looked through it. It was as good as no longer there. He didn't think much, at present, about how long he might have to be here, in this place—he didn't expect it to be long. It was another temporary situation, another version of the hospital stays, which, despite his many resolves, he terminated each time, by getting up from the bed, putting on his clothes, and simply walking out of the building.

How long he'd been here—he wasn't entirely sure. His arrival was a fragment of time set off by itself—the incident faded, already submerged, like an old memory. His recollection of the trip in the sheriff's car surfaced and blanked. He remembered miles and miles of poor, piney country, no habitation to speak of, just worn fields and slopes of streaked yellow clay. Then finally, an entrance with square, brick pillars. A long, tree-lined stretch. Then the building. Out of nowhere. It rose out of the ground like a behemoth, three-storied, with a dome and stained glass windows. Lower and upper porches, then a third story. Long lines of white columns. Wings on each side, with bars at the windows. Henry recalled thinking that it looked more like a palace than a crazy house.

Right here, behind his own wing—he had asked permission to be here, at the far edge of the grounds, where he could look out over an ordinary site. And he considered the permission granted, although that wasn't exactly the case. He'd singled out Nurse Compton, who, together with the orderly Hollis, rolling the medicine cart, accompanied Dr. Spivey on his rounds. The nurse, a soft, maternal type of woman, was the only person so far that Henry conversed with, to speak of.

Dr. Spivey was detached and brusque, his conversation minimal.

"Morning, Mr. Gray. We'll just need to let Mrs. Compton get your pressure, here. Appetite all right?" He didn't pause for an answer. "Set you up to begin with Dr. Levy, one the staff psychiatrists." Already Dr. Spivey was moving past Henry's rocker. He continued down the porch.

By contrast with the doctor, Nurse Compton was effusive. And it was genuine warmth—Mr. Gray seemed a courteous sort. She pumped up the bulb and released the air, watching the needle. "Now, you'll like Dr. Levy—such a nice young man."

The subject of the psychiatrist didn't interest Henry much

at this time. But his walking, being able to get out and move around—that was critical. "Would it be all right if I walked—just walked, yonder, along the fence?" Henry gestured.

The doctor had moved further down the porch. "Well, I don't see why—." Mrs. Compton's answer had been spontaneous, but she stopped herself. "I'd have to ask the doctor." She had forgotten to ask, but the tone of her voice was all the affirmative Henry needed.

So he walked at intervals throughout the day, always first thing in the morning, again at late light. The first time Henry left his room in this manner, unauthorized, Hollis had seen him but had ignored him. And because he had done the same on subsequent occasions, Henry concluded that Hollis would give him no trouble—the one gesture of human feeling the man made toward Henry. Henry figured that Hollis was too nervous for much fellow feeling, a thin and tense kind of person.

"We scare the fellow. That's what it is," Henry thought. "He can't tell one of us apart from another."

But Henry gave little thought to Hollis. The thing that interested him at this time was not, strangely enough, the idea of where he was, but the depth of his exhaustion. Like a trail of dead weights. He couldn't remember being exhausted in a way that a night's sleep wouldn't repair—no amount of rest seemed to restore him. But it was all the same, for the present. Henry's life had been brought to a stop. He'd had no say-so in the matter. But the time hadn't come, yet, when he would think of the situation as being locked up. No, as a matter of fact, for the moment Henry felt an odd relief. The bodily tiredness had a pull all its own. He gave in to it—Henry looked forward these days to his nightly rest like someone else might anticipate a good meal. And during the day, except for the walking, Henry tended to sit in his rocker or lie on his bed. Not trying to sleep, exactly; just feeling safe in the knowing that no one would disturb him. Henry sank into that bed, very conscious of its physical support. For the time being, there was no more struggle to make. It was good to be still, just still and quiet. To at last be released from the struggle. Only a mild curiosity had prompted him to walk the porch corridor of the two-story, clapboard building, which was set back a distance on the grounds. The rooms were small, each with a window looking out onto the porch. Inside each were a bed, chair, and bedside table with Bible. Beside the door to each room were rockers, all identical, all painted black. There was a kind of recreation room, not very large, at the end of the corridor. A ping-pong table stood in the middle; both paddles and balls were missing. The room wasn't used much—a few of the men played cards there. But there was one curious thing. At one end of the room was a shelf of *National Geographics*, all of them tattered and loose. Henry never saw anybody reading one. There were comic books, and those were read and re-read. But the magazines—Henry supposed that some doctor had brought them in for the pictures—each day they ended up on the floor, trampled-looking, with more pages coming loose. Henry restacked them once or twice. Then, on one pass by the room, he noticed a man sitting against the far wall, by himself. Young, with a blank face that looked at nothing in particular. As Henry watched him, he produced tiny objects one at a time from his shirt pocket, positioning each one carefully between his thumb and middle finger. Then they flew. Spitballs. Made from pages of *The National Geographic*. Aggravated, Henry took the magazines, himself; but he didn't read them. Only felt rich in the hoarding of them—he stored them in the suitcase under his bed. Felt a little smug about it, in fact, like the time he had "borrowed" the books from old Miss Lewis. He was saving the magazines. He couldn't have read anything just yet—didn't have the mind for it. For the present Henry rested—he didn't know when anything

had been so comforting as this rest. His walks near the back property line were slow, aimless strolls. The odors of spring were still
locked up, the March air not yet warm enough to release them.
Henry gratified his senses on simple sights, absorbed the small,
ordinary sounds of the lot and pasture.

David Levy had come from Ann Arbor to do his residency
at Bryce's, and he was not having an especially easy time with
Southerners. The voices, alone, were enough at first to give him
pause. The women had the most noticeable peculiarity. The feminine voices seemed to be raised a pitch or two, with a curious flatness to the sounds; they crooned and cooed, with odd inflections.
In the beginning, the speech had come across to David as a form
of affectation—he kept expecting it to be discarded, at some point
in time. But then he realized his mistake. Gradually, he'd come
to understand that this was ordinary speech, not contrived—that
the sentiments expressed in this manner were in fact genuine.
Southern women were, if anything, over-solicitous, fluttery. With
the men, however, there was the bluff joviality that he couldn't get
past. And to most of them, he suspected, his branch of medicine
was no more than a refined form of Voodoo. He couldn't get near
the men. In the first place, he didn't hunt, an aberration generally
attributed to his being a Yankee. Neither did he fish. The game of
golf could have provided a link, but he wasn't very good at it—
Southern men took their sports very seriously. He was asked to
social gatherings and attended, to be honest, from a sense of duty.
On such occasions he contributed a mild and congenial presence.
The gatherings could have, in fact, interested David a good bit,
if he could have done what he wanted to do, which was sit unnoticed and simply observe—Southerners he found to be rich

objects of observation. Of course, he couldn't just sit back and watch; but he did take the opportunity to pay attention to hands. David had always paid attention to hands, and when he could do so with a patient, he often began with the hands. This wasn't a professional strategy, just a thing that he liked to do. Hands had an expression, almost like faces.

David Levy was the serious sort, always had been. Over-serious, to tell the truth—a thing which was at present a certain social liability. His face had a single unusual feature, the mouth. When relaxed, the face gave the impression that he was smiling slightly. This was because Levy's mouth had lines on either side, little half-moon shaped grooves at each corner. His own hands, if anyone had observed, were attentive. As Dr. Levy looked over his notes, he laid a hand over the pages. And David Levy made copious notes. He was fairly strictly Freudian—not because this would have been his approach of choice necessarily, but because he had been extensively schooled in psychoanalysis. Nor had he yet occasion or experience enough to substitute one methodology for another. To his mind, as a whole there was no field short of preservation of life itself more important than his own. He was an ardent spirit. And he was lonely.

Henry had forgotten any mention of the psychiatrist. It was Nurse Compton, as she trailed behind the doctor that morning, who reminded him. And as it turned out, Henry had most of the day to think about it. So, he was going to have his head examined—maybe they hadn't taken him to be sane, after all. The fatigue that had dragged against Henry these past weeks was lessening, with his rest. He spent a greater part of the day walking. There'd been a couple of warm days, already, and from one of the rooms Henry could hear the droning of an electric fan, a tranquil sound. His mind was like that, for the most part—blank and tranquil. Henry didn't stop to consider that the medication he was given may have been responsible for his state of mind. He let himself be. So it was with tranquil interest that Henry allowed himself to be led to his appointment that afternoon. A mind doctor. He'd read something about it somewhere, this thing called psychiatry. Mind doctoring. He didn't know, frankly, if he held with it. But he was curious.

Levy sat behind his desk—he didn't stand up, at first, to greet Henry. His office was small, one of the many, closet-like spaces built into the west wing. Levy spent a good amount of his private time there, so it was there that he'd brought his philodendron, a plant grown out long enough to make a thick leafy coil. Levy had trailed it around the window, up, across, and down again, with its dangling lateral stems: a little oddity that pleased him, and an unexpected sight for the patient. It stopped Henry at the door. Each man used that brief pause to make a quick, visual study of the other. Levy noticed that Henry held himself very straight, that he wore a nubby flannel shirt, although the days were warming. Henry noticed that the doctor was surprisingly young, that he had the look, somehow, of a minister about him. He seemed to be smiling a little. Levy rose to introduce himself, shook Henry's hand, and then both sat. There was no feeling of hurry. On the desk was a folder containing papers on Henry. Levy laid his hand over it for a moment, and Henry noticed the gesture.

"How are you managing here, Henry?"

The use of his first name startled Henry somewhat, coming from a man that young. The question seemed deliberately personal.

"Oh, I'm making out all right, I guess."

Levy saw the deep creases beneath the man's mouth. He had sorrowful eyes. "I'd like for you to begin, if you will, by telling me about yourself."

Both the suggestion and the phrasing of it were new to Henry, who had prepared himself, so he thought, for all manner of questions. He studied a few moments, then fell into an obliging recitation of the facts of his illness. Levy waited until he could politely interrupt.

"I've familiarized myself with your medical history, Henry." He gave a small push to the folder. "There's no need for you to go into it for me. Your medical history isn't our subject, here. Our subject here is you."

This too struck Henry as odd. He chuckled, a delaying tactic. Levy was accustomed by now to the conversational chuckle of Southerners of a certain age. Henry had never, to his recollection, been asked to talk about himself as the subject of a conversation.

Levy saw that he was having some difficulty. "Can we start at the beginning?" He nodded, urging Henry.

Henry made a stab. "Well, I was born in '92. Folks started out as farmers. No big crops. Some cotton. Corn." Henry leaned forward on his knees as he talked. He'd prepared himself to tell the story of his illness—to be totally honest about it. But he could not have said for sure when it was that his life had first gone dark, then blank, like days strung out in a dream sequence. Some of it nightmare. Henry had left the little abandoned gray house on Range Street that morning for the floors of Strayer's, the empty warehouses or lots, any odd corner where he could lay down his body. Himself and Drefus and all those faceless others. He didn't speak about that.

Levy was a soft-spoken man. "Family history isn't what's important here. Let's focus on you—as a member of your family, if you'd like to."

There was the chuckle.

"Try putting your life into story form for me. Start at the beginning. Just tell me the story of yourself."

A story. Well, he could do that much, he imagined. "A story," he repeated. An odd notion, to make a story about himself.

"That's right. From the beginning. As much as you can remember, especially from your childhood. We'll want to concentrate on your childhood."

His childhood. That seemed a peculiar topic to dwell on, under the circumstances. "Well, there were the five others besides me. I have a brother, Drefus." Henry relaxed a little now. He could enjoy talking about Drefus. "Now, my brother, Drefus—he's a character, all right. Lives over in Uniontown these days. Married a widow named Bea. We had some times, Drefus and I did." Here Henry could have told the man some stories, for real.

Levy gently interrupted. "Let's keep the focus on you."

On himself. Henry was as good a one as any for conversation, but a conversation had to be *about* something. A person didn't just go on and on about himself. "Well, what exactly would you be wanting to know?"

"Let's begin with your relationship with your parents and family." Levy was persistent. "Your mother. What was she like? Tell me what you remember about her."

Henry's mind caught a swift picture of his mother, standing in her apron, hands on her hips—they were sturdy hips. The mild, half-smiling expression, the sudden switch to scolding. There seemed to be nothing outstanding to tell. She'd been a little severe.

Levy persisted. "Describe her for me."

How to describe her. "She was a little heavy set. Had brown hair, gone to gray."

It was not going to be easy. But, then, it seldom was. Levy's hand twitched, holding his pen "Let's try it like this. What were your parents' names?"

"They were Annie and Joe."

"Well, start by telling me about Annie and Joe. How did they meet each other? What kind of people were they? Tell me about their marriage and children."

Henry examined Levy's face, for any sign that the man was making some sort of sport with his questions. Levy's eyes were attentive, not making fun. He simply waited. Henry had the sudden impression that the young man was kindly.

"There was a man named Joe who was married to Annie," Levy began for him. For the first time, Levy smiled outright. He tilted his chair back, now playing with his pen. His feet moved.

Again, Henry was surprised at how young a man the doctor was. Under ordinary circumstances, it would have seemed perfectly natural to address him as "son." What he wanted must be some sort of mind game, Henry decided, finally. And he'd always been able to tell a good story.

"Well," Henry chuckled. "They say Annie was a pretty sort of woman. Laughed a lot. Had a lot of callers. And Joe, he was a serious young fellow, churchgoing type. Think my Pa said they met at a church social. She gave him a time of it, made him chase around after her a lot." Another chuckle. Henry was trying to get into the spirit of the thing, but his mind wouldn't stay there—it moved instead to the picture of Lillian, herself young, wearing a white dress. The perfect mouth. The way she sometimes covered it with her hand when she laughed. The way she laughed so hard at times that she doubled at the waist. Then the mouth drew down at the corners. Henry would have liked to talk about Lillian, the sight of her. How it had pleasured him. Her little ways. He paused.

Levy observed the hesitation and entered a note on it. And this made Henry catch himself, attempt a switch back to the subject of his family. There were of course Olive and Myrtie, of whom he'd been fond. Henry wanted most to tell Levy about Drefus. Now where in the world to begin about Drefus, when there never had been a time when Drefus wasn't there. Once started, he could have easily talked the whole time about Drefus. And there was too the imagining of how things would have been without this brother. Henry wondered, frankly, if the drinking would have ever begun. But Levy had already noted Henry's tendency to take off about this one brother—and stopped him.

"There were others."

There was Jay. Henry wondered if he ought to tell the man about Jay. The quiet face, the faraway look. He decided to risk it—Jay's invisible folks and their carryings-on would make for a good tale. But the tales and the story, Henry's own recollections, got all mixed up, about that point. For Henry, there was no particular connection among the things he remembered from his childhood, just a string of images, like small claps of light. There were the woods and the meadows and creeks. There was that secret spot behind the cornfield. There were the stolen books, his first treasures—he couldn't tell the man about those. There was going outside alone in the mornings, just to watch, think about things. There was the slow river; the quiet, waiting woods. Henry looked, now, into his memory, seeing these things—he said nothing out loud. He couldn't say much of anything, without coming back to Drefus. And that led Henry unaccountably to think of the boy. He hesitated again. Levy noticed. He would have liked most, at that moment, to talk about the boy. But he realized it wouldn't be part of the story. He knew he had gotten lost somewhere on the part about Jay.

Again Levy made a notation. But he wasn't dissatisfied with the session, so far—or especially impatient. Henry seemed to enjoy talking, and Levy was aware that between the spurts of talk, the man's mind was working. The puzzling thing was that Levy couldn't place Henry as a type. His clothes were poor, the clothes of a ruffian, but Henry wasn't rough. His posture alone gave that away—there was a certain poise in the way the man held himself, whether standing or sitting, a dignity even. The speech offered no very specific clues. The accent was heavily regional, the language informal, in the local manner. But Levy noticed that Henry made none of the usual grammatical mistakes. He wondered about the man's education, if he had had any—that information wasn't included in the folder. It crossed his mind briefly to ask if Henry read, but he had learned by now that intellectuality was suspect in the South—it wasn't likely. Looking at Henry, Levy could pick up on no single clue that would give him an idea of the man's personal history—except that he had fallen on hard times. But most of the South had done as much, these past several decades.

Levy stood and leaned against the window for a moment, biting his thumb, as he sometimes did when he was thinking. It was the same, the same issue, always—it came up with each one of them. Was he going to be able to do anything for this man?

Henry sat with no self-consciousness while Levy stood, biting the tip of his thumb. Already an atmosphere had been established of a certain ease, an absence of hurry, an intentional thing on Levy's part. Neither man appeared bothered by intervals of silence. Henry folded his hands and rested them on the edge of the desk, and that was the first opportunity Levy had to look at them. Southern men tended to throw their hands around when they talked. But Henry's were still. They were rough, work-thickened hands, enlarged at the joints. The nails were not clean. But then, they may have been different hands, at one time—Levy knew that years of the man's life had been laid to waste by his illness.

As a matter of fact, Henry was fairly meticulous about his hands; he borrowed scissors or files from Nurse Compton when he needed them. But the hands couldn't be made to look clean, at least not yet. There were black lines around each nail, which he could scrub out, a little at a time. But where the nails had split into the quick and the black lines followed—there was nothing he could do about that.

As Levy looked at Henry, he knew that the question was coming, that he should have withheld it, that he was going to ask it, anyway. That the wrong answer would stay with him, plaguing him, for days, maybe longer.

"Henry, do you have visitors?" Henry seemed to be looking off at some distant spot.

He came to attention. "My brother, Drefus. He comes with his wife." Levy would learn that although there were others, the words, my brother, referred only to Drefus. "And my daughter, Betty Kate. She comes each week."

Levy felt an enormous relief, though he noticed that the old gentleman was studying on something. It was that Betty Kate wouldn't bring the grandchildren, Ellen and Rallie. He missed the boy badly.

Now Levy sat again. "I take it that you have no contact with your ex-wife."

"She lives in London with my daughter, Mary."

London. That was unexpected.

"Mary always did say she wanted to live in London. Said she wanted to see Rome." Henry's voice dropped off. He let his hands fall back on his knees. Then he continued, "Lillian wanted to go with her." He made a noise probably intended to come out as a chuckle. "Said she wanted to float around Venice, Italy on some kind of boat."

Grieving. Was the man grieving?

"Can you say a little more about that?" With time Henry would become familiar with the question.

"Never was satisfied to live here, Mary wasn't. Went to Montgomery, first, then Washington, D.C. Always planned on getting to London. Started up about it when she was still little."

It wasn't the line of thought that Levy had hoped to follow.

"And your ex-wife?"

"Oh, she likes it fine over there. Seems to suit her. Betty Kate tells me about it."

Always, Levy had to slow himself down. This was enough for a beginning. Levy stood for a final time. Again, the men shook hands.

It was a beginning, and a fairly good one, as beginnings went. The two men had taken a liking to one other, although neither of them could have been sure of the other's feeling in that respect.

When Henry walked the fence line that evening, he thought of his meeting with Levy. The truth was that he'd thought of nothing else since he'd left that office. As he walked, he pulled on the ends of a branch that trailed over from the other side of the fence. An old live oak. A few new leaves came off in his hand. The evening air was soft. Sounds were muffled, even the heavy clink of dishes and utensils, sounds of cleaning up from the dining hall. Henry smiled to himself. The meeting—it had stayed with him like something set apart at a distance. He had the peculiar sense of having traveled. He felt different all over. He felt an immense goodwill toward the young doctor. The man interested Henry. And more: made him suspect that there was something he, himself, hadn't gotten to. Was it possible that there could be a whole world of something out there, that he, Henry, hadn't gotten to? With that ministerial air, the odd smile, Levy made him suspect it. Henry sensed that this man knew things that he didn't. Important things. It was education—must be—that made the difference, a different set of chances all the way around. So, there were men, then, ordinary men, who were different in this way, who understood a world of things that he, Henry, didn't know. He'd have to study on that.

Our subject here is you. Himself. The statement was odder, even, than it might have been, up against his thinking of recent days. After almost two decades of stillness, Henry's mind had begun to stir. He'd had a notion, something that at one time would have struck him as a streak of imagination, gone a little wild. And the notion was this: he was nobody. Maybe the idea had come to him in the walking out by himself, when he pictured himself from across the grounds, as anybody looking out through a window would have seen him, an aging man in worn-out clothes, wearing taped-together glasses and a none-too-clean felt hat. Nobody. Nobody that anyone knew. Here, in this place, a person looking out on one man by himself wouldn't know if he were sane, if he had a past, a family, people who knew him—a name, even. Then it occurred to Henry that everyone was nobody to the world of people who didn't know him—even though the world went on, every bit of it, inside those other people, just like it did inside himself. The world was made up, in a manner of speaking, of nobodies. What that came down to was that he, Henry, was of no more account than the next fellow. And, funny thing, it didn't make any difference—the notion had its appeal, even, in a way that he couldn't quite figure. Now Henry thought of telling his idea to Levy, if he could have explained it just so, so as to make the gist of it understood for the both of them. Would it be part of the story he was supposed to keep to? Again Henry smiled. He hadn't been paying much attention to where he was walking, which was the whole length of fence that ran along the pasture. It was warm enough for a few crickets to have started. A soft, whisper-like noise. Henry gave his attention briefly to the sound, then started back across the yard.

Chapter 31

Within a week or so following his return to Clanton, Henry and the boy had their routine down pat, to the full satisfaction of each. Henry picked up the boy soon after supper. The thick summer dusk was long; they would have plenty of daylight left. When he heard the truck, the boy would rush out of the house, yelling. These days he wore his cowboy getup: a hat, boots, and holster belt with cap pistols. He fired a greeting, causing Wolf to give a warning growl as the dog jumped down from the truck after Henry. The boy had several fresh rolls of caps in his pocket. He was a happy child—the fact that just minutes before he'd had a temper tantrum had nothing to do with that fact. Betty Kate had already given him his supper—she and Ellen, the boy's sister, would wait for Frank. The old Griffen Motor had by now been transformed into an automobile dealership.

"I guess Frank's got a car deal." Betty Kate spoke with her back to Henry, who took a seat in the kitchen, from habit.

"Want a cup of coffee?" Betty Kate was already making the preparations for it. She and Henry drank coffee together at any hour. There was always some small or large news of the household, the dealership, or the children. It seemed that the boy hadn't been particularly attentive in school that year. He had caused no special trouble, merely sat through his school days with his mind somewhere else, dreaming vaguely until his release. Betty Kate wasn't seriously worried—he was after all just a first grader. She'd run into Rallie's teacher, Miss Jewel, at church that Sunday.

There'd been some little murmured concern—Miss Jewel was elderly—followed by equally mild and murmured reassurances. Just about any story on the boy, good or bad, caused Henry to chuckle roundly.

"Well, I wouldn't say it's so funny." Henry knew there was no real reprimand in Betty Kate's voice. But Frank—now, Frank was another matter. He was cheerful enough, but beneath the good spirits there was always something else. He and Henry were amiable towards each other. Henry had the two sons-in-law—Mary hadn't married—with whom he had no quarrel. In fact, he had everything to be grateful for in the two men. Both were generous. Henry didn't yet draw Social Security, and the generosity was frankly needed. Henry knew neither young man well, George because he seldom saw him—the Yeager place was some fifteen miles out of town.

He couldn't have said that he really knew Frank, either, although the young Griffens lived just a few minutes down Alabama Avenue from where Henry roomed. And this was because—well, Frank was just Frank. He was invariably polite to Henry, never failing to address him in a warm manner, usually rather formally, "How're you today, Mr. Gray?" Later, the form of address was softened a little, to "Grampaw." But the shining politeness was like an upraised palm, and Henry stayed at his distance. Frank was different. Words like "fine" and "upstanding" came to mind at the mention of Frank "Buddy" Griffen. Frank bristled with it, those qualities—those and competence. Frank was smart, they said. Frank was exceptional. People depended on Frank. All of them, even the old man, worked at the business. The brothers were partners, and the old man was nominally the head, although he hadn't pretended to do much of anything since Ned was killed in the war. Whatever it was that made Frank distant, he had no doubt come by it from the old man, Henry imagined. He remembered Ralston's glaring, from the time when the families were neighbors.

But hard and standoffish as the old man was, he'd shown some surprising behavior—Henry heard all of the Griffens' news from Betty Kate. They said that when word came about Ned, Griffen had put his garage in order—it was still a garage, then—put away his tools and machinery, all arranged just so, then locked the door and left. He never went back. He spent long hours, light or dark, isolated in his garage shed at home. Henry would have never imagined the man capable of that kind of attachment, although he understood that the family had set a special store by Ned, who'd begun college on an athletic scholarship when he was sent overseas. Frank had declined the partial academic scholarship he was offered. He remembered how the woman's face would change at the mention of her boys. Her he knew to be a woman of good, kindly feeling; it had all eventually come out from Lillian—the "trading" for eggs, the gifts on moving day. He knew the woman would have taken a son's loss hard. After Ned's plane went down, Dr. Mabry arranged through the Red Cross to have one of the brothers—Frank—sent home. It was called a hardship case, with all four of the boys in the war at the same time. Alone, back in Clanton, Frank had gone over the books, re-designed and relocated the business.

Henry reflected on Frank; there was a quality—there was something unforgiving—in Frank. If he didn't like—even despised—Henry, of course Henry couldn't in all fairness blame him. Everyone who ever saw them together knew how it was with Frank and Betty Kate. They were crazy about each other. Frank had suddenly seen Betty Kate, whom he'd known for years as one of those three little girls next door, just once—that is, really seen her. It was a January evening in 1940; Betty Kate was eighteen that year. They were on the pavement outside the Wilby Theatre,

Betty Kate and another girl, with their arms linked together, and laughing. Betty Kate skipped a little as she walked. Right then, he decided—Frank always thought, later, that he had decided, from just that one look.

He went to Emma first, with his news.

"The little Gray girl!" Emma beamed at Buddy. "Well, I sewanee." Then she was suddenly thoughtful. "I always did wonder what happened to them." Emma had never learned to drive an automobile; but Nettie often took her to town on Saturdays, sometimes just to sit in the parked car and, as they put it, "watch the people go by." Every now and then she thought she caught sight of someone who looked like Lillian. She never caught sight of anyone resembling Mr. Gray.

"What happened to them, Buddy? Back in the Depression." Emma jumped ahead. "Where are they living now?"

"Well, they aren't all of them together anymore, Mama."

"What happened?"

"It got bad with Mr. Gray. They had to separate."

"The drinking."

"Yes'm."

Emma looked off. "Well, where is he now? And where are Lillian and the girls?"

It surprised Frank a little to hear his mother refer to Mrs. Gray by her given name. "They live over on Alabama Avenue. Mrs. Gray works at the hospital." Then Frank paused. "I don't know what happened to *him*."

"Well, I hate to hear that it went bad for him." Emma held steadfastly to the opinion she'd formed of Henry that day he'd walked over and taken the hoe out of her hand. "He *was* a nice man."

Buddy looked at his mother strangely. She could come out with the oddest things, sometimes. "Betty Kate doesn't much like to talk about it." Emma saw that at the mention of the girl's name, a smile started in Buddy's eyes that swept all across his forehead.

"You'll have to give me some time to get it fixed with your Daddy." The words had a familiar ring.

But Emma had not been able to fix this one. Ralston was outraged—that his oldest son should marry into a family like *that*! With a reputation of the kind that man and his brother had! There was no reasoning with him. And for a while, the house had been dark with his anger. It had been Betty Kate, herself, who had fixed it, after all—when Buddy, never doubting her ability to make an impression, resolutely brought her home for a formal introduction. Home again, almost, for Betty Kate—there on Water Avenue. To Betty Kate Frank let on nothing of the dissension in his household. And even Ralston couldn't fail to fall in with the courtesy demanded by that occasion. Because Betty Kate charmed him—or came as close to charming him as could be done with Ralston. It was not, after all, possible to disapprove of her. She was sunshine in a room. Privately, Ralston continued to frown and clear his throat with the family members. But all of them caught on to the changed attitude—for a sure fact when he introduced Betty Kate to raw oysters with hot pepper sauce. The purchase of a barrel of fresh oysters became a special sort of occasion for the two of them.

His daughter's wedding: Henry couldn't get any of it back. It was lost to him, in the long blank of years. If he could have chosen one thing to relive, it may have been that occasion—of seeing his best loved daughter radiant and fulfilled. They were married before Frank went overseas. But by the time of the war years, Henry's mind was a void. He remembered nothing of the ceremony—which was not a wedding as such, but a simple exchange of vows in a church. It was Drefus who had made him presentable and sat with him, in a back pew. Henry didn't remember, then, that the daughter who resembled him was as perfect and composed as a portrait of herself, in her cream-colored suit—the single expense the family could make for the wedding. That, and the corsages for both of the mothers, who to everyone's amazement greeted one another like old, dear friends. Nettie had talked Emma into cutting and perming her hair. Emma had just been to the beauty parlor, and felt a little self-conscious but pleased with herself. Behind each ear she wore a dab of *Evening in Paris*. And Henry didn't remember whether or not Ralston had glared at him. Which Ralston hadn't done—he ignored Henry altogether. Or that Emma had come conspicuously to the back of the church to greet him, while Ralston stood down front, with a mottled and furious face.

Frank was arriving. Neither Betty Kate nor Henry heard the car enter the back yard. Frank always drove an automobile that had that sweetish smell of a new car about it, a silent and smooth company demonstrator. The boy was yelling again. Wolf barked a couple of times. Then Frank himself came whistling across the yard. An exuberant, high-pitched whistle.

Henry chuckled. "Looks like he made the deal."

Frank flashed a greeting to Henry, as he entered the house, the smile of a consummate salesman. The boy was suddenly clamoring to be off. Rallie had the grocery bag, neatly folded, that contained his pajamas and toothbrush. The pajamas were never used; the toothbrush wouldn't see use before the following morning, if at all. Henry, too, was ready, but one quick deviation from routine was necessary. He had a tadpole with arms and legs that he'd caught in a jar for his friend Louise's boy, John Earl. At the Bluebird he pulled around to the back and left the truck engine running. Betty Kate was emphatic that Rallie not be taken inside the Bluebird—it was no fit place for children, she said.

Then they were on the Orville Road, driving out of town, past the Live Oak Cemetery.

Rallie stood on his knees, next to Wolf. "Can we fish all day tomorrow, Grampaw? All day long? Can we?"

Henry made a turn. "Boy, we'll fish from can see till can't see." Rallie squealed, which prompted a growl from Wolf. Henry, grown slightly hard of hearing, didn't pick up on the growls. The truck had turned off in front of a scaling clapboard store.

"What d' you want for breakfast, boy?"

The boy's nose wrinkled a little when he grinned. "I want a Butterfinger!"

Rallie had meant to go into the store with Henry, but there were objects outside that required shooting. Henry emerged shortly with his purchases: bread and milk, peanut butter, a package of cinnamon rolls, and a double Butterfinger. They drove a gravel road to the spot at the cattle gap, which before had been a flimsy, barbed wire fence. The thistle-strewn pasture was no longer in use. They drove, now, where Henry and Drefus had once walked. A tire path angled off to the right, past the old Catalpa, which was dying back, the branches all gray on one side, the other side heavy with flat leaves and frilly white blossoms. Henry drove right up to the porch of the cabin, which had come into some disrepair during his years at Bryce's. Some of the steps rotted and a window ledge gone. He had to pull down a netting of honeysuckle that covered one side. He'd cleared briar bushes and masses of poison ivy. Then it was almost as though no time had passed. As he stepped down from the running board, Henry removed his hat and passed a hand over his head, now gone almost completely bald. In the hot weather, they had to walk the milk down to the spot below the house where Henry had made a hollow in the branch bottom. The path still required careful climbing. But the boy followed at a rush, and loudly; then he froze.

"Did y' hear that, Grampaw?"

"What's that?"

"Lissen."

Henry stood up, leaving the bottle of milk resting in the water. There was nothing to listen to but the boy's imagination.

"Lissen!" Henry's and the boy's eyes met. " 'Spect it's a wolf?"

Henry held back the laugh. "Don't know if a wolf would be about by day."

"Well, I 'spect it's a wolf."

"Reckon it might be." Henry chuckled.

Chapter 32

Bryce Hospital
Tuscaloosa, Alabama

The mild acquiescence of those first weeks came to an end, as Henry's medication was phased down. He felt betrayed. Angry. Above all, he felt shut up. He had realized, of a sudden, that he couldn't get out. And he *had* to get out! But he couldn't have plotted an escape without Drefus—and Drefus was one of them, now. It was his own Betty Kate that had done this thing to him. She and Elizabeth—Elizabeth, at least, he could have understood. But Drefus—.

The change came to Henry first at night when he lay down. Sleep was no longer a comforting thing—he had little enough of it, now, at all. Just the weariness—a kind of twitching, nervous weariness that sleep wouldn't touch. Beneath the sheet, he felt hot—the room wasn't hot. Hot and dry. The little dry, scratching sounds of mice or rats moving inside the walls annoyed him. His eyes burned. There was an uncomfortable emptiness in his belly—food didn't stay long with Henry. There was something he needed, some soothing, cooling, immersing thing. Drink—he needed a drink. He was frenzied for alcohol. And he knew what lay ahead of him: the struggle, the spiraling argument, the wild swings that exhausted him. The resentment that this affliction had come to him, when other men—his own brother, even, made sport with their drink.

He could no longer sit or stand still for any period of time. The place maddened him, all the little familiar things about it. The porch corridor, the shabby recreation room with its useless ping-pong table. The peculiar, indistinct smell of the place—all of it was over-familiar—the sounds, sights, smells of the place grown suddenly hateful. He had by now examined each foot of the chain-link fence. There was no way to scale it. Rows of barbed wire lined the top. He told himself that if he could just once again be outside these hateful grounds, outside this place, just that one thing by itself would be enough. But he knew it wasn't altogether so.

Alone, he went into rages. At his worst times he needed someone to blame. And it was the daughters. Betty Kate and Elizabeth had met privately with the probate judge, to have him committed. He knew nothing of it until that day the sheriff's car arrived. Had seen the car at a distance, inching down the steep slope that wasn't really a drive, to the little tar paper-covered house. He'd left the Burroughs', hadn't waited to be asked. There'd been a scene there, an ugly one—but he remembered almost none of it. It came about on an afternoon towards suppertime. He'd had a case of the shakes. Been sick to his stomach. The real trouble started with the fish—they had come back. Henry became aware, all of a sudden, that they were in the room with him. Silent and stealthy. The water in the room was murky enough at first that he couldn't see them all. He knew that they weren't real—he tried to remind himself of that. Then he discovered that there was one just next to him, very still, shadowy in the water. An enormous one, deep-bodied and immovable. He saw the blank, filmy eyes. He bumped against it. The cold surprised him, layers and layers of wet cold. Then the terror had come so suddenly that he almost gagged—he was paralyzed with it. A stinging thing, moving up from the different bones of his feet along the backs of his calves. He knew that he must have made a lot of noise, didn't know if he had done any damage to the room. For the incident blanked, there, for Henry. Later, he learned that during the blank he'd been jailed. At his release, he would have gone directly, out of some improbable courtesy, to the Burroughs' to collect his things; but Betty Kate had already been there.

He remembered little, now, about the rented tar-papered house that stood just beneath the river bridge on the side opposite from town, a shoddy structure that let in the weather. Gradually the pieces came back. There something had gone wrong—he couldn't exactly recall. He knew that he'd taken to forgetting things. Like that morning, still too early for most folks to be up and around, that he'd meant to walk across the river bridge to the Green Front store. He'd just walk on across, he told himself, before the traffic started. In his haste, he'd forgotten to put on his shoes. He'd also forgotten his glasses. And on his way home, at the foot of the bridge, the traffic light was down. He'd paused just long enough to help straighten things out a little. He stood at the center of the intersection and attempted to direct. The police were called. Then Betty Kate was there. There was some physical difficulty—he couldn't urinate. Betty Kate was angry—kept asking how long it'd been since he had eaten. And angrier than that about Wolf—no one had been feeding him, it appeared, and the dog had met up with a rattler. His head all swollen, the skin split and festering in places. That part of the story had been told to Henry—he didn't remember. It was too stinking foul a thing to think about. But coming as near as he did to remembering made him realize that he would be wrong to turn on Betty Kate. His resentment toward her left him.

Drefus, however, he could have pummeled to powder. But he couldn't even speak his mind, let alone tie into his brother, because Drefus' wife Bea was always there. Wily old Drefus—he hadn't been caught, like Henry had. Drefus sat in the room sedately, one loose leg crossed over the other, ankles touching. He'd had the nerve to tell Henry that he wasn't *ready* to be discharged. Preachy, downright infuriating—and not to be borne. Drefus had become an old maid in britches since he'd married Bea. He could have blasted his brother with profanity; but oddly enough, this woman Bea had a calming effect on Henry. At first Henry couldn't see for the life of him why Drefus had married her, when Drefus—why, Drefus could have enticed anybody alive. Drefus liked women plump, but Bea wasn't plump in the way he usually liked them, just kind of slack around the middle, like any woman out in a yard slinging feed to her chickens. Drefus was a fool for the children, but Bea wouldn't let him bring any of them along. Henry understood why.

And Levy—he'd turned on Levy a few times. Henry didn't like much to admit this, but he knew it was so. For if there was a side to be on, he knew that Levy was on his. The way Henry saw it, you had to admire a man with a mission, even if you couldn't see it, yourself. And it was a rare thing, kindness—the sort that Levy had. He'd come to accept—thought that he had—Levy's peculiarities, which were many and puzzling. When he felt frantic, these same behaviors infuriated him. For one thing, Levy wouldn't answer a question. He had a way of turning a question back around to Henry. Sometimes he did this with a particularly annoying question of his own: "What do you *want* me to think about it?" Henry began to suspect this boomeranging to be some kind of strategy, on Levy's part. Levy had an odd slant on things, in Henry's opinion, to say the least. He often asked how such and such an incident had made Henry *feel,* when to Henry's best recollection, there'd been no feeling involved, one way or another. He had a special interest in dreams. Was always after what such and such an object appearing in a dream *reminded* Henry of. He couldn't do so much as dream of, say, eating an apple, without Levy carrying on about what an apple reminded him of. For the most part, Henry had few dreams; or if he did, he forgot them within the hour.

There were several unscheduled, night appointments during this troubling time. Henry paced Levy's office, running his hand roughly down the back of his head and neck as he talked. Levy leaned against his desk and watched him. At Henry's first such irregular appointment, he was a little startled at the sight of the doctor without his white coat. He'd had a phone call: Mr. Gray was extremely agitated; it looked as if the situation could become difficult. Levy was needed at once. It was a miserable, early evening toward the end of October. Just about every day, it seemed, for weeks, there'd been rain. A dark, noisy rain. From inside Levy's office, the sound of the rain hitting the gutters was loud. If it had been a routine appointment, Levy would have all the same approached Henry differently. Something was happening to his patient. And Levy didn't try to calm him—that would have been a mistake. It was time to let him be, let the man say whatever it was he felt so urgent about saying. It was simple surrender. They'd been caught up lately in a kind of war, it seemed, the two of them. The change that had come to Henry, from submissiveness to rage—Levy had all along expected it, watched for the signs. The initial calm had given way to something frantic and fever-like. Levy could see it, like something clawing inside the man.

He was trapped. Trapped and locked up. And betrayed. He had tried, once, to explain himself to Levy. But it hadn't really come out. "I'm a woodsman, son"—neither of them seemed to notice the familiar term of address. He was mad for outdoors—to fill his senses with light and air and earth. To see that bright plane of water, sudden as a shout. Things he needed as he needed food for his body.

Once he directly confronted Levy. "What's the point of all this talk about childhood and such? I can't see the good of it, myself."

The question made Levy urgent. He leaned forward in his seat. But that wasn't enough. He walked around the desk and squatted, putting a hand out toward Henry.

"It's like this." The hand moved closer, briefly made contact with Henry's. "I know you don't understand why I devote so much time to talk of your childhood. You see, that's where it all begins, really, for each of us. Unresolved childhood conflicts, things we think we've forgotten—that we *have* forgotten, for all practical purposes. Our compulsions, our fears"—he hesitated—"our addictions have their roots there. If we can just get back to the conflicts, resolve them, we become free, Henry. We free ourselves. It's a kind of miracle. Don't you see?"

Henry wanted to answer that yes, he did see. But he didn't. As he saw it, his conflict began as he grew *out* of childhood. But what he did see was the other man's sincerity—a passion, it seemed to amount to. Levy believed what he was saying. If he'd had less respect for Levy, Henry would have lied to him, out of gratitude. And this despite the fact that Levy continued to perplex him, frustrate—almost fail—him at times, although he couldn't entirely account for that impression. At times, to be truthful, he felt like throttling Levy. All this talk about childhood and dreams had nothing to do with any real life situation. Levy just didn't grasp it. The years—his years. All of them made up of days and hours, hours in which Henry knew he had eaten and slept and worried and sported. Hours as impossible, now, to recall as some dream in the mind of a stranger. And there were those times, too, when he wanted to talk about things that Levy would have dismissed as unrelated. The boy, for instance. He didn't know quite how to put it, this special thing about the boy. That in the world there was something new. A clean sheet of paper not written on. That at odd moments, Henry *was*, almost, the boy. Seeing it all—all over again. New and fresh. As though he, too, was there inside the boy, looking out.

But he had to say this about Levy: when he was troubled, Levy knew how to back off. He let Henry rail. The sessions ran long overtime; and there were many of them. Levy sat back in his chair and simply watched. During these times, his eyes never left Henry's face, though he said very little. An occasional comment: "They were afraid for you." "They were trying to take care of you." "The Depression hurt a great many people." The remarks would stop Henry in his pacing—for seconds, only. He'd look back at Levy. Something might begin to stir, not a full thought, before the anger took over again. He was halted, too, by Levy's expression. It was odd that the man could look so sorrowful at moments, when all the while he had that little smile on his face. When Levy looked troubled, Henry was instantly mollified. He wondered, at one such time, if Levy had ever loved a woman. Loved her so that the lobe of an ear or the shape of her mouth were little sights to almost hurt a man's heart.

He didn't turn again on Levy.

When the rain stopped, the season brightened to its fullest, the first November air tonic with the remembered scent of winter. Henry began to come back to himself a little—his mind reached out. He removed the *National Geographics* from the suitcase under his bed—he had pretty much forgotten about them. But now he looked forward to them greedily. The hoarding of them, in itself, had gratified him, as he'd long ago been gratified to get those books out of the schoolhouse, right under the nose of old

Miss Lewis. At first he only looked over the pictures in the magazines; then he went back and studied them. He began to read with an intensity. It took him out of himself; it took him back to that windbreak spot behind a cornfield, a time remembered like a single image torn out of a dream. In the pictures there were strange-looking plants and bright-colored insects. Waterfalls and wide, vapory rivers. Brown-skinned men in turbans and white loincloths, men with mud coating their spindly legs. Women with bright patterned shawls wrapped around faces and throats. A fountain, where a small, green lion's head with a pipe in its mouth spewed a thin arc of water.

The Faces of Man.

Henry smoothed the crumpled pages, was infuriated by the missing ones. The magazines were his, by his lights—he had practically memorized them. He read through the paperbacks that Betty Kate brought him, most of them Westerns. And these Henry enjoyed in the way he enjoyed a good smoke or a stick of chewing gum. He read the Bible that was placed in the room. At first he read with no special purpose, letting the old, familiar words trickle over him like water. The cadence of them was comforting.

Without his knowing it, his mind had begun the slow work of repairing itself. Henry read and he walked, and between these activities and his meetings with Levy, his periods of intense private cogitation, time began to pass again without his particular attention. He walked the fence line, ankle deep in the litter of leaves, to think over what he had read. He made biblical comparisons. There had been so many countless, nameless numbers of men, and so many years. It had been thousands of separate years since a psalmist took pleasure in lying down in a pasture, just as Henry lay now where the sun hit, for the pleasure of it, the warmth. His energies were engaged in this process of new understanding. He listened and watched, like he had done as a schoolboy. This earthly place was a world full of business. His own particular business didn't matter in the least to that world, which would go on without him, just as it was—which had gone on without him all the way back to wherever it was that time began. The world for Henry and for the psalmist was the same world, that old world that kept on going. That was the thing, then, that mattered. Not anyone, in any certain place, with a name—like Henry. And surprisingly, little pointless things mattered again. His first taste of coffee in the morning, his first draw of tobacco.

Levy observed that for a time Henry's crisis had passed, and he took heart, again, himself. Levy suffered in the wet, furry heat of Alabama summers—they challenged his endurance and sapped him. But the change in season returned Levy to the peak of his energies. He would start over with Henry, as many times as were necessary.

And for his part, Henry made a new resolve to cooperate with Levy. Gradually it came to Henry that there was some grievance Levy seemed to be leading him to discover, something he could call up from the past that would shed a revealing light on all his difficulties. The idea of Henry's mother absorbed Levy. It was true, Henry reflected, that his mother had not been one to understand too much of what a person was feeling. Henry didn't think that he held that against her—it was kind of like a person's not being able to sing. But he searched his memory for any small detail of her—he had an idea, by now, of the sort of thing that interested Levy. There was his mother's fussiness about her smooth, white bed, her tyrannical protectiveness of her flower beds. That time that she worked herself into such a swivet about her kitchen plots that she hitched up Joe and Jay to the plow. Levy looked thoughtful and tilted back in his seat.

"Lillian—how did she feel about Lillian?" Levy once asked.

The question brought a chuckle from Henry. "Tell you the truth, I don't think she cared much for Lillian."

"Why was that?"

"Oh, she thought Lillian put on airs, I reckon."

"Well, did she?" He had slipped. He'd asked the question from simple curiosity. Now he'd never get Henry back on track.

Henry laughed outright. "I expect she might have, back then." He thought a moment. "She had a way about her, Lillian did. She had her own special way."

Henry didn't hear the sigh that escaped him, then. But Levy did—the sigh and the longing. He understood he was looking at loneliness. There was no therapy, he knew, that could remedy that.

And for once, Henry spoke his full mind to the man. "I wish I could tell her now that the truth of it was, I just didn't *know*. I didn't know a thing about alcoholism. I couldn't square with her. I'd never squared with myself—didn't even know how to. I didn't keep anything from Lillian. I just didn't know, that was all."

Levy recognized this moment of self-revelation for what it was. What the man was telling him was right at the heart of his life story. Levy himself wasn't schooled in how to manage problem solving—his task was to understand origins. And Henry wouldn't follow him, there. But he asked, all the same, "Do you think you could tell her now?

There was a hesitation. "No. Not now. It wouldn't make any difference, now. It was too long ago. Too much has happened. Lillian had to save the girls." Henry thought to himself that above all, Lillian had to save Elizabeth. "No. No difference, now."

Chapter 33

"It's just not safe, honey." Buddy's brow was creased. The two of them, he and Betty Kate, stood in the kitchen, Frank all spiffed up in a suit and tie and smelling of shaving lotion—ready for work. He was troubled. It was the old man. There was always something, with the old man. Himself, he didn't know but what the old fellow still tippled. And with a child along, anything could have happened. His, Frank's, child—the very sun of Buddy's existence.

"Bryce's helped Daddy, Frank. I didn't know if it would, but it did. You don't have to worry."

Buddy cleared his throat—a habit, Betty Kate noted, that he'd picked up from his father. Parenthood had made a change in Frank's personality. At times, he took things over-seriously, in his sanguine young wife's opinion.

Betty Kate smiled, using her eyes. "Frank, Daddy's sober. He's been sober for more than two years, now. And *we* grew up with him. Daddy never took us anywhere that he wasn't tippling. And we survived."

That much was so, Frank had to concede. And so it went on, this sort of small argument.

Himself, he didn't trust the man—would never forgive him for the hurt he had brought to Betty Kate. But she seemed to have forgotten all about it, going on about the old man's never having had a son. That Rallie brought him a world that he'd missed out on. Buddy wasn't particularly moved at the idea of what Mr.

Gray had missed out on—the man had squandered what he had. But that face of Betty Kate's. She could talk him into anything, with that face.

The sun had dropped. It would be hot on the water tomorrow, that kind of heat that drove right through to the bone. The two of them, Henry and the boy, would suffer some, but there was a contentment in summer, strong and thick and hot, that Henry felt move into himself. He felt it around him now, in the dusk. He was sitting from habit, in front of the dead fire ring. The boy had worn himself out and was, by that time, asleep in the cabin. Henry never requested that the boy go to bed—camp had none of that sort of discipline. Rallie simply disappeared when the need for sleep came upon him. The boy amused Henry hugely. Even with the lamp unlit, he could see that Rallie lay as though he had made a sort of leap. One foot, cowboy booted, dangled over the edge of the bed.

With the boy off asleep in the cabin, the place lost its feeling of isolation—not that Henry minded that feeling. Night solitude on the river was a thing he enjoyed. The failing light was crazy with sound, tree frogs and cicadas. Henry waited, as he did in the evenings, for the air to lift, for the old smell to lift off of the river, sweetish and rank. The cicadas were screaming, and that sound and the smell and the falling night got all mixed—Henry liked the slow blend of first dark. It was at these times that he chose things to take out of his mind and examine. On some occasions, he chose simply to remember.

Talk. Henry was lonely for talk—which would have been an odd thing to mention to anyone, when there was talk every day all around him. Henry talked daily to his friend Louise, and to his daughter Betty Kate. Betty Kate was someone whom Henry could have talked to, in the way that he wanted. But he'd never talked with any great frankness to his family—there'd been too much to avoid. There was his shame. There were things he'd have never talked of with Dreyfus, although their lives had been a running conversation, left off and taken up whenever they saw each other. He had always been one for congenial talking, Henry imagined. Now he realized that what he had thought of as talk had been only rote conversation, tale-telling or news. Men bragged or joked. Told stories—Drefus was at his peak when telling a story. They talked of card games, crap shoots, catches or kills. They were good enough boys, good men. But their company and talk was identical enough to make them interchangeable, almost to a fellow. And women seemed to always have things going on in their imaginations, concerning that role they felt they had to play. Lillian, he knew, loved the girls and himself with her whole heart. But he understood, too, that her life role was to be a lady, not just the mother of children. There was that one from time to time, like the farm woman, who seemed not to have given herself any particular role. This woman he enjoyed talking to—she talked simply of what mattered to her. People wanted things. And wanted to do things. But no one ever seemed to talk about it.

He thought of Levy. He'd done plenty of talking to Levy. Levy had a whole world of thinking inside him, silent on it as he was. And he had questions, too—he was a young man. But there were always those times when Levy stopped Henry's talk. And stopped himself, too. Levy hadn't allowed himself to talk—Henry understood that it was part of the rules. But he remembered how the man's eyebrows would pull together. He'd return Henry's words with a stare. Henry had learned to see so well when Levy was thinking that it was second only to talk. But Henry failed to realize that he'd conversed with the young psychiatrist as much or more in his mind as he had in his sessions. He had come, in his imagination, to try on his most private thoughts with Levy. And in his mind, Levy heard them. So that Henry was hungry, now, for such talk again. And had begun to look for this special thing in other people. People warmed to Henry; and anyone warming to him, he liked at once, in return. But it was the others who did most of the talking. And that rare thing was always absent.

Or almost always. There was the young fellow named Robert who walked up the steps to the Burroughs' porch one afternoon, carrying a Bible. He plopped down beside Henry.

"Do you believe that mankind is basically good or evil?" No preliminary. Odd, that Henry had tried to bring up that same question with Levy.

A Jehovah's Witness, then. Henry thought about chuckling the question off. But he answered. "Guess your idea about that depends on what kind of folks you've run into." Robert's young face fell into sudden interest. Henry didn't know that generally people made no attempt to answer the question—or allowed Robert more than a few short moments at the door.

Henry took out a cigarette and tapped it. "Guess a lot depends too on how comfortable a fellow is." His mind went back. The faces waiting beside the tracks for the boxcars. Hungry faces, all twisted with worry. The huge and empty night.

"Hadn't thought of that. But it's part of what I've got to find out. I want to know about things, you know. Know things." He bobbed a knee up and down when he talked. And there began a brief but enjoyable friendship. Robert's mind worked live with questions—Henry discovered that, that first afternoon. He had a special fondness for the phrase, "did you ever notice." It was endless. Henry came to enjoy seeing Robert enjoying himself. When he was worked up on a subject, Robert fairly twitched with excitement. Henry egged him on a bit at times, then as often again was grave and ruminative with him. They talked on any number of subjects. Robert had a playful, wandering sort of mind.

Then there was that day that Robert walked up the front steps, his face looking odd, a little crooked. He was wearing a t-shirt and denim instead of the usual Sunday suit. He had joined the army—so young a fellow, having decided to part with everything that was home. He dropped down beside Henry, his arms dangling free. "See? I'm not carrying it around, anymore." Robert held up his hands, empty of leaflets or Bible. He made an attempt at small conversation, a thing that was unlike him. Then it came out. "You know, Mr. Gray, I don't know if I really believe in it, anymore."

"The religion?"

"Yeah." Robert's face was red to the point of looking scalded. He had suffered, then, Henry saw. And he understood that for the boy the loss of his faith would be a blow, as well as a scare. Then Robert abruptly hit his knees with the flat of his hands, as if slapping down what he'd just said. He was uncomfortable. He stood up to go.

Henry watched the young man walk back down the sidewalk, shoulders hunched over, hands pushed deep into his pockets. He didn't know if he'd ever see him again. He hadn't been able to give Robert an answer that amounted to anything—he felt in no real position to comment. There was nothing of the churchgoer left in Henry. It had been years since he had prayed as he'd been taught to do, as a boy. But strangely enough, something that felt like prayer seemed to come of its own, at times, to Henry. Gratitude. For no particular thing. Just gratitude. A feeling that had come to him first by himself on the grounds at Bryce's. And a matter he had wanted to examine with Levy. If Robert had stayed, Henry would have most likely tried to describe it for him. The whole matter of religion needed a good thinking through—and good talk. It seemed an angry and alien thing to Henry now, the religion that had been presented to him, growing up.

He'd done some thinking along those lines at Bryce's—Henry was grateful that his mind had begun to work again, during the ordeal of Bryce's. Before that time, there were most of two decades gone blank—alcohol did that to a person. Henry's mind went dark, trying to grope back over those years. He could get back certain disconnected pieces. Mostly, he had to jump back over those years altogether. At Bryce's he began to see and notice things again, much of it having to do with Levy—or with that world of ideas that those talks set off. And there was another matter besides the talk that emerged for Henry. There were people like Levy, who wanted to serve—Henry guessed he would have used that term. He hadn't expected to come across that again—had it been that he just hadn't noticed?

Before Bryce's, he would have felt no particular curiosity about the old Negro man, although he would have seen him often enough during the long years of the blank. And this man, Maxine's old father, turned out to be of far greater interest to Henry than Robert—than anybody else, as it happened. For all the fact that the old man would have nothing to do with him, there was an air about the old gentleman that intrigued Henry. Here, maybe, was another man of ideas: someone who would have acquired learning, one way or another. Or someone like Levy, who wanted to be of service.

Maxine was Henry's closest neighbor at the river place—closer by water than by land. He and the boy would go to Maxine's by boat, for their meals. She listened for the sound of the outboard motor. She would be there, then, at the bank, with the breakfast—lunch, whichever it was—in a basket covered with cloth: eggs and bacon and biscuits—heavy biscuits made with lard. Henry and the boy loved the biscuits. It was an arrangement of some years' standing, back even before Henry was taken from Clanton. He and Drefus had always crossed the land Maxine's house stood on, to hunt. And on the occasions when they passed near enough, there were neighborly greetings and exchanges. It was in '50, during the big flood, that the acquaintance turned into a friendship—that is, with Maxine herself. Her house, a tenant house like Henry's cabin, sat on the bank high above the water, at about the same distance from the river as Henry's. But the rising river was now inching onto the land at both sites. Henry walked only a few yards beyond Maxine's clothesline. He hunted alone, now—had done, since Drefus got married. On that afternoon, the weather was sunny. Light traveled and bounced along sheets of water standing in the fields, fell through branches on the bank onto more standing water.

"You still dry?"

Maxine laughed. She was shaking out clothes, with a popping sound. "We's still dry!"

Henry noticed that her woodshed was on the side of the house next to the cotton rows. Himself, he didn't have a woodshed, just a pile covered with planks. He'd been negligent; the truth was that he'd been blank. Henry's wood had been soaked through, when the rain had flown in all directions. Now he thought of the squirrels—there were seven—that he had in a croker sack slung over his shoulder.

"You like squirrel meat, don't you?"

"We sure do."

"Tell you what. My wood's all wet. You take these. 'S more than enough for both of us. I'll be leaving for town directly. Could you make me a meal?"

And Maxine had come out of her back door even before Henry brought his truck to a stop. She had a heaped plate, the squirrel pieces dipped and fried. She'd made grits and cornbread. There were pickled peaches on the edge of the plate. Henry ate sitting in his truck and brought the plate and fork to the back stoop. It was then that he noticed that there seemed to be something secretive about the interior of that little house. Maxine was protective of it in some way.

There was rarely a sign of the old man, even back then. It was only now that he'd come back from Bryce's that Henry recalled that he'd never seen the man dressed for fieldwork. And that his shirts were white to the point of brilliance when he stood outside. Maxine's protectiveness was about the old man, Henry concluded. What he didn't know was that Maxine's abiding fear was that her father might get himself killed. The family had to keep him out of the white sections of town. He wouldn't do things like step off a sidewalk, wouldn't use words like "boss" or "captain."

Maxine never gave Henry time enough to enter the house. Once, standing just outside the kitchen doorway, she had shushed their conversation. They were speaking of groceries.

"*Shh!*" Loudly. And seeing Henry surprised, "Daddy's at work. We got to be quiet, you know."

Henry looked interested.

"He's a reverend—well, used to be a reverend. Now he's most retired. But he'll be speaking on Sunday."

The air of seclusion around the old man made Henry curious, and the curiosity was noticed. The two men became very aware of each other. Then Henry committed a violation. He'd come by on foot, with his shotgun, at a time when Maxine wouldn't have been around. He stepped up to the back stoop and spoke. No one answered. Henry stood for a minute at the steps. On the little stoop, a dishcloth hung smoothly over a string. The yard and kitchen garden—everything about Maxine's house—was precise and orderly. Henry walked up the steps and into the kitchen, where the newspaper-plastered door stood open. The old man was in the front room, sitting. There was an open Bible lying across his lap, but Henry could see that he wasn't reading it, merely holding it, like a kind of ritual. It seemed that his mind was at work.

When Henry spoke, he was already halfway across the small, front room.

"Morning, Reverend."

The reverend sat in a large, stuffed chair, with a doily draped over the back. He looked at Henry with no expression: completely white-haired, elderly enough now to assert the right to look this white man directly in the eye. For all of his age, his look was not the slack-faced, drowsy stare of the elderly. And this aroused Henry's interest in a way that the young Robert had not. Henry felt that he looked straight through those eyes into the old man's mind, all the way through to the force of his feeling. Which was ageless, like all the years of earth and rock. And just as unyielding.

"Maxine's in town." The voice was bass, a little gravelly, which was surprising.

The answer was clearly Henry's dismissal, but Henry hadn't come by to be dismissed. The old man's face wasn't hostile, only closed—he was not going to make idle conversation with Henry. Stalling, Henry looked around the stuffy front room. There was the armchair, a small table with a straight chair pushed under it, and a bed, sheets drawn tight, at the other end of the room. The walls were white-washed. There was only one decoration, an ornate oval frame with the portrait of a man and woman, the likenesses grayed over with age. Then the newspaper, a double sheet, not plastered for insulation but carefully tacked to the wall. Henry walked over to it. It was a double center page from *The Atlanta Constitution*, and it had been carefully folded at one point into many small squares. The young preacher, King. There were photographs, a very formal close-up, a shot of a church, another of a house.

The old man watched Henry, who turned, with a tentative smile. "This young fellow, King. You think anything'll come of it?"

For a part of a second—Henry wondered if he imagined it—there was that quick intake, that piqued interest that would have under other circumstances led into good conversation. Then the old man did a peculiar thing. He jerked and brought a cupped hand to his ear, clapping it, as though he hadn't made out what Henry said. It was as studied an act of deception as Henry had ever seen. Henry already knew that he wasn't going to talk, but knew, too, that the old man had floods of words inside him. If he'd had the nerve, he'd have tried to pick up on some sort of topic. Himself, he could see why the Parks woman had done what she did, for example. But the old fellow may have thought Henry was baiting him. No. Here was refusal, proud and unyielding.

Henry was surprised at the strength of his disappointment. "Well, tell Maxine I came by." Over his shoulder. Already on his way out. The slighting was after all, he told himself, no more than he should have expected. If he felt he could have gotten beyond it, he'd have come back. But there was no way of getting beyond it.

Chapter 34

Bryce Hospital

Tuscaloosa, Alabama

Henry had understood for a good while, now, about Levy—the young doctor had only fooled him in the beginning. He knew that Levy was a talker, he suspected a great talker, who would not, in his role with Henry, allow himself to talk. From the beginning, Henry understood that talk was what the business of psychiatry was all about—he hadn't counted on the fact that it was he who was supposed to do all the talking—or that there would be all the rules.

"I'd like to make a change in the focus of our discussions." Levy looked up at Henry without raising his head, rocking back in his seat and playing with his pen.

"If you're agreeable to it, that is." Neither man had laughed. But it wouldn't have been out of place to laugh. Both of them knew that Henry was more than agreeable. Levy'd felt like gagging Henry at times, in his effort to keep him on track.

"I'm agreeable."

Meetings with Levy were becoming for a fact more gratifying these days, had finally come to resemble conversations, on occasion. Henry was pleased—he supposed that he'd been promoted. If it had been grade school, he could have said he'd moved up a year or so.

"We've concentrated on your childhood." Levy didn't use the word, conflict—he had a special liking for that word that Henry didn't share. How Levy had worded his proposed change Henry couldn't exactly recall—something about the shift into adolescence, young manhood. Henry looked interested.

"Should I ask the questions? Do you want to begin?"

Now that, too, was a switch. Levy waited, with that little smile at the corners of his mouth. "Your work, for example," he prompted. The phrase, "your work," struck Henry as flattering, as though it had been work in the way that Levy had work. Something with a plan. A thing of importance. The truth was that of the four boys, Henry was the one his father had pulled out from behind the plow. As simple as that.

"I mean back in the beginning, before the Depression." Levy corrected himself.

Then it was Henry who was obliged to correct himself. Comfortable, pleased with the subject shift, he'd launched into an enjoyable spiel on the subject of child labor and mill conditions. He didn't realize that he'd started off wrong until Levy got that look about him. So, Levy still had his plan after all. One way or another, Henry always seemed to interfere with the plan. But it didn't annoy him anymore when his answers disappointed Levy or went wrong somewhere. He understood by now that it had to do with the plan.

"If we could, just—." Levy interrupted, batting his eyelids, a mannerism that appeared whenever he had to redirect the focus of a session. "Your early plans. Let's talk about your first plans."

Henry wasn't quite sure what Levy was getting at. "My plans." He repeated, looking at the floor. "Well, what sort of plans would you be talking about?"

"Your—well, your ambitions. Your early ambitions."

"My ambitions." The word felt foreign to Henry's tongue. He

shifted in his chair, crossed one leg, then the other. "I don't know as I had any ambitions, to speak of."

Levy was unruffled. He knew he was going to be losing Henry, that Henry was going to be released. The man's family had been called in to discuss the possibility of taking him home, but Levy didn't know if Henry had been made aware of that yet.

"Okay, your dreams, then." Levy smiled at the word. "Let's talk about your dreams for your life."

Now Henry sat up straighter, stalled on his answer, no longer so sure he was pleased with the shift. "Don't know as I could say I had any of those, either, tell you the truth." *Dreams.* Levy just didn't have a right picture of things. Maybe he couldn't be held strictly accountable, being from up North and all. Now Henry dropped forward, his elbows resting on his knees. "Don't know as any of us were in much of a position to think about that sort of thing, back then. Dreams." He shook his head. "We didn't have much, in those days, you see. Nobody else had much, either. I just did whatever it was came along I could do. It was my Pa put me to work in the mill." Henry thought back to the mill. He thought back to himself and Lillian in that first little cottage. He thought back even further.

The academy's for those who plan to be doctors or lawyers and such.

He thought he had forgotten.

Then Levy stood up and opened his drawer, holding out something for Henry. A little blue book without any printing on the cover. "I'd like for you to read this." The actual title, *Alcoholics Anonymous*, was printed on the front leaf. It was that anonymous-looking little blue book that had blown Henry's preconceived world into fragments. And in his urgency to deal with that, he had been forced to wait. Levy was planning to leave around Christmas. This time he'd announced the absence. There had always been occasional missed sessions. But Henry was never notified in advance. In the beginning he'd asked about the missed meetings, but the most that came back was something with the word, "conference." And now Henry understood that even that much had been a kind of indulgence. Levy didn't give those sorts of explanations, as a rule. And he gave none for his December absence. Henry wondered if Levy had gone home for a visit, wherever home was. For Christmas, or New Year's—he recalled that Jews didn't celebrate Christmas.

On a cold morning of pale sunshine, Henry walked the line of back fencing. January 6, 1955. He remembered when the words, nineteen fifty, had sounded new and strange to his ears. Nineteen fifty five. He didn't say the words aloud. The phrase moved pleasurably across his mind—he liked the ring of it. Also agreeably, he thought he'd picked up the odor of wood smoke, a good smell. But these things were the sum of what pleased him that morning. He was worse than anxious to see Levy. There was so much to talk about. The book: the book had seemed to Henry to validate his own thinking—all along he'd known that liquor didn't mix with his blood as it did with other men's—that there was some unaccountable physical difference. But there was more to it than that. Maybe much more. Somewhere along the line, he'd gotten lost. Or was it a matter of a thing not found? And questions like these, unaccountably, brought the word "God" to mind.

It had taken him over a week to finish the little blue book. Not because the reading was difficult. Once he picked it up with the intention of finishing it, he read it through in a matter of hours. Levy didn't know what he had put into Henry's hands. That he had offered Henry his first medical understanding of his disease—Levy would have been aware of that. But that part, important as it was, wasn't the biggest thing for Henry. There were ideas here that he'd never heard spoken of before, had never come across anywhere in print. There was this word, "agnostic"—Henry didn't know the meaning of that word. And it was necessary that he know. Yet he had no way of finding out. He indulged his pride in refusing to ask Levy about it, not wanting Levy to know, for some reason, that he didn't understand the meaning. The anonymous writer spoke of such things as a Power, a Creative Intelligence, a Spirit of the Universe. Henry had never heard such inspiring—such mysterious—phrases. There was also the recurring phrase, "God as we understood Him." It was taken for granted in the world that produced Henry that an ordinary person didn't understand God, didn't even make the attempt. No one had that privilege. God was handed out whole and unmodified, by those who did understand Him. Revealed uniquely to His ministry. You took this interpretation as you found it, liked the idea or you didn't. Hell itself was the consequence for questioning. But these folks from the book, whoever they were, were doing that very thing, with no apologies. If God could be as a person "understood Him to be," then everything else was open. There would be nothing, then, that could not be held up to the light and scrutinized. Right away Henry felt the need to talk to Levy.

But Levy was away.

It occurred to Henry that there were things that he and Drefus, even, had never talked about—maybe couldn't have talked about, in any easy sort of way. *As we understood Him to be.* Henry took his walks for a while with his hands shoved into his pockets, studying the ground. It was important, now, to make the effort to get this concept down—of another, higher power: some strength that he could tap into. He had occasions of a feeling he'd have called blessedness: a sense that just sort of came over a person—of the blessedness of things. Ordinary things. And there was a presence—a sense of presence that couldn't be explained.

Whatever this presence was, and along with whatever else, it was right down in the earth, directly. The scriptures said something about an abiding place, a resting place. From inside the earth something moved. Henry imagined, at times, that he heard the water moving, the water deep down, invisible below the soil. Like molecules. Molecules of water and soil and roots, all slow and dark and knowing. And all of it moved by the sun, making tree branches stretch up toward the light. Maybe trying to pin it all down, like he was trying to do, wasn't a matter for human understanding. How could you squeeze down into a single notion a thing that was everywhere—something bigger, older than you were yourself. Older than rocks and stars. Older, even, than time. Yes, he had to speak to Levy, just as soon as possible.

By afternoon he was outright fidgety. Nurse Compton had come by with the doctor—Dr. Spivey didn't always stop for Henry these days. She'd fussed around Henry in the maternal way that she had, confirmed for him that Levy was back. Around three o'clock Henry was called. He nearly ran up the stairs to the west wing. And at the door he didn't knock. Levy was standing, facing the window when Henry entered. When he turned, Henry saw that he looked different, healthier—sunnier, some way. His face shone. Funny thing was that Levy looked suntanned, right there in the middle of winter. He smiled, beamed, at Henry—Henry had never noticed that he had very white, regular teeth.

Levy had been afraid that by the time he returned Henry may no longer be there.

Henry dropped into a chair. "Been to a conference?"

Levy laughed. "No, not a conference this time. I've been to visit my family." Levy leaned back against the window ledge.

"Well that's good to hear. Thought you might have taken a notion to visit your family. What part of the country're you from, anyway?"

"Michigan."

"Michigan?"

"That's right." Levy still smiled.

"Reckon it gets cold up there, huh?"

"I reckon it does." Levy had unintentionally pronounced the word, "reckon," so quaint to his ears, with a Southern accent.

"Well."

"So, how have you been?"

"Oh, me. I'm all right." Henry had brought the little blue book with him. He didn't know how to begin.

Levy nodded down at the book resting on Henry's knees. "I see you brought the book. Did you get a chance to look over it?"

"I read it." Again Henry hesitated.

Now Levy sat down, all serious again. More his usual self. "Did you get to the case histories?" He was starting to get that urgency about him.

"I read the book."

"So, what about the case histories?"

"Well, that part was all right." The "all right" had a tone of dismissal to it.

"Did you find yourself relating to those accounts, in any way?"

"Oh, they were fine." Now Henry was clearly dismissing the topic.

"Well—." Levy looked disappointed.

Henry broke in. "You see, this thing about God as you understand him—."

"Oh, that." Now Levy laughed, looking relieved. He had in turn interrupted Henry. "Don't think a thing about that." It had been Levy's biggest concern that Henry might be put off by the quasi-religious tone of the writing.

"Not think about it?"

"Not at all. Henry, it's not the purpose of the organization to foist any religious ideas on you."

Foist. Now there was an interesting word. "But the thing about a higher power—."

"Like I said, don't think a thing about it."

"Well, why not? There was an awful lot about the subject, seems to me."

"But Henry, none of that's the point." Levy was smiling broadly again, relieved to have identified the problem.

"Well, then what *was* the point?" Henry felt himself getting piqued.

It was one of those times when Levy left his chair and walked around from behind his desk. "There's fact, Henry, and human reason"—Levy knew that he didn't have time to go into that, now. "The point is that once you leave here, you'll need the help of other people. You can't try to contend with a thing like alcoholism alone. But there's A. A. There's the help of others who know your experience."

Henry hadn't paid much attention to that aspect of it, the A. A. meetings and such. He returned stubbornly to his own train of thought. "Seems to me there was a whole lot that wasn't fact or reason. And the religion thing—."

"Don't think a thing about it." Reassuringly. Kindly. "All this business about religion and the hereafter—I wouldn't give a nickel for it." He walked over to his window again, looking out. "You know, Henry," now he was biting his thumb, "human beings. They can break your heart."

Henry had never heard that tone in Levy's voice. But at once Levy brightened. "Anyway, back to the book. I had hoped you would get a lot out of it."

"Oh, I got a lot out of it." Henry prepared to launch in. Then he had a thought, something from the book that made him feel a little smug. "Says in the book that being an alcoholic is kind of like having an allergy."

"That's right."

Now, that response was a surprise. Here, all along, Levy seemed to have been hanging it all on some kind of childhood conflict, as he would have called it. Henry had expected him to argue. Henry went on, "Myself, if I had to say, I'd say it was something in the blood."

"You could put it that way."

Again, an unexpected answer.

"My man—." Henry had never heard Levy use those words. "I've got to cut us short for today. I'm trying to at least give a few minutes to everybody who's missed."

So, he was not going to be able to talk to Levy at all that afternoon.

And Levy's cheerfulness was a sham. Once Henry left, the brightness left his face. There was something about Henry, something he had missed. A factor he'd not yet come across. He was not going to have the time he needed with Henry—he would never have that time. But it wasn't just a question of time. There was something—Levy felt it must be an essential something—he'd never quite gotten to with Henry. It struck Levy that this time he had missed. And that the miss should have been this particular time, this patient—that was the worst of it. There was a quality of mind about Henry. Levy wondered at times what his life would have been like, under better circumstances. And the idea hurt him. He loved the old man.

It was on a weekday that Drefus and Bea showed up, all dressed up in church clothes. Henry was sunning himself in his rocker. He'd had to put on two shirts, to stay warm enough. He was the only one sitting outside.

Henry laughed when he saw Drefus in his best suit, a good cut of a suit, too. Spare and upright as ever, Drefus moved with that old self-assurance that was his birthright. Beside him, Bea, who was not a tall woman, walked along smoothly, plumply, her hips and backside swelling and rolling under the slippery material of her dress. It was a best dress, blue-flowered. Her hat was decorated with what looked like little blue pansies.

Henry laughed again. "Looks like I'm all mixed up. Didn't know it was a Sunday."

Bea had already gone into Henry's room, and Drefus ushered Henry inside. "It's better than Sunday for you, Brud. It's Christmas Day! We've been over to the other building, with Dr. Dawes." Henry knew Dr. Dawes only on sight. "You can get out your suitcase." Drefus leaned against the doorjamb, leg crossed, the tip of the shoe poised on end. Pleased and congratulatory, waiting for the words to sink in. He saw Henry's mind starting to operate.

"Suitcase. They're gonna let me out for a visit."

"They"—Drefus stressed the word—"are gonna do nothing. You're out of here, Brud, to stay."

Bea made a cooing sound and held out a hand, which didn't quite reach Henry. "Henry, I'm so glad."

Henry must have looked incredulous. "Well, wait a minute. How'd all of this happen?"

"Simple as pie. Just a little talk with the doctor. Some papers and such. You're all ready."

Henry told himself that he'd waited the whole two years for this moment. Now that it was here, he felt an odd lack of conviction that it could be happening. Bea was opening drawers.

"Don't tell me you've gone and gotten attached to the place."

Henry's answer was a chuckle. It was beginning to sink in a little. He stepped over to the closet where his one good suit hung. Wait until he saw Levy's face about this one—Henry smiled to himself, thinking about it. But the smile reversed itself. Hold on—there was something he hadn't thought about. Maybe he wasn't going to see Levy. Maybe they were leaving right away. Right then. That minute.

"What do we still have to do?"

"Not a thing. It's all done. Every bit of it."

"Hold on a minute. There's somebody I've got to see."

"Nobody, Brud. We've seen 'em all for you."

"Drefus, there's somebody I want to see before I leave here."

Drefus picked up at once on the changed tone of voice.

"It's a Dr. Levy. I'm gonna have to talk to him before I go."

They were old men, now, the two of them. But Drefus still humored Henry at times like a younger brother. "Well then, you'll see him. I'll go and get him for you."

Drefus had to walk all the way around the long west wing, to get to the main entrance of the building. He could have knocked at the walkway door, but he knew better, even though the long way was a good five-minute walk. At the reception desk in the main foyer sat a nurse in uniform. Middle-aged. Drefus assessed the type.

"How are you today, ma'am?" He was the soul of politeness, an exaggerated politeness intended to come across as a way of putting the other person at ease. Drefus knew that in these situations it was best to act as though he were the one in a position to confer favors, not asking one, himself. It worked every time.

"I'm here to see a Dr. Levy." He gave a beneficent smile.

The nurse was looking through a chart. She wasn't really on duty at the desk. "Janine!" She called into the office behind her. A different woman walked out, in everyday clothes. Drefus nodded at her.

"Did you have an appointment, sir?"

"No, Ma'am. I didn't think of calling first. Should have, I guess."

"Oh then, I am sorry. Dr. Levy's not expected back until Saturday. Do you want me to set up a time for you?"

"That'll be all right." Drefus replaced his hat, giving a little push to the brim.

They were running, moving through the woods with loud, crashing sounds. That is, Henry was running. The boy seemed as slight as a kitten all straddled across Henry's shoulders, the cowboy boots flopping against Henry's chest. Rallie held up his air rifle high, and Henry zigzagged, to avoid the branches. Rallie was squealing. Henry laughed. The briars and brush made a crushing sound, even though it had rained the night before. Henry had known it would storm when the birds went quiet all of a sudden. The rain had been hard enough to drum against the tin roof, with little popping explosions. When Henry and the boy first walked out that morning, a mist streaked up out of the ground and into the branches, the sun a single white spot.

"Hold on, now."

There'd be low spots in the brush. Holes. Henry had to keep up his pace, trying to explore with his feet at the same time. But it didn't matter. He knew they wouldn't fall. And if he did lose his footing, they wouldn't go all the way down—he could right them, again. At that instant one foot did go into a hole covered by old brambles. Henry dipped and swerved, chuckling. Rallie shrieked with pleasure.

"I see one, Grampaw!"

"Course you see one. They're all over the place." Henry felt a squirming on his shoulders.

"Got 'im!" Rallie had fired the air rifle before Henry could stop him.

"You won't get one of 'em, shooting off that-a way, boy." Henry stopped then, stood stock still. The boy had to learn how to be still. Wolf was tied back at the camp, for this lesson. "Now when you aim, keep your eye on the sight." Henry tilted over to one side, as if his leaning might be of some assistance to the boy. "You got to get the sight right on him, now, just up under him. You don't want to hit a wing." Henry didn't much like hitting a songbird, but the boy had to learn how to shoot. Henry had a 410 shotgun he wanted to give him. There was a sudden whoosh, then that little thud-like noise made when a BB hit its mark.

"*Now* you got you one!" He lowered the squirming boy, who took off running. Henry watched him go, his clothes snagging, making ripping sounds through the whip-like brambles. It was a good time. It came to Henry that it was one of the best times. Walking out into the steaming new morning, Rallie crashing around, yelling, the smell of the damp earth beneath the brush, the air crazy with the racket of birds. The sky was a bird's egg blue, like a saucer flipped over. Henry thought he would have known there was a river nearby, even without being sure where they were. It was in the lay of the land, the old earth smell that drifted up from a river. And the quiet. Between the noise of Rallie, the frantic chirping, Henry thought he could hear the quiet. That's it. Or, that's it—he'd find himself thinking at times. That huge concept that he'd tried to make clear for himself and Levy had become simply "it," now, in Henry's mind.

"Come look-a here, Grampaw!"

"I'm coming, boy."

He'd had to wait all week long for the boy. It seemed that Rallie had gotten into trouble at Sunday school. Into each pocket of his Sunday jacket he had slipped a crawdad, just a couple of the small, dark ones, not the red, lobster-looking kind—the pockets wouldn't have held one of those. The crawdads were produced during the Sunday school lesson. Old Mrs. Pettus had gotten heavy on her feet. She'd had decades of Sunday school classes. Not as much as a dry twig of humor was left. The boy had to be punished. And consequently, Henry was punished. Rallie had to stay inside until he could, in Betty Kate's words, learn a good lesson. What the lesson was, exactly, or how long a time would be required for the learning of it, was unclear. So Henry waited it out. He went over to the house during the day and simply sat, watching Westerns or cartoons with the boy, drinking coffee with Betty Kate.

The cartoons were reruns. Henry sat at the table in the kitchen with a cup of coffee in front of him. He tasted it, put it down, and added another couple of teaspoons of sugar. As she sometimes did when they were in the kitchen together, Betty Kate had her back to Henry. Now she stopped what she was doing and turned around. She inclined her head a little. Lillian used to do that.

"Daddy, are you all right?" It was a question that Betty Kate had reserved for just the right moment. And Henry had anticipated the question.

He took another sip of his coffee, sugary now, like he liked it. He chuckled—Betty Kate knew the chuckle. How to explain it—Henry had some difficulty, here, not with the answer itself but with how to put it. He never had discussed his problem with family members. It seemed a little late to start now—would be frankly, he admitted, against his habit. A biblical verse came to mind. *I have learned, in whatever state I am—to be content.* Betty Kate was waiting.

"I'm all right, Betty Kate. Don't worry about me." He sipped the sugary coffee. "You could say something like—." Again, prompted by a Biblical phrase, "Maybe I'm just sitting under my own fig tree."

Chapter 35

November, 1971

The hallway looked dark when Henry closed the door to his room. All the doors closed onto the main hallway. The panes over the front door were of colored glass. A single bulb hung from a long cord in the little back section behind the stairway. There Juanita was mopping the floor. And now Henry noticed that the whole hallway was wet—drying at least. He didn't want to interfere with Juanita's mopping job. She spotted him, although he hadn't made any sound at the door.

"Well now don't you look spiffy this afternoon, all dressed up for Sunday." She grinned at him, speaking in that slightly singsong, almost caressing way that some people habitually spoke to the elderly. Juanita was a tall, very dark woman. When she did housework, she tied a kerchief around her head. Otherwise, it was topped by a dark frizzy halo of hair. Henry thought the haircut looked like something that belonged on a boy.

"Got to go to a funeral this afternoon."

"I am sorry to hear that, Mr. Gray." Her tone changed.

Henry touched his hat brim and walked through the front door onto the porch of the Burroughs' house—that is, Henry thought of it that way. The Burroughs had not owned it for many years. Mrs. Burroughs herself had passed away, Henry heard. The house had changed hands a number of times. A couple of the downstairs roomers, like Henry, had lived there for a very long time—although Henry's stay had been interrupted and resumed. He stood for a few minutes on the porch, thinking about what to do next. He had gotten dressed too early. As he stood there he looked out across the post office lot. The block that he lived on had changed. The old post office had been torn down. And now this new building—it looked like a series of shoeboxes, Henry thought, flat and squat, with no roofline—and surrounded by two city lot's worth of concrete. Henry didn't feel much like taking his rocker. He felt a little uncomfortable in his clothes, especially the shoes. He smelled like shaving cream and lotion—he was that spit and polished, he thought to himself, though he'd nicked himself shaving. He knew he was going to be warm in the jacket. It was one of those November days that would be warm until the sun dropped.

Emma Griffen had died. The funeral was not until two o'clock, and it wasn't quite one, yet. He decided to go on ahead, anyway. He'd walk up and sit a while with Lillian and Mary, who lived not many blocks from his own street. He walked past the Skinner house where Betty Kate's family lived without looking—he knew that she wasn't at home. The family would already be at the funeral parlor. And Betty Kate had been in and out all morning. Billy's wife, Eileen, had called early. It seemed that there was some sort of difficulty with old Mr. Griffen—seemed, in Eileen's words, that he'd gone all to pieces. No one could get him to put on his clothes. And for once, Nettie was in no condition to do it.

It was a good day for a funeral, breezy and ringing with sun—make it easier on the family, Henry thought, as he walked up Alabama Avenue in the direction of the Vaughn Memorial. Lillian and Mary lived in the first house on Union Street, which sat directly behind the old Philpot home and looked directly into that yard. It struck Henry that here life had drawn a small circle. Mary had brought Lillian back to Clanton a few years earlier. And at first Henry hadn't known quite what to do, how to handle the fact of their being there. It occurred to him to question whether he would be welcome. Then he had settled on the simple thing, walked over and made a friendly call. Lillian was delighted to see him, welcomed him with all the warmth due any family member.

"Why Henry," she beamed out at him—her voice hadn't changed an iota—"how wonderful to see you. Do come in."

And she ushered him in, in that way that she had.

"How *are* you?" Lillian made a gesture toward a chair and Henry sat down. She herself stood in front of the heater, with her hands clasped behind her. It was a thing she had taken to doing, even when the heat wasn't burning—she always seemed to be a little bit cold.

"Well tell me about yourself these days."

"Oh, I'm fine. Doing just fine."

"How's Drefus?"

"Drefus's doing okay, he and Bea. Both of them fine. And the family."

Lillian gave Henry the gracious attention she would have given any visitor—more, even. She was sincerely glad to see him, and continued to be, each time he came—which was frequently. She listened to his news, lately of how his hearing—the loss of it—was bothering him, with a concerned little face. He knew the face so well. But then she'd remember what it was she'd been looking for. She'd interrupt.

"*Now* I know where I put it! It's in my handbag." Lillian always had to do some looking around for the handbag itself, although it usually sat within sight of her.

"I'll only be a minute." She'd sit then and go through the contents of her purse, first pushing things around on the inside, then, as her frustration mounted, emptying the contents—there weren't many—into her lap.

"But I know I haven't lost it!" Now Lillian was getting vexed, a little distraught. Mary, overhearing, walked in from the next room.

"Mama, what is it you've lost?" An even and unsurprised voice.

"Well, it's my medicine." This was a tiny cylinder of pills. Fairly often it was the medicine. Sometimes it was her compact. Or a letter.

"I've *got* to have my medicine!" Lillian's voice rose. It was becoming querulous.

"Now you know you haven't lost it." The voice grew soothing. "We'll just have to go back over every place that you've been in the house, until we find it."

"But I've already *looked!*" Now Lillian threw her hands up. Her mouth began to quaver. She was frustrated not quite to tears.

Henry was well accustomed now to these little scenes. The misplaced object was usually located within a matter of minutes. Often, it would have been in the handbag all along.

Henry sat and smoked. Their conversations never picked up where they left off. But, calm again, Lillian would take up their visit. The white rosebush was still blooming in the side yard. Had Henry noticed? Elizabeth was having such a hard time with William. Young people were so different these days.

Then Lillian edged over in front of the heater, which may or may not have been burning. She was tiny, still, seemed even tinier to Henry. Her hair was a pristine white. Like flower petals, he thought sometimes. Lillian had developed the slightest suggestion of a little paunch, emphasized when she stood with her hands clasped behind her. It was the fruit turnovers. Lillian didn't eat sweets, never had; and of course Mary understood this. Therefore, the frozen fruit turnovers were baked but never brought out from the kitchen. Mary left them in the toast tray on the stove. Lillian ate a turnover—a while back, it had been oatmeal cookies—standing in the kitchen, when no one else was around. That way, she couldn't really be said to have eaten one. Mary never mentioned the turnovers. Neither did Lillian. They didn't exist.

As Henry walked into the yard of the house on Union Street, he could see that the Plymouth was not in the drive. It wasn't a particularly well-organized household that Mary and Lillian ran. They seemed always to be in and out of the grocery store, for some little overlooked something, bread or milk. They would be back directly. Henry entered the house through the screened front porch. Everybody but Henry seemed to prefer the front porch and swing, when the weather allowed. But Henry preferred the front room; as a matter of fact, he liked the room best when he was alone in the house. It was fairly often the case that he sat there alone. Today he looked forward to that little bit of quiet, by himself. He liked the interior of the house. There was something about it. A kind of atmosphere. It had a definite smell—Henry had analyzed that—of fresh air and clean, laundered cotton. The sun slanted into the front room, morning and afternoon. At this time of day, it came in through the far side, near the sofa, an upholstered Victorian piece. The windows stood open. Mary had very sheer draperies that she kept pulled back. They billowed a little away from the walls. Squares, rectangles, of light fell in and moved over objects and floorboards. There were no carpets. Mary had a couple of oval-shaped rugs with soft, mingly colors. When the sun moved over the rooms, the colors were brighter, and sun-stippled. There were objects Henry liked in the room. A huge piece of old furniture—a hutch, Mary called it—with dishes lined up on it, ones that she didn't use. This was her Wedgwood. There was a tea service on a platter, sterling, that she didn't use, either. The sunlight was especially bright on that spot. The blue of the dishes changed color when the sun moved across them. There was a good feeling, a calm, in the house. Henry absorbed something from it.

Inevitably he'd discovered the bookcase, and there Henry helped himself. He liked to read when he was alone in the room. He returned, always, to his favorites—it didn't matter how many times he had read or looked over them. There was a book on ancient history. One on human anatomy. The one he chose now, on geology—that one might be his favorite of the three. As Henry picked up the book, he smiled, as he always did, at the bird. The two pictures over the bookcase didn't match, although everything else in the room seemed to match. One was of a woman with a pitcher. Vermeer's milkmaid. Henry didn't find that one particularly interesting. But the bird—this was a little black and white picture, in a small black frame. Henry didn't know that Mary had cut the picture out of a magazine. Morris Graves' "Bird Singing in the Moonlight." Now, why would an artist want to make it look like that? The bird wasn't even pretty. It looked like something you'd see in a cartoon picture. It had its head thrown back, with its mouth open. And around its head was a cascade of white marks made on the dark background. Henry always looked at the bird.

Sometimes when he sat alone in the house, he thought about Mary, the one daughter he thought of with regret. He'd missed out on Mary, in some way, and had never been able to make up for it. She moved to Montgomery as soon as she graduated from high school, and had taken a job with the government. Everybody, including Henry, had thought she would marry the Eisenberg boy. The Eisenberg boy certainly thought it, although there were plenty of others attendant on Mary, who as an adult was nearly blind without her glasses. But she had mastered the trick of re-moving the glasses quickly, then glancing down. When she raised her eyes, she widened them. It was long enough for the effect to be felt. The eyes made her many conquests, conquests Mary nev-er seemed particularly interested in keeping. From Montgomery there had been Washington, D.C.; and from there, London.

Mary was in everything in the room, but Henry didn't think to look at it that way.

The funeral was simple. At the gravesite the minister recited the Twenty-third Psalm. There was no other sound but from Nettie. The old man looked at the ground. Henry avoided looking his way, out of respect. He found himself looking over Betty Kate's family, all of them seated together in a row. The girl, Ellen—she was a young woman now, Henry corrected himself—held onto her father. Rallie and his wife clasped hands. David leaned against his mother. Betty Kate had had a later son, who was adolescent. The boy looked on, with that blank expression of children in the presence of something too solemn for understanding. The boy David was a sight, Henry thought—if he hadn't been careful, he could have let himself grin. The boy's face was beautiful to look at. And the looks puzzled Henry. A throwback to someone or another in the family—who, was the question. On the Griffen side, it could have been Ned. No, not Ned. Another face came to mind. The narrow, aristocratic-looking face of Lillian's father.

There were not a whole lot of people at the graveside cer-emony, and the group departure was almost silent. The old man, calm now, it seemed, let himself be led. It was afterwards, at Billy's house, that the trouble began. People started to arrive—these be-ing mainly friends of Emma's adult children—all bringing food, to be added to a table already loaded with covered plates and casserole dishes. The talk was a pleasant hum, an undercurrent, that offering to the family of warm company before the hard business of grief set in. It was the appropriate time for affectionate stories about Emma, but no one outside of her family had known Emma—no one alive and present, that is. Except Lillian and Henry Gray—Henry, who would have never opened his mouth, on any account. His hearing had grown too feeble to overhear conversation in a room.

Ralston sat in an armchair, alone. At first it sounded like he was mumbling to himself; the mumbling grew louder. Then he was talking. Now shouting. Not to anyone in particular. Just shouting. The same thing, over and over. "I didn't." "I never did." "Oh, but I didn't." It went on. Guests and family tried to ignore the outbursts, carrying on the polite conversation as though nothing out of the way were taking place. The shouting grew frantic. The old man began to cry. Not a quiet sort of crying. Ralston wailed. He let his head fall back, his mouth hanging open. The thin mouth turned down in a bow. He didn't bother wiping his face—he may not have known it was wet. Ralston may not have realized, even, that he was talking out loud—for a fact, he didn't care. He had no more thought for the people standing around in that room than if they had never lived. "I didn't." "I never did."

The situation was becoming embarrassing. Now Ralston's sons stood together, by themselves, not looking at anyone, not looking at each other. Nettie had long since gone home. There were a few people present who felt like reassuring Ralston in some way. Whatever horrible thing he felt he had done, that anyone had accused him of doing—they knew he hadn't done it. It was all right. But the completed statement was not what anyone would have expected; and it did eventually come out. He had never told her he loved her. It came out that one time. It came out again.

Once Ralston came out with the whole of it, his raving went on and on. Now that his meaning was clear, the daughters-in-law could approach him, attempting some kind of reassurance. She had known. People always knew, they said. The old man who had been so taciturn was willing, now, to talk to just about anybody, fairly clutched at people passing, grandchildren or old church friends. But the talking seemed to have quieted him. He settled down. It would have made anybody there ashamed to admit that they had forgotten the old man. Until he started again, as he did off and on, in spurts, over the next several hours, first quietly, then gradually raising his voice.

"My God, I can't live without her." "Oh my God, I *can't* live without her!" No one was able to do much about the crying jags that followed. He seemed to doze off in between.

Henry knew the story of Emma's illness—not the usual sort of illness, according to how Betty Kate described it. It sounded to Henry as much like a decision as an illness. Frank told the story in detail to Betty Kate. Her adult children had developed a pastime of telling stories on Emma, often in her presence. For some time, the topic had been the way she'd taken to disputing Ralston, which amused all of them a good deal. Ralston still conversed by fits and starts, more or less brooding in between. At those intervals, Emma contradicted him. She would allow him his comment. There'd be a few moments of grace. Then, the complacent but emphatic, "Well, I reckon it ain't," to whatever point he had made. Frank laughed out loud about it. Nettie and the brothers repeated the comment no end, themselves laughing about it. Frank went by often, sometimes daily—too often at suppertime, according to Betty Kate, who held the family supper. Emma had each new convenience or appliance as soon as it came out—her children saw to that. That evening she removed a custard from the oven. They had bought her a stove with the oven placed above the burners, so she wouldn't have to stoop. Emma wore a quilted glove. Frank noticed that her arm shook as she removed the pie. He tried to do it for her. She fussed at him and sent him up front.

The pie hadn't had time to cool down before Emma walked up to the living room.

"Buddy, I want you to take me to the hospital." Matter-of-factly.

"What for, Mama?"

"I don't feel so good. Been sick to my stomach." Emma had, in fact, several times been violently nauseated, but with no sort of nausea she knew from previous experience. Only the doctor would hear about that.

"Well you don't need the hospital for it."

"I'm going." Emma turned.

"Pshaw, Emmalie." Ralston cleared his throat. He had a leg crossed. The raised foot jerked a little. Ralston had narrow feet, and the shoes he wore were expensive. Nothing else moved but the foot. It was useless these days to argue with Emma.

Shortly, Emma came back into the room with a suitcase, and Frank took it from her. He had hoped she'd let the matter drop. He and Nettie could do more with her than anyone else, when she was contrary like this.

"Now Mama, you're tired today."

"I am tired. And I want to go Home." Emma was as fond as always of phrases of religious rhetoric.

It was apparently one of those times when she would not be budged. Frank gave in.

"Well, maybe the rest will do you good."

"Pshaw," Ralston added again, without much force.

Frank tried—it was his habit to make the best of a situation. "You'll feel better when you get back."

"I'm not coming back."

Ralston moved a foot and cleared his throat.

Henry sat for a while at the house that afternoon, after they came back from the Billy Griffen's. Lillian and Mary went about their own business, as they often did when Henry was there. No one felt much like talking. Henry had some thinking to do, and that was best done while walking. He'd go back to the room, change his clothes, and walk a while before supper—he hadn't eaten anything at the gathering. He'd have his supper early. Then he'd go over to check on Grindley, an A. A. member who was losing his own private battle, and with whom he'd offer to sit up the night, if need be.

As Henry crossed Broad Street at the foot of the bridge, he wondered where it was that Grindley roamed around during the day—except for the club room, he was homeless. There were plenty of vacant buildings. The old waterfront blocks on the east side of Water Avenue were in a sad, neglected state. In the lot of the St. James Hotel, empty too, the grass was so thick that the crickets were singing. That fall cricket noise; loose, leaf-like spangles of sound. He paused, decided to walk down to the water. Now he thought of Emma Griffen. The way it had happened for her—he wondered about it. Could it have really been that easy? Was it ever that easy for anybody? But it surprised him less in her than it would have in somebody else, the woman herself being as natural and easy as soil and rain.

She'd had something, Henry reflected. A thing he could catch sight of in her face as she moved around her yard. The letting go like she had: his guess was that satisfaction would have had something to do with it—but not in the sense of what anyone had given to her. The woman had taken what she had and made it sufficient for herself. Whereas he, Henry, had never been satisfied.

This, of all of it, was his truest accusation against himself. He had wanted more. He didn't know why. Certainly not more in the way of a wife or children. Other people had been satisfied with what he, Henry, had had. A time or two it came to him that the fault may not have been with himself. But here, Henry knew he was out of his depth. To follow through on an idea like that, he'd have had to unravel his whole life, backwards.

Henry realized himself to be in a strange state of mind that afternoon. It must have been the effects of the day, the funeral. Everything that he looked at seemed to have some kind of meaning beyond itself. Maybe everything did have, one way or another. From where he stood Henry could see the surface of the river, the floating light splinters, gliding, breaking apart. He could look across to the dark green quiet of the other bank. But that wasn't close enough for him, on that particular day. He walked all the way down—it was paved now—along the bend of the landing. Right away he caught the smell of the water, a slightly decaying odor, an odor strong, too, with life and vegetation. Betty Kate complained about it, said that the river was dangerous, that it was a dirty river. And this much was true. But where did it come from, this muddy old river, from where back, Henry wondered. Fed from the earth, fed from all the way back to that first ancient soil and rock. And without itself knowing why, this slow brown power glided, always to the sea. It had run, too, Henry thought now, through all the days of his life. If it had a voice, it could have told his story. It was an old, old earth Henry walked on. And the river remembered. Then a thought struck him—that one day the course of this river might be only a trace, a scar of something. A geological memory. Now, there was an idea. That all of it, that slow power, that memory of light and green and sky and water: all of it could disappear. But he supposed, after all, it wouldn't matter. All rivers were one river. And this one would be there. At least, it would be there long enough for him, Henry. Of it all, it was what he had seen and felt of something close to eternal. He stood for a while and watched it go by.

Henry walked back to the Bluebird in going-home traffic. The restaurant, too, had changed hands, he didn't know how many times over. Funny, no one had ever thought to change the name of it. He was still a little early, but he wanted his meal. As Henry walked through the door, at first the restaurant seemed dim to his eyes. Millie was having a smoke. She sat at the back stool, where Louise used to sit. She was a small, shriveled sort of woman. She seemed to like Henry. When she saw him, she smiled, raised her head, blowing out a long spume of smoke, then called back to the kitchen.

"Special for Mr. Gray."

CPSIA information can be obtained at www.ICGtesting.com
Printed in the USA
BVOW01s1828270814

364441BV00003B/792/P